THE BOOK

THE KEY

&

THE CROWN

Jennifer Eve Cipri

ISBN 1502552949
Italian Americans—Fiction. 2. Cosimo Medici—Fiction. 3. Emerald
Tablet—Fiction 4. Ancient Babylon—Fiction 5. Hermes
Trismegistus—Fiction 6. Child Abduction—Fiction

Summary: A powerful crown is hidden in the city of Redemption. A
secret brotherhood is desperately searching for it and a girl from a
broken home finds herself tangled in the web of their sinister plans.

This book was typeset in Garamond.

To the great storyteller, Anthony Carpenito & to the one who believed in me from the start, Marian Bauer

Endless gratitude to Anthony Carpenito. You took care of me so I could write this book. I'm forever indebted to you. To my sisters, Heidi and Angela, and my brother Tim, for loving and supporting me. To my sister Sara, for lighting my way. To my friends and family who nurtured my dreams. To my Aunt Shirley and Uncle Nunzio; my Uncle Mario, Aunt Lorraine. To my Uncle Mike, my Aunt Rita. I could write a book on each of you that would change the world for better. And to all my aunts and uncles who have passed on—there are many. You are my mothers and fathers. You have taught me who I am. To my nephew and niece, Timothy and Mikayla for showing me magic again. To my coworkers at Weed Library for being my family. For Lorraine Castelluccio who insisted I get my book out there. For Renu Sharma, my cover artist; your success inspired me. To Steve Zampino and Ricci Rondinelli for your gracious guidance. To Hernan Restrepo for helping me claim my space as an artist.

This is what we proclaim to you:
what was from the beginning, what we have heard, what we have
seen with our eyes. 1 John 1:1

The Sweeper	8
Stori	16
Priscilla Van Patten	39
Stori	63
Priscilla Van Patten	86
Stori	92
Priscilla Van Patten	119
Anna	139
The Sweeper	144
Stori	149
Priscilla Van Patten	178
Stori	192
Joe	202
Priscilla Van Patten	211
Stori	220
Priscilla Van Patten	237
Stori	245
Bilhah	269
Stori	275
Priscilla Van Patten	287
Joe	305
Stori	311

Frank	327
Sweeper	342
Soldier Sonny	354
Stori	357
Priscilla Van Patten	363
Stori	368
PriscillaVanPatten	384
Stori	394
Bilhah	412
Tony Carp	420
Stori	423
Lone	427

The Sweeper

The boy sits reading by the fireplace. Stone quiet, he stays this way for quite some time. I watch him from the shadows, waiting for him to put the book down and rise. But he is lost inside those pages. Far far away from this world, in another place and time. Ah, the magic a child can bring to the art of reading. If I try my hardest, I might just remember what it's like. But even if I wanted to remember, I couldn't. For I've sold my soul to the Brotherhood. My life and my memories and my magic belong to them now.

The front door groans opens and a tall man is ushered in by a gust of wind. Outside snow is coming down hard and a dusting of snowflakes sweeps into the entryway. The man leans his weight against the door as he shuts out the storm. He stands there for a stiff moment, wary of the intrusiveness of his snow-caked work boots. When he spots the boy on the far side of the room he calls out to him in a hushed voice. "Benjamin."

At last Benjamin startles. When he sees the man his face breaks open with delight. In an effort to keep his page he lets the book close over his thumb and flies over to the man with open arms.

Ah, the love between father and son. I can remember that one too if I try. I know I shouldn't be telling you this, but sometimes I do it, even though I'm not supposed to. If the Brotherhood found out, they would surely have me killed.

His father lifts him to himself, only to set him back down and stiffen again, his face realigning into harsh utilitarian lines. I note from his grimy clothes and exhausted eyes that he's a laborer of some sort and although we are in the Italian slums of the Valley, he looks to be some kind of Eastern European.

Mr. Galafortuna shuffles over with a welcoming grin. "Mr. Bak. Don't be shy. Please come in." Mr. Galafortuna is a short, plump man in his late seventies with a youthful, lilting voice.

The boy holds out his book and says, "Tato, Tato, look!"

"What is it Benjamin?" the father responds wearily.

Mr. Galafortuna is more curious than the father, for he cranes his neck to take a look. "Benjamin. What is it you've found?"

I take this opportunity to dart from behind the shelf of paperback biographies to the turning rack of comics and then over to a tall shelf that is conveniently situated by the front door. Mr. Galafortuna's book shop is older than he is and the floorboards creak in some places, so I have to take special care of my footing. If Mr. Galafortuna spots me, he will surely question my presence in his establishment. I used to read a lot. But ever since I joined the Brotherhood, I don't have the time or interest to bother with books anymore.

"Ah yes," Mr. Galafortuna says. "The Miraculous Journey of Edward Tulane. A magical one indeed."

I pull a book out of its place to create a peep hole. The business of Snatching is a bothersome waiting game and if I can help it I like to keep myself entertained.

Mr. Galafortuna smiles down on the young boy. "Would you like to take it home with you?"

Benjamin nods eagerly. "Yes, please."

"No," the father interjects. "He leaves it here."

"But he's nearly finished!" Mr. Galafortuna insists.

"He'll come back tomorrow."

"The story can't wait."

Mr. Bak wavers and then at last, the confession comes. "I don't have the money to pay."

Mr. Galafortuna makes a face. He puts a hand on Benjamin's head and gazes regretfully at the book. "I mean no disrespect, Mr. Bak., but I'd like the boy to have it. It's on me."

"Oh, please, Tato," Benjamin pleads. "Please."

Mr. Bak finally rests his eyes on his son and the harsh lines are gone.

If I'm going to feel bad for what I'm about to do, I guess I should start now. But nothing comes. It's been a while since I've felt guilty about anything. Ever since I signed my life over to the Brotherhood I don't have to worry about regret anymore.

"Very good," Mr. Galafortuna says, beaming. "Please come to the register and I'll get you a bag for the way home. They said a storm was coming. They said it will last all night."

After they complete their moneyless transaction with Mr. Galafortuna and wave goodbye as they make their way out into the cold evening, I wait for the old man to turn his back to me. When opportunity arises, I dart from behind the shelf, and steal out the door after my precious Ben.

****

The next afternoon at Sunny Days Elementary, I, Samuel Sampel, aka the Sweeper, am equipped with a face to forget and a janitor's broom. I whistle a pleasant melody as I make my way along the busy corridor. Children are screaming and throwing things and slamming locker doors shut as they gather their belongings in a rush and head out for the buses.

But the boy Benjamin is not among them. I find him in the darkness of the small theatre working on a contemporary piece with his dance instructor. I gaze down on him from the back row. Upon the stage, he moves with Lady Gaga's "Applause." His body is lithe and his movements are effortless. He has everything that makes a great dancer: control, power and the ability to completely let go. But the music overwhelms him or maybe he senses an extra set of eyes on him. Whatever the reason he leaps too far and falls.

The teacher steps to the stereo and turns the music off. "You're not concentrating," she tells him sternly. "You have to start focusing, Benjamin."

"I'm sorry Mrs. Dax."

"Tell me. What are you thinking?"

"Edward."

"Edward who?"

"Tulane. He fell overboard and Abilene, the one who really loves him with all her heart, needs to get him back."

After a few false starts it finally dawns on her that he's not talking about an actual person. "Your books can wait," she says tersely. "The All State Competition is in two weeks. Don't you want to win and make me and Principal Victor proud?"

"Yes," he answers dutifully and full of apology.

"Maybe it will help if you repeated our city's Declaration. I myself have found it quite freeing when I've been encumbered by unwanted worries. Go ahead. Say it."

Ben gets up and stares out into the empty seats. He squares his shoulders and positions his head with a slight tilt to the right. "Future Forward. Free From the Past." He looks at her hopefully. "I am ready. To try again."

Mrs. Dax is pleased. She puts the music back on and taps her foot to the rhythm as Benjamin works his magic.

Watching him move in all his brilliance I know he is the one. Not only have I found and avid reader, (which is what the Brotherhood is greatly lacking) but I have happened upon one gifted at dance at well. Ah, my masters will be proud. I've found a diamond in the rough for sure.

When he's done the teacher congratulates him and reminds him of his overnight assignments. I can tell she has great hopes for him and has invested much time in his progress.

Little does she know she will never see him again.

The halls are empty now, devoid of the screaming children running wild. The emptiness they left behind is a stark contrast to the echoing madness that ushered it in. Their madness still rings in my ears as I trail behind Ben. I have made little mounds of debris along the edges of the corridor. Paper and dust and dirt, mostly. You cannot believe how much paper and dust and dirt there is in this world. By this hour tomorrow there will be the same amount for me to sweep into neat little mounds.

He halts to take a book out of his backpack. He opens it, flipping through the pages to find his place. When he finds it he starts walking again. I follow him toward the science labs where he stops at his locker, I presume. He doesn't open it right away. Once again, the story has him entranced.

I drop the broom and it claps hard against the linoleum. He looks up, startled. "Oh," he says, closing the book. "You scared me."

"Damn broom," I complain. I reach down for it. But then I jerk my torso upright and seize my lower back. "Ouch! My back!" I am quite the performance artist myself.

"Are you alright?" the boy asks.

"Don't ever get old," I warn him, maintaining my stiffness.

"Here. I'll help you." He hurries over, takes the broom in his one free hand and holds it out to me.

When his heavily lashed eyes meet mine I no longer have a face to forget, but have bared the other side of me. The side that no longer sees the boy as human.

He goes white with terror. He's still holding out the broom, but he drops the book. *The Miraculous Journey of Edward Tulane*.

There is nothing left to do but snatch him. A hand over his mouth, an arm enclosing his body, I drag him from the hall and stuff us both away in the passage from which I came—the broom closet.

Oh the sweet rush of triumph that comes from taking a child without asking. What does it feel like, you wonder? It feels like all the memories I wish to blot out are finally no more. A slate has been wiped clean.

I have forever known life as a series of aimless wanderings burdened by the weight of unfulfilled dreams and unanswered prayers.

But not with the child underarm.

When I steal the child I am no longer forsaken.

Inside the broom closet, I switch on the light and kick an empty paint can aside. I move to the back where a life size poster of Tony the Tiger giving a thumbs up to a bowl of frosted flakes covers most of the wall. I pull the tape up from the bottom corners. The boy kicks wildly. But he is no match for the strength of a Hound. I only need one arm to restrain him.

Behind Tony and his cereal is a door. It is not a magic door. It was installed by the underground construction workers, the ones most citizens of Redemption know nothing about. I fumble in my pocket for the key. I slip it into the keyhole. The door unlocks. I jam the key back into my pocket and open the door.

"Say goodbye," I tell him. "Say goodbye to the light."

Stori

"Give him back, Richie!"

Richie's lapdogs have me by both arms as I fight to break free. Richie flails the papers in my face and says, "Watcha got there, Sullen?"

"You're gonna be sorry," I threaten.

Richie strokes his imaginary beard and reads, "Missing. Frank Putzarella. Five hundred dollar reward." He laughs, his breath fogging the air. "Man. You're dad's dead. He's a wackadoo."

Everybody's saying he's dead. Even my own mother. But I've got this gut feeling that he's alive and he's out there somewhere. That he's suffering something awful and he wants to come home.

"And you're a coward," I fire back. "Say it again, with

my hands free."

"I ain't scared of you."

"Prove it."

His face loses some of its resolve. He grits his teeth in resentment. "I saw him smack you once in front of the whole neighborhood. Don't deny it. Like you got a daddy better than the rest of us?"

Okay, so maybe he wasn't the best dad a girl could have; maybe he ignored me sometimes, maybe he even hated me. But none of that matters. He's the head of my family and a family will fall to ruins without its head. "You mark my words, Richie Ramera. I'm going to find my father. I'm going to get him home."

"Good luck with that." He tosses my papers in the air and skips off down the street. He blows a sharp whistle and his pathetic dogs release me. I can land a shot on one of them for sure. But revenge will wait for now. I've got to get those flyers.

It's a gloomy night and even though it feels to be about 20 degrees, I swear I just heard thunder. After I snatch my last runaway flyer from the cobblestone street I continue my march down Kindred. The wind howls from inside an alley and my spine shudders. I'm trying to focus on the task at hand, but Richie got me all shook up. It doesn't help much that every block or so a little helpless face stares out at me from behind the plate glass of a storefront. They're like sad ghosts. Someone kidnapped them and none of them have been found. I try not to look into their eyes. Those kids are somebody else's problem. Not mine.

Many of the shops are still and dark. But the lights to Funicelli's Shoe Shop are still on. Mr. Funicelli's at his workbench, tapping his slender hammer on the heel of a leather shoe.

Bells chime at my entrance. Mr. Funicelli glances up, but goes right back to work. "Good evening, Miss Putzarella," he calls over his tapping.

"Hi Mr. Funicelli. Sorry to bother you. But I thought maybe I could put up my dad's picture in your window. Next to that kid."

He pauses his work and grimaces. Removing his glasses he looks at me earnestly. "Why would you even ask?"

"Sorry, Mr. Funicelli." I take out my masking tape and rip off a piece between my teeth. *Up you go, Daddy. Up you go. But don't worry. It's not for long.*

"You're father was a good man," Mr. Funicelli reflects nostalgically.

"He still is."

"He was proud to be a mason, as his father before him. It's the only way we survive, Stori. Honoring what went before us. Why, do you even know how long I've been in business?"

Like every other store or restaurant in the Valley, this place has been in business since the late 1800s. So I tell him.

"That's *after* immigration. But before that, my father's father's father and so on custom made all the shoes for Pontius Pilate and his queen. Why with this very hammer and lath."

If Mr. Funicelli ever had aspirations for a more glamorous vocation he's never once alluded to it. I'm not sure if I should feel sorry for him.

It's like he can read my mind for he says, "There's no other job out there that would make me happier. It's an honor to do it." He waves his ancient hammer at me. "Change is for the rest of Redemption, Miss Putzarella. But not here. "

I work my way down a good portion of side streets, taping him to any piece of dry wood, glass or stone I can find, and return to the cobblestone where I began. This is the main artery of the Valley and the street I grew up on— Kindred Street. Most of the apartments sit atop Mom and Pops shops below. The buildings are squeezed tightly together and fire escapes serve as front porches.

There was a heavy snow storm last week and some of the cars are still snowed in, their owners too lazy to clean them. The sky rumbles. Halting in the middle of the street I gaze a charcoal cloud closing over the rooftops. A thunderstorm would be odd this time of year, but lately the weather has been quite unpredictable.

A boy with a big smile stares out from Golden Threads Fashion Boutique. Ben Bak. I know that kid. Mom's Italian and Valley-born, dad's Polish. Ben's into ballet and books. Polite as they come. Never bothered a soul. Poor kid.

I better look away.

That's when I spy something at the lip of a nearby alley. It's a girl my age; I don't recognize her face. She wears a lavender dress with lace embroidery. It softly billows about her in the wind and smog. Barefoot she steps out of the alley and comes into the middle of Kindred and just stands there. A halo of lavender light surrounds her.

"Hey," I call out. "Where's your coat? And your shoes? It's freezing out here."

She doesn't answer but points to Ben. Then she looks at me and with a finger over her mouth, signals me to silence. Then she turns northwest where the sky is still clear, and points into the distance. She's indicating the billboard. The massive one of the sexy model in the red dress. It's the biggest billboard ever erected in United States history. Right here in the city of Redemption. There was even an article in the New York Times about it; "Advertisement or Assault?" was the title.

"What about it?" I ask. She cups her hands around her mouth and whispers something. I can't hear, so I move closer. She's telling me something I need to know. I can feel it. Maybe she knows about my father. "What are you saying?" I ask her, now only feet away. "Speak louder," I demand, getting aggravated.

Then her gaze darts to something behind me and she goes white with terror.

I whip around to see what it is. A tall black shadow is there, just inches from my face. But like a picture on a television screen being snapped off, it disappears. I whip back around to the girl but she's gone too.

Damnit. It was just another one of my visions. I get them sometimes. Especially when I stop my medication.

I've forgotten that I'm standing in the middle of the street, but reality comes crashing back in when a car slams on its breaks and swerves around me. "Get out of the road you crazy nut!" the driver cries from a crack in his window before he speeds off.

A smoker's voice calls from under the awning of Rita's Tavern. "Who's that?"

Someone answers back. "Just one of them crazy Putzarellas."

"Should have known," the rasping voice returns.

I'm about to hurl a massive F-bomb at them when another car comes out of nowhere. Its horn blares as I dart out of the way, tripping over the curbside and sprawling onto the sidewalk. It is not easy being crazy in a sane world. Somehow I always end up on my hands and knees. This time I'm in a freezing puddle.

I rise to kneeling and snatch up my flyers yet again. I'm scared to look up and still see that girl. I cover my eyes with the flyers and cry, "Go away! Leave me alone you visions!"

Laughter erupts from the other side of the street. "Come over here and say it to my face!" I dare them.

They won't come over. I know they won't. People call me crazy pretty often. But one thing they never do is step to me to fight. Mano a mano, I have never lost a battle in my life. I may be just an average sized sixteen-year-old girl, but don't let that fool you. I can step to the toughest brawler, banger, or cockeyed fool in the Valley and just look at them and they know I'm the real deal. You can either let people walk all over you in this life or you can stand up and give them hell for it. I choose the latter. It has *never* failed me.

Just great. My dad's flyers are soaked. "Damnit!" I growl with teeth gritted. "Now look what you've done."

To add insult to injury the sky opens and it starts to pour.

Here in the Valley streets flood quickly. I take momentary refuge under the narrow portico of Tony Carp's stoop, pasting my back against his door. One of my rain boots has a nickel sized hole in it. My sock is wet and my toes are frozen to the bone. Not to mention my palms and knees are raw and stinging from the fall. I hunch my shoulders against the cold and wait patiently for the storm to pass. *Just a few more streets*, I tell myself. *Just a few more.* I dig in my back pocket for a little motivation. My father's goodbye letter, folded into a precise square. I unfold it and read:

Dear Family,

Goodbye. I am never coming back. Forget me and move on. I have a credit of $14.65 at the bakery. Oh, And you better bless the kitchen table when Easter comes.

Love,
Frank

The sound of the deadbolt from the door behind me catches me off guard. I leap off the stoop and whip around to see an old woman staring down the barrel of a gaming rifle—aimed right at me! It's Tony's grandmother.

"Nana Lu!" I shout into the din of the storm. "It's just me, Stori."

"Stori? What in God's name are you doing out here on a night like this?"

I show her my sopping wet flyers. They sag miserably and I'm ashamed. "I made missing signs for my dad. I gotta find him."

She scans the street suspiciously, like she suspects I'm not alone. Then she lets the rifle fall to her side and invites me inside with a nudge of her head. "Take off your shoes and come in. Dinner's ready."

Here's where I better explain something about my people, the Calabrese of the Valley. We take sinning seriously and there are three unforgivable ones, resulting in exile:

1. Swearing at your mother or father.
2. Admitting you think you're better than someone else.
3. Refusing to eat when someone offers you food.

All other transgressions can be absolved with prescribed penitence: Adultery, theft, even murder. I know it sounds odd. But the Valley is odd by nature and it has been for over a hundred years.

Nana Lu's apartment sits atop a store called Novelties and a Doctor. Mr. and Mrs. Neri are the owners and they sell all kinds of odds and ends. In addition they have a corner in the back of the store designated for treating the ill. It's a compact space backed by a wall of medical books. Mr. and Mrs. Neri don't dispute the efficiency of the Other Mothers in the Valley who are wise in the ways of natural remedies and old prayers. But if ever the Other Mothers fall short, as sometimes they do, the Neris are there with their medical library and a hidden stash of illegal pharmaceuticals.

Nana Lu leads me up an enclosed staircase to the

second floor. The first door on the left of a long hallway is her home. Entering Nana Lu's is like stepping back in time. An antique grandfather clock in the foyer looms over me as I leave my boots and socks on the corner of an already full shoe mat. I welcome the comforting warmth after the cold outside.

Nana Lu picks up my socks and sucks her teeth. She brings them over to the radiator in the living room. An Enzo Caruso vinyl is playing on an antique Victrola. (I know it's him because my mother listens to him all the time. His voice sounds more like a ghost's than a man's.) A Persian rug cushions my feet as I glance at the countless black and white photos adorning every tabletop and windowsill, sitting atop little clouds of Queen Anne's lace.

It is 2014 for the rest of our city, Redemption—the one that's GPSing, texting and LCD TVing, the one that's Future Forward. But here in the Valley it's still 1910. This place is a technophile's worst nightmare. There are very few computers, hardly any cell phones. Our people have a deep seeded mistrust in all things foreign to the Old Country. Many who disagreed left the Valley seeking out a more modern life. They worked hard and bought houses up in the Ridges. Our people call those deserters 'Merigans. (Slang for Americans.) I'm not saying this kind of attitude is right. The desire for progress is part of the human condition and our city's new Declaration is just a reflection of that. I'm only telling you how it is here.

I hope Tony's not home; I'm not in the mood to see him. But for some reason I ask, "Is Tony here?"

"No," Nana Lu says. "That boy lives at the gym nowadays."

I'm disappointed. *Hey, I thought I don't want to see him. Okay, maybe I do just a little.*

Nana Lu leads me into the kitchen, where she takes my flyers and spreads them out on the linoleum floor next to a cast iron stove. The air is scented with lemons and roasted garlic. I'm suddenly starving, but I lie and say, "Nana Lu. I already ate. But maybe I'll take something to go."

"Nonsense. You have a minute to sit for a decent meal. God knows your mother isn't up to it. That poor woman, what she's been through."

She orders me into the dining room, where her son, Arty Arm, is seated with two of his bookie friends. All three are about my parents' age and know my father well. Arty pulls out a chair as he and his cronies offer their condolences. The name Arty Arm is a perfect fit for this man. He forever has a folded newspaper tucked into his armpit and it's rumored that when he breaks bones as a Collector for the Tommy Tapparelli Family he's so strong he doesn't even bother to put his paper down; one arm is enough.

Some people think guys like him are cool. Even Tony who calls him the baddest-ass uncle in the world. But in my opinion his uncle is a scumbag who hurts people for money. He's not worth a minute of my time and I would just love to tell him. But I have to be polite as he offers his regrets and keep my judgments to myself, lest I commit the Valley's sin number two.

"Thank you. I'm hoping he'll come back soon. There's been a social worker to my house. She's from CPS and she talked to my mother about putting me and Regi in a foster home."

A roasted Ham is the centerpiece of the table and the men swirl spoons in steaming bowls of wedding soup. A bowl is placed in front of me and I don't wait for Nana Lu to join us to start eating. The hunger in me is ravenous. Her voice travels into the room from the kitchen, "I remember when my grandson, Tony, lost his parents and had to leave his house. I never saw a child so solemn."

Tony's parents were killed in a car accident when he was eleven and Nana Lu took him in thereafter. A picture of Tony is framed on a buffet table by the window. He's standing in the middle of a boxing ring with a referee who holds his gloved hand up into the air in victory. His muscular chest glistens with sweat and his boxing shorts accentuate his narrow hips. Tony Carp is a senior; he's tall, tan and rocks a spiky high fade that makes my knees go weak.

I look at his picture and endure the nasty sting of tears behind my eyes. The pain is so sharp that I almost enjoy it.

Oh, Tony. You broke my heart. Do you even know it? A broken heart is a bitch to lug around all on one's own. It's an injustice really, that I'm carrying the cross of my thwarted love and the one who set it upon my shoulders is completely free.

There's an awkward silence and I know why. The Arm and his friends are looking at me like I'm the saddest person alive. I want to use my spoon to gouge their eyeballs out of their sockets, but I try to concentrate on my soup.

Finally Nana Lu sits down next to me. "Soup good?"

"Delicious. Thank you, Nana Lu."

She's pleased. She smiles and puts a cushiony palm on my cheek. "Arty. What are you doing? Give her some ham."

Arty fixes me a plate and I thank him.

I'm almost afraid to ask because I'm scared of the answer. But if I'm going to find my father, I have to know the truth. "Mr. Arty?"

"Yeah, kid."

"My father was kind of distant the last couple of months. Like not home much." I take great care with my next question. I have to pose it as delicately as possible. "Could he have gotten mixed up in something, you know, with your guys?"

"Absolutely not. Your father was proud to be a working man."

I nod and let out a sigh.

Nana Lu puts a hand on my knee. "You know, Stori. Sometimes men don't always do the right thing, when it comes to family."

I put my spoon down and look her full in the face. "His family was his life."

She smiles apologetically. She knows she crossed a line. But since she's old, I'll forgive her. "Nana Lu," I ask. "Why did you come outside with a gun?"

She drops her hand from my knee. She goes to say something but stops.

"You might as well tell her, Ma," Arty says.

"For what?" Nana Lu barks. "She's just a child."

"People need to know," Arty answers grimly. A gust of wind and angry rain rattles the window panes.

"Tell me," I insist, verging on a tone that could be considered disrespecting my elders. Still I take the risk.

"Lying about it won't help," Arty tells his mother. Then he looks at me. "People have been talking. There's something evil going on in Redemption. We're not safe anymore."

His friends nod regretfully, mumbling disapprovals under their breath.

"What do you mean?" I ask.

"This place always sleeps with one eye open. Don't you find it odd that no one ever saw anything?"

I do find it odd. "What do you think happened, Arty?"

"Something otherwordly might have taken him."

29

"I don't believe in ghosts."

"Not a ghost," he corrects me. "A man. Dead but still living. By the name of Cosimo the Corpse."

"Cosimo the Corpse?" I ask. "He's not real. He's just a myth to scare children."

"My grandmother used to talk about Cosimo," Arty's friend says. "He been looking for a crown since the Renaissance. It's called the Crown of Final Sight. Anyone who put it on their head would become like God or some shit."

"They would be granted the wisdoms," Arty clarifies, like he's an expert on the subject. "To unlocking the greatest mysteries of the universe—like life and death and heaven and stuff like that. Cosimo wanted to use the crown to take over the world, since he already had Italy on lockdown. But he was murdered before he found it. Lucky for him, his lovesick witch was able to keep him alive; but she couldn't fully bring him back to life until the crown was found, placed on his head and an immortality spell was said over him."

"I heard it too," Arty's other friend chimes in. "My Great Aunt Helen told me. That crown is out there and Cosimo and his witch need it to bring him back to life. Aunt Helen even whispered it's here in the Valley."

"He's real," Arty insists, jamming a stubby finger into the table. "And so is his lovesick witch and her creatures, the Hounds. They're all a part of the Night's Council."

I refuse to believe it. "People talk," I say. "People get bored and they talk. To fill up time. I don't believe in stuff like Cosimo the Corpse."

Arty's unshaken by my disbelief. "If you were to ask Mayor Vaughn he would say this city is safe. He's got us all distracted by the casino and this robot lounge he just built." It's what everybody keeps talking about. On the very top floor of Strive will be a member's only club where robots will cater to all the member's needs.

"Gotta tell you. I could make good use of a robot," his friend says.

"Bet you could," the other quips.

Arty isn't amused. "But I'm not distracted. There are some real evil things going on in Redemption. I've grown up with thugs and bone-breakers my whole life. And let me tell you something, they can do ugly. But even crime has a code. Some ugly's off limits. Like stealing children. You tell me. Where did they all go?"

I'm used to my people, the Calabrese, being a bit paranoid. They often get involved in conspiracy theories about the police and government. They don't trust anyone, really, outside of the Valley. As a result, they employ Other Mothers when ill and give birth right in their own beds. They settle disputes through old-fashioned fistfights, and cultivate their backyard gardens for fruits and vegetables and make their own wines.

"It's happening." Arty insists. "It was predicted too, by

the old folk who remember the prophecies. Most are dead now, but I remember hearing them talk when I was a kid. They said Cosimo has been looking for the lost crown. That it's somewhere here in the Valley and he will stop at nothing to find it. Once he does, that's when the final battle will begin—between us and the Night's Council. And people will have to decide which side to fight on. The Corpse has evil plans. Maybe your father knew something. Maybe he tried to get in Cosimo's way."

"Enough!" barks Nana Lu. "I don't want this talk at my table. You'll spoil the food!"

The room goes quiet.

I don't know what to make of the Arm's suspicions. I still think he's paranoid, but now he's got me wondering. So I turn to the oldest and wisest in the room. "Nana Lu. Do you believe it too? Why did you shush him?"

She gets up and goes to a china cabinet. She takes a loose photo off the bottom shelf and comes back to the table. "Stori. You remember my brother's wife, Concettina? She lived on Windy Way? She died last week. They found her lying on the kitchen floor. She had the magic plum tree. Do you remember?"

"I don't know if it was magic," I say.

"Nonsense. It fed every hungry child in the Valley. All summer long."

"I guess," I say just to be polite. I don't really think it was magic though. Concettina was just playing a trick on us, the way adults always do. Yes, there were baskets upon baskets of glistening fruit, each and every day of summer. More plums than any tree could ever produce. But there was also a cellar nearby and one day the door was opened and I peeked down there and saw an empty crate from Rolling Farms. That's how I knew it wasn't magic. But I held my tongue because my little sister, Regi, believed. I didn't want to ruin it for her.

"Dead on the floor."

"Oh. I'm sorry. I hope she didn't suffer," I say.

Nana Lu jabs my shoulder with the hand holding the photograph. Her bony knuckles hurt and I have to contain my irritation. God. Old people are so pushy sometimes.

"Look. Look at her picture," Nana Lu says.

I take it so she can stop poking me. A black and white, dog-eared shot of a young girl in an ankle length skirt sitting at the lip of a grotto. I don't know why, but the picture makes me long to go back to that time. To sit there in that grotto with her and ask her things. Things like…well I don't really know.

Nana Lu stands over me wiping her face with a cotton napkin. "Why don't you believe in magic, Stori? Don't you believe?"

"I'm not a little girl anymore, Nana Lu. Tell me more about this guy Cosimo."

"Oh, I don't believe Cosimo's here in the Valley. If he were it would mean death for us all. But something must be done soon to ensure that wherever he is, he won't get his hands on that crown. We…" she points to Concettina. "who still have the ancient magic to keep the Night's Council at bay. When we have all passed, then Cosimo just might find it. My dear, my dear. What will you poor children do when we are all gone?"

The word *gone* sets an awful aching inside me. *Not gone. Not gone.* "Nana Lu. Have my flyers dried yet?"

The rain seems to have let up a little. I better get back out there.

She glances into the kitchen. "Of course. They're only but paper. You're in a rush. I understand. I'll fix you something to go." She gets up and returns to the kitchen.

Before I follow her I look at Arty, sensing he has more to tell.

He lowers his voice, so it doesn't reach the kitchen. "Just ask Miss Beppy down the street. How come she can't walk no more. There's a war out there, Putzarella. An ugly one that nobody can see. At least not for now."

Back in the cold wet night, the rain's picked up again, coming down hard.

Rising waters stream down into the gutters. I see one of my father's flyers sail by. Then another. I bite back a scream. *Oh no. Here comes the dark side of me.* With a mighty thrust of my arm I fling the rest of them out onto the sidewalk. Stomping right over them I march my way south in the direction of the abandoned warehouse.

The Cage isn't for everyone. I would never want my sister down here. Or my mother, or my best friend, Ernestine. But for me, the Cage is just fine. I like it. The forbidden pleasure of being somewhere illegal. The blare from the crowd. The shouting is so loud I can't hear my own voice. I love that feeling—of speaking and no one can hear me, not even myself. Thoughts get drowned out too. The only thing that matters is the diamond in the center of the room.

I like to see the blood when they're fighting. If skin doesn't break what's the point? The more bloodied and battered they are the better satisfied I become. Sometimes I get lucky. Sometimes there's another girl who wants to fight. If the ref checks her out and weighs her and deems her a good match, he'll give us a couple rounds.

Tony Carp is sitting with a few girls, some of his Black friends from the Hills and Richie Ramera, that asshole. When Tony spots me talking with the ref he stands.

The ref's got a girl, he tells me. "You got your gear?" he asks.

I heft the bag at my side. Replacing my textbooks and my doll, Amanda, are my sneakers, mouthpiece, gym shorts and a tank.

The ref turns and looks up to the booth. "Put her on the list," he shouts. "Putzarella."

My name goes up on the screen by the booth. Stori Putzarella vs. Christina Dexter.

Tommy Tapparelli's boys are in the corner taking bets. It's not an official business. They don't make too much money off it. They just do it for fun.

On my way to the locker room Tony grabs my arm. "What are you doing?"

I wheel around to face him and the tears are already falling down my face. "What does she look like?"

I told him I loved him at the New Year's Ball at school. Right in the middle of the dance floor I said, "I want you to be the first to kiss me, Tony. I love you."

He looked at me like I had hurt his feelings or something and said, "I can't Stori. I'm sorry. My heart belongs to another."

It can't be. Don't you think if I could just get him to see how my heart beats only for him, that I could make him love me?

"Please, Stori. Don't."

"Who is she, Tony? Is she prettier than me?"

"That's not fair. You can't do that."

"Just tell me."

"Okay. Okay, fine. It's Desma."

I'm crushed. Desma is one of the prettiest girls in the Valley.

I wrench myself free of him in utter disgust. "Typical. Going for the bimbo with no brains. I hope she gives you an STD."

Tony never reacts to my anger. That's part of the

reason why I love him. "Don't fight tonight," he pleads gently. "You're not a boy, Stori."

I like that he doesn't want me fight. It shows that he cares. But I'm still raging with jealousy over the thought of him being with Desma. "Don't tell me what to do. You're not a man."

As I walk away he shouts. "You're not made for this. Trust me. You're made for something better."

When my name is finally called and I'm inside the diamond I step forward and face my opponent. The ref goes over the rules but I'm not listening because I've done this already. Plus, I'm not a rule breaker like that. I never play dirty. But I *will* beat her. This much I know. It's not that I'm cocky or anything. It's just that I understand what it takes to win a fight. Fearlessness and Crazy. I got plenty of both.

Someone is shouting, "Cat fight! Cat Fight!"

Tony stands and turns. "Yo! Shut the fuck up, man!"

I don't have time to think about him anymore. All that matters now is the adrenaline. It's pulsing through my veins. Filling me to the brim. I'm bouncing and getting ready to make my first strike. She starts to move. She's sizing me up. Her form is tight. Head tucked. She's been formally trained. She knows technique. But I know the beast. And there's no formal training for the beast.

I take a good jab to the ear and a foot to the calf. The first ones always sting. I like to take a few hits just to get numb anyways and what's more I've got this thing about never being the first one to strike. Another one to the ear again and then a combo to the midsection.

That's when I let the beast go and take a sound body shot. I hear the breath go out of her in a deep grunt. She backs up.

It's good I took a pill this morning. I've decided I'll start the pills again. I'll get the crazy right out of me. Get a little disinterested. Disinterest is great for fighting. I don't want to know you. I don't need to know you. I just need to overcome you. I need you to submit.

I land a good one to her nose and she falls. She's wide open on her back and I drop over her, straddling her tight. I pound and pound and pound and the noise gets louder. I don't know how to stop myself. Once the pounding starts, I can't quit.

The ref comes between us and shouts. "That's it! That's it!"

I stand and look up. People are cheering. Whistling. Howling. Tony Carp is out there somewhere but I can't see him anymore. I only see the light. A different one than the light that edged the barefoot girl standing on wet cobblestone. It's the cold fluorescent glare above my head. I imagine myself just being born. Coming out of my mother's womb. Bloodied and triumphant and filled with a screaming that has a very life of its own I look up and the first thing I see is the beautiful fluorescent light.

Priscilla Van Patten

Not in my wildest dreams did I ever imagine this. I had no idea, the night I decided to stuff a single dress and a tracksuit into a duffle bag in that hellhole of a trailer park I once called home, that I would end up here in the city of glittering lights, dining in a snug corner of a five star restaurant with *Redemption's Most Eligible Bachelor*.

Nate is seventh generation aristocracy. His family has their legacy in oil.

I occasionally reflect on the girl I was before I met him and find myself snickering. I used to order prime rib at Applebees twice a month and shop at Target for my underwear. But that wasn't my fault. Back in Erie I was a total ignoramus. I didn't know there was another life out there. A better life. Until Nate stepped in and showed me.

This Friday evening we are dining at our favorite revolving rooftop restaurant, Le Chíc, perched high above downtown Redemption. It's always packed here, with a fast table turnover and a happening lounge where a DJ spins every Friday and Saturday night. The kitchen serves a combination of mainstream and exotic fare. Nate and I are friends with the owner, Tyler. He went to NYU with Nate. Tyler came up with the name in his junior year on one of his trips abroad. Le Chíc. Doesn't it just sound young, hip and brand spanking new?

The clientele here are what Nate and his dad call Newbies (or New Money). Flashy business men and women who like to spend their money as soon as they get it. (And make sure all of upper class society is nearby to see.) They're predominantly young, white and attractive. Like Trish over there, standing with the hostess, whispering something in her ear. She's a natural red head with pretty long legs and well turned ankles. She's a model. She got the contract for that massive billboard hanging over the I-95 expressway. It features her with a bubbly champagne glass in one palm and a pair of die in the other. Neck craned, mouth parted, she's staring straight ahead with a sickening little satisfaction on her face. Casino chips shower around her. Above her are the words: FUTURE FORWARD. *STRIVE FOR BETTER AT STRIVE CASINO.* Yes, Trish is a dish and everyone knows it. But she's too thin if you ask me. If she's so sure being a stick is hot then why do I catch her nervously eyeing my ass every time I walk by? My ass screams WOMAN. *Take a bite of this*, it says. Nate loves my ass. And so do I. There are lots of things I love about myself. You know, the *me* that always was. The me that was me when I was just a nobody packing up a duffle bag in Erie. I'd like to think that as far as I've come I've kept that girl with me.

"I started a new case today," I tell him over the new age techno pumping softly from the surround sound. "In the Valley of course."

"Slumming it again?" he asks grimly.

"Uh huh."

"God. Can't they assign you to some boring domestic dispute in the Ridges? Get you away from those third class heathens?"

"They could. But I'm good at what I do. And they need me down in the trenches."

"I guess." Nate is looking particularly handsome tonight, wearing a periwinkle button down and skinny jeans. "So what's this one all about?"

"An Italian family with two young girls."

Nate lifts a fork of linguine, dripping with white clam sauce, into his mouth. He listens blankly as he chews. Nate has no patience for the people I deal with at work. He calls them The Walking Dead. I try not to bring up my cases with him, but I can't shake the Putzarella one; it's been keeping me up at night. "The father took off and the mom

41

stopped working because she's so upset."

"Deadbeat," Nate manages through a bite of sourdough baguette.

"I'll have to remove the two daughters from the house." Just saying it gives me a dreadful feeling in my gut.

"Desperate times call for desperate measures," Nate comments passively.

"But the oldest daughter, Stori, swears he was kidnapped. Some of the neighbors do too."

"Mob?"

"No. Cosimo the Corpse."

Nate looks confused. "Cosimo the What? Who the hell is that?"

"I never told you about Cosimo the Corpse?" I can't help but laugh a little at the absurdity of such a notion.

"No. You missed that one. But do tell."

"He was in the Medici Family. They say he's undead and he's hiding in our fine city of Redemption, and has evil plans to take over one day. They're all afraid."

"You sound like you've taken stock in this Corpse, my love."

"Oh no. Of course I haven't."

"So the father's not a deadbeat. He's just been kidnapped by a dead guy from the Renaissance? Poor baby."

"I know. It's absurd."

"I gotta tell you. Those people sure have some

inventive ways in making excuses for their degenerate proclivities."

I only half agree with him because I used to be one of those people—a degenerate. My family was very similar to the Putzarellas and I know how hard it is to rise up out of scum. Nate doesn't know that about me. He thinks I came from Buttress, a quaint town just outside of Erie. He thinks my parents were schoolteachers and we lived in a modest raised ranch behind a white picket fence. I will die before I let him know I lived in a trailer park with an unemployed, Jesus freak mother and a compulsive gambler lush of a father. I reach a hand over the table and caress the smooth skin on his knuckles. "Trust me. I know."

"And only ignoramuses would believe in someone named Cosimo the Corpse," he adds through another mouthful. Nate is a glutton when it comes to food....and sex...and money...and me. The *me* part makes me smile. "You're sexy," I tell him. "I hope I say it enough. That I think you're incredibly sexy."

Nate winks and wipes his mouth with his linen napkin. He places it back in his lap. After a sip of ice water he says, "So if you think the father's gone off with this dead guy, close the case, get it off your desk. And get it off your mind. So we can get back to planning our amazing future. You know too much stress will give you wrinkles in that perfect skin of yours."

Nate has always told me how beautiful I am. God, I

thank my lucky stars for being pretty. It was the golden ticket that sold me out of the dump I came from. God was merciful to me, and I try to remember to thank Him.

"I don't want to stress, baby. But something is holding me back from closing this one. I mean, there's definitely serious neglect and the entire family is loony. But there's also..." I'm not sure exactly what it is, so I think on it. "There's also love there. The oldest daughter is going around the neighborhood putting up his picture everywhere. She said she won't give up until she finds him. That's some serious love."

"Love," Nate repeats robotically, opening his mouth so I can see what he's chewing.

"Don't be gross, grossy."

We both get quiet. I can't shake all the thoughts about Cosimo and bad fathers and love and Nate doesn't want to deal with it.

"Listen, Pris. I know you're an emotional person and that's one of the reasons why I fell in love with you, but let me give you some advice, okay?"

"Okay."

"The Valley is hopeless and the mayor needs to expedite his plans on razing all those old houses and shoving those backward people out of the city."

"But the Valley is all they have. And so many of those people helped build Redemption."

"Who cares? What I've learned in business is that in

order to climb the ladder to the top, one can never look down. Ever. I mean, isn't the city's new Declaration and booming economy proof positive of that same sentiment? Future Forward. Free From the Past. If they want help, let them get on the ladder just like I did and climb."

I'm not sure how much climbing was actually involved in Nate's success, seeing how he's been heir to a fortune since birth; but that's not to say he's not super ambitious, educated and always looking for ways to improve himself.

Anyways, he's right about the Valley. I'm going to close the Putzarella case as soon as possible. People like that shouldn't be allowed to even have children. The girls would be better off in a home. "You're right," I concede. "Everybody can help themselves."

He frowns and my heart flutters. Damnit. Why did I upset him like that? "I'm sorry, babe. Look at me, not even appreciating this wonderful meal, letting my soup get cold."

"You know you don't have to work anymore, Pris. I've got us. Don't you trust me?"

"Of course, babe. But I like my job. And it's good for me to stay busy." I can't tell him the whole truth. That I'm scared of being dependent on him. What if I fuck up? What would happen then? I'd have only a duffle bag and a ticket back to Erie to fall back on. Or worse—what if he fucks up? I can't even bear the thought.

But what if the rumors are true? The ones about Nate still being in love with Trish. I catch her glance over at me with those icy blue eyes. She smiles and waves as if she's only noticing me now. Then she mouths something to the hostess and they both have a nice giggle. Skinny bitch. Stay your flat ass away from my man.

"Keep it then," he says. "If that's what you want. You don't have to do anything anymore, Priscilla, that you don't want to."

Nate has a knack for relaxing me. I lean back and take a healthy sip of wine anticipating a nice buzz to kick in soon. "Life is good," I say to no one in particular.

Just then, I catch a bright blur of something in the corner of my eye. A flurry of movement draws my gaze across the room to silver white hair, thicker and longer than Trish's, sprawling over both sides of a white ermine cape. The cape is full length, draping almost all the way to the floor and is fastened around her neck in braided red velvet. She's entered from a side entrance. A door just beside the small bar at the cocktail lounge. I stifle a gasp, unable to explain the sensation that I've just witnessed a ghost in motion.

Nate twists in his chair. "Well I'll be damned."

The woman makes her way across the room, escorted by Tyler himself. Four busboys trot past them carrying a table for four, a single chair and all the accoutrements necessary for civilized dining. Before she even reaches the west window, her table is plopped down close to the glass; it's draped in white linen and plated in a flash. A chair is pulled out for her and waiting.

"A queen," I say involuntarily.

I want to be that woman with every ounce of my being. As she passes our table she doesn't look our way, but Nate and I are openly oogling her. She looks to be in her early forties. Her face is not pretty, yet it possesses a kind of triumph that makes her stunning. Statuesque and fluid in her movements, she's quite possibly the most elegant thing I've ever seen.

When she reaches her table she unfastens the velvet to let her fur fall into the hands of an eagerly awaiting busboy. He hurries off with his treasure with a terrified expression on his face, as if he's carrying a bomb seconds from detonating.

The woman is all the more glorious now that she's shed her outer shell to reveal a lean yet curvy body under a blush pink satin dress.

"Do you know who that is?" Nate says with scandal.

"Who?" I've never been more eager to learn about someone in my entire life.

"She's the buyer of Pilgrim's Island."

"The one with the old stone mansion on it? The one that was up for auction last spring?"

"Rumor has it, the bidding lasted all night. It went for seven figures. To her."

"Who is she? She looks exotic. Is she the daughter of a duke or something?"

"Nobody knows."

"Is she from Redemption?"

"I don't think so."

"What's her name?"

"Smyrna. Smyrna something. I can't remember the rest."

Just the sound of her name and how it slips out of my boyfriend's mouth like a delicious little rumor, makes me tingle right down to my toes. Finally, I tear my gaze from her and return my attention to Nate. "I just want to know everything about her," I say. "I think she's quite fabulous. In an odd yet beautiful way."

He turns back around to the table and shrugs. "She's probably just some dead rich man's benefactor."

"Hey wait a minute. I heard something else about the mansion in the office. Bill said the woman who bought it is gonna donate an entire wing to orphaned girls. There's a lottery to get in. Maybe I should go introduce myself. Ask about getting the Putzarella girls in."

"I thought we were finished with those people. And besides, I don't think she wants company tonight. Oh look. There's Deb and Jerry. I invited them to meet us for drinks."

I turn to find a well dressed middle aged couple coming in through the front entrance and making their way over to the lounge. Nate waves to catch their attention. "I'll be over in a minute," he mouths with a big grin. Jerry waves back and Deb blows kisses in the air.

"Jerry. Is that the Wall Street tycoon?"

"Yes."

"I thought you said Jerry is one of the most pretentious people you've ever met."

"I did. He's also wealthier than God. He's got a share in the casino and my dad and I are trying to get a piece. Pris, I haven't told you too much about the casino, have I?"

"I already know about the Member's Only lounge."

"Yes. But there's more. Are you able to keep a secret? I mean, I really shouldn't be telling you."

"I would never tell a soul. You have my word."

He leans in close and lowers his head along with his voice. "There are some powerful people behind this Member's Only. Like very powerful."

"You mean the mafia?"

He scoffs. "Fucking slimy mobsters are at the bottom of the food chain."

"Really." I say amused but unconvinced.

"Yes. Really."

"So who's on top then?"

"Jerry is one. And my father is close to getting in."

"Like a country club?" I attempt. I don't ever want to look ignorant in my beautiful Nate's eyes.

"No." Glancing left to right he whispers, "Like the illuminati."

"You're pulling my arm." I don't know if I believe in

stuff like the illuminati. I mean of course there are powerful behind-the-scenes people in government, but nothing as sinister as the illuminati.

"Men so powerful you wouldn't believe. They are right here in Redemption."

"Does the mayor know?"

"The mayor is one of them."

"You lie."

"Well he works for them at least. Which is just as good as being one of them. The men of Redemption are going to rule the world one day, you watch."

Well, if Nate believes in this, I guess I'll just go along. "And where will you be when this happens?"

"On a yacht with dad and Jerry and the rest of the Brotherhood. Living the good life. And you of course. That is if you want to join me."

"I would go with you anywhere, Nate Rodney Harrington the Third."

He smiles and winks again. God I can't take it. "Good," he says. "If you stay on your best behavior with Deb and Jerry later, maybe you'll be my lucky charm."

"Don't worry, baby. I'll behave."

I work in an office on the tenth floor of the Henry Stein building in downtown Redemption. As I exit the elevator, quiet welcomes me. I'm grateful for it. Not that I don't like my coworkers. Sometimes I just need emptiness to get my thoughts together. I remove my Vince Camuto slingbacks from my aching feet. Hanging them on a crooked finger I pad down the hall toward my office.

I wasn't too thrilled about Nate needing "alone time" to talk his business with Jerry, seeing how Trish was still in the lounge shifting her ginger waves from one shoulder to another, still acting like she barely was aware that her x-boyfriend was in the same room. If Nate is secretly seeing her, I'll die. I'll pick up everything and go back to Erie.

"I hope you won't be too long," I said. "Will it take long?"

"Maybe an hour or so. But I'm getting under his skin. I can feel it, babe. I don't want to rush this."

"Okay. I'll be home waiting for you. To tuck you into bed. Feed you bread and aspirin if you get too tipsy." I kissed him and pressed my forefinger to his lips.

I have to go home and practice being a good housewife. I'll empty the dishwasher, set up his coffee for the morning and turn down the bed. And I'll lie myself naked, ass up in it.

But first thing is first, I have to empty out all these pesky thoughts swimming around inside my mind. Pesky thoughts ruin all fun and leave me prey to vultures like Trish. I wish I could have left that part of me, the part that thinks too much, back in Erie. The sexy me sure does not appreciate her.

There's one other workaholic in our office—my boss, Bill. As I move down the hall I notice his light's on. "Hi Bill," I call out cheerfully, so as not to startle him. My mood is lighter in this moment, and I attribute it to the alcohol.

"Priscilla?" Bill is about fifty. He's a tall, slouching man with big, brown eyes framed in outdated glasses that don't flatter his face.

"Do you ever go home, Bill?" I ask leaning on his doorframe.

"You know me. I think much better at night."

I shouldn't have asked him that. How insensitive. Bill's wife committed suicide three years ago and ever since he's been glued to his desk.

He takes off his glasses and looks at me in earnest. Bill is super considerate. He's the kind of man who, even if I did hurt his feelings, wouldn't show it so as not to upset me. "So what's *your* excuse?" he asks. "You've been here a lot of late nights yourself."

"Too many cases. I can't keep up. I've got a couple drafts to write up."

"What's the most recent?"

"The Putzarellas."

"Putzarella. Oh yeah. Heather told me the mother might be hard to get to."

"The mother's a closed door. And the oldest daughter's in denial. It's not gonna be easy."

"Look. If you'd like, I'll see if one of the other girls has space to take it."

I'm suddenly relieved, like a hundred ton weight has just been lifted from me. "Yes. I would love that. Thanks, Bill. That would be nice."

The office I share with six other women was just newly renovated. I won't admit it to anyone but the office was part of the reason why I moved to Redemption and took this job. It's all clean lines and sterile furniture with not a hint of oldness anywhere. And the view. God, the view. I switch the light on and step over to the windowed wall. Downtown Redemption is lit up against a black sky. The new casino, Strive, is glowing in neon purple and stands at least forty stories taller than all the other buildings in town. Some people call it unoriginal, as it was designed after the Lisboa in Japan, but I think it's a work of art. Nate is planning on renting one of the penthouse suites there in a few weeks, for the grand opening. "Just for fun," he said. "Because you deserve it."

I wonder for a moment if this is a guilt gift. Like maybe he did something wrong. I don't want to ask him about Trish because that will make me look needy and insecure. God, why can't she just go away or die or something.

My thoughts shame me.

I narrow my eyes onto my own reflection imprinted upon the city. "You're beautiful," I tell myself. "And you're enough. He loves you."

Dropping my coat over the back of my chair I start in on my assessment: *The Putzarellas live in a two bedroom apartment on Kindred Street in the Valley, above a restaurant named Mama's Door. The oldest daughter, Stori, was reluctant to let me in, but out of duty, observed the Valley custom of unbiased hospitality. As she made a pot of coffee and prepared a tray of cookies I observed the kitchen to be clean and orderly (no strong odors, no dirty dishes in the sink) Although the mother was ill in her bedroom and not fit for visitors, Stori insisted her mother cooks for her and still takes care of the house.*

I stop typing.

I search my memory for little details that will help me present my case. I'm not bragging or anything, but I'm pretty smart when it comes to the nuances of the interview. The big story can always be found in the minute details. A word spoken or a wayward glance can open up an endless closet of bones. I've gotten things out of people I never dreamed I could.

But I knew from the start that Stori was gonna be hard.

Sitting at her kitchen table in her brown brick kitchen with its quaint wall sconces and mahogany window frames, I tried my best:

"So are you originally from Redemption, Stori?"

"Lived here all my life."

"And have you always been in the Valley?"

She nods.

"And your parents. Are they from the Valley as well?"

"All of us are Valley-born."

"It must be nice to have your roots so deep in a place. That is, as long as you like it."

"I like it."

"Have you ever traveled?"

"I've never been more than maybe ten miles from the Valley."

I dread the thought of having to remove this girl. Any number of things can happen as a result: Stori might get violent, seeing how she's been suspended from school on numerous occasions for fights. She's also bipolar. There's one report, which I'm still waiting on, that documents a hallucination that resulted in a two week stint in the hospital psyche ward. (I'm gonna have to have a police escort when the time to remove her comes.) Or she might try to run away, or worse, she could even kill herself. I've witnessed all of the aforementioned and for some reason I don't think I'll be able to handle any of them in the case of Stori and her family. As tough as she is, there's something undeniably vulnerable about her. I feel awful for her already.

"Stori, I just want you to know how sorry I am about your father."

She dunks a lemon frosted cookie into a steaming cup of coffee. "Sorry for what?"

I dunk my cookie into my cup and allow for some silence. I can't help but notice she's pretty boring in the looks department. Maybe it's that big shock of bright burgundy hair that overwhelms her small face. Or maybe it's the God-awful mauve sweatshirt that does zilch for her olive skin. She wears no makeup and her eyes have dark circles under them from either a poor diet or lack of sleep. The girl needs an ambush makeover and she needs one bad.

Shallow, I know, focusing on such superficial things while she's obviously going through something horrible. I hope I'm not becoming a jerk. I have to remind myself that just because I live in a penthouse apartment with the winner of last year's *Redemption's Most Eligible Bachelor*, I don't have to let that go to my head. After all, there's something to be said about a woman who's risen from the gutter, but still has reverence for her roots. Looking at the forgettable face of Stori Putzarella is like looking at my roots. I decide to be kind to her. "Stori, if you'd like, I can set up some counseling for you at the Child First Center to help you get through this."

"I don't need counseling. For what?"

"To help you deal with your loss."

"It's not a loss Miss Van Patten. He's not dead. Look, I know you think my father's not coming back and you think my mother's gonna unravel to pieces. I know you think me and Regi are being neglected. I bet you even started your paperwork on us or whatever it is you all do when you come in and wreck these families to pieces."

"Now hold on a minute. That's not fair."

"But I'm telling you my father did not run away from us. Something bad happened to him. Like a kidnapping. And I need you to believe me."

"Stori, what evidence do you even have that would suggest he was kidnapped?"

She gets up and grabs a tin from the kitchen counter and brings it back to the table. She opens it and says, "Take a look at *this*."

I look inside and see more lemon cookies. "What is it that I'm looking at?" I ask.

"These are my father's favorite. He asked my mom to make a double batch the morning before he went missing. Why would he have asked her to do that if he was gonna just leave? Do you know what goes into making these things?"

"Stori. I know it's horrible thinking your dad might not have done the right thing. I've looked into his background. So I know he tried to kill himself once at the dam. If it makes you feel any better my father—"

"—I told you already lady. He was kidnapped. Don't you have any cop friends? That can help?"

I do. I can nudge one of my friends on the force, but I've become quite the skeptic over the past few years. Her dad either skipped town or overdosed.

"I'll look into it," I lie.

She's looking me over, and I suddenly feel self-conscious. I straighten in my chair and hook my hair behind my ears.

"You're lying aren't you? You're gonna take me and Regi out of here."

"No. I'm not." Another lie. "But I need to make sure you both are safe. Stori, if you have to leave this place just remember there's a whole other world out there beyond the Valley. Even in this very city. Redemption's growing rapidly and Mayor Vaughn believes we're gonna be one of the top booming metropolises one day. I can help you with college, get you into a respectable career. You can have a great life. Future Forward. Remember?"

She sneers. "Stop talking lady. You just reminded me of why I hate when people talk. And FYI. There's no such thing as the future."

Okay, Pris. Calm down. She didn't mean to be rude.

That's when I notice something on the floor. A pair of eyes staring up at me out of Stori's book bag. "Is that a doll?" I ask her.

She looks down and I can see she's embarrassed. She goes to reach for it, but it's closer to me. I'm already pulling it out of the bag.

I hold it into the light. It's a handmade doll the size of a newborn infant. Her head and torso are sculpted of clay, but her arms and legs are of stuffed cotton. I finger the green velvet dress, pinch the lace embroidery and rub it softly. I caress the Tussah silk hair, drawing it back from her shoulders. I have never seen something so finely sculpted, so elaborate. "This is exquisite," I say. Taking closer note of the facial features I have a small epiphany. "She looks just like you, Stori. The resemblance. It's uncanny." I guess Stori can be pretty after all. Somewhere under all that gloom and doom there's a loveliness too frightened to come out.

"Regi has one too," Stori says snatching it from me and placing it back in her bag. "My father had Mr. Funicelli, the shoemaker, make them. He sculpted and painted the faces himself."

I can't help but be impressed. "Really. It's a treasure."

"I know," Stori snaps in her oh so charming fashion.

I would never suspect someone so tough to be carrying around a dainty doll in her book bag. I have to remind myself that people in the Valley do very unexpected things. They're somewhat of an enigma. I know the doll has no bearing on my case and I shouldn't be wasting time, but I can't help it. I can't help but conjure a Christmas when I received my own doll. My father, on one of his sober mornings, watched as I pulled the wrapping paper off and squealed in delight. He was beaming with happiness and flicking away big round tears, as big as raindrops, from his face. That doll is long gone, but the memory lives on without her.

How do you forget someone who is unforgettable?

A horrid sound is coming from outside, down below on the street. An ugly sustained caterwaul.

"What the hell is that?" I ask, wanting to cover my ears.

"Wailing women," Stori says. She doesn't bother getting up, which tells me that women wailing in the middle of the street must be an everyday occurrence in the Valley. But I'm dying to see what's going on, so I get up and go to the window. Looking down I see a group of about ten or eleven women, approaching the house, walking in the middle of the cobblestone. All of them are dressed in black and carrying their own picture frame. I can't make out the face but I know it's a woman in the frame. A priest in black, carrying a bible trails reverently behind them.

"It's Concettina I bet," Stori says. "She lived here for almost a hundred years. She died."

They're directly below me now and I'm about to pull the blinds closed on this most morbid sight when all of a sudden something just behind the women catches my eye. There! In the alley behind them! "Oh my God!" I exclaim, covering my mouth with a quavering hand. My heart is caught in my throat.

"What?" Stori asks in alarm. "What is it?"

"Do you see that?"

"See what?"

"Come here. Quick."

By the time she's looking to where I'm pointing the alley is barren. "I don't see anything," she says.

"He was just there. I swear it. There was a man in the alley down there. A man with fur all over his face. And he was laughing."

"You mean a beard?"

"No. Not a beard. Fur. Like all over his face. Dark brown like bat fur."

"You high on something?" she asks.

"Of course I'm not."

"And you're worried about me, lady?"

I hear a light wrapping on solid oak and I am no longer in Stori's kitchen but back at my desk in the office. Bill pops his head in at the door. He puts an arm through an outdated tweed jacket. "Just out of curiosity. Did they ever locate the father?"

"No. He's still missing. I've talked to some neighbors. People say he was never the same after the accident. I think he's gone for good."

"It's a shame," Bill says. "Too many people going missing lately. And most of them children."

"We do our best…" I remind him, being the optimist I always try to be, "…to keep as many families together as we can."

He smiles. "Good night, Priscilla. Don't work too late."

"Good night, Bill. I won't."

Damnit. Nate's already home. The lights are on. I come into the living room and drop my things on the couch. Quietly I step inside the bedroom and find him under the covers, snoring loudly, *The Art of Seduction* lying open on his stomach. I place the book on his nightstand, pull the covers up to his chin and creep back outside, closing the bedroom door behind me.

His cell phone is on the coffee table. I sit on the couch and go to reach for it. But then I don't. There has to be trust if this is going to work. *I'm worthy. I'm worthy. I'm worthy.*

When my silent mantra is done, I reach past his phone and grab the remote. Scrolling the DVR I select my favorite show—Big Bang Theory. A smile creeps across my face and I lean back and exhale. This is all I need. A little laughter. And Sheldon Cooper always does the trick.

Stori

Oh God. Out of everyone in the Valley who might know about Cosimo the Corpse, does it have to be Miss Beppy, dumb Desma's paralyzed aunt? I hate Desma. I don't care if it's wrong. She lives next door, one floor above us. Our families share a clothesline; it runs from a pulley attached to our front fire escape and crosses a narrow alley, slanting up to her fire escape pulley. Mostly everyone in the Valley hangs their clothes out to dry, even in the dead of winter. Kindred Street is cluttered with rows of billowing cotton during midday, waving like friendly flags above our heads. My mother insists if her family leaves their stuff out too long and I need the space, I am to take it down and fold it for them and bring it over to their apartment in a basket. It was never a problem before, but I'm more than sour about it now as I lean over the side of the fire escape and draw her bobbing dish towels toward me. I'll pull them in, but I am NOT folding them for her.

Rumor's out. How I've put a mark on her out of raging jealousy.

Cradling a whicker basket of hand towels and oven mitts I make my way down to the street. Once outside, I come down the three concrete steps of my stoop and up the three steps of Desma's. Desma lives atop My Fair Lady Beauty Salon. After ringing her buzzer I try to ignore the biting cold by peeking inside the salon. A few old ladies sit under dryers and Lorraine, the manicurist, is at her work station warming her hands around a steaming coffee mug. Her sister, Loretta, busily sweeps the floor. Loretta glimpses me from the corner of her eye and waves hello. "Don't forget your mother," she mouths.

I nod and wave back.

Loretta wants to treat my mother to a complimentary shampoo and setting and have Lorraine give her a full mani/pedi—on account of Mommy being really sick.

Finally I hear the deadbolt of Desma's door go *klock*.

When she sees me her face drops. "I...I..." she stutters.

"Oh please. I'm not here for you."

"You're not?"

"Don't flatter yourself, Desma."

"I didn't mean to…well it's just that people were saying you had beef with me…I'm sure it's not true. I mean it's not like I stole your…" She bites her lip.

"Tony was *never* my man. And I never liked him."

The first statement is true. The second is an outright lie. Her bottom lip is bright red from her chewing on it so hard. I can't help but recall another rumor that's been circulating—that Desma is a great kisser.

Yes, a great kisser! I hate having to even say it, because it makes me so fucking jealous but rumor is spreading faster than HPV that she can make out with the best of them and that's why he fell in love. I heard most of the story from Ernestine. You see, Ernestine is a little faster than I am when it comes to boys. Sometimes she goes to those stupid make out parties when she knows a hottie's gonna be there. Turns out Tony was at the last one she went to, cause he's such a horn dog. Ernestine said that Tony and Desma were making out all night and after the lights came on Tony couldn't stand. His friends tried to lift him off the couch but his knees kept buckling. "She killed me," he said. "That girl is the best kisser I've ever had."

Now all the guys are in love with her and everybody's talking about how she has the kiss of death.

I'm not too sure, but I think I'm a horrible kisser. I mean, I've never really done it before so I must be horrible. I wanted to learn so bad that I stole a Seventeen magazine from the media center at school; it had this article on the art of kissing. Ever since then I've been brushing my lips once a week with a toothbrush to exfoliate them and I put Vaseline on them every morning. I practice at night in bed after Regi falls asleep—I roll my tongue around in my mouth to get a feel for of how it would be like—I run it under my lips over my teeth. (I got all that from the magazine.) Sometimes I use my fingers for practice, pressing two of them together as pretend lips. But it's just so hard to know. I mean what makes a good kisser? A part of me would love to ask Desma but I would rather die than admit I suck at something she's good at. I despise giving other people the upper hand.

Looking at her now, getting an up-close of those lethal lips, shimmering under a gleam of strawberry lip gloss, I feel so inadequate. Like I'm just a child and she's ten years older—already a woman.

You're probably going to think I'm the biggest loser you ever met now, but I wish I was Desma instead of me. I wish I looked like her, acted like her and had her man. I wish instead of being the toughest girl in the Valley I was the best kisser in the Valley. God, what an honor it would be. I would never wish for another thing again. Except my father of course.

Now I have to ask her permission to come in. Could this get any worse? "No beef, Desma. I'm here to see your aunt."

"Oh." She smiles and I note the small gap between her

two front teeth and her slight overbite. Even her imperfections are pretty. "Aunt Beppy?"

"Yeah."

"She's having lunch in the den."

"Can I see her?"

"Of course, Stori. You're always welcome here."

Stop being so nice, damnit. I don't want to be your friend. I want to imagine you as the evil man-stealer you really are.

She leads me upstairs into her apartment. Aside from the spotless linoleum kitchen the whole place is covered in wall to wall carpet. It's a pinkish salmon kind of color with not the slightest stain or cigarette burn. Plum drapes frame the windows and radiators, sweeping all the way down to the floor. Desma's mother owns the flower shop a few blocks from here. Potted ivy and gardenias sit in the windowsills, all of them gleaming and neatly trimmed. Her apartment kind of feels like being inside a red flower.

Through a small room a door leads out to another little room. Unlike the rest of the house, with its muted glow, there are no curtains in here. Sunlight streams in from every direction. Desma's Great Aunt Beppy rests in a cushiony rocking chair, her legs under a blanket. Half a sandwich is on a plate in her lap and a napkin's tucked into her collar. She isn't much of anything—maybe ninety pounds at best—I'm not sure if I'd even give her that. Her long arms are roped with purple veins and splotchy with sun marks.

"Aunt Beppy. You have a visitor."

Aunt Beppy stares straight out the window into the blaring light. "Who is it dear?"

"Stori Putzarella."

"Putzarella."

"Frank and Anna's daughter. Remember?"

"Oh yes. Come in dear. Sit in the sun. The birds aren't back yet from the South. But at least we have the sun."

Desma puts an armless chair in front of her aunt and I sit. I wait for Desma to leave but no luck there. She goes over to the corner and sets herself on a footstool, placing my whicker basket in front of her. She places a hand towel on her lap and says with a smile, "Go ahead. You can talk to her."

If she's waiting for a smile back, she's not getting one. I ignore her completely and look at her aunt. "Miss Beppy. I'm here to see you because…well my father is missing, Miss Beppy. He disappeared in the middle of the night. I was at Miss Lu's house last night—" I glance up to see Desma's reaction. I guess I'm not a threat to her the way she is to me. "—and her son, Arty, said Cosimo the Corpse had something to do with it."

She stiffens like she got stung by a bee.

"I don't know if I believe in Cosimo, but—"

"—Stop right there," she demands. She starts choking a little bit. She can still use her one arm for she takes the

napkin out of her blouse and puts it to her mouth. She
clears her throat. "Desma. You better not be playing no
tricks on me."

Desma puts her folding down. "No auntie. I swear."
She turns to me wide eyed. "Stori, I'm sorry. But we don't
talk about that person in this house. Not never."

I ignore her again. I lean forward on my elbows and
hunch down so I'm much lower than Miss Beppy. This is a
sign of respect and I hope it will assure her I'm not here to
play tricks or hear a good story. "Miss Beppy. I'm so sorry.
I would normally never ask you something like that, but my
father—he could be in danger. He could be dead, Miss
Beppy. My mother's not good either. If my father doesn't
come home soon we can be in a lot of trouble. Please, Miss
Beppy. I'm scared." I'm forced to say it. Even if now
Desma knows I'm all around pathetic. But I don't care
anymore. The more I think about my father not coming
home the more I understand how nothing else matters but
getting him back—nothing—not even my pride.

Aunt Beppy closes her eyes and says, "Who saw him?"

"I don't know if anyone saw him. But that's what Arty
Arm told me."

She starts nodding her head, eyes sealed tight. She
reaches forward and grabs onto the pillowed arms of the
rocking chair. Gripping tight, fingers pressed into stuffed
cotton, she begins to speak. Weird words that don't make
any sense. A language I have never heard before.

Desma looks terrified. "No, Aunt Bep. Stop it."

But the words come spilling out, faster and faster and faster. Her voice rises, booms off the walls. My heart is racing. I don't want this woman having a heart attack or anything. Or falling out of her chair and getting hurt. I reach out and put my hand on top of hers. "Miss Beppy, take it easy. Please."

Then her eyes shoot open and she stares wildly at me. "It wasn't him. But one of his Hounds was here. He came right over my bed. Have you known evil, girl?"

Desma stands and knocks over the basket. She rushes over to her aunt and kneels before her. "Please, Aunt Beppy. Let it go." She looks up at me. "Stori. You have to leave. You don't understand."

Man am I spooked now. Maybe I don't want to know what she has to tell. But my father. My father. I look away from Desma and back to her aunt. "If I haven't, I want to know."

Desma's panting as if she's going to pass out or something but her aunt pays her no attention. "Cosimo and his lovesick witch sent their Hounds in the night to kill me. One of them came right over my bed and put his hands around my neck. He had the claws of a pigeon."

My toes cringe and my spine tingles the way it does when I sense someone behind me might grab me. I have to straighten and tighten my shoulders to fight it. "What did you do?"

"I prayed for him, Stori. I prayed good and hard. He couldn't get my life, but he took my walking away. That much he was able to get. But he and the other Hounds will be back. They won't stop until all the Braves in Redemption are dead."

"Oh. So this is about the Braves?" I'm disappointed. This is just another one of those old people myths.

Here's where I better pause to tell you a little more about the Valley. I was hoping I could kind of skim right over it, seeing how utterly insane it sounds. But there are some who say they're from the lineage of the first people. Like Adam's people. I know. It's insane. Noone is able to trace their roots back that far. But nonetheless some old folk here claim they go back to some tribe that descended from Eden.

"I am of the lineage of the Braves. There aren't that many of us left in Redemption. The Braves are the oldest tribe to walk the face of the earth. They have been around since the time of Babel and before. They were on the boat with Noah."

"But Miss Beppy. How do you know?"

"Well I know the stories. The ones I tell on my front stoop to the children." She points at me. "You never come and listen."

"Me?"

"I know the old tales of how my people came to be our most powerful in the city of Shinar, when the tower of

71

Babel was being built. I know about the making of the crown. All of it passed down, Stori. Passed down. A thread as thin as spider's silk that has never been broken. Why don't you come and listen with the other children?"

"I don't know. How can stories last that long if they were never even written?"

"Oh, some were. In the book. The book that has the spell that saved Cosimo from dying. But no one knows where that book is. But there are other ways, far better than a book even, to preserve history. Just as the places still exist where our ancient mothers walked so are the lives they lived. Nothing in this world can ever die. Whether we know they're there or not, the stories remain. And we can preserve them. Why through each other, of course."

"I won't hear the stories," Desma says all defiant. "Aunt Beppy tries to tell me the stories but I won't hear them."

Miss Beppy frowns. "Why Desma? Tell me why?"

"Because look at you! All hurt and sick. And just because you wouldn't stop telling those kids that one about Bilhah."

"Bilhah?" I blurt out, having completely forgotten my rivalry.

"Yes," Desma insists, clutching my forearm. "Aunt Beppy told that story to some kids from Soda Can and then that night that *thing* came in here."

"I knew it was only a matter of time," Miss Beppy

says. "He don't want us telling them stories. Knowing who we are. Where we came from."

"The old and the new?" Her eyes darken. "They are going to kill me. But before they do, I just want to pass the stories on to Desma."

"I won't let her," Desma insists. "The stories are dangerous. They should never be told. Ever ever again."

"Let's call the police." I say. "Or maybe we should tell the Tapparellis."

"It's beyond the police. The Tapparellis can do nothing. Your father's missing? Pray for him. The dawning of the Dark Age has begun. And the final war is being waged this very moment. I don't think the good side will be able to win, with all I've heard and seen. There are only a few of us left now. Just a few who have the stories of the Braves. If the end is coming, and Desma won't hear my stories, then I just want to sit here in my sunroom. Why isn't that enough?" She points out to the brilliant sky. "Look at the sun. My God. Look at that sun!"

"Miss Beppy. We can't let this person just come in here and hurt us like that. We are the Calabrese of the Valley. We're stronger than him. Where do you think he is now? Where does he hide?"

"You foolish girl. Go ahead and call for him. He'll send his Hounds to come and eat you up alive. Do you know his power? Get out of here! Get out of here! Get out!"

Desma takes a step forward. "Stori. Please. She can't take it."

I get up and look down on the woman. I want to say sorry but she's so mad at me I don't even think it will help. I rush out of the house as quickly as I can.

Back out on Kindred Street Desma calls out to me from her stoop. "Stori wait."

Once I'm on the sidewalk I turn to face her. I feel better already, not being on her turf anymore.

"I won't tell anyone what happened in there, okay? I just want to be friends."

"I'm not your friend, Desma. And I don't need you doing me any favors. Tell as many people as you please."

She pouts. Looking at her and her perfect lips feels like double failure.

This is the way I'm gonna go out. My obituary will read: Getting pouted at by the mouth that kills. She puts her hands down by her sides and turns her palms out. She spreads her fingers wide. In the Valley if someone shows you their palms it means you have their submission. And their trust.

As much as I hate Desma I don't think she stole Tony out of spite. I think she gets how bad it's hurt me and she wants to make amends.

My little sister is across the street with a few of her friends, playing double dutch. Regi turns the ropes on one side as her friend Sammy gears up to jump inside. He rips off his coat and leaves it at his feet. The young ones never get cold it seems. As he waits, they all sing:

> Down in the Valley
> was a boy named Sam
> Traveled to the alley.
> One called Soda Can!
> Man came out to bite him
> Bite him in his hand
> Jaws just like a lion
> Even though he was a man
>
> Sammy got the curse now
> Send him to the fire
> Burn it out and spin him
> Get the beast real tired

Sammy bolts inside the ropes and starts jumping.

I nudge Regi's shoulder with two knuckles. "Mom up yet?"

Regi is petite so she has to reach her arms up to keep the ropes aligned. Her plum puffy coat makes swishy noises as she works the ropes. She's panting a little from the effort and her breath comes out in white puffs against the winter air. "She's still in bed. She doesn't want to be our mommy anymore. Just like Daddy."

"Don't say that."

"Well I'm hungry."

I think of this Hound that could have possibly been in our house and can't help but worry about Regi. It's bad enough my dad is gone, but if anything ever happened to my little sister I couldn't deal with it. "I'll make something. What do you want?"

"French toast and sweet sausage."

"Yeah right. We're having chicken."

"You're boring."

"And you're a pain in my ass. I'll be right back. I'm going to the market. Don't leave the front stoop."

"I won't."

On my way to the butcher's Richie Ramera falls in step next to me. "Sup Sullen. Pretty day for a cold one."

I hate small talk. If you've got something to say to me, say it. Otherwise get out of my face.

"Don't call me Sullen. And I should beat your ass for messing with me the other night." Aside from being a punk-ass bully, Richie is the Valley pervert. He took my best friend Ernestine's virginity last year. She said she didn't want to but he had some big dirt on her father. I told Ernestine it was rape. But she said, "Please. If that's the case, every man breathing is a rapist."

"Ok. Fine. I'll call you Stori then. Your man, Carp, don't like that name either. But I don't care what Carp likes. I care what you like."

I stop and face him. One thing I've learned in my sixteen years on this planet is when someone shows you evil, you should never run from it. No matter how uncomfortable it makes you, you have to face it dead on and never look away. "Look. I'm wasting time here. In case you haven't noticed, I got stuff going on."

He narrows his squinty eyes and licks his lips. "You're untouched, aren't you?"

I have a clean shot on him. But Richie's big. It could get ugly.

"Them lips," he says. "They never been kissed."

I shove him hard. It doesn't move him much. He laughs and lets me go, calling out. "It'll be our little secret!"

The bells chime at my entrance to Mr. Delfi's Butcher Shop and the young man at the counter looks up and smiles. "Hello. How are you today?"

I don't recognize him from the Valley. It's odd to see him in Mr. Delfi's place. I approach the counter. "Where's Mr. Delfi?"

"He's taking the day off. I'm his son in law, Jeffrey. You'll be seeing a lot more of me from now on. So what can I get for you?"

I can already tell I don't like this guy. He's a phony. "Chicken. Two thighs and some wings."

He smacks the countertop with both hands. "Coming right up."

"Wait a minute. I changed my mind. Sausage. Four links. Sweet."

"You got it."

Over in the corner is a table set up by a small black and white television mounted to the wall. There isn't a shop in the Valley that doesn't have a table set up for Tommy Tapparelli's crew. Tommy runs the streets here. His business is big—heroin, gambling and the bunny ranch on Liberty Road. Tommy's crew makes big money, and in order to make big money one must have big bodyguards to keep others from trying to take it.

I see Arty Arm sitting with a man named Mo.

Mo wasn't made for blending in. I'm talking six five with twenty four inch forearms. His presence is a major imposition wherever he goes. He has a way of filling a room with whatever mood he happens to be in at the time. If he's happy the room is happy. If he's quiet the room is quiet. At the moment he's relaxed and I must be insane for disturbing the silence. My father knows my temper so he's always given me strict warnings about staying on Mo's good side. "Your tough," my father would say, in his slow speech. (Almost drowning caused him a little brain damage.) "But not enough for some things. You see Mo on your side of the street, cross over to the other side."

Mo threw a baby down a flight of stairs once just because the baby was crying. The baby died.

My father would be very upset right now if he knew I was walking over to Mo while he was enjoying a fresh cold cut sandwich and a can of Pepsi.

"What do you want?" he snaps through a mouthful, shredded lettuce trying to escape his brutal maw.

Arty puts a hand up, "We're busy kid. Not now."

I guess I'm not thinking rationally, what with everything that happened at Desma's house. "I'm sorry to bother you, Mr. Mo. I just was wondering if I could tell you something."

"Talk."

"I was just at Miss Beppy's house and she's upset about this guy named Cosimo who sent some guy she called a Hound into her house to attack her. Arty knows who I'm talking about, don't you Arty?"

"Yeah," he sais. "But now is not the time."

"I've heard the Arm's horror stories already kid. Don't worry."

"So then you know too. I thought maybe you guys could do something, since you protect the streets and—"

"Fuck that old lady," Mo snaps. He chuckles at his own insult.

I hate Mo. I don't know why the Tapparellis allow him to run around the Valley and treat everybody like shit. It's not fair.

Arty scowls at me, shaking his head. "Told you to scram, Putz."

"Something should be done," I insist. "About Miss Beppy. About my father. And those kids too. Your supposed to protect the streets, remember?"

Mo looks up and says, "What do I care about some old bag who's a day from croaking, or these snot nosed shits always asking me for change? Fuck 'em. Let your corpse and his hounds take 'em. They ain't making me no money."

I'm fuming now. I dart my eyes on Arty. "Nana Lu know you sitting with this guy?"

Arty hides his shame as best he can.

Mo leans forward on his elbows. "You know, girl. You got the features of a mouse. You know how them scientists in the lab kill their mice for research? Grab 'em by the head and tail, pull at both ends like this."

Arty closes his eyes as if he's fallen into prayer. His nostrils flare.

Mo glares at me impatiently, waiting for an answer. Mustard is caked in the crevices of his mouth. I normally make it a point not to look at people too long—you know, in the probing kind of way. God only knows what I might find. But desperate to make sense of Mo's indifference, I peer back at him and search deep into his eyes, his face, his body, his atmosphere. The harder I concentrate, the clearer I can see the monster inside him, rolling outward so that it pulses like neon light all around him.

I've never searched Mo before so I only half believed that story about him throwing the baby down the flight of stairs. But looking at him now, I know it's true. And it breaks my very heart.

He would do just what he said. He would hurt me bad

and feel no remorse. I've always known there were people like that in the world but I never imagined I would ever have to face one.

Until now.

The bells chime as a few more customers walk in.

"All ready!" Jeffrey shouts. He whistles. "Young girl. Your order's ready."

I pay for my purchase at the register, but before I go I look across the room at Arty. I wait for him to meet my gaze. When he finally does I let him have it. "Facce Due!" It means two face in Italian. An insult in English is one thing. But an insult in Italian is the ultimate disrespect.

I leave Mr. Delfi's Butcher Shop utterly defeated, disgusted and something more—I feel like I've just lost faith in the world—in its goodness, its honor, its innocence. In a matter of just a minute, I'm not a little kid anymore.

I share a small bedroom with Regina. We have two twin beds—hers is by the double doors of the closet, mine is under the window facing out into the alley. There's a little fire escape outside my window and the potted pine tree strung with Christmas lights that my father bought at Thanksgiving is still out there. The lights are blinking and I take comfort in them as I try to drift off to sleep.

Regi's fed and fast asleep, I tell myself. *You need your rest for tomorrow's mission. As soon as school's out, you've got to find Uncle Joe.*

I close my eyes and after some time my arms and legs get heavy and before I know it, I'm in blackness. But not for long.

I wake again. But this time I'm not in my own bed, but in a large canopy with soft duvet covers and satin sheets pulled over me. Wearing some kind of silk dress I never even knew I owned I sit up and take in my surroundings.

This is definitely not my room. This is definitely no room in the Valley. Why, this place looks almost like a castle.

I pull my legs out from under the duvet and dangle them over the bedside. The cold of the stone floor whispers just below my feet. I shiver and hold my arms about myself for warmth.

A bay window in the far corner shows snow falling in big white flakes. They sail by, and with the moon behind them, make shadows upon the grey stone sill. Then comes a great wind and suddenly two doors burst wide open. In another corner are French doors draped in linen. The linen whips about in the gusting wind. Snow flurries into the room and makes a dusting over the floor.

"Where the hell am I?" I ask.

Out there, in the far beyond is Casino Strive. It's all lit up and quite beautiful, sitting under a big white moon. "I'm in Redemption," I tell myself, still shuddering from the cold. "But where?"

Before I can get off the bed and go out to the balcony I am being awoken by my sister. "You're in you're bed, Stori. You're home. With me and Mommy, still. Like always."

It was just a dream, of course. The face of my sister in all her innocence and alarm comforts me. But it also scares me somehow. She's headed for some kind of sadness. I can just feel it. I would do anything to protect her from it. I would do anything to know my sister is never harmed.

In the morning, before I put her on her bus I tell her, "Now remember what I told you. If anybody, even your friends, asks about us, you tell them nothing. Got it?"

"Got it."

I want to kiss her on the top of the head, but I don't. She's too soft and needs to toughen up. I have to be more stern with her now. It's for her own good. "Get on the bus. And remember what I said."

A couple of her friends skip over. "Hi Regi!"

Regi brightens. "Hi Britt, hi Maria."

"I love your new shoes," the one girl says.

"Thanks," says Regi.

"Oh!" the other girl says. "And look at your curls. Did you use a straight iron?"

"I only used bobby pins!" Regi is a sweet girl and has tons of friends. She's all hyper and giggly; she's whispering some kind of boy gossip with them. She's totally forgotten me. I feel a little left out. I think I'm actually jealous.

I get to my bus stop early so I can board first and get a seat right in front. I used to sit in the back with Tony but ever since he hooked up with Desma I avoid him like the plague.

He gets on with her. "Hi Stori," Desma says as she passes.

I don't answer.

"Hey Stor," Tony echoes.

I don't answer.

Tony's not pleased. He stands over me. "Come on, Stor. Why you sitting up here? Come in the back with us, kid."

"I like the front," I tell him and turn to look out the window.

"Fine. Have it your way." Tony's not used to people rejecting him so I know it's just burning him up inside. Good. Give him a dose of his own medicine. Guys are so good at dishing shit out but horrible at taking it. There you go, Tony Carp. Dissed first thing in the morning. I hope it burns you up so bad it gives you chronic indigestion. I know it's not right to wish bad things for another person, but I just can't help myself. Thank God for my best friend Ernestine, who slips into the seat beside me and distracts me from my loathing.

"Hey, Stor."

"Hey, Ern."

"I saw the missing sign you put up outside my house."

"Yeah. I was up late that night."

"I would have helped."

"It's okay. I know you're going through you're own thing."

"I'm sorry about your dad, Stor."

"It's okay."

Finally the last of our students have boarded. The doors bang shut and the engine roars.

"Did he start drinking again?"

"No. That's the thing, Ern. He was doing so good. Working overtime. Taking us out to dinners. Bringing us home gifts. It just doesn't make sense."

"Hey. He might come back then. At least you have hope. My dad's up against 10 to 15 and the public defender said this time it's gonna stick."

Ernestine's father was arrested before Christmas for holding up a pawn shop in the next town over. He said he needed the money for gifts. Her mom is legally blind and isn't able to work so Ern might get placed in foster care.

"CPS been by your place?" I ask her.

She rolls her eyes. "Every day."

"They came to my house two days ago."

She reaches over and puts her hand on my knee. I put my hand on top of hers and we ride the rest of the way to school in silence.

Priscilla Van Patten

Stori's little sister sits alone in the principal's conference room.

I set down my things and take a seat across from her. "Hi, Regina. My name is Miss Priscilla. I work for the city and I'm here to ask you a few questions. Do you think that will be okay?"

"Are you that lady from CPS?" she asks.

"I'm a social worker, yes. I help people."

"I'm not supposed to talk to you. My sister, Stori, told me."

The family's a locked volt. But I'm not deterred a bit. If there's one thing I'm good at it is tapping that vault and listening patiently for the little clicks.

"That's okay, Regina. I don't mind." I let a moment of silence pass, then continue. "You know something? I like you Regina. I can tell you're a very smart girl."

"You can?" she asks.

"Yes. I can. So I'm going to help you out, okay? I'm going to be completely honest with you. I was sent here to find out about what's going on at home. And what happened the night your father left. But since you don't want to upset your older sister, we won't talk about those things, okay?"

"Okay."

"But I do need something for my notes, or else I'll get in trouble with my boss, so maybe we can just talk about other things."

"Like what?"

"I don't know. I'm sure we'll think of something."

"What's a social worker?"

"It's someone who helps people who are having a little bit of a hard time. Families mostly."

"And kids?"

"Oh, yes. Lots of kids."

"Like sick kids?"

"Some of them are sick, yes."

"Are any of them blind?"

"Some. Why? Do you know anyone that's blind?"

"Not really. But there's a woman on our street with a seeing eye dog. And every time I see him helping her cross the street I want to just give him a big hug and tell him I love him."

Sweet. I wasn't expecting that. "Those dogs are very nice, Regi." Her conversation is quite enchanting but talking about seeing eye dogs won't get us far. "Why don't you tell me about your friends at school?"

"I got lots of friends," she says proudly.

"I bet you do."

She's nothing like her older sister. She's slight and tender and unassuming. I decide I like her. But nonetheless, I'm here for one purpose and one purpose only: to get to the bottom of things. "Tell me about one of your friends."

"Well, my best friend is Alexandria Madonna Adams."

"That's an awfully long name."

"Her mom said she came out shining when she was born, like the Madonna. She's the captain of the modern dance team. She's really nice to me, but sometimes she yells at other girls. Well, she's not that nice actually. I'm a little scared of her."

"It's not nice to yell at people," I comment. She's finally stepped onto my stage and I don't want to scare her off by too many questions.

"Yeah. I don't like it either. Alexandria picks on this one girl, Netty. Netty's brother disappeared and he never came home."

"What is Netty's last name?" I ask her. I might need this for later.

"Bak."

I jot it down. The name sounds familiar. I think our office handled a family by that last name.

"That's very sad," I say.

"I know. So I like try to be friends with her, but Alexandria doesn't like her and she's always yelling at her at dance practice. You see, Netty can't get the steps right even though she used to be a ballerina."

"That's strange," I say. "If she was a ballerina wouldn't she be able to get the steps?"

"No. She wouldn't. Cause after her brother Ben left he took the dancing with him, so she lost all her moves. He was a ballerina too, and he was gonna win the All State Dancing Competition this year but then he disappeared."

"I see. Maybe that's why Alexandria doesn't like Netty. I think maybe Alexandria feels inferior, Regi."

She leans forward, her little palms pressing down on the sides of her seat. She whispers, "If I tell you a secret do you promise not to tell anyone?"

I lean forward, elbows to knees. I whisper too. "Of course."

"Today at practice a flute started playing all by itself and it floated over right to Netty."

"Are you being silly?" I whisper back. Now we are whispering friends.

"Uh uh. Principal Victor told us if anyone sees an instrument playing by itself we have to report it right away."

"Did you report it?"

"No."

"Why not?"

"My heart told me not to. Mr. Victor is in charge but my heart is too."

I get up and close the door. Enough with the whispering. I sit back down and say, "Now no one can hear us. Regina. Why did your father leave?"

She looks up at me and says, "The night my father went away I saw a witch in the house. I think it was Cosimo's witch. She was the one who put the note on my kitchen table."

I half believe her. I don't know why. But I quickly return to my senses. "What note, Regi?"

"The note that daddy wrote."

"What did it say."

"I'm not supposed to tell you. Stori would kill me."

"I promise I won't tell anyone."

"Well…Daddy said he's leaving and never coming back. Oh, but don't you think you'll find him and tell him to come home?"

I've got my information, but for the first time, I'm sorry for it. I don't want to know any more. As soon as I get back to the office I'll have Bill give this to Heather.

"Well, I assure you there's no such thing as Cosimo or witches. Sometimes, we see things, Regina, when we really don't. When we're super scared our minds can play very powerful tricks on us."

She doesn't answer and I don't expect her to. I don't want to leave abruptly after having made her tell her secret. But I have to get away from her. I pick up my briefcase and place a hand on her shoulder. "I have to go. But please know everything will be alright."

As my hand turns the doorknob she asks, "Are they sad?"

"Are who sad?"

"The blind kids."

"No, actually, most of them are very happy."

"But they can't see the sunlight."

"I know."

"If you don't see the sunlight you can't be happy."

"But I just told you, they are."

"Are you sure?"

"Yes."

She takes some satisfaction in that, then says, "They must have sunlight inside them. We must all have sunlight inside and we don't even know it." She's drifting off into her own thoughts and she likes them. She stares beyond the wall and says, "They must have their own personal sunshine."

Stori

"Tell me a story," my mother begs ninety year old Other Mother, Rose, who stands at her bedside. Rose has just administered a sticky ointment that smells like tree sap and vinegar to my mother's temples and wrists. She's one of the best Other Mother's in the Valley. She once healed my chicken pox overnight by making me drink a tea that looked like soot and tasted like tar.

Prisicilla Van Patten is sitting in the winged back chair in the corner of the room, keeping a respectable distance, yet paying close attention. She knows she overstepped her boundaries by being in here. But my mother allowed it. (I can't stand Priscilla.)

"Tell me a story about the Braves," my mother pleads in a weak voice.

Rose tucks the quilt under my mother's chin as my mother looks longingly up at her. "How they lived. And the Other Mothers."

Rose gives a defeated sigh, "My mother knew more stories than I can remember. I should have written them down. I can kill myself that I didn't write them down. So stupid of me."

"You know some," Mommy says. "Tell me."

I spot Priscilla reaching for her purse. She wants to take out her stupid notepad and pen. When she catches me glaring at her she snaps her hand back to her lap. Good. I've shamed her. She oughtta know just what an ass she is.

Rose sits on the corner of my mother's bed. She's so tiny she doesn't even make a dent. "The Braves lived off the land in southern Calabria. They migrated there after the Tower of Babel was destroyed. For many many years they made their home by the waters in the Sila Woods.

"They lived as they always had from the beginning of time: all belongings were shared. No man or woman had more food, clothing, or shelter than the next. And their children ran about in happiness and freedom. The adults had different jobs; some hunted, some gathered nuts and herbs and fruits, others tended the animals and the homes. But no matter what the daily profession was, they all shared the common goal of providing for the whole of the tribe, which they called *The One*. Every day the same toils were performed while the children ran about in happiness and freedom. To tend and grow the togetherness of *The One*. To feed and shelter, wash and heal and love *The One*.

"And they never grew tired of this task. Of toiling for togetherness. Of loving one another.

"At the end of each day they would build a great bonfire under the night stars. There they ate and danced and prayed. And the children ran about in happiness and freedom. The mothers gave their little ones the last sucklings before bed. And if one mother was too tired or unwell to suckle her child the closest nursing mother would snatch that baby from her and put him to her breast and that baby would not hesitate to suck from her because when he looked up into her eyes he would see her very soul shining down on him. And she could see his soul, because she loved him just as much as she loved her own child. And inside of that Other Mother's love he would drink from the fount of indiscriminatory love. And right before he drifted off to sleep she would whisper 'All is well dear child. Good night.'"

"What if their mother died?" Priscilla's voice is unexpected and sounds strange when spoken in my mother's room. I glance over and notice tears welling up in her eyes. "What if both parents were dead?" she asks.

Rose answers in a flash. "There were no such things as orphans. Your mother was the closest woman to you. Your father the nearest man. This is how the Tribe of the Braves lived. And they lived for a very long time. Until the great flood that killed most of us. The flood that sent the rest of us here, to America."

"Stori," my mother says. "Come closer."

I don't want to go closer. I'm afraid of what she might say. But she's my mother. And I have to obey.

She wrestles free from the quilt and takes my hand in both of hers. "It's deep in my bones, the freezing."

"You have to fight it, Ma. You have to be strong and fight it."

Even though she's telling me something, it feels more like she's asking something unsaid. Like permission. Permission for what?

"Did you ever just feel so tired, Stori? Like you might lie down and never get up again."

"I'll make you something. You need nutrients. And Rose's tea will start working soon, won't it Rose?"

Rose looks doubtful. "Our remedies are but a shadow of the Great Mysterious and His ways."

The last person I want to hear about is God. I know enough to know that whenever people start talking about God and His *mysterious ways* that somebody's about to die.

"She'll be fine," I insist, finding myself looking over to Priscilla for support.

"Of course she will," Priscilla agrees, nodding. For a fleeting moment, I'm glad she's sitting there.

"It's not that kind of tired," my mother says. "Tea won't help. It's the worst kind of tired, Stori. I hope you never have to feel it."

She can be so dramatic sometimes. Sometimes I think she secretly enjoys her moments of misery, so she can just feel sorry for herself. But life isn't about feeling sorry for yourself. You can't just lie there and cry and expect other people to come and save you with their pity. Life is about picking yourself up, wiping your tears away with your own hands and saving yourself. The world is a cruel place that does not care. You can't wait for other people to come and save you. "What are you trying to tell me, Ma? You wanna just give up?"

"Don't be mad at me."

"Daddy's gone and you're too tired to care. Don't be mad at you. Of course not."

She closes her eyes and says, "I need rest now. Go make something for you and Regi."

Thankfully, Miss Van Patten doesn't put up a fuss when, back in the kitchen, I tell her it's time for her to go. She slips out of the apartment with Rose, after placing her hand on top of Regina's head. "It was nice talking with you today, Regina."

Regina shoots a worried look my way. *She better not have.*

Since my mom has been in bed for a week there's not much in the fridge or pantry, so I decide on keeping dinner simple: grilled cheese sandwiches and Ovaltine. The butter starts to hiss in the skillet, telling me it's time to drop my sandwiches in. Cooked butter smells sweet and it makes me even hungrier than I already am. Regi's perched atop the radiator staring out the window to the dying sun. "Hi purple. Hi orange. Hi blue. How are you?"

"Who are you talking to?"

"The angels. Do you want to come talk to them with me? There's one right here on the fire escape."

"No. There are no such things. But speaking of *talking*, what did you tell Miss Van Patten today?"

"Huh?"

"What happened?"

Regi gets quiet.

"I really hope you didn't tell her anything about us. Did you?"

She presses a finger into the glass and makes tracing motions. "Hi purple," she says to her imaginary friend. "I hope that's not true. I really like it here."

I've come to the conclusion Regi's not normal and it occurs to me she might be having visions the way I sometimes do. I don't want to think about it. Someone like Regi couldn't handle visions. Will she end up in the nuthouse by the time she's my age? I get so pissed at her I see myself picking up the skillet and bringing it down over her head.

"I'm gonna eat real quick and then I'm hitting Soda Can," I announce sternly.

She looks at me with eyes wide open. "Soda Can

Alley?"

Good. I've distracted her from her fantasies.

"Why are you going *there?*"

"To see Uncle Joe."

"Daddy said to stay away from Uncle Joe. Uncle Joe does bad stuff in Soda Can. I heard daddy talking about it. Why would you go there?"

She's right. Uncle Joe's shady and a 'Merigan besides. (He quit the masonry with my dad when he got a job working for the city and moved out of the Valley.) Nevertheless I have a gut feeling he might know something about my father's disappearance. Regi can tell me not to go all she wants, but she doesn't get that no one's looking for Daddy. Yeah the cops came and took a statement and told us they would do their best. But they were just lying. The police don't care about people like us, and they never will. Next to the Blacks who live in the Hills not far from here, we are last on their list. And Miss Van Patten—even though I'm sure she could pull a few strings with those pretty little legs of hers—she won't do much to find him either. So I tell Regi, because she needs to grow up a little and start thinking with common sense. "Who else is gonna look for him Reg?"

"The cops are. They said they would."

"The cops were too busy sniffing mom's underwear to even care."

"They did not sniff her underwear!" Somehow this

statement has put her on the edge of rage. I almost want to laugh, but I'm too tired for laughter.

"Yes they did, Regina. So don't talk about the cops with me. Don't you get it? We don't live in the Ridges. We don't have a fancy house like Uncle Joe. We are nobodies to them. If we wanna find Daddy we have to do it ourselves. And we have to stick together and not let anyone get in our way. Get it?"

She sulks. "You're negative." She's still young enough to be an optimist and my words have a crushing effect. I almost feel bad. I don't want her to grow up too fast, but what else can I do? Hard times call for even harder measures. "The social worker will be back, Regi. Thanks to you, she thinks Daddy left us for good."

She looks like she wants to say something, but then she changes gears. "Who eats grilled cheese sandwiches for dinner?"

"Girls who talk to social workers do." I say dropping her sandwich onto her plate at her place setting. "Now come eat."

She turns from me, gazes out the window again. Her back is so narrow and fragile—her little spine standing out under her shirt. "I'm not hungry."

I've hurt her feelings. I feel like a bully and I hate it. "I'm sorry. Come and eat your food."

"You would feel better," she says, still turned away from me, "If you came and talked to the angels with me.

They can tell you all about Daddy."

As I wait for her to come eat my thoughts return to the Other Mothers. It's hard to envision a time when people lived like that. Everything's so separate in 2014. Maybe not as much here in the Valley, but in the rest of Redemption it is.

If I had to leave my home, I would really know what it's like then, I bet. Just how separate everyone is. There's the rich and the poor, the happy and the starving.

Priscilla keeps saying I can be happy. Just like her. She's successful and smart. She drives a nice car and has beautiful clothes. She's pretty too. I bet she's got a boyfriend. I bet he bought her all that stuff and really loves her.

I bet her father never walked out. I bet the love of her life didn't diss her for another girl. I bet she never wanted to hit her little sister over the head with a frying pan.

A wave of sorrow almost doubles me over. An unwanted thought worms its way into my mind. *We are never going to get out of this.* He left us here. He left us behind. I'm so sure of my family's demise I have to hold myself back from caving in and crying.

I better take a pill right after I eat something. I can feel another vision coming on. But this time I feel a dark one. They don't come as often as the good visions, but when they do, everybody watch out. Like last week in history class. I was sitting there listening to Miss Wheaton tell us that very soon we wouldn't be reading history anymore. The Board of Ed was replacing those books with biographies on our current time's most influential people.

As she was explaining this, rather regretfully, it happened—the seizing of my very soul. Everything went silent. Miss Wheaton was speaking but I no longer heard her. Her mouth was moving but really slow. That's when I saw her in her death form—the way she will look when she is six feet under and rotting.

Have you ever wondered if there really is a God? Have you ever wondered if this life is but a fantasy or a dream and you are about to wake into the true reality of nothingness? Annihilation. No time. No space. No color. Just vacuum. No past or future. No memory, no light.

I don't want to scare you because so far you've been a good listening friend. But I have witnessed annihilation. I have been to that place where there is nothingness. No God.

If I could have screamed I would have but in that place I myself didn't exist anymore. No soul, no spirit. Just floating out there in the bottomless pit of what I assume is hell.

People try to say the devil will take you to a fiery place where monsters will take pleasure in playing with your feet. But it's not even that good—trust me.

Hell—this is what hell is—it's the dark one leading you away from the world you know and sending you through a door, shoving you straight through it. What's on the other side is not fire to look upon and the company of monsters. It is absolute nothingness—your whole life snuffed out and you're left to hang in the absence of all things—a big empty black hole—for the rest of your existence.

I get so scared of hell sometimes it makes me shiver. I don't want to be having these thoughts. I want so badly to get rid of the darkness in me.

I am that person right now, although I try to fight it. I am full of a shaking, shivering, decaying hatred-fear. I don't believe there's hope for my family anymore. I see my sister becoming a nutjob, my mother dying in her bed, my father rotting in a pit somewhere and myself roaming the streets with a hunger to destroy every living thing I see.

I know it's morbid.

I have to remember my condition. I have to tell myself it comes in waves—to just ride the wave, get through it, and let it go.

But the anger I feel when I'm inside all this darkness changes me—the way those people in the movies change into werewolves—I'm not me anymore. I'm full of hatred and thankful for nothing. I don't want to live anymore when I'm in the darkness. Yes. Even though I've seen what's waiting on the other side.

The only thing that saves me from the annihilation is a single thought. Escape.

It wouldn't take long to pack a bag for me and Regi

and hit it. I could take care of us. We'd stow away in one of the freight trains going out West.

Although it doesn't feel like a possibility, as I've never slept a night outside of this house, I make up my mind to formulate plan B.

I pull Regi's chair out and sit on it sideways. "Reg. Come over here. Now."

She slides off the radiator sulking and takes heavy steps in my direction.

I pull her close, between my legs. "You and I might have to leave this place."

She hangs her head. "Not without mommy."

"Mommy's not well."

"I'm not going anywhere."

"You need to look at me."

Her eyes come reluctantly to mine.

"If anything happens to us—like we get separated, if you go somewhere you don't like, or somebody's not nice to you, just run away okay."

"I'm not going anywhere." She hangs her head again.

"Just listen to me. We have to have a meeting place. That only me and you know about. Our own secret place."

"Our own secret place?"

"Yes. We'll meet at the dam."

"Where daddy jumped?"

"Yes. Where daddy jumped."

"How will I know you'll meet me?"

I don't have an answer, but I'm convinced that I love her so much that if she did call me I would somehow know. "When you get there, tell it to the stars. I promise I'll hear it and I'll come."

"But we're not getting separated, right Stor?"

I kiss her on the forehead. "No. Now eat and then finish your homework. I'll be back."

I yank on an army coat from Forever 21 and an old pair of Adirondack boots and make my way outside. The wind is whipping about through the narrow tunnels of Kindred Street and flurries of snow feather down out of the darkening sky. The air is crisp and I breathe it in deep. I shift where I stand and allow a minute to just be. The kiss I placed upon my sister's head is what I want to think of. I allow myself a minute to just live in that memory.

In less than five minutes I'm at the piazza, which is a small courtyard where in the summer children play in the fountain and men sit on the benches playing chess or discussing local gossip—or both. The fountain is frozen and the courtyard is empty save for two crooked cops commiserating with one of the hooker girls from Madam Scarlet's bunny ranch. The three of them stop to look at me and then the cop nudges his head for me to get lost.

As I pass the rambling stone church, which is tucked in the back of the piazza, behind a hedge of manicured bushes, I see Father Ash Chenasi eyeing me as he stands before the front doors. (The church was built by the men of the Valley in the late 1800's. Free of charge they spent many weekday evenings and weekends chiseling and laying stone. Even the bell in the bell tower was hand crafted by our men—my father's father was one of those men.)

My family is like many others in the Valley. We don't always make it to church every Sunday as we sometimes like to pray the ancient ways. A succession of dissatisfied priests came before Father Ash, some of them even calling us heretics. But Father Ash finds our ways amusing and calls us Relic Christians. The Valley has been grateful for him as he's good at holding judgment, unlike his predecessors.

"Good evening Miss Putzarella. Out for a walk are you?"

I stop to address him respectfully. "Good evening Father Ash. I'm headed to Soda Can Alley." I don't know why I tell him the truth, but I figure it's not good karma to tell lies when I'm looking for the truth myself.

He picks up his eyebrows and nods his head as if he half understands why I would be going to an awful place like that. "Is there anything you'd like to ask me?"

I'm not sure what he means. But it probably has something to do with the Word. Right now I don't want to hear it. The Word is not going to help. "No father. I don't have anything to ask."

"Very well. Have a nice night." And with that, he steps back inside the church and closes the door on me.

He's a little strange sometimes.

About a hundred yards or so beyond the piazza is the train tracks and farther beyond is the outskirts of the Valley. Here the streets are paved and lead out to the Interstate I-95. There's a junkyard lot called Soda Can. A dye factory was knocked down ten years ago when the plans for the casino were approved. (Even though they ended up using a different lot.) Two thousand people were laid off—many from the Valley. They live here now in Soda Can. Yes, the desire for progress is intrinsic to the human condition, but it doesn't seem to come without a cost.

Soda Can Alley is the cost of the casino.

It's situated under the overpass where the billboard of the model in the red dress is standing. The Canners are bottle and can gleaners. They spend their days scouring downtown Redemption for recyclable containers, stacking them into stolen shopping carts. At the end of the day they bring them here to the Alley where the city set up a line of recycling machines. The Canners live entirely off the profits from the machines. It's not much and some days they don't even eat. "Stay away from hungry people," my mother always tells me. "They can get awful ugly. Keep your butt out of Soda Can."

But the hungry Canners are just a front for what really lies under the overpass and the billboard of the beautiful girl. There's an office building called the clubhouse that belongs to the mob boss, Tommy Tapparelli, who runs Redemption's City Carting. He lets some of the mayor's city officials use that building for their unofficial clandestine meetings.

I'm not so educated on politics and what it takes to run a city but I do know one thing: there's not a city in the world that doesn't have dirty secrets. Every politician out there is hiding something. Our mayor brags about Redemption's clean streets and upright citizens, the promise of our rapid modernization, our booming economy. Redemption was voted one of the top ten cities in the United States: clean air, great schools, lost of jobs, nightlife and five star restaurants.

But they left out the part about the rampid drugs and prostitution and the illegal gambling. The mayor and his officials sweep all that under the rug so they can enjoy the spoils of such crimes.

My Uncle Joe, head of the Park's Department, uses the clubhouse every Thursday night to screw his mistress, otherwise known as his "gumad."

By the time I step to the lip of Soda Can, it's after nightfall. It's littered with trash and instead of parked cars are shopping carts abounding with stuffed trash bags, Canners resting wearily beside them.

I brought my bookbag, and Amanda's inside. I thought I would bring her along for moral support. "Okay, Amanda. Here goes nothing. You keep your eyes peeled for the Dobermans." I tune in to their sharp barking in the near distance and I pray to God they're chained. An intruder like me would be prime meat for them.

Then I step forward and start my way in.

The air is about ten degrees colder here than in the rest of the Valley. I zip the open part of my coat up to my chin.

That's when I spot something in the shadows. My heart jumps into my throat. Something small and fast darts out from behind a garbage container only to vanish behind another. A child's laughter sounds. Not knowing the direction it came from, I whip around like a madwoman. The laughter comes again. I plant my feet for battle. Then a young boy steps into view. A few yards from him a little girl appears. They're gaunt and wearing tattered clothes. "Brother," the girl calls out. "Sister," the boy responds. The boy digs into his jacket pocket and brings something out. He inspects it closely, holding it less than an inch from his eyeball. Then he hurls it in a high arch into the air. I catch it on instinct. It's a gaming chip. One for placing bets. It's black, engraved with little white hearts and spades. Etched in the center is the word STRIVE. On the flip side is the unsmiling face of Mayor Vaughn. I've heard of these chips but it's the first time I'm seeing one. An advertisement went out a month ago in *Redemption's Tomorrow* about how anyone who finds a black chip will get a free buffet dinner and one night's VIP access to the Member's Only robot lounge called Heaven.

I send it back to him. "You can keep it," I say. I'm not interested in the mayor's lounge and the boy needs the buffet dinner more than I do.

He laughs. The girl does too. "Do you have any toys for us? I want one."

My mind flashes to Amanda. No way!

Shit. Now I feel guilty. She needs the doll more than I do. But Amanda is staying with me.

When I don't respond she straightens with pride and says. "Let's go, brother." She scampers off to the right toward the overpass. The boy pivots, looks back, motioning me to follow. They lead me to where the reverse vending machines are. They stand next to a woman who's feeding her cans methodically into a machine. The boy yanks on her coat and she shoos him away impatiently.

I look up to the bridge and the massive sign towering above it. The largeness of it is frightening and somehow obscene. The woman is like King Kong and I almost expect her to come alive, reach down and grab me. I wish she weren't there. I can hear the whir of speeding cars above on the overpass and this makes me all the more dizzy.

No one else seems to mind her or the noise though. They're too busy feeding the machines and organizing their cans. As I watch them I note a heaviness to their movements and a hunger in their eyes. Their bodies are draped in soiled rags. They don't look like people to me. They look like rubble. The ruins of humanity.

I imagine I must stick out like a sore thumb. "Hey!" a man shouts. "Hey! What are you doing over here?"

He wears layers of red cloaks and they billow out around him as he thunders over to me. He's tall and massive but I don't flinch. I have learned in the art of battle, that size doesn't really matter. It's what's in the eyes. So I gather myself and stare him down with all my might. I don't really want to get into a tussle with a Canner. Who knows what kinds of diseases he carries.

Luckily my fearless eyes halt him in his tracks.

"You don't want a piece of this," I tell him.

He's not old but his hair is grey and he stinks so freaking bad it actually smells sweet. I give a dry heave and say. "You stink."

"You got a lot of nerve coming in here uninvited! Who do you think you are? Didn't you see the sign? Canners Only! No Trespassing."

"I go where I please. Now step off."

"Get out!" he insists. "Or I'll set the dogs on you!" His rage edges him a little closer. "I'll do it, I swear," he promises.

"I didn't come here to fight," I say. "But you are really trying my patience old man."

He fumes. "Old man? Old man? You think you're better than me, don't you? Don't you? You sinner! You sinner, you!"

"That's no way to welcome a guest." I'm cool as ice on the outside but inside I'm sizzling.

But then a hand falls on my shoulder. I don't know who it belongs to. For all I know it could be another Canner ready to crack my skull in. But for some odd reason, I feel relief from this touch.

It's Soldier Sonny. He's frowning. "Don't be like that, Stori. Please."

Sonny wasn't too sane to start with, before he went into the Army. And after he served three years in Iraq he's been pretty touched. You would think with all the combat he endured (he even has a purple heart) he would come back and nothing in the Valley would faze him. But it's just the opposite. Sonny is scared of everyone and everything. He's like a little girl now. "Please," he says again.

"Fine," I tell him. "Fine, Sonny." It's strange to see such a big guy, with a bandana tied around his forehead and hands as big as oven mitts acting like a whining little girl.

Sonny never smiles but I know when he's happy. His eyebrows go up like he's just discovered something. "That's better. Fighting ain't the answer. Trust me, Stori. You've got to trust me."

I don't want to stay long in his presence. For starters, I

think he might like me. And what's more, he's super depressed. I think he might kill himself one day, to be quite honest. Whatever happened to him over there in Iraq, he carried it back with him, and he can't handle it. Now he's homeless, and some of the nicer Canners take care of him.

"Stori," says Sonny. "You shouldn't be here. A place like this isn't safe for a lady like yourself."

One thing about Soldier Sonny. He's real respectful with girls. I like him for that.

"Sonny. My dad's missing. Have you seen him?"

"Frankie Putz?"

"Yes."

"Last I seen him he was over at Rita's having a Heineken. I wasn't drinking, you know. I was just beating the cold. Drinking makes people do ugly things. Horrible, disgusting things."

"When was that?"

"Couple weeks ago."

"Before Friday, the 3rd?"

"I guess."

"Well did he look okay? Did he say anything?"

"He was talking about his job, I think. About some pretty tigers in a cage and how they asked him for a cookie."

Oh God. Why did I even ask him?

"You know, Stori. I had a brother once. And he was my friend. But he's far away now." He shakes his head desperately. "Sometimes in life you have to take different paths. To get where you're going, Stori."

"I'm sorry about your brother."

His face brightens and it almost looks like he's gonna smile. "Thank you beautiful lady. And I don't mean that in a nasty way. I mean you're beautiful in a spiritual way. These other guys, I know why they say it. They're disgusting."

He makes a face like someone just stole his chocolate pudding. "I just wanna go, home, Stori. I'm scared and I just wanna go home." Sonny is way worse off than me. He has no one.

I grunt like someone punched me in my belly.

I fear for him. Someone that vulnerable isn't safe. Not in the Valley, not beyond the Valley. Not anywhere. The world seems to do very bad things to vulnerable people. I wish there were a number I could call. There should be places for people like him. Where he could get gentle care and help with all his mental issues. But I don't know of anything other than the shelters, and they're just holding cells. I don't want to think about Sonny's bleak future anymore. It's only going to depress me. "Well I better get going."

As I go he calls behind me, "One day I'm going to have a beautiful woman just like you! That's my dream."

Don't dream, I want to yell back. Sonny, this world is not made for dreaming.

As I knock on the front door of the building I can hear a woman's laughter inside. It halts and there's silence.

I knock again, louder this time.

"Get the fuck out of here!" It's my Uncle Joe.

I lean into the door and holler, "It's your niece. Stori. I need to talk to you Uncle Joe."

A discussion ensues, between my uncle and his mystery gumad. Then I hear a chair scrape against the floor and a door slam.

Quiet again. Is he going to answer me?

Finally the door cracks open an inch and I see my uncle scowling through the opening. "What do you want?"

"I need to talk to you."

"No time."

"Uncle Joe…" It sounds weird just saying it, seeing I haven't had contact with this man for over three years.

He doesn't like the sound of it either. "Just call me Joe."

"Fine. Joe. You know my father is missing, don't you?"

He casts a paranoid eye into the room with a look on his face like he's constipated or has to pee real bad. Then he turns back to me and says, "Yeah, look kid. I'm real sorry about your dad and all. But I've got things to do here."

He slams the door in my face.

I won't let him get off that easy. I lean into the door

again and holler, "The man back there said he's gonna sick the Dobermans on me. It'd be a shame for the cops and the press to have to show up here tonight and find a dead girl's body, and whatever else might be going on behind these closed doors."

"Ahhhh!" he bellows and then the door flings wide open. "Like anyone would call the press for *you*! You got two minutes."

There's a desk in the middle of the room and it's covered in a disarray of papers. A refrigerator is next to a file cabinet by the windows and there's a table with a hot plate and a bare bones sink connected to a rusty pipe. The light bulb in the ceiling is pale orange and the dark wainscoting doesn't help to brighten the gloom.

The linoleum floors haven't been mopped in what looks like months and dust rises from a stack of papers as he pushes them aside to take a seat at the desk. The room tells me women don't visit often and the ones that do aren't the domestic type. Which reminds me of his gumad. There's another room in the back and the door is closed.

"Is someone else here?" I ask.

"What's it to you, Nosy? Now get it over with."

Uncle Joe's not a bad looking guy but today he must be tired because his eyes are all red-rimmed. I don't want to think it's because he does drugs. Even though I hate him and everything he's still my uncle.

"My dad's been missing. Cops came by, took a

statement, but I don't think they're really looking."

"Give them time."

"I don't have time. A social worker wants to take me and Regina out of the house. Mom would die."

"And how does any of this involve me?" He's all jittery, leaning forward, then back, running his fingers through his straight black hair.

"Uncle…I mean Joe. Don't you care at all? Don't you remember how close you and daddy used to be?"

"That was a long time ago. People grow up, Stori. People change."

"Not family. Family doesn't change."

"I haven't seen your father in over a month. Okay? So can you let me get back to my business?"

"Cosimo!" I shout, surprising even myself.

His eyes bulge wide open.

"People are saying Cosimo has been in the Valley. That he's the reason why people are disappearing. You could be next."

Uncle Joe suddenly looks sad. "Cosimo. I'm sick of everyone talking about Cosimo. There's no such thing."

"Listen. You're the only person we've got now. You know people. People will listen to you. I think—no, I KNOW—he's still alive. Deep in my heart, Joe. I can feel him, his heartbeat, right up against mine at night. In my dreams I hear him calling out to me. Calling out to my mother. Wherever he is, he's very lonely and he's very sad and he doesn't wanna be there."

Joe gets up and paces the room. He speaks to the sticky floor, "I told your father to do a lot of things. But he never listened. If he would have listened he could have gotten out of the Valley. He would have made a better life for himself."

"We like the Valley. We don't want to leave."

He stops pacing and faces me. "I'm sorry about your father. But there's nothing I can do."

There's no hope here. Uncle Joe has been gone from the Valley for too long. It is said once a person leaves they lose the part of their heart that feels loyalty. Somewhere deep beneath that jittery mess I can see he's searching for it, trying to locate it inside himself. Or maybe he's fine living the way he does. A part of me is disappointed, knowing he will be no help, but another part of me is relieved. Now I can finally tell him how I really feel. "You were one of us, once," I tell him. "And my father loved you. He would have cut off his right arm for you if you asked him. Good luck finding a friend like that again. That's the kind of man my father is. He risked his life for me once. I wonder if you would do the same for your own daughter. But looking at you now and smelling your whore in the other room I don't think you could even do that for yourself. 'Merigan."

In less than a flash he's up in my face and I rocket back, my head slams into the wall. Thank God for my backpack for it absorbs some of the blow. Pinning me against the wainscoting he slams his fist right through it just beside my head. It makes a hole and I hear stuff crumbling and falling to the floor. "You dirty little piece of shit. You think your father is better than me? Why don't you go ask that whore, Butterfly, if she thinks he's better too. The one he was fucking behind your mother's back."

I foist him off of me with all my might. He staggers back, stunned by my strength. He moves behind his desk, opens the front drawer and pulls out a pistol. He aims it right at me. "Stop looking."

I duck at the sound of the first pop. I'm out the door and down the steps by the time I hear the second.

As I'm pounding my way out of Soda Can Alley, the Doberman's barking, bullets zipping by my head, the only thing I can think is this: My father cheated on my mother and my uncle is trying to take my life.

Priscilla Van Patten

A young man in his budding twenties stands on the curbside, staring up at a window above The Golden Thread's clothing boutique. He's accompanied by three older men. One sings a dusky rendition of *Fools Rush In*. The second squeezes the melody from an old accordion. The third delivers soft and lingering notes with a saxophone.

The young man's dark features are obscured by the shadows of dusk, but the window in his sights glows orange from within.

I'm a half a block south on the other side of the street, making my way closer. My car is parked directly across from him, in front of Rita's Tavern. Stori's house is just a few blocks from here. When I get to my Jetta I climb inside but leave the door ajar so I can still hear the song. I rub my thighs vigorously to generate some heat.

The young man and his music making entourage have attracted attention not only from me but from some of the locals. A group of smokers under Rita's awning keep their eyes pasted on the serenading quartet with whimsical expressions on their faces. A car heading north hits the brakes and parks in the middle of the street. The door swings open and a man steps out with one foot and throws an arm over the hood.

Middle aged couples and young children lean out from nearby stoops, windows and fire escapes. All of us are rapt by the young brave soul who looks to nothing but the orange where he awaits a glimpse of his love.

Finally the curtains part and she appears. She opens the window and sticks her head out and shakes a fist in the air. "Freddy Ambitore!" she hollers. "What are you doing?"

He comes down on one knee and lifts a bouquet of flowers with both hands. Men howl and women shout, "Hooray."

Another girl appears in the window. She's younger, most likely the sister of the girl being serenaded. She smiles down on the kneeling suitor declaring his love for all to see. "You foolish boy!" she cries joyfully. "Haha! What a fool."

The older girl retreats into her apartment and it feels like time stops. The air braces. Waiting inside of eternity I pray she doesn't leave him kneeling there. I'm convinced if his love goes unrequited he might freeze upon bended knee. Cursed to spend eternity as a sad monument of failure where all will take their young ones to tell his cautionary tale. What a horrible end to the story that would be.

But just when hopes might turn sour the door beside the boutique opens. She steps onto her front stoop, wrapping herself in a wool coat.

Freddy stands and she flies down her stoop into his open arms, her coat falling to the ground behind her.

As they kiss the audience claps and hoots and shouts BRAVO. The young lovers stay wrapped in each others arms, center stage. The newborn night sky is showing its first glimpse of stars and suddenly the moon appears.

This is a magical place—the Valley of Redemption. I don't care what Nate says about it. I know of nowhere else that stops everything just to get a glimpse of a man and woman in love.

And how about that Freddy? Mad props to him. Nothing like showing the entire world you like someone, before you're even sure they like you back. Most guys nowadays just throw you a text or try to ask you out sideways by inviting you to group events. Sometimes you don't even know you're on a date until your naked on all fours and then you're like—Hey, I think this guy likes me.

I'm not saying it was like that with Nate. He's *Redemption's Most Eligible Bachelor* for God's sake. I mean he's got some serious game. Not serenading, down-on-one-knee game, but c'mon—that shit's pretty much extinct outside the Valley. Nate made it just as exciting if you ask me. Here's how *my* love story went down:

I was looking for full time work after college and Heather, a friend of mine, convinced me to take the five hour drive northeast to Redemption for the weekend. She was already working for Bill and knew he needed extra help at the office. Since all those children had been disappearing, (I think there's about fifteen of them now) CPS was slammed with cases.

After my interview with Bill I wasn't quite sure I wanted to pursue the job any further. Even though the pay was decent and the office was pristine, something about Bill made me hesitant. He reminded me a little of my dad. He rarely smiled and the few times he did it didn't seem sincere.

"You don't have to make a decision right away," Heather told me. "Come on. Let's go for a sexy drink."

We ended up at Le Chíc. Working on my second Dirty Martini I wandered alone over to the windowed walls and strolled from the west wall and it's glorious view of the casino over to the east where the massive billboard hung over the expressway. I took a cleansing breath and read the words. "Future Forward. Strive for Better."

"Do you like it?"

There was Nate. Six two, dirty blonde hair falling in

tousled locks just past his ears and big brown eyes. A sight for sore eyes but maybe a little too young for my somewhat seasoned palette. (I tend to like them older.) "It's a little large I would say, but your city's motto is quite catchy."

"It's called a Declaration. You might not believe this but I gave Mayor Vaughn the idea. We're friends. Here in Redemption we're building a new city. A Future Forward City. We don't stay stagnant in the past."

Hearing it come from Nate's mouth, abundant with glittering optimism, it dawned on me what that Declaration could impose upon my battered life. "That's nice," I replied, taking note of the way he held his gin on the rocks so confident yet casual. I already wanted him to save me.

"I like it too," he said puffed up with pride. "Do you like the girl? The model?"

"She's very pretty," I answered stiffly, not sure where he was going with such an inquiry. (My *ménage à trois* days were over. I was preparing for something more meaningful.)

"I used to date her."

My heart did a little flutter. If he was trying to make me jealous it was working. If I was on the fence about liking him just moments ago, I sure as hell wasn't now. I rolled my eyes in my good-old Erie girl fashion. "So what."

I decided not to look at him anymore. But I could feel his eyes on me and was quietly pleased. "You're prettier than her. Like a goddess."

I tried so hard not to do it. I tried so hard. But Nate was good. Oh boy, was he ever. So I smiled.

Nate's face disappears at the sound of my cell phone whistle. A voicemail. It's my sister, Grace. I tap her name and listen.

"Where have you been? Why don't you ever pick up? God, Pris, ever since you left Erie you act like you don't have a family anymore. What are we only gonna talk on facebook now? And by the way I can hardly recognize you in your pictures. Since when did you start dressing like Paris Hilton? Don't think I'm jealous. Cause I'm not. You're living the good life and that's fine by me. But just so you know, Dad is dying. *Dying*, Pris. If you wanna come and say your goodbyes you better do it soon."

I delete the message as soon as it ends. I don't need my little sister telling me what kind of person I've become. I deserve a better life, Goddamnit. Just because she's okay with that backward town we came from doesn't mean I have to be. So now that dad's dying I have to drop everything to run by his side? Where was he when *I* was down and out and needed a father? If I let myself go back I'll lose it. I want to call my sister right now and tell her some of the horrible things my father has done. Things she was too little to know about. Why should mom and I have to carry the burden and not her?

My heart's racing. I have to get a hold of my emotions. They always interfere and I refuse to let them tonight. But I just can't help myself. Another memory comes crashing in like a ten foot wave and despite my best efforts to run for dry land, it washes over me and pulls me back to the bottomless waters of the past. I can't fight the current so I let go.

I'm five years old again, standing on my front porch, watching as three men chase my father toward the house. Before he can reach the steps they catch up to him. One grabs him by the neck, punches him in the back of the head and shoves him to the ground. Then they all crowd around him like vultures settling over fresh death. That's when the kicking begins.

I blink and I'm in my car again. I wipe at my tears and shut the door against the cold. Freddy and his lover are gone and so are his entourage and the crowd.

I slip my key into the ignition and meditate on the task at hand: figuring out what to do with the Putzarella case. I know Nate wants me to focus on only him and having fun and not get too caught up in my work, but I can't stop thinking about the witch Regi said she saw in her house. Their mother's gonna die. The least I can do is spend an hour at the office investigating if maybe someone did kidnap the father. If there's a way for them to get him back, I should at least give that option an hour of my time.

Back at the office, as I plunk the Putzarella file on my desk and settle over it, Bill peeks in from the hallway. "Knock

knock."

"Oh, hi Bill."

"I talked to Heather. She has an opening. She can take the Putzarella case. Do you have the first assessment?"

Heather's my friend but she's also notorious for being a no-nonsense unforgiving social worker. If this file lands on her desk, those kids will be out of that house by the weekend.

I stare at the file. The mere thought of Heather taking it sets a panic loose in me. I slam a territorial hand on top of it and say, "I'm not as behind as I thought. I think I just might keep it."

"You're not behind? It's seven fifteen already. You've been here since 6:30 this morning."

"I had some errands to run in the afternoon."

He swings his body around and comes into the office. "Priscilla," he says in a more authoritative tone. "I noticed you've been a little stressed lately. Not your normal self. If you're overworked, you should tell me."

"Don't worry about me. Really."

He taps the desk before leaving. "Think it over. Heather's ready when you need her."

"Bill," I say, suddenly remembering the man with the hair on his face.

He stops and turns to face me. Bill is mostly about business but he occasionally offers a conversational side.

"Do you believe in the devil?" I ask him.

He hesitates. "I have known darkness," he says. "So yes, I do. But I don't believe he's some fantastic demon lurking the streets at night. I think he is me, and you. He is all of us. When we choose to do what isn't right, that's the devil. And then there's God. And he is me and you and all of us. When we choose to do right."

"Are some of us just born bad?"

He grimaces and ruminates some more. Finally he says, "Bad is just good that's forgotten."

"Forgotten what, Bill?"

The cleaning lady has started the vacuum down the hall.

Bill glances back at the noise and then returns to me. "What it was when it first came into this world."

"You make a lot of sense."

"Good night Miss Van Patten. Don't work too late."

I wish I can take his advice. I think again of the Cosimo rumors, the hairy faced man and Regina's witch. Could one or all possibly be involved in Frank Putzarella's disappearance? And the missing children including the Bak boy? Maybe there have been other witnesses who've seen something.

I go to the cabinet where we keep our *Closed* files. I don't find a file on any Baks but I do find some other files of children who've gone missing, from the Valley and beyond. I bring them back to my desk and start to sort through them.

After about an hour I can't seem to find any statements involving Cosimo or anything extraordinary from anyone else.

I lean back into my chair in utter defeat. I blow a strand of hair out of my face. "It's just a stupid myth, like Nate says. Regina must be crazy. And if I spend any more time on this, I might go crazy too."

But then something pops out at me. An analysis of a ten year old dyslexic girl named Jasmine. *A pleasant little girl who loves dancing and participating in the da Vinci Theatre of the Arts for Children.*

I open another file and rummage until I find another assessment of a boy with Bell's Palsy. *Tyler is an avid reader and writer and enjoys composing his own songs as well as performing them for his friends and family.*

I go to another file. *Melissa finds her outlet for her speech delay in the modern movement courses she takes at the YMCA.*

And then of course I remember what Regi told me about the Baks. Singing and dancing and writing... Performance! This is what all the missing children have in common.

I slam my hand on my desk again and stand for battle. My chair goes *thwack* as it hits the ground. My discovery has ignited an unexpected fire in me. I know my duty is to pass the information along to Bill so he can notify a detective. That would be protocol. Let the police do police work and focus on my own job, getting Stori and her sister out of neglect's way.

But ever since I've been in Redemption I can't shake this feeling that the city might be in danger somehow. Whether it be terrorists, or mafia stuff, or even a serial killer, I've just got to find out. I won't stop at just these files. I've got to do more snooping. I've got to go somewhere where people know a thing or two about this Cosimo guy.

Back in front of Rita's Tavern I turn off the ignition, snatch my purse and open the car door. The icy air has a vicious bite so I hunch my shoulders against it. I slam the door shut, press the alarm button on my keychain and make my way inside.

One thing is for sure about the Valley, these people care nothing for décor. None of the furniture matches and there's barely enough lighting, as candles upon wall sconces are the only source of light. The air in here is thick with must and dust and regret. I wade through it all and make my way to the bar where I take a seat, leaving a respectful two stools between me and a burly man in a nubby sweater. The middle aged woman at the bar, who I assume is Rita, does not even acknowledge my entrance. Very bad customer service if you ask me.

"I'll have a Gin and Tonic," I say politely as I wedge my purse between the backrest of the stool and my ass.

She still doesn't look at me.

I give her a minute and then repeat, "Gin and Tonic when you get a chance."

She huffs like I just asked her to take out the garbage or mop the floors and makes me the drink begrudgingly, only pouring a three count of gin. I don't say anything because I already know my presence in her establishment is not appreciated. She wipes the counter down with a dishrag and sets my drink in front of me. "You looking for that Molly shit, honey, you come to the wrong place. We're not that kind of gig."

Oh my God. Did I come off as copping? I hope not.

Frantically, I plead my case. "I'm not looking for anything like that. I was just in the neighborhood and wanted to beat the cold."

She gives me one of those *bitch, please* looks and saunters off to the other end of the bar. One of the first things I learned about people from the Valley is they are not inclined to faking pleasantries. Here it's all about straightforwardness and transparency. If someone doesn't like you, you'll know it instantly.

The barmaid does not like me.

Who cares, I tell myself, resenting her for making me feel I have to ask permission to be in her shitty bar. She's nobody. She must not have any friends, too. She's like my sister, Grace. Never giving people a chance. I, on the other hand, have plenty of friends. And as a matter of fact, I will soon have more. Nate's taking me to the grand opening of Strive. Lots of important people will be there and Nate knows them all.

If you want to get anywhere in this world, you have to have lots of friends. And in order to do so, you can't be like this woman—letting people know how you really feel. You have to hide that stuff. You have to make people believe you want them in your world.

Good thing men are much easier to win over. I take a sip and smile at the guy next to me, "Boy, is it cold out there."

He only grunts.

That was stupid. Can't I come up with something better? I note a local newspaper tucked under his left arm. "I see you have the paper. Anything good today?"

He glances sideways at me, and I can see a meanness in his face that can only mean one thing—mafia. "Some good. Some bad, but who knows if any of it's true."

"Awww. Don't get him started," a man grumbles from a table behind us.

"Yeah. We don't need to hear the Arm's fairytales tonight," adds another man.

"You wish they was fairytales," the Arm says, unmoved. He's obviously too tough to be threatened by playful teasing.

"I like a good fairytale," I say fully aware of how absurd I must sound. Lately I'm used to dinner parties where I'm exchanging meaningless platitudes with Wall Street tycoons and Broadway producers. They're not nearly as hard to talk to. But nevertheless I persist. "Tell me a good one."

The man, Arm, gives me a once over and says, "Little girl. You ain't got ears for the fairytales I been telling. Plus you ain't Valley-born."

"I'm a Putzarella," I lie. "A cousin." I stammer a little. "Fro...from the mother's side. Anna. It's just that she's been so down and out I can't really talk to her. Have any of you heard anything about the father?"

"You mean your cousin?" he corrects me wisely.

"In-law. We weren't that close."

I don't think they're buying it; I'm going about this all wrong. *Come on, Pris. You're an Erie girl. You can do this. You're gonna have to take that old girl off the shelf and give her a good dusting.*

"Whatever, don't believe me." I drink my rum deeply in a blasé movement that's eerily reminiscent of my father. (I must have learned it from him.) Then I slam the glass back on the table and say, "I've seen them for myself anyways."

"Seen what?" Arm asks.

I stay wordless, taking up my drink again with two hands, listening to the clink of the ice.

"I said seen what?"

I take my time to reply. "A man that had a face of a

bat. He was laughing at the wailing women. The ones mourning for Concettina."

Arm blinks. His mouth opens a little and in these slightest of movements I know I've got him. This is what I was trained to do. People. I do people. And I do them well. I've thoroughly regained my confidence, so I lean in confidentially and say. "Motherfucker looked like a bat. And he was laughing. Good and hard. Laughing."

Arm nods his head meaningfully. "Hounds. Sold their souls over to Cosimo and his lovesick witch."

My ears prick at the word witch.

"No blood runs through their veins," says Arm. "They take the form of their totem when they're in attack mode."

"That's right," I comment pretending I know the story well.

"Nobody outside of this place would believe it. But we've been hearing about the Hounds since we was kids. Noone has ever seen one. Until now. If what you say is true."

"I swear on my mother and father."

"Ghost stories," comes a voice from the shadows.

"Bloodless vampires," comes another mockingly.

"Not ghost stories," someone interjects, taking Arm's side.

"You nonbelievers should be ashamed of yourselves," Arm chastises. "You were all raised here. You know what our ancestors taught us. This isn't some Twilight shit. The

Hounds exist. For whatever reason they're back and they're in *our* hood." He looks at me full in the face and says, "You look around this place. Look up to the storefronts and tell me what you see. Children. Missing children."

"Kids are bad nowadays," someone offers. "They run away."

Arm shakes his head. "No. Not like this. Never to be seen again. Our children were always safe. No matter what kinds of dirty was being done in these streets. The children were left alone. I'm telling you. It's the Night's Council. And their Hounds."

I didn't take time to notice before, because I was too busy judging the checkered tablecloths and floral print curtains, but it's rather toasty in here. I unzip my coat and loosen my scarf.

The barmaid is frying chicken on a stove. She sets the cooked ones onto sheets of paper towels covering a plate. As she works a fresh batch into the oil, she reads a book held open in her other hand. Lost in its pages a delicious little smile curves her plump berry-stained lips. I find myself envying this woman's contentment. In life there seem to be only moments of happiness—so fleeting, yet so sweet. You know, the deep down sincere moments. I have not felt one in what seems like forever.

"I bet that witch is at the helm of this Night's Council," I put in knowingly, even though I'm blindly grasping for information.

"Ah. Haven't they said it, Cosimo's lovesick witch. They say she's got the book that keeps the show going. The one with all the spells."

"She's running the show," one of the believers offers.

"Nah," says another. "It's the Brotherhood. You ain't heard about them?"

"I believe it's Cosimo who runs the show," the Arm says. "He's the one to watch in my opinion."

I lean into Arm and speak only for him to hear. "What's his last name, Cosimo?" All I need is a name and I can pass it to someone on the force.

"Medici," Arm responds, straight-faced. "Medici the undead."

Just then, abrupt popping sounds outside in the near distance.

Gunshots. I know them. From my father, when he used to get so wasted he would run outside and try to shoot the aliens. The aliens that were coming to take us all away.

My spine shivers. "Oh my God," I say.

"Soda Can," Arm says dismissively.

The barmaid has stopped reading; she's shaking her head in disapproval. She notices me eyeing her as she returns to her chicken and throws me another one of her charming little looks.

Then the door opens and a monster of a man steps inside, each footstep declaring its beastly presence. He owns the room as soon as he's in it and he knows it.

He's as big as the Incredible Hulk. He lumbers over to
the bar and wedges himself between me and the man
named Arm, placing two vulgar forearms on the lacquered
wood. His breathing is audible and his fingers are scabbed
and raw. It takes me back to my hometown, Erie. I know
it's wrong of me, but poor people disgust me. They have
bad hygiene and never wear clothes that fit right. It's so
fucking depressing.

Without warning he turns and looks at me directly. His
eyes hold not a speck of light. Instinctively I understand
that he would hurt me bad if he could. And he would like
it.

"Fresh Meat?" he asks. (There's a whorehouse only
blocks from here.)

I'm unable to answer. Luckily someone does it for me.
One of the men in the shadows says, "She's Frank's cousin.
Wanted to know if any of us seen him."

Mo picks up his eyebrows like he's interested.

I don't think I'm breathing anymore.

"What do you think you're doing exactly?" he asks.

"Huh?" I act confused because I really am.

"Coming in here, pretending you're one of us. Asking
questions about poor Frank. What are you some kind of
cop?"

"Me? A cop? God, no. I hate cops."

He slides his hand out and pulls the front flap of my
coat back, taking a look at my skin tight Lulu Lemons. I

curse myself for always needing to look cute.

He sucks saliva from his teeth and grunts. "That is one fine ass pair of legs you've got hiding under there."

I'm too frightened to snatch my jacket back.

He leans closer so I can feel his hot breath on me. "If you ain't five-O then…" He inhales deeply.

I still don't speak. Showing fear could make things worse.

"I don't smell nothing," he whispers.

"Are you supposed to?"

"Blood. Human blood."

Finally I snatch my jacket back and slide the bar stool back. I reach for my bag but he grabs my wrist with one hand and snaps a switchblade open with another. He puts the blade to my cheek.

"Somebody help me," I say calmly, yet firmly.

No one moves. You could hear a pin drop.

"You one of them Hounds ain't you?"

"I don't know what you're talking about."

"There's only one way to find out."

As fast as lighting, Arm slams his paper down on the counter. "Please, Mo. Enough!"

"Yeah, Mo," someone else says. "You can't do that."

"I can do whatever I want." Mo answers.

"It'll be trouble," the Arm advises.

He lets go of my wrist and I jump down off the stool. Rushing out the door I hear him call after me, "And don't come back."

Anna

I just want to sleep and never wake up, but someone comes into the bedroom and shakes me by the shoulder. I open my eyes and see a face that is terrified.

I sit up with great effort. "What is it Stori?"

"You lied to me."

How could I be so stupid, believing the girls wouldn't find out eventually? Still I hope maybe she's talking about something else. "What are you talking about, honey?"

"You know what I'm talking about. Why didn't you tell me daddy left us for another woman? Why did you let me look like such a fool putting up his picture all over the Valley? How could you do this to me?"

I don't know what to say because I know she's right. I should have been honest with them from the start. But how do you tell your children something like that? How do you destroy the most important thing in their lives—their vision of their parents? "I just couldn't," I tell her. "I just couldn't do that to you. Or Regina."

"So you think me finding out on the street is better?"

"It's complicated. How would I start?"

"How about with the truth. The truth isn't complicated. It's easy."

"Not always, honey. For grownups, the truth is very complicated."

"Not for me," she says and turns her back on me. She goes to my bureau and looks at herself in the mirror. Her hair is disheveled and I notice her pants are dirty. As a mother I want to ask her where she's been, but I don't think I have the strength for her answer. My little girl, Stori. I knew she was going to grow up way too fast. I knew she was going to become the hard, angry girl I see before me.

I want to tell her: *Don't ever have children Stori. Because the moment you do, you will understand how insignificant you are. You will never be able to protect them from the cruelty of this world. You will never be able to mend their broken heart. Your father thought making you tough would protect you. But I always knew he was wrong. Even though you're so much tougher than Regina, I worry for you the most. Because deep inside, I know you're the weakest. I remember when my mother died last year, your sweet Nonna. You used to sleep in her bed with her when I let you stay overnight. Even when you were too big to fit—you would insist. After she died I saw how you slept with her picture in the bed with you. Right between you and Amanda. Even though you were nearly grown, you still needed to be somebody's baby. And you still do. You need the Other Mothers. You need the Tribe. The things that are just memories to us now. The things long gone.*

"Not for me," she says again. "The truth is easy, Mommy. Daddy's a scumbag and I hope he never comes home. I hope he's happy. I hope he's really happy with what he's done. He always ignored me anyways."

"You don't understand. He was trying to protect you. There are dangerous people in this world, Stori. Your father new too well about them."

If I tell her what her father whispered to me the night he disappeared she would never believe it. Maybe it was all a lie—a distraction from what he was about to do. Oh, Frank. Why did you tell me of such evils, only to leave?

"It's not easy being a parent," I tell her.

"Don't tell me it's not easy being a parent. I think it's only hard because all you adults have forgotten how to be decent. I will never speak his name again."

A quote by Graham Greene comes to mind as I watch my oldest daughter, almost a woman now, studying her own face, the face of a brokenhearted girl: *There is always one moment in childhood when the door opens and lets in the future.*

I realize all the doors that have already been closed in Stori's face and I fear like I have never feared before for her future.

Oh, Frank. I remember the kind of man you once were.

Do you? Do you?

I remember that Christmas years ago, before you took that bullet, when your coworkers chipped in and bought us a little color TV. The girls were so excited and so were you.

One night you had a show on, I think it was CSI or something like that. They were just getting to the part where they were about to arrest the killer and you were so enthralled. Just then Stori came into the room and wanted to show you how her popovers came out.

But you shushed her.

She didn't fuss. She only said sorry and left the room.

But you did. You woke from your trance and looked at me and said. "Something's not right here."

You went over to the TV, unplugged it and picked it up in your arms. I followed you into the kitchen and watched in horror as you opened the front door and flung the TV out into the avenue.

Then you came back inside and looked at Stori and said, "I'm sorry, Stori. Now get out some butter. Me and Mommy want to try your popovers. Go ahead. Get the butter honey. Everything's alright."

You were a good man and a good father. But I guess that television was just the start. Of things to come and interfere. Things to come and take away what we had together. Oh, Frank. You've broken my heart. You've left me here all alone and I am dying without you.

The Sweeper

It might take another day to get there. The manmade tunnels under the city spider out from there traveling for miles in all directions. I have been carrying the child for hours and I'm getting tired now.

Beyond tired, I am hungry. Yes. You heard right. I'm hungry. You might think that a man like me, who sold his soul over to the Brotherhood and signed his name in the book, wouldn't be bothered anymore with such a base desire. But you would be wrong.

They're worse now; the pangs. It's as if a big gaping hole lives where my belly once was and it is bottomless.

And don't let me get started on the thirst. I can drink five gallons of Poland Spring in one sitting, yet I am far from quenched.

I'm coming up on a checkpoint now. The tunnel gets wider and there's a woman sitting at a booth behind the gated entrance. "Name?" she says, flipping through a fashion magazine, chewing on a wad of gum.

"Samuel Sampel."

She flicks a few pages of her magazine. She slides a glass plate and a razor blade under the open slot. "Verification."

"Don't you see I'm carrying something?" My patience is running thin. If I don't get some food in me, I'm going to collapse right in front of her.

Her false eyelashes flutter and she rolls her eyes. Then she turns to someone in the shadows behind her and indicates me with a nod of the head.

At the sound of an electric buzzer a corner of the iron gate flies open and an armed guard in all black (aka a Black Boot) comes out and unburdens me of the child. For a fleeting moment, I don't want to let him go. He carries him inside and the gate slams shut again.

"Verification," she repeats, the gum sloshing around in her mouth.

I take the blade and cut. I always get nervous when I have to do this.

She pays close attention. Her lips are curling into a delicious little grin as she anticipates my failure.

Checkpoint girls. Dime a dozen. Empty headed and

always looking to delight in another's misfortune. Oh, and they live for gossip. Their unguarded whispers have been quite informative—I know more about the Night's Council than they would ever suspect.

The plate takes a few drops. She looks up and pouts. "What's a matter baby? Who you got up in that pretty little head of yours?"

If we remember, we can still bleed. I am not supposed to remember.

"No one. Now let me in."

She drags her head from side to side. "Now you know I can't do that."

"Listen. I'm starved lady. It's just a girl, alright. A dumb cunt like you who's not even worth it."

"Ohhh," she cooes. "Poor baby. But don't you worry. I'll get you all hooked up and forgetting. I'll get you feeling nice in no time."

"Do it then," I bark.

She blows a big bubble until it bursts. The pink skin sticks to the bow of her lips. She reaches over and presses something. The gate pops open again and two Black Boots step forward to usher me in.

Inside the checkpoint I'm patted down, emptied of all electronic devices, then led to the cafeteria where I sit amongst other Hounds, too famished to speak, plowing bland rice and kidney beans into their mouths. I eat three plates and ask for another. The guard tells me no. I gulp down the last of my tepid tap water and find the bathroom to pee.

I'm never sated, never quenched, but it's enough to get me through another day. They tell me it gets better in time. That soon a plate and just one jar will be enough. How this body is my prison I can never describe. I really hope it gets better soon.

In the doctor's office I sit in a steel chair and a nurse in starched white flicks a syringe full of the potion.

"All you have to do is remember."

It takes the better part of an hour, because I don't want to think of him.

But eventually I grow too tired to fight. I'm struck by a blinding flash and then suddenly I'm walking up the hill toward my home after a long day at the office. There she is, the only woman who ever loved me. My second chance in life. She is standing on the front porch holding my ten month old son in her arms. When she spots me trudging up the crest of the hill, she throws up and arm and waves. She points to me and takes my son's small hand. She brings it up into the air and he begins to wave too.

I can feel the drug taking it away. The memory. He is fading now. My limbs get heavy. The quilt of annihilation falls slowly over me. I let myself go. I let myself get taken down into blackness.

When I wake I'm sitting in the middle of a movie theatre. People are seated on all sides of me, chewing popcorn, hypnotized by the screen. I look up and see the blue white projector beam stabbing through the blackness, dust dancing in its trajectory.

I turn back to the screen and of all things to feast my eyes on, I see me. I almost jump out of my seat. I want to yell out. "Oh my God. That's me! That's me!"

I search every visible face in my vicinity to see if anyone is aware that the star of the movie is sitting right amongst them. But they're transfixed.

The big me, the me on the screen reaches out and touches a girl lightly on her face. "You've been good to me. I'll always remember that." I reach down and pick up a suitcase and walk away from her.

Women in the theatre clutch their chests and sigh.

I walk with purpose into a crowded airport. The bustling people swallow me up and I'm gone.

Behind me, I hear a woman whisper, "Don't go. Please don't go."

Stori

Drifting off to sleep my eyes suddenly fly open at the sound of someone or something outside my bedroom window.

They're coming up the fire escape.

I sit up and instinctively check on Regi. She's sound asleep.

My heart starts to pound wildly. (Thank God He created rib bones. If He hadn't my heart would surely beat itself right out of my chest.)

Okay, motherfucker. You back for more? Who do you want this time? Me? My sister? I'll never let it happen. I rise to kneeling and fling the curtains open. My ferocious rage fully convinces me that my words alone will send this predator on his way.

Intent is a living thing. In this flash of adrenaline I fully understand that intent is even better than a fist or an elbow or a wrist.

But the person outside my window is a pretty girl with a big old smile on her face and an expression like she's just come over my house for a cup of tea.

She's at the top of the landing, and she puts a foot out near the potted pine. A red stiletto heel gets stuck in the grates.

Suddenly I remember her. She's the girl I saw the night I was putting up my dad's missing signs. She wears the same lavender dress and no coat. But, again, she doesn't look cold.

What is she doing here?

I crack the window open. "Go away," I tell her. "Go away you crazy visions."

She doesn't though; she only looks at me with earnest. "I put shoes on. Like you told me."

I push the window further up its sash. It bumps and jerks and I have to hold it up with one hand so it doesn't come crashing back down. "Go away," I demand. "I'm done. I'm done being crazy."

"I've come to tell you something," she says.

"So tell me fast. And then get lost."

"There's a treasure hidden here in the city of Redemption. And there's a girl who will find the treasure. She will hold it in both hands and in that moment the purple moon will rise."

I can't do it anymore. Tomorrow I have to refill my other prescription at the pharmacy. Even if those pills make me feel all numb and weird I'd rather be numb and weird than a lunatic who gets hallucinations. "I said go away!" I bark. I let the window fall and yank the blinds shut.

Regi's sitting up now. "Stor? What happened?"

"Shut up," I tell her. "It's nothing. Go back to bed."

Friday morning cleaning is ritual in my family. I usually wake before sunrise. By this time my mother will have already cleaned the bathroom and started dusting the rest of the house. But today as I open my bedroom door there is no Enzo Caruso drifting into the hallway from the living room and no scrub bucket glinting with sudsy water on the hallway floor.

In the bathroom I don't find the customary pink cleaner in the toilet for my pee to turn orange. My mother never misses her Friday cleaning, even when she's not feeling well.

I pad down the hall to her bedroom door and crack it open. She's still asleep. I feel bad for last night and I want to say sorry. But I'll wait till she gets up.

I head to the washer tucked in the back corner of our hallway and start a load of whites.

As the wash is running I light the kitchen stove with a

match to warm the kitchen for Regi. I start a pot of coffee. I set up two slices of bread in the toaster oven and take out the cream cheese and jelly from the fridge.

When the wash is done I bring it into the kitchen and put out the clothesline that hooks to the side of the cabinets and runs along the middle of the room to the window. I could go out to the fire escape fronting Kindred and hang the stuff out on the line. The weather is starting to thaw and winter's sunlight is just as good as summer's. But I don't want to run the risk of Desma getting my stuff down before I do. If I don't have to see her and her lethal lips for the rest of my life, I will be just fine. As I'm clipping wet underwear and white t-shirts to the line Regi appears yawning, her face still puffy from sleep. "What were you doing last night?" she asks.

"Nothing. Couldn't sleep."

"Where's Mommy?"

"Sick. Don't wake her. Your bread is out already. Get it going."

Regi doesn't listen. She plunks down at the kitchen table in the chair closest to the stove. Our kitchen faces east and orange sunlight spills through the windows. The pussy willows on the center of our table cast grey shadows; they creep over Regi's face. My mother always has some kind of centerpiece in the middle of our table. To cover a bunch of scratches my father made with a pocketknife one night when he was bored and wasted. My mom always said it was impossible keeping anything nice with him in the house. I used to defend him against her badmouthing, but not anymore.

Regi sits on her chair sideways and leans her head against the rungs. "Did you find Daddy yet?"

I flap a crumpled towel out into the air. "Daddy's gone, Regi. If he wanted to be here he would."

Today is Valentine's Day and Miss Wheaton, our History teacher, took the day off to spend it with her fiancé. She takes a lot of time off now ever since the mayor's been talking about replacing our History classes with something called "Stories to Light the Future." We have a sub today. She slips a DVD into the television and switches off the lights. "Not that it's gonna make a difference," she announces over a massive wad of gum. "Soon you won't have history at all. But here's Ghengis Khan. If you feel like it, get out some paper and take notes." Then she goes to sit at Miss Wheaton's desk and pulls out her cell phone and starts texting.

Liliana is from the Ridges and she and I are friends. She's sitting next to me and after she empties out her Red Bull with a prolonged gulp and a thirst-quenching gasp, she puts the empty can down on the desk and says, "Oh, Stori. Don't you just love Valentine's Day? The one day out of our 365 dedicated to LOVE?"

I shake my head and roll my eyes. "Who is it this time,

Lil?"

"Well that's the thing. I don't know yet. But I can just feel it. He's coming, Stori, he's coming. My prince charming. I can't wait to meet him!"

This is the last thing I want to be hearing after the night I just had. "You sure about that?" I ask.

"Well of course I am silly! I mean don't you want to know who *your* soul mate is? Your one and only?"

I sigh and tell myself it's not worth the effort to reach across the space between our desks and smack her in her mouth. Besides, Liliana is a nice girl and she wouldn't deserve it. But she does deserve the truth. So I turn to her and say, "Do you want to know what I really think? I think all men are pigs. I think men are the reason why there are wars and starvation and global warming and why everyone in this world is all FUCKED UP."

She sits there stunned. I've never been rude to Liliana because I know a sweet girl like her can't handle it.

The sub clears her throat. She puts her cell phone down and gives me a look of warning as she picks up the remote and turns up the volume. The female narrator of the film says, "Ghengis Khan was so notorious for his inhumane acts that women elected to throw themselves off of high towers rather than to be raped and murdered by him and his army."

"You see," I tell her, silently thanking Genghis Khan for helping to drive my point home.

Liliana is speechless. She snaps her mouth shut and turns back to the television.

I'm a horrible person. I've just ruined her day.

Tony Carp is waiting for me by my locker after fourth period. Great. The last person I was hoping to see.

"Hey Stor," He says with a forced smile. "Happy Valentine's Day."

Is he kidding? There's nothing more detestable than fakeness to me, so I don't even respond.

"So no hi back?" he asks like I've hurt his feelings.

I shove my world history book into my locker and slam the door shut. I face him and say, "Hi."

"Nice fight with Dexter. I told you not to do it."

"I don't have to listen to you."

"Richie Ramera been by to see you?"

"Why?"

"Stay away from him. That's why."

"You sure do have a lot of orders."

"Look," he says, putting his hand against the wall so I can't get past him. "Just because it didn't work out the other way, doesn't mean I don't care. You're like a sister to me, Stor. I can't see it any other way."

The word sister burns like acid. But I won't show him. No, I will never show him how I feel. Never again. It was the stupidest thing I could have done, telling Tony Carp that I loved him.

I guess I thought he and I had something in common, both being great fighters. He used to fight in the Cage too but he got so good that he had to stop. (He says it would be inhumane.) He's been training with the twenty and thirty-somethings in Nardo Nuckles' boxing gym. Nardo is his coach now and everything and people are whispering that Tony's gonna be the next big thing.

"I get it," I tell him, loathing his paternal paw on my shoulder.

"Any word on your pops? I wanna help."

I want to tell him not to bother because my father is with his whore now. But I hide the truth because I'm sick of always being the pathetic one in Tony's eyes. "No sweat. Got it covered."

He wipes a palm across the back of his neck—his signature move when he gets nervous. "I seen all them pictures you put up. You should have called me. To help."

"That's alright. I know you've been busy with training and with Desma." I can't help the last word dripping bile from every syllable. I don't want to expose my pathetic jealousy, but I'm horrible at hiding my feelings.

"You should give her a chance. I would love it if you two could be friends."

Desma with the mouth that kills. I wish she weren't so nice, so that I could get a really good hatred brewing for her. But sadly I can see why Tony likes her. If I were Tony I would probably choose her over me too.

"But just cause I'm seeing her, doesn't mean anything changes between me and you. I'm never too busy for my best bud." He claps my shoulder again and I consider punching him in his nuts. "I'm sorry about your dad, Stor. I just can't get him out of my head."

I know it's earnest. Tony is an earnest guy. And I know what I'm about to say next isn't right, but despite my heart I say it. "At least I still *have* a father."

He takes his hand off me. As I shoulder my way through the hall and seek refuge from the tears that are flooding behind my eyes he calls out behind me, "That's real mature of you, Stori. I won't forget that."

To love a man and know he doesn't love you back is a hurting thing. But if I have any say in it, I'll make sure it doesn't hurt just one—I'll make sure it hurts both.

I head for the closest girl's bathroom. Any girl my age can tell you that high school bathrooms are notorious for all kinds of drama. I'm sure the noise in here will eat up my pitiful tears. What I don't expect is that my best friend, Ernestine, has beat me to it. She's alone, heaving deep sobs over the sink. I drop my bag at the entrance and rush to her side. A hand on her back, "Ern. What happened?"

She looks up into her reflection, her smoky eye design streaming down her face in murky rivulets. "It's impossible. This life is impossible."

Here's another thing you probably will need to know about the Calabrese of the Valley: we don't make friends, we make family. I'm not saying I have many friends, because I don't. Ernestine is my only one, really. But I'd rather have one real friend than a thousand fake ones. The day I became family with Ernestine a girl twice her size was smacking her repeatedly and telling her to like it. I stepped between them and punched that girl dead in her throat. She fell like an imploded tower. Nobody fucks with my homegirl Ernestine. "Tell me right now," I insist. "Who made you cry, Ern?" I can feel her straining heart like it's my own. I forget my own sorrow completely and become lost in hers. She gasps for air and tries to speak. Greif has knocked the wind out of her but she manages to get some words out. "They placed me." Snot bubbles out of her nose. She leans forward and turns on the faucet. I gather some paper towels as she splashes her face with cold water. She takes the towels and blows her nose into them. "My dad skipped bail. That horrible woman, Heather, came and told me to pack a bag. That was it. She just walked straight into my bedroom and said, 'Pack a bag with a few things. Most of it you won't be able to take.'"

"That's horrible. Let me ask my mom if you can stay with us."

She shakes her head. "It doesn't work like that. CPS has all these rules. I'm at The Girl's Home."

"Which one?"

"The Mansion. On Pilgrim's Island."

"The Mansion? Why didn't they put you at the

convent, closer to home?"

"I don't know. My name got picked from some stupid lottery or something."

I try to find a silver lining. "It's only temporary. Till your mom gets out of rehab. Well it must be nice in the mansion. Isn't it?"

She's having a hard time meeting my gaze and I don't know why. "It's nice."

"Do you have your own room?"

"Yeah."

"Well maybe you'll end up liking it."

Ernestine glances from right to left, making sure we're alone. She goes over to the bathroom door and kicks the stopper up. Then she takes me by the forearm and brings me into a stall. Locking us in, she faces me and whispers, "Mistress Smyrna is in charge. She feeds me every night and she doesn't hit me, but the other night I couldn't sleep so I crept out into her quarters. I saw a light coming from her bedroom. The door was cracked open a little and I could hear her talking to someone. When I got closer I saw it was Mayor Vaughn. 'Wives. These will all be my wives,' he said."

"I don't understand," I tell her.

"Us, Stori. Me and the other girls. He's planning on making us his wives."

"How is that so? The Mistress would never allow it."

"No. That's the thing. She's not like other women. I

peeked inside. And do you know what I saw? The Mistress was listening to him at her vanity table. And she had a knife. She sliced herself right across the neck. The skin opened, but there was no blood. Then she started laughing and she said, 'My darling mayor. I think that's a wonderful idea.' Then the hole closed."

"You were dreaming," I tell her, brushing her stray hairs back behind her ear. I caress the side of her head to soothe her. "You were having a nightmare because you're far from home. And you miss your parents. It would happen to any of us."

"No. You have to believe me. Stori, the mayor and her are bad. There's something evil going on! These people, they're not human!"

I don't know if I should believe her. But there's no way a dream would make her this upset. "Maybe we should tell one of the SROs. They'll go and arrest them."

"No!" she insists. "If they know I snitched, they'll kill me. You have to keep this between us."

"So what do we do?"

"Do everything in your power not to get placed, Stor. I know you. You won't be able to deal with it. If they don't find your dad and they place you, take Regina and run."

"Run where?"

"As far away from Redemption as you can."

Boarding my afterschool bus I look over to where

Ernestine is boarding hers. She casts a downtrodden glance back at me, puffy eyed, and tries a smile before she gets on. I try one too and board my own personal misery: Tony Carp in the back making out with Desma, the bus driver, Jim, who openly glimpses my ass in his rear view mirror, people laughing and shouting like life is one big party. And me on the outside of it all. It never bothered me before, that I don't have many friends. But right now it's all I can think of. I've never felt so far away from the world around me. I've never felt so lonely.

Every street that passes brings me closer to the place I do not want to face; it brings me closer to my broken home, devoid of my father. I dig in my pocket and pull out twenty five dollars. I was going to buy some lengths of synthetic silk and have the seamstress at the boutique make me a dress pattern. I'm not too shabby with the sewing machine and my mom is even better. Combined we could pull something decent together for the prom. But seeing as I'm not going anymore, I decide I'll use the money for what's more important. I feel bad for upsetting my mom last night. It's not her fault that my father left. I'm going to make it up to her by making her favorite meal—stuffed hens.

I let myself out at the first stop in the Valley. I head for the general market to get my ingredients for the stuffing. As I stride Kindred I see that new faces of missing children are hanging up along with my father's. Children going missing. The old me would keep my head tucked and keep walking. But this time I have to look up. I want to see their faces. I look at all of them. The children. And I realize the atrocity of what has been going on in my city.

How do I restore my family back to what it was? How do I become the kind of person to do such a thing?

At the general market Mrs. Buzzi only charges me for the onion and celery and gives me a stale loaf of bread for free. I make sure to thank her profusely as I leave, walking backward out of her store. (This is the ultimate sign of respect.)

Next stop is the butcher shop. I'm really hoping that Mr. Delfi's son-in-law isn't there; that pork he sold me, that shit was all water. He probably thought because I was young I wouldn't notice the difference but I knew it was different as soon as it hit the pan. Watered down stuff makes a distinct hissing when it's cooking and it gives off extra steam. I came back the very next day and told him I wanted my money back and a true Calabrese would never rip off one of his own. I was this close to calling him a 'Merigan.

Unfortunately he's working again today and I lay a sharp eye on him as he weighs my stuff; he would probably put his finger on the scale if he had the chance.

Honest people. There aren't that many left in this world.

It's been weeks since my family sat down and had a

real meal together. The way we always have. As I make my way home I envision what dinner is always like: My mother moving quietly from stove to table, serving us. My father waiting with patience until we all have plates and my mother sits down. Lights off, a single candle in the center of the table, we hold hands and bow our heads to pray. My father is the one to start. "Ancient of Days, our Lord Jesus Christ. Knower of all things, maker of the lands far and wide, we thank You for this food, and we ask You to bless the land it came from. We are forever Your servants, Great Ancient of Days, Jesus Christ."

And we all say, "Amen."

It hurts like hell that my father won't be with us tonight to say the prayers of gratitude. But at least we can keep the tradition alive without him. "Put ice in the bag," I tell the little crook. "I'm not going straight home."

I won't be walking out of this place backward.

Madam Scarlet doesn't want to let me in to her bunny ranch, and I personally would prefer eating dirt over being here, but I'm not going away until I see her. "I told you already, I'm not here to cause any trouble. I just want to ask some questions to the lady called Butterfly, that's all."

She finally relents and lets me in. We walk up two flights of stairs to the third floor. She has me wait in the front room that's covered in red wallpaper and draped with gaudy gold curtains. The coffee table features an ESPN and Esquire magazine and a glass serving tray with empty glasses and a bottle of Southern Comfort.

I know this is gonna sound pretty pathetic, but I'm not here to give the whore a piece of my mind. I just want to see her. Like—what does she have that me and Ma and Regi don't? What kind of beauty and magic does she possess?

That's half the reason why I went to Desma's house that day. Of course I wanted to talk to her aunt. But I also wanted to get up close to Des. To her lips. Her clothes. Get a whiff of her. I just wanted to see what it is that I just don't have. Maybe to torture myself. Maybe to wallow in pain. I can be kind of morbid that way. A little bit like my mother.

It takes a while but finally a woman appears.

I stand and survey her head to toe. She wears a big smile that, to my astonishment, kind of disarms me. "Now who is this here says they need a word with me?" she asks in a voice that sings instead of speaks.

I'm utterly confused, as she's not nearly as pretty as my mother. Her hair is brittle from too much bleaching and her roots are slightly orange. Her face is orange, too, from what I assume is tanning spray and her powder blue eye shadow is just plain wrong. *This* is who my father left us for? "Have a seat, honey," she says, gesturing to the couch.

Even if I wanted to hit her, or spit on her at least, I know it's not going to achieve anything. Up until now my strength has always been able to solve my problems. But this one is different. Hurting her won't keep my mother's heart from being broken. Hurting her won't get my father back. I sit back down already feeling defeated. It makes me tired. She sits next to me and says, "Now what can I do to help you?"

"My name is Stori Putzarella. I think you know my father, Frank."

Her smile dissipates and she looks at me regretfully. "Oh," she says. "I wasn't thinking. I'm sorry."

I stare at the shaggy brown rug. It's got potato chip crumbs in it and a knot of blonde hair. Have these people ever heard of a vacuum? "Sorry for what? Being a home wrecker?"

I expect her to get defensive. People always get that way when you hurt their pride, but she doesn't. "I understand how you feel. I had a father once too and it wasn't easy."

She sits forward and pours herself some Southern Comfort. She rests her elbows on her knees, cupping her drink in both hands and gazes toward the only light in the room streaming through a small slit between the curtains. "I heard about your father. I'm sorry, Stori. I'm really sorry. I can see your heart is heavy. If you'd like I can listen. To whatever it is you want to say."

If she thinks she's gonna be my therapist she's got another thing coming. "I don't need you. Or my father. I'm just here because I wanted to send him a message. Tell him we're fine without him. That Mommy's doing great—better than ever. She got a job already. Tell him not to come home."

Butterfly gives me a look of pity. She may be washed up but she's not stupid. Plus I'm not good at faking. "Oh, honey. I haven't seen him in a while."

The *in a while* part stings. "So he *was* here." There was a part of me that was hoping it wasn't true. I brace myself for her answer.

She bites her lip and I think of Desma. So far my life has been a series of lip biting women stealing away all the men I love. "Damn," she says. "I shouldn't have said that. I'm sorry."

"I already know everything. What do you think we wouldn't find out?"

She's pensive now. She hunches her shoulders and sighs. Then she sits straight and her eyes come to mine.

I don't want to look into hers but she's staring so intently. I'm looking for it. The evil. I want to hate her. I do hate her. But I read people well and I can see she's not evil at all.

"I'll tell you everything if you want me to. But I don't want to hurt you."

"You can't hurt me. Even if you tried."

She takes another sip and winces from the burn. "Your father was here. He saw me a few times. It wasn't right. And he always knew that."

"I knew it. What a pig."

"He wasn't Stori. He really loved your mother. In fact, he told me he loved her the last time he was here. And that he would never be coming back. He just got caught up in life. Lost. And he drifted away. But he was coming back to you guys. Said he was gonna do right."

"Don't lie to me. I can't take any more lies."

"I promise you. He's only a man, honey. Men make mistakes. But the good ones come back and make up for it."

I return my gaze to the potato crumbs. Sadly they have been my saving anchor through this whole conversation.

I've always thought that if someone loved another person with all their heart they would never be able to do something as horrible as cheating. But maybe my mother was right. Maybe love is more complicated than I thought. "So he didn't leave my mother for you?"

She laughs like it's the most ridiculous thing she ever heard. "Honey, please. I'm a pastime. A placeholder. To get them through what's rough. That's all."

"God. How can you live like that?" I ask her. She's pathetic to me now. "I mean, doesn't it make you feel bad? All those men using you?"

"Sometimes. Yes. Sometimes it makes me feel awful bad."

I shake my head. If she were a friend of mine I would have a whole lot of things to tell her. I would make her quit this job. I would demand it.

I imagine all the smelly men who haven't showered that just walk into her room. What would it be like? Having to touch them, having to let them touch me. In the most private of places. I get the creeps and I cover my coat tight over my front. "How young were you when you lost it?"

Butterfly lights a cigarette and takes a puff. Her eyes get bleary, out of focus. They've drifted somewhere far beyond this room. "Fifteen," she answers.

"Fifteen," I repeat, finding it hard to believe, even though lots of girls I know this age aren't virgins anymore. I'm still a virgin, even though I don't want to be. I would have given it to Tony. If he hadn't broken my heart.

She's still far out in space. "Why you asking me that?"

"My mother told me I should wait. For marriage."

She smiles and takes a deep puff. "You're a Valley child alright. That's nice, Stori. That's real nice."

"Who was he?" I ask. I know I shouldn't be talking to her like she's one of my friends, but my curiosity has the best of me.

"Honey. You don't want to know. It wasn't one of them fairytales they tell you on TV. It was real life. Real life is hard."

"Tell me."

"Better that I don't. You still got young in you. I can see it. Better keep it while it lasts. You couldn't hold something like that in your young head. It would swim around there in circles. Get mixed up with all the pretty things. Simple things."

"I can hold way more than you," I dare her. She doesn't know what I've already been through.

One thing I've noticed about Butterfly, she doesn't get upset when I take a shot at her pride. That's a rare quality in a person. "I bet it's true. I forgot what you young ones are up against nowadays." She leans in and lowers her voice. "Those missing kids, God that's something scary. I was one of them once, Stori. I was one of them."

"You were?"

She nods her head up and down vigorously.

"What happened?"

"Ran away. Wasn't more than a week, when I got picked up. He was handsome; had the whitest teeth I'd ever seen. When he smiled it was like the sun was shining. He said 'Hey. What's a pretty girl like you doing on these streets all by yourself? Don't you got a daddy?'

"'A daddy,' I said. 'I ain't never met my daddy.'

"He looked me up and down like I was a prize. Made my heart do somersaults. 'That fruit is ripe for the pickin',' he told me. 'You're about to be plucked.'

"'I can take care of myself,' I said. But who was I fooling? I was just playing hard to get.

"'You gonna need a man like me in your life. Teach you things. Or this street's gonna eat you up and spit you out.'

"'I wanted to learn from him, you know, Stori. I thought he was my boyfriend. He took me to eat at the Marriot. Bought me a satin dress. Never forget it. Then one night he took me to a party. Locked me in a room. Two men came in there and raped me. That was my first time."

"You left that man after that?"

"No. I stayed. He made me feel like it was all my fault. Eventually I did leave him, though. And here I am."

I think of what Ernestine told me about the mayor and I almost start to tell Butterfly.

I need my father. I can't let him go. I can't. "I guess that fucked you up pretty good. Made you hate men after that right?"

"Mistrust, yes. But hate, no. Hatred is a toxic thing, Stori. Once it seeps in, tears your organs all apart."

"How did you keep from hating people?" I ask her.

She thinks on it and I wait for the answer. "Well, I heard a voice."

I hear my name being called. Someone outside is yelling, "Stori Putz! Your mother been calling for you!"

I know I have to wrap things up but I'm curious about Butterfly now. "A voice?"

"Yes. It was a tiny thing, slight as a hummingbird. But I could hear it every now and again. It would pop up just like hummingbirds do in a backyard on a summer day. One minute it's not there, the next it is. You never see where it comes from. Just jumps up out of thin air, all pretty and perfect and beating its wings. And it says, 'Hey girl. Don't you know you are somebody's baby? Somebody out there needs you! They need you like the grass needs rain, like the earth needs sun.' Not every girl has that voice inside her. That's why I look out for the ones that don't. I can't make them stop what they're doing. Hell, I never stopped myself. But I can be their hummingbird. Only if they want."

"A hummingbird," I say.

My name is being called again. "I gotta go," I tell her. "But I have one more question."

"Shoot."

"Well, I've never kissed anyone before."

She laughs one of those regretful laughs that adults do when they're holding back anger. "That takes trust. Trust I don't have. I haven't kissed a man in a very long time."

On my way down Kindred street she pops her head out of the fourth floor window and calls after me. "Don't stop looking for your father, Stori. I promise you. He loves you. Listen for the hummingbird, Stori. You're a sweet girl. A good one too."

I walk alone again, along the cobblestone avenue. This time I have no missing signs and masking tape, no job to do but go home and tell my mother there's no one to blame. There is no big bad wolf preying on our family. No point of reference, no target to set our aim.

I thought the whore could be the answer in that I could assign the blame on her and place all my hatred there.

But she's suffering just as bad as I am.

I guess in life, there's really no one to blame for our hurts. We are all under the same curse. I can see the curse now. It's everywhere. It hangs like an unwanted coat on everything. It's a living breathing thing. I wade through it and carry it along with me. And everyone else does too.

How sad it is to know that no one is the answer to my problems.

So if there's no one to answer for my pain then what do I do with it?

I'm awfully lonely. I wish I had someone to walk alongside me. Hold my hand. It's not easy being forgotten and afraid.

But there is also something else here in the Valley.

If only you would come, come closer to where I stand now. Do you see it? Do you feel it?

It's here. Something magical. A heartbeat under the city. Buried deep inside; it beats to a song that is neverending. A wonderful promise that has yet to be fulfilled. The best that we've ever seen. It fills me with hope, with patience, with understanding. I am transformed.

And I am neverending. And you. And he. And she is also. The woman coming upon me weighed down by her grocery bags—she is neverending. "Let me help you!" I tell her with a big smile.

"Move out of my way," she hisses.

I let her go. I'm looking at her small back and a bone

crushing love for her takes over. I want to run to her and gather her into me and tell her just how I feel. "Well you have a wonderful day!" I call to her.

She doesn't respond.

Watching her go, I get this strange notion that she and I are not even two separate people—that we're actually the same damn person. The mere thought blows my mind and I can't help myself from calling out to her. "You are mine! You are mine!"

Now I'm at Nardo Nuckles' gym. There's a small frosted window at the entrance and I glance inside to see Tony in a white wife-beater wrapping a hand with great concentration. I wish to be with him, be him, and never to have met him all at once.

Seeing Tony makes my mood take a nosedive.

Nothing is yours, a mean old voice insists. *Nothing.*

Tony spots me and I duck from the window and rush away. But now I hear his voice calling me.

I turn to find him standing on the sidewalk with a big smile. Tony's very forgiving. Maybe the most forgiving I know. "You came."

"I didn't mean that," I tell him across the space between us.

He comes over and takes one of my bags. "I know. Come on. Just come inside and stay a while. I want to show you what I've been learning. You won't believe how quick I'm getting, Stor." He starts to shadow box with his free

173

arm, making little pfft, pfft sounds with his lips shriveled up tight.

Some kids are drawing a wooden wagon over the cobblestone street. They're delivering wood for some of the houses that have wood burning stoves and those on the side streets that have chimneys. The two smallest, maybe six or seven-year-olds, carry bundles up a front stoop and bang on an unsuspecting door. Pregnant Marie answers and promptly shouts back into her house, "Wood's here. Boom Babies!"

I study the group waiting in the street by the wagon. None of them look familiar, so I suspect, as Marie has, they are the children of Forest Boom. "You ever seen them before?" I ask Tony.

"Nah. You?"

"Uh uh. You think they're Boom Babies?"

He sucks his teeth. "You mean the Peter Pan kids from the forest?"

"Yeah."

Legend has it in Forest Boom there's a secret place where time and death do not wield their powers. Some little ones chose this secret place over their own parents and left the Valley to be young forever. It's not an easy place to find for Ernestine and I looked several times. (Not that I would ever leave my parents. I was just curious.) But the only thing we ever came across was poison ivy and a near death experience with a falling tree. The forest is said to be cursed and not many people go in there.

"Don't believe it," Tony says. "They're probably from Soda Can."

I'm sure he's right. But one of them, the oldest, notices me watching them and we lock eyes. He's tall, onyx eyed and shining. His skin is the color of my mother's morning coffee. A gust of wind tunnels into the street from the North. It picks up his long, blue-black hair and sends it twirling above his head. Blades of black silk whip across his face and his slanty eyes narrow in on me. I gasp, despite myself. "Beautiful," I whisper like a bedtime prayer.

Tony's saying something; but it's muffled like he's behind a wall or locked in a closet somewhere. I think he's saying, "Hey, Hey. Hey Stor." But I'm too transfixed by the dark beauty who stares straight at me.

Tony's voice starts to come in louder and finally I hear, "Stori. Are you listening to me?" He sounds pissed.

I'm kind of like stupid from the trance I'm in. "Huh?"

"I said. What are you looking at?"

The sharpness in his voice is like a knife and it cuts me loose from my trance. I look at Tony. I try not to smile because I know he's pissed about me looking at another boy in front of him. "Oh. Nothing."

The two young ones kick down the steps joyfully. Free of their wood, the boy has cash in his hand. He gives it to the dark beauty who, in turn, jams it without counting into his pocket. He hitches the wagon and starts off down the street, turning to give me that spooky look one last time.

"Sup, Wild Man!" Tony calls out to him. The boy cuts him a look that almost looks welcoming and he smiles.

"Keep walking!" Tony threatens.

"Hey!" I say. "What did you do that for?"

"He was staring. He don't know you."

"Well maybe I wanted him to stare."

"Why? You like him or something?"

"That's none of your business. You don't own me, Tony. I'm not your girl."

"But I can still look out for you, as a friend."

"Oh really?"

"Yeah really."

"Well guess what? I'm not your friend. So butt out of my life." I snatch the bag out of his hands.

He doesn't call after me as I go. I bet he really hates me now. Good. I hate him too. And just for an added bonus I hate the world along with him. Thanks to him, I'm back to hating everybody again. Just like that, the loving girl is gone.

I don't see Soldier Sonny leaning up against the side of my building so when he greets me I get startled. "Your momma looking for you."

"I know, Sonny."

His eye is swollen. "What happened to you?"

"People are ugly, sistergirl. They only know the beast inside them. They only know how to strike and hurt."

"You have to fight back." I'm trying not to raise my voice, but it's hard. I want to scream at him now. "You're strong, Sonny. You can defend yourself."

He shakes his head and a tear rolls down his cheek.

"No. Don't cry. You're a big boy. Don't do that."

But the tears keep coming and my heart does that unwanted thing where it feels like it's just been pinched. "Please, Sonny," I whisper.

"Fighting is bad, Stori. I don't want to see it anymore. I don't want to see it."

"Life is a fight. Life is two fists like this." I raise my trusty fists to show him. "These have never failed me. Go ahead. Put them up. Take a shot."

He won't. I know it. "I saw your little sister the other day. What a good kid she is. I know a good kid when I see 'em. I want to have a kid, Stori. I would be a good father. But I need to find a girl first. I went to see the old woman who lives in the tower."

"What woman in the tower?"

"The one she got magic."

"What did she tell you?"

"Told me I ain't never gonna have kids, Stori. That's what she told me."

"You don't know about the future, Sonny. Just one day. Take it one day at a time. I gotta go. I'm sorry."

He reaches out and strokes my face. "That's alright. You go. You're better off getting away from me."

Priscilla Van Patten

I'm on my second serving of coffee with Mrs. Anna Putzarella when Stori finally arrives home. She bursts through the front door and scowls as soon as she sees me. (Don't get into social work if you want to be appreciated. This is a thankless job, if ever there was one.)

"Stori, hon," her mother, says.

Her face changes when she sees her mother. "Ma. You're up?"

Her mother is still weak but decided after some coaxing from me to try just another day. She nods with a smile. "Priscilla convinced me to get up. I called for you."

This place is an anthropological goldmine. There are many fascinating codes of conduct here in the Valley. If a child is out in the streets and their mother wants them home all that mother has to do is open any window and call out the child's name. It doesn't matter the distance between mother and child. The call will be heard. It will travel far, as hustler will pass it to hooligan, hooligan to welfare bum, welfare bum to street sweeper, street sweeper to sedentary veteran and so on.

It's an unbroken chain linked by something stronger than steel—an absolute reverence for the bond between mother and child.

"Stori, You remember Miss Van Patten."

Stori drops her bookbag and coat on top of the radiator and kicks off her boots onto a brown paper bag on the floor. She gives me a half-assed hello and brings her own bag to the kitchen counter and begins to empty its contents. "Where's Regina?" she asks.

"Taking a nap," says Mrs. Putzarella. "Miss Van Patten brought her to the da Vinci School of Arts today."

I take this opportunity to size her up while she's not looking at me with those razor sharp eyes of hers. Broad shouldered, slim waisted, and her leg muscles are defined under her black leggings. It's a natural strength she possesses, one of someone born to be strong. Not of someone who works for it at the gym. I wonder if she had been raised under different circumstances, if she would have harnessed her physique into becoming a gymnast or a runner. I ponder what I consider to be her wasted talents and surmise that the end result is the hard, unforgiving girl I see in front of me.

She must sense I'm checking her out because she turns and gives me a look that makes me fear for my safety. This girl can obviously beat me up and if she has a chance to get away with it, she probably would. She grins with satisfaction like she knows exactly what I'm thinking. I can see it gives her great pleasure intimidating people. I come to the conclusion that this has been her coping mechanism in her most recent years. If one can't enjoy the finer pleasures of this world, like I have been fortunate enough to, one must at least be able to make that same world suffer.

"How you feeling Ma?" she asks.

"Better today. I even got dressed and everything."

"I got some hens from the market," Stori tells her. "Your favorite."

As Stori busies herself about the cabinets and fridge her mother tells me, "Stori's a wonderful cook."

"Did you teach her?" I ask, warming my hands around my coffee mug.

"Just what I know. But she's got that Calabrian blood in her veins. She cooks with the passion from the Old Country." Anna's pride in her daughter is sincere, and although I don't believe that culinary skill is inherited I envy her adoration.

For some reason, whenever I step foot inside this

rickety old apartment, I always get distracted by things irrelevant to my case. I have to remind myself to stay business minded. I have specific questions I need to ask. About Anna not paying her bills, about the possibility of placing the children in a foster home.

But there are other things I'm curious about. Like the strange rumors in Rita's Tavern and Regina's secret. I decide to ask a question or two to sate my curiosity. "I was at Rita's Tavern the other night. And some people were talking about very strange things. Like this man Cosimo."

In a minute's time Stori has chopped a head of celery and an onion. She angles the chopping board over a heated skillet and scrapes only the celery in with her knife. She jerks the skillet a little to get the onion where she wants it; the oil sizzles. Then she grabs a stale loaf of bread and starts to cube it.

It's kind of hard to explain without making myself look like a hypocrite. (Seeing how I don't like Stori.) But I feel kind of soothed sitting here while she's cooking. She's totally in charge and I must say there is nothing more calming than being in the presence of a capable woman in a kitchen.

I had that once. Back in Erie. Before stuff got bad with my dad. Afterwards my mom wasn't up to cooking I guess. She got involved with this nondenominational church and spent so much time there that I hardly ever saw her. I really resented her for that. Putting her church friends in front of Grace and me.

"What about Cosimo?" Stori mumbles.

"Have you heard things about him, lately? Being here in the Valley."

Stori shoots a look of warning to her mother and her mother straightens in her chair.

"I assure you, I'm only curious. It's not for the case. I just found it all hard to believe. But they were dead serious about this man."

"Cosimo hasn't been seen in the Valley or anywhere for hundreds of years," says Mrs. Putzarella.

"So you do believe he's walking dead."

"Listen. I know you think our ways are strange. But lots of stranger things have happened beyond the Valley. You can't fault us for our beliefs. They were passed down from generation to generation. Like our naming day."

"Yes," I say. (There I go again, getting distracted.) "I find that one quite lovely. To be named at first light under a tree."

"By a prophetess no less," Anna adds. Her smile makes *me* smile. She's a soft woman, nothing like her daughter. She reminds me a little bit of my own mother. "Tell me," I say. "What was it like when Stori was named?"

"Stori was born in the middle of a blizzard. I labored for four hours right there in my bedroom. She came out wide-eyed and screaming. The next day we gathered under the sycamore in the backyard and the prophetess, Caroline, who lives somewhere secret came. She held Stori up into the light and sang an ancient psalm and then she named her: My beloved. I will write your words upon my book. In an ink of permanent. Pages ever turning. My beloved. I will lay open my heart, become the book. And you will write my story."

"It's gorgeous. What does it mean?"

Stori's interested too, as if she's just hearing this for the first time. "Yeah, Ma. What does it mean?"

"It means that Stori's special. And her destiny is waiting," Anna answers grandly.

I turn the words over in my head as Anna beckons Stori in for a kiss on her forehead. There's something so submissive about her naming song, yet also it's infinite, it's soaring.

What would the prophetess have sung when I was born? Something infinite as well? I would only hope so.

"Ma," Stori says, wiping her fingers with a dishtowel. "I've never seen that lady Caroline. Is she for real? People say she's in some tower and hasn't come out for years. Is that true?"

"She's real. She stays hidden. And she's a hundred-thirty-years-old."

"People don't live that long," I insist.

Mrs. Putzarella shrugs. "People can live as long as they choose to, I assume." She puts a hand up to her forehead. "Oh no. I have to rest. I have to."

"What is it?" I ask, my heart fluttering in my chest.

"The pain."

I hate seeing people in pain. It gives me a sour feeling in the pit of my stomach. "Of course. Please. Let me help you to your room."

Stori hustles to the fridge and says, "I'll get her some water."

In her bedroom, as I help her into bed and close the blinds, Stori comes in and places a glass of ice water on the bed stand. "We should let her sleep," she whispers.

"Of course," I whisper back.

I follow Stori out but on my way Mrs. Putzarella calls for me.

I feel guilty standing over her bed while she's lying there in discomfort.

She puts a pleading hand on my forearm and whispers, "Have you ever been in love, Miss Van Patten?"

"In love?"

"Yes. In love."

"Yes. I love my boyfriend. Very much."

"Would you die without him?"

"I don't know. I've never thought about it."

"Cause that's what I'm doing. I'm dying here without him."

"You could move on," I tell her.

"No."

"You *should* then. For your children."

"Miss Van Patten. How can I forget about someone who is unforgettable?"

Oh, Daddy. Don't die. Please. I wish I could come home.

"If he wants to leave me, that's fine. But I just need to see him one last time. He cheated on me, and it tore me up. I just need to tell him, before I die, that I forgive him. If you find him, you tell him to come on home. You give him that message for me."

Jaded as I am, I know I will not have a chance to relay the message but I lie to make her feel better. "I'll try my best to find him and tell him."

"Oh thank you. You're a good woman. Thank you so much."

Back in the kitchen I decide I don't want to bother this family any more. I start to collect my things when Stori says, "You can stay for dinner if you want." The room smells delicious and she's stuffing the hen with her bare hands.

Against my better judgments I put the coat down and sit. Evidently I do want to stay. Evidently too many memories of the good days back in Erie have been resurrected in this kitchen. Funny how memories can haunt. Like ghosts. Like real things. Living and breathing memories. Mine are of days when the sun was spilling through the windows and the floors had just been mopped and my mother was humming over the stove.

I watch Stori wash her hands vigorously with a bar of

soap. She covers the pan with the hen in it with some foil, dons a pair of oven gloves and shoves the pan inside the oven. I almost feel like a little girl in her presence.

"Can I help?" I ask.

"You wanna chop the broccoli?"

"Sure."

A cutting board of Broccoli Rape is set before me. I pick up the knife. "I heard once about angels too. Not in the bar. But from a case I had last spring. The youngest daughter ran away from home. The mom thought she was looking for the angels."

Stori's sautéing garlic in another pan. "A legend Miss Van Patten."

"Well I would like to think they are real because we sure do need some angels in this world."

She turns, holding her wooden spoon, her strong but slender hands glistening with water. She does something that almost knocks me off my chair. She smiles.

"Do you believe in them?" I ask hopefully.

"Even if I did, I don't anymore."

"Have you ever seen one?"

It looks like she wants to tell me something. Something she's been holding in her heart for a long time.

"Go ahead, Stori. You can trust me."

She sighs as her gaze cuts across the room to the window. "Yes. I do remember them. But I would never admit it to Regi. It would just make her sad to know they're all gone. But when I was young, they were everywhere. On a winter's evening like this, they would show themselves in the moments when I was having the most fun. Like falling in love with a single snowflake or racing out of my house to dive off my front stoop into a mountain of snow.

"And in the summer. They used to meet me on the rooftop when I was up there star gazing. They loved to talk. Tell secrets. They liked to tell silly stories, too and have a good deep down belly laugh. Angels are really just kids at heart. Grown ups who never grew up. Who went to heaven still never grown up. And so the Lord made them into Night Lights. To hover over rooftops where children rested and gazed at stars. And dreamed of peaceful things and felt at one with the whole wide world.

"You could find them, too, if you ran wild and free in the open field skirting Forest Boom. (It's not too far from here.) Chasing after fireflies and pressing your bare knees into the coolness of the grass. How perfect and clean is one blade of grass. So clean you can pluck it from the earth and put it in your mouth and chew.

"It's been said that the angel's were vital for the Valley. That the magic created between angel and child was what was holding the neighborhood together and keeping the darkness at bay. But then the angels started to disappear. The children started to get sad and bored. They started begging for video games and expensive toys to fill the space. I, myself, begged my mother for my doll, Amanda.

187

Some kids couldn't take the loneliness. So they ran away from home and vanished into Forest Boom. It's rumored there are still angels in the forest." She gazes out the window and sighs.

"Thank you, Stori. I loved hearing that. I wish I could see an angel."

"Miss Priscilla. If I tell you something do you promise you won't share it with anyone or use it against me?"

I don't want to promise, because God knows what might come out of her mouth and the bearing it could have on the case. "I promise."

"My friend Ernestine was placed at the Pilgrim's Mansion. The one that woman named Smyrna runs."

"Really? I've yet to meet this woman. Well you're friend is lucky."

"No. That's the thing. She said the mayor wants to make all the girls his wives. And she also said the mistress isn't human. She cuts herself and doesn't bleed."

I get a chill that runs from the nape of my neck all the way down my spine. I shudder.

In some way, I believe her. Ever since I've moved to Redemption I've known something wasn't right about this place. But what can a girl like me do? Or even Stori? People like us don't have any power to change things.

"I got this feeling, Miss Van Patten, that there is some real bad stuff going on in this town and my father got caught up in it. Maybe someone can check out the mansion and the mayor and stuff."

"Stori," I say, determined to forget all the things I've learned in the past few days. "Your friend is probably going through a hard time adjusting. I think people would know if someone as visible as the mayor was planning to make an illegal commune in the middle of Redemption."

"I knew you wouldn't believe me." She takes the cutting board from the table, turns back to the stove and tosses the broccoli into boiling water.

"Stori. I know about what happened at the dam," I tell her. "The report from the hospital came in. Your father didn't try to kill himself. You did. He jumped in to save *you*. I just want you to know it's not your fault that you have a mental illness. Your father walking out on you guys, it's not your fault either. I know you think the world of your father, because he tried to save you that day. But you and Regina are the innocent ones. Your father and your mother have not been doing a very good job at taking care of you. They both need help and in the time being I think it would be in both your and Regina's best interest—"

"—Stop," she says. "Just stop your talking because I don't want to hear it anymore."

"I know this discussion is tough but we have to have it at some point. Stori, look at me. Please."

She turns.

"Forget this place. It's destroying you."

"It's home."

"It's not. Stori, I like you a lot. I can help you if you let me."

"You don't like me. You think you're better than me."

"That's not true."

"Please. I could see it the first moment you walked in here. You're just a lying, deceiving little bitch like everyone else in this world. And by the way, that top looks horrible on you. It washes out your face."

Our tender moment is destroyed; I'm back to secretly hating her again. Except this time I don't bother hiding it. "You know. I'm trying to be your friend here. But you're never going to make any friends with that horrible attitude."

"What does someone like *you* know about friends?"

"Me? I have lots of friends. I know how to make them and how to keep them. And it definitely doesn't involve being a sour puss with everyone I meet."

"Phaa."

"What, you don't believe me?"

"Lady. I sized you up the minute I laid eyes on you. Them fancy clothes and jewelry. What a front."

"What are you talking about?"

"You are trying to be someone you're not. Trying to fit in with a crowd you don't even like. It's just cause their popular, and have lots of money. It's not cause you really like them."

"There are lots of very nice rich people in the world."

"And you don't know any of them."

"You know nothing about me."

"Why are you getting so mad, then, if it's not true?"

"Because you shouldn't be making assumptions about people."

"So you're allowed to come into my house and make all the assumptions you want? Is that how it works?"

"I'm trying to help."

"You lie. We're just another case to add to your file. You don't care about us."

"That's not true."

"You don't care about anyone. Not your job, not your friends. So who do you care about, Miss Van Patten?"

"I don't have to take your shit." I get up and grab my things in a hurry and make my way for the door. "You know maybe you're right about me not having any friends. But at least I'm not a bully!"

She turns back to the stove satisfied she's won the battle, but deep in her heart she knows I will win the war.

Stori

Minutes after Priscilla's gone, someone's ringing the bell from the stoop. I bet it's her, wanting to say sorry. I fly downstairs and fling the door open and say, "What?!" But to my shock and horror it's Uncle Joe!

I try to slam the door shut, but he uses his patent leather shoe as a wedge on the door saddle.

"Get the fuck out of here. Or I'll call the police." I'm fighting against the door with all my might, kicking at his shoe. I don't know if he still has his gun, but I'm sure if he makes it in here it's not gonna be good. "I'll scream," I warn him. That's all it would take in the Valley. When a neighbor screams everyone comes running. Uncle Joe knows it. "Wait. Just wait. I'm not here to hurt you. Please, Stori."

"You tried to kill me."

"A bad time. You caught me at a bad time. I was all

jammed up. I'm here to make it right."

"I don't believe you."

"You have my word, Stori. I give you the word of the Valley."

The word of the Valley. It is used in lieu of contracts, more binding than any legal document, even from the courts.

What is he kidding me? He hasn't lived here in over five years. His word is garbage. "You don't live here anymore," I remind him.

"So what are you saying? I don't remember? I didn't grow up here? My mother didn't die three houses down the street? I'm *not* a 'Merigan, Stori."

"Well you sure aren't one of us."

"Fair enough. I'm not one of you guys either, okay? But I ain't no 'Merigan."

I ease up on the door, but still block his path inside. "Anything you have to say to me, you say it right there. Mom and Regi are sleeping. There's no way in hell I'm letting you inside."

"Fine. Have it your way." He backs off and curses and paces up and down the steps. He's all jittery again, the way he was in Soda Can Alley. What a skitz he is. I'm starting to wonder if maybe he does do drugs.

I come outside and shut the door behind me. It's freezing out here and I hug myself for warmth. "You better make it quick."

"I just came to say I was sorry, that's all. Things got a little out of hand, and I'm a man of honor and I know when to admit I'm wrong."

"Ok. I forgive you." I really don't and he knows it. "Can I go now?"

"Come on," he pleads. "Let me in. You're freezing."

I whistle to Donny and Christopher, Tony Carp's boys, across the street. They're leaning on the bumper of a Monte Carlo, smoking. They look over and nod.

"I'm going inside now with my wonderful uncle!" I tell them.

They salute me and Donny yells, "Enjoy!"

I cut a look at my uncle that says, fuck with me and Tony Carp's boys will be on you like flies on shit. He's not appreciative. I know, deep inside, he still wants to belong here. Even though he's too far gone.

Inside the kitchen I don't offer him anything to eat or drink.

He sits at the table and laces his hands in front of him. "Okay. So there's something else I need to tell you."

"About my dad? You know where he is?"

"No. I don't. But I do know that there were some people looking for him. People he owes money to, from his gambling days."

"Who?" I ask. "Tell me their names."

"Are you crazy? Stori, I know you're young but I'm sure you're aware of the way things work around here. I'm

sure you know about the Tapparellis. They control the cops
and they pay the mayor and his cronies good money to
keep their noses out of things."

"So what are you saying?"

"Stori. I don't know how to put this. But if your father
owed money to the Tapparellis I don't think he will ever be
coming home."

"So your saying he's dead. Mo killed him."

"I'm saying, guys like that, in debt, who can't control
their impulses—they can get into some really deep trouble.
And it's not safe for you to be running around the Valley
asking all sorts of questions. Because you just might come
across some knucklehead who thinks he knows something.
And then well…" He acts like I know what'll happen next,
swooping his arm out to his side like he's ushering the very
truth into the room. I do know where he's headed, but I
feign ignorance just to annoy him.

"Look," he says, bristling. (My uncle is known for a
raging temper) "You know damn well where it will get you.
Trouble. Okay? So just stop looking. And stop asking
questions."

"Why do you care, Uncle Joe?" This time I really want
to know. He was a good uncle once, when I was about
Regi's age. I remember him bringing me to the arcade
downtown and getting one of his mobbed up gumbahs to
slip him the key to all the games, so I didn't have to play to
win. He just opened the glass cases and let me reach inside.

"You used to be a good uncle," I tell him. "But not now. So why do you care?"

"I still am!" he shouts. "Damnit. I still am. A good fucking man. Just because I'm not in the Valley anymore, what does that make me scum?"

You sold your soul to the devil, I want to say. But I only give him this: "You left my father behind."

"I'm a good man," he tells me, looking like he might cry. "I deserve what I got in life. I deserve the money. I deserve the house. Don't I? Stori. Don't I?"

What did my uncle Joe mean by all that stuff he said? Is he trying to tell me that my father was killed by Mo and if I go asking questions Mo will kill me too? Is my life in danger? My sister's? My mother's? Did my dad do something that could have put us in harm's way?

I'm so confused.

I pull on my coat and boots and head to the street. Tony Carp's boys are still hanging by the Monte Carlo. I come down my stoop and cross over.

Donny and Christopher are tatted, scarred and tough as Teflon. "Hi Donny. Hi Christopher."

"What up girl?" Donny says indifferently.

"What up Putz?" says Christopher. "Where was that crazy ass uncle of yours off to in such a hurry?"

"Who knows," I say.

"You looking for Carp?" Donny asks as if he's already

trying to get rid of me. One thing about guys from the Valley: if they even assume that you're talking to one of their boys they will treat you like a leper. Every since me and Tony got tight all his boys barely talk to me. Once, one of his friend's cousins asked me out and Tony had a conniption fit. At first I was kind of flattered by his reaction and thought maybe it was because deep inside he had feelings for me, but Ernestine knew better; she was outraged. "Are you fucking kidding me?" she squealed right after I told her. "He doesn't ask you out himself but won't let anyone else either? What does he think, you're his property? That's so freaking sexist. I'm sick of all these guys around here treating us like we belong to them."

"It's kind of a respect thing, I guess," I told her, not wanting to believe Tony could do anything wrong.

But Ernestine wasn't having it. "That kind of mentality objectifies women and is unfair. He's patronizing you!"

Donny's kind of cute and I could see myself having a crush on him if maybe I got to know him a little better. Anyways, Tony's tied up with Desma. I'm sure Donny knows. Just in case I'll set the records straight. "I'm not looking for Carp. He's probably with his girl. I actually wanted to talk to you guys."

"Go 'head."

There's really no segue into what I'm about to ask so I just put it right out there. "I need a piece."

They exchange mischievous glances, smirking like I

just told them a joke.

"I'm serious."

Christopher puts his pinched cigarette to his lips and takes a hit. "What you need a piece for soldier?"

"That's my business."

"You ever even held one before?" They snicker, all condescending.

Normally I would say something ugly but my pride has been having to take a back seat lately. I stay cool. "No."

"Go 'head girl."

"So I'll need you to show me how to use it too."

Donny shakes his head. "Nu uh. Carp gets wise he won't be too happy."

"Tony isn't my father," I snap. "Since when does he decide what I choose to do?"

"Trust, kid. He got his eye on you."

"He does not."

"You wouldn't know if he did." They start to snicker again, that infuriating little *guys-only* snicker that says *Your just a dumb girl and don't know any better, but we do*. It always makes me want to scream.

"Yes I would. He's with Desma now, didn't I just say it?"

"That don't mean shit."

I'm starting to understand Ernestine's aggravation now. I'm sick of everyone acting like I belong to Tony or something. What kind of shit is that? Like he can just label any girl he wants his and they don't have a say? I'll rip that label right off and shred it to pieces right in his face! "Listen. Last time I checked I'm a Putzarella, not a Carpenesi. I'll pay you. Whatever you need. I got it."

"It's gonna be a few bucks, Putz."

"I said I got it." I don't really have it, but I'll figure that part out later.

Donny's shaking his head.

"Man, that's trouble, bro," Christopher says turning his face into the street, a sign he's officially dismissed me.

"He's right Putz. You better scram."

Back inside my kitchen I turn the flame on again under the skillet. My broccoli isn't done yet. I want to make a salad, but what's the point? Regi isn't gonna wake up and neither is my mother. I set the table for one. I put the lamp on over by the window. I sit on the radiator and stare outside just wishing that someone will come and rescue me from this loneliness.

Someone's walking by. Of all people. It's Sidewinder—the man who called my father retarded. They call him Sidewinder because he walks in zigzags down the street, never walking in a straight line—he says it's an OCD thing, but everyone knows he's a hopeless drunk. I hate Sidewinder. I don't think I can ever forgive him for what he did to my father.

My father didn't respond to him. I know he wanted to,

but it's hard for him to get the words out. I wasn't going to let Sidewinder get away with it so I hit him. Hard. He fell to the ground, coughing and laughing. Then he got up and pulled out a knife. It didn't take a millisecond to know what to do. I stepped forward, pushed my cheek into the knife, grabbed my wrist and broke skin.

Sidewinder pulled the knife away, looking like he saw a ghost. "What?" I asked him. "You ain't never seen LOVE?"

As Sidewinder pounded pavement, my father grabbed me by the shoulder roughly and smacked my wound. "Why?" he demanded. "Why did you do that?"

"I love you," I told him, shaking all over. "I would die for you, Daddy."

"No," he demanded. "No. I'm going to take you somewhere."

He brought me to the Cage. It took a while but he convinced the ref to let me fight. The first round was a nightmare. I took a terrible beating. In the corner my father yelled at me, "Where's the fighter in you now?"

I told my father, "I want to stop."

"No you don't."

"I don't like this. I don't even know her. Why would I hurt a stranger?"

"Because you can!" he told me.

"Please Daddy. I wanna go home."

And that's when he said it. The thing I will never get

out of my head. "Look at me!" He hollered. "I can't talk! Look what you did to me! I should have let you drown!"

The day I jumped off that dam, I wasn't try to kill myself. I was actually happy that day. So happy that I leapt off that dam without a care in the world. So happy that I forgot my father would jump in after me. That he couldn't swim.

I grab the vase of pussy willows at the center of the table and hurl it against the wall.

Joe

I sit down in the shoe shiner's chair outside of the Funicelli Shoe Shop and Mr. Funicelli's grandson comes out.

"Like a shine, sir?"

"What do you think?"

He stoops down and starts his work.

I'm really getting tired of it. Of everyone's undying loyalty to the Valley. They treat this place like it's the Garden of Eden or something.

But what did the Valley ever do for me?

I'll say it cause I ain't scared like the rest of them. It lied.

The Valley with all its codes of honor and righteous pride lied right to my face and thought nothing of it.

The day I discovered that I had been duped was in

seventh grade. I was playing hooky with Mo and his boys. Yeah, Mo. The one who threw a baby down the stairs just because it was crying. I've known him since even before that baby and let me tell you, he was just as mean. There was an all girl's private school three blocks from ours and one of the girls was famed to be frisky. Mo said she was gonna meet us in the playground right after recess and even though I took a pass he dragged me along anyways. Even back then, there wasn't saying no to the guy. It wasn't like today, where bullying is a crime and shit. The kids today don't know what it was like. Being on the street with no parents around and some sociopath telling you if you don't come see a girl he's gonna go see your mother later. Back then, kids like Mo ran the streets. Even the cops was scared.

I was still a little green at the time, if you know what I mean, and I suppose I was embarrassed about banging in front of my friends. Plus, my mother was a teacher at the school so I was all shook up about getting caught so close to her job. My mother was no novice with the wooden spoon. You think that thing is only used for stirring sauce, then you never grew up with an Italian mother. When she whipped me in the face with that thing I could have sworn it was full of lead. "Out with the demons!" she would yell. My mother was always talking about the devil waging his wars in our hearts and how we had to take up our swords and fight him. But I never believed any of that shit. There was never any harm in having a little fun, even if it got you in trouble sometimes. My mother was one of those women who never smiled and was always moaning over her bible. Made me sick.

Turned out the girl was a no-show. On our way out of the parking lot someone spotted this old woman wearing an apron. She was picking up trash with a gloved hand, shoving it into a trash bag.

"Hey trash lady!" Mo yelled. "Suck on this!" he grabbed his crotch and we all got a good laugh.

Ha ha. Poor lady. She didn't deserve it. But it was still funny.

But then the woman turned around to face us. You wanna know who that old lady was? Do you? Do you!

It was my mother.

That's right. She was a trash picker. She lied to me the whole time, telling me she was a schoolteacher. My father lied to me too. That lazy bum let her rummage through maggots all day long and then sat his fat ass on the couch at night while she served him dinner. Chuckling at Ralph Kramden from the Honeymooners, sipping on a beer.

When I got home later that day I wanted to call her out on it. *You're a trash picker and Pops doesn't even care. All that praying you do ain't shit.* I was hoping she would hear those words and take out that wooden spoon and beat me with it. Cause I would stand there the whole time and not feel a thing. Nothing she could say or do would ever hurt me anymore.

But I didn't say a peep. Only that I wasn't hungry. I never ate home again, or at least at the table with them. My mother put up a fuss for a while, but eventually she let me be. She said, "If those hooligans want you more than Him then let them have you." At least she had my brother Frank. He was her prize you know.

"You're wrong," he said one day. "Not sitting at the table with us."

"Mom's a trash picker. In case you didn't know."

I thought that might shut him up good. But do you know what he came back with? "I know."

No way. "You knew?"

"Of course. Mommy didn't want to tell you because she knows how sensitive you are."

"We're living a lie man. This ain't no American dream."

"We're living. And we have each other. We have the Valley."

"Fuck the Valley. You're a fool," I told him. "You're a Goddamn fool."

The Valley lies. That's what it does best.

So I want you to tell me this—what is so great about a fucking place where decent women have to pick trash for a living? Where they have to lie to their sons? If you can find one redeeming quality about this shithole I want you to tell me. And don't say honor, respect for family, all that. Cause

I don't want to hear it.

Here's what I'll do then. I'll do me. Doing me is what I'm best at.

Life is short. Have a little fun.

I'm at Rita's Tavern, now. I kick back in the corner, away from the Arm and his men arguing over their conspiracy theories. I'm sick of everyone talking about all these missing children and how they think Cosimo the Corpse and his Night's Council have something to do with it. I don't know why everyone is getting all excited. If you ask me, people just need to take it easy and enjoy themselves. If you think about everything that's going on in the world you'll only drive yourself crazy. All I'm focused on right now is getting my buzz on, and figuring out if I want to take a stroll over to the Madam's ranch in a while.

Cheating. Fucking cheating. Yeah I do it. Yeah. I know it's wrong. But there are a whole lot of things that are wrong in this life. Like the mayor and those sex slaves he's rounding up in that mansion on Pilgrim's Island. I'm pretty tight with the mayor. He pays me well to keep him safe and advised. I would have never thought he would have confessed his secret to me, though. But come to think of it, for every man I've known, no matter how discreet, there always comes a time when they need to fess. Let them demons right out, like my mother would say. Just so happened I was telling Mayor Vaughn about my own little down-low dirties. About how sometimes I like to dabble in the underage girl thing. It's kind of like half bragging, half-confession, I guess. It's like, yeah I'm a bad boy but doesn't the evil just taste so damn good? And he was all like, yeah I get you my man. I get you. I'm down with the same damn thing.

But who can judge us? We are born right into a swarming sea of iniquity. It almost drowns us before we even take our first breath. Nobody asks to be born into this world. It just happens. And you've got to deal with it. So this is the way I deal with mine. The bottle, the women, and the money. Oh yeah. The money.

The mayor's liaison takes a seat beside me and orders a White Russian. "Did you get any more information?"

"Been busy," I tell him.

"We all been busy. The family. Do they know anything?"

I should probably tell him about my niece, but I don't. She may be a nosy little brat, but it's already bad enough I tried to kill her. Anyways, she won't find out nothing. "No," I tell him.

"You're lying. We know about the girl. She's been to you and she's asked you about your brother. And about…him."

Great. What now? Don't tell me they wired the clubhouse. Goddamn this new age we live in and all our shit being monitored all the time—fucking Dragnet Nation and shit. The clubhouse is my only place left to unwind.

"Who told you that?"

"A contact."

"Yeah. So what. She's just a little shit. You can't blame her for trying to find her pops. Can you?"

"She mentioned Cosimo. She might know things."

"Trust me. She doesn't know anything. People tell ghost stories around here all the time. Even The Arm."

"But The Arm is not the daughter of the man who is missing."

"She's still just a little kid. Didn't I tell you that? What are you def?"

"What about the house. Have you been in the house?"

"You don't understand the Valley. I can't get in there that easy. Besides, you all were in there already. And you didn't find anything."

"We didn't have much time. But you know the family."

"They consider me a "Merigan. I was just in there today and they kicked me out before I had my coat off." I remember the aromas in the kitchen. God, it smelled good in there. I wished my niece would have at least offered me a bite or even a doggy bag or some shit. "I was only in the kitchen, but I didn't see no crown."

"Shhhhh," he whispers. "Don't say it out loud."

"What the hell is it anyways? Why is it so important?"

"You will find out in due time."

"When do I get to meet your boss anyways?"

"He's not well. He's not having many visitors."

"Well I'm getting tired of waiting. All these promises. Couple bucks you been tossing. Ain't enough. I can make my own."

That's when he slips something across the bar. It's a DVD. It's titled "The Final Boss."

A guy who looks like a real bad ass is featured on the front. He's like some kind of a gangster. Relaxing in a study with his legs propped up on a desk. He's smoking a cigar and looking straight into the camera. The guy is *me*.

"Where'd you get that?" I ask.

"Why? Do you like it?"

"That's *me*," I tell him.

"Yes. It is you. Do you want to be famous Joe?"

I reach out to take the DVD, but he slides it down the bar out of my reach. Motherfucker. "Do you want to be famous?"

I get it. I'm not a fool. This is like some kind of a pact. A choice has to be made here. "I'll keep looking. For that crown. I'll keep looking for the one who has it. As for my niece you can check her out yourself."

"I can't. She's hot with something. I can't get near her."

"Watch yourself, bro. She's just a kid, bro. And still my niece."

"Keep an eye on the Putzarellas. Let us know every step they take, especially the hot one."

"She ain't hot. But I got my eye on it." I want that DVD. I want it for myself. But he ain't giving it to me. He gets up and leaves a twenty—a charitable tip for the White Russian he barely touched. And he and my fame and fortune make their way out into the night.

Priscilla Van Patten

Bill is poring over some kind of encyclopedia looking book; he's so lost in its pages that he doesn't even notice me standing an inch from his desk. "Five," I say.

He jolts upright; his glasses go crooked on his face. "Pris. You startled me."

"Five more, Bill. Five. I spoke with one of the officers downstairs. Internal reports were made, but no investigations. I checked the paper. Nothing. Why has it not been made public?"

He takes his glasses off and heaves a deep sigh. He looks like he hasn't slept in days. "Priscilla. Sit."

I'm not in the mood. I just want an answer. I just want a number to call. Someone to go to. To lodge a complaint. Why is this being swept under the rug? But if Bill wants me to sit, I'll sit.

"Prissy. We're friends, right?"

"Of course."

"Ok. So what I'm about to tell you is not between professionals. It's between friends."

I get it. The stakes are higher. Whatever he tells me cannot go further than this room. I think of what friendship means to the people in the Valley. I respect their loyalty and I like to think of myself as being of that same moral fiber. "It will stay in this room."

"Mayor Vaughn's liaison was here. We spoke. The reports were sent to the office. We sent our people to the homes and they're dealing with the families. Offering whatever support they need. But the mayor insists this doesn't get out."

"But this is children we're talking about. People need to know."

He shakes his head decidedly. "No. No one is going to find out. It's out of our hands."

"But why?"

"Mayor Vaughn is quite the opportunist, Pris. More than anyone knows. This casino—he's obsessed with it. We're just a week away from the grand opening and he wants every headline to be about that. These reports would smudge his image, would put a bad taste in people's mouths. What's more, he's running for governor next election."

"I've never heard of this before."

"I'm sure it happens everywhere. I'm sure it's not the first. And it certainly won't be the last."

"It's wrong," I say. I want to cry. I want to bury my face in my hands and cry. "Bill, please. Let's do something. I'm sure there's something—"

"—Pris. I resigned."

"What?"

"I'm only finishing out the month." He closes his book and I see the cover. It's Shakespeare.

He caresses the cover. "From my college days. Had it on the shelf for years and kept telling myself I would pick it up one day and start reading again. Now is the time."

"No, Bill. We need you here. *I* need you."

"It's time, Priscilla. For me, it's time."

I stand. "Give me the names at least."

He shakes his head. "I don't want you getting involved. You're too emotional."

"I promise I won't make a fuss or get you in trouble. I just want to know who they are."

He considers my request. "I won't give you their names," he finally decides. "It's for your own protection. But I will tell you this. They all had scholarships to the da Vinci School of Arts. I don't know if the people there should be advised on keeping a closer eye on their students."

The da Vinci School of Arts for Children is a wonderful place. An old humanitarian couple named the Hillanders who have lived in Redemption all their lives funds it. A plaque honoring them is in the front office right above a picture of the two of them standing outside of the building. How nice. If I had that kind of money, I could see myself giving back to the community. Every time I'm in here I make it a point to look up to their picture. It reminds me that there are still good people in this world.

Today I've brought Regina with me, with the permission of her mother of course. Aside from her being my excuse to come here, I think a girl like her, so open and sensitive would benefit from immersing herself in the Arts. And there are scholarships for the underprivileged. I'm sure I can pull some strings to get her full tuition.

Today we're meeting with the head master, Miss Janice Brine, to take a tour of the school.

Janice is about my age. She's in black cargo pants and a white wife-beater. She's got the smallest waist I've ever seen and her body is toned like crazy. Her skin glistens from a sheen of sweat and her cheeks are flushed. "You came at the perfect time," she tells us as she leads us down a corridor with children running and skipping carefree. "I just finished my Hip-Hop class."

"I love Hip Hop!" Regi exclaims skipping alongside her.

"Sounds fun," I say.

"Oh. It is." She winks at Regina.

Regina winks back.

We stop outside a classroom where children are painting on paper canvasses propped up on easels. The teacher is in the front of the classroom twirling to classical music.

"What's she doing?" Regi asks.

"She's the movement. The students are trying to capture her."

"Interesting," I muse.

"Capturing movement," Janice says, still observing. "How do you do it? Where is the movement? Is it in the color, the angles? Or is it in the still places?"

"I think it's in the twirly stuff all around her head!" Regina says. "I could paint that!"

"I bet you could," Janice agrees with a hand on Regi's head.

"Smart," I comment. "And fun. Do you have classes for adults?" I ask.

She smiles. "There should be, that's for sure."

We continue down the hall and Janice says. "Next I'll take you to our modern movement class. Regina, if you'd like you can join the girls there. See what you think."

"Okay!" Regina's all excited and for a brief moment I'm almost sorry I brought her here. I don't want to get her hopes up with too much fun. I've already started up the paperwork to take her and her sister out of the house. But maybe this school will be a saving grace. An anchor for her in her life.

We reach the studio and Regi looks inside. There's a girl Regi's age dancing in front of the mirror. "Hey. That's Alexandria Madonna. Hi Alexandria!"

A woman standing and watching the dancing girl shushes Regi with a stern finger to her lips.

"That's Alexandria's mother," Janice explains apologetically. "She's a little bit of a stage mom."

"Lovely. I'm sure she's a charm."

Regi whispers. "That's Netty over there. I'm gonna say hi."

"Okay," Miss Janice approves with a gentle nod of her head.

Miss Janice lets Regi in and closes the door behind her. We move to the glass wall and look in on Alexandria dancing.

"Miss Janice," I say. "There were a couple of your students who went missing recently. I'm sure you're aware of it."

She straightens her spine. "Yes. We lost them."

"And now the five from the Valley."

"Yes. The five."

"And the Bak boy before that."

"Yes. You knew him?"

"Our office didn't handle his case. But I'm privy to some of the details."

Regi sits against the wall with the little girl Netty. She whispers something in Netty's ear and Netty bites her bottom lip nervously.

"Is that why you're here?" Janice asks, suddenly getting defensive. "To investigate?"

"No. To be quite honest, this is nonofficial. I won't be documenting my visit. I really am here to get Regi registered. But I'm also here because...well I've got this feeling that someone might be targeting specific children— ones who are into the Arts. I'm not sure why, but I thought maybe you might have an idea."

"I couldn't think of any reason why. These children don't pose a threat to anyone."

"Did the Bak boy?"

"No. In fact, Benjamin was profound when he danced. He was born to dance, Miss Van Patten."

We watch Alexandria move across the dance floor, executing perfect little bounds and spins.

"She's quite good herself," I note.

"Her mother sees to that," Janice says sardonically. "She's obsessed with competitions. Winning them. Between you and me it makes me sick. That whole *I can do better than you* phenomenon. Our kids are up against it, you know. I try to protect them as best I can." She looks up to a picture of Leonardo daVinci hanging just beside the front door. "Sometimes I wonder if he would have been as great if his mother was at his back all the time demanding he beat everyone around him. How can true art come from cunning? It can't, Miss Van Patten. It has to come from…"

"Where?"

"Well I don't know. That's what we try to discover here. Where it comes from. All I do know, is in order to access it, one must have freedom." She stops and her jaw drops open. "My God. There it is. Thatagirl Netty. Thatagirl." I look and I see Netty gliding across the floor, her arms like two ribbons billowing out around her. Regi stands clapping in joy as she watches her. She hops up and down in excitement.

Alexandria has stopped dancing. She's just standing there with her arms laced in front of her. She glares at her mother and then back at the girls, her face beet red.

Her mother rushes over to the stereo and slams her hand down on it and the music stops.

Janice shakes her head and looks at me. "Damage control," she utters resentfully. "I have to deal with this. If you have any more questions feel free to call."

Is it possible that Alexandria's mother is involved in the missing children? Could she be getting rid of them to knock out all the other competition? I'm about to pull out of the parking lot when I see Alexandria's mother heading toward a white Tahoe SUV.

"Wait here, Regina," I say. I get out and approach her with a big smile on my face. "Hello," I say.

She's digging in her purse and doesn't even look up to acknowledge me. "I saw your daughter dancing in there. She's quite talented."

"Thanks."

I think she still might be pissed about Netty stealing her daughter's thunder. "I was thinking of my niece. Maybe enrolling her here. Is there any way I could maybe get your number in case I had any questions? Maybe I can introduce my niece to your daughter."

"She's busy. She doesn't have time for any more *friends*. Ask the secretary for a brochure."

Stori

I rocket up the stone steps, and yank at the red doors. They're locked. I pound with a closed fist.

No response.

"Father!" I yell into the door. "Father!"

I pound again.

While I anxiously wait for him, I turn back to the desolate piazza and ponder what I might do if he doesn't answer. Where else can I go? Who could help me? Nothing comes to mind.

Thankfully I hear the doors unbolt. I whirl back around and there's Father Ash. Just the sight of him makes me want to take his pale face in my hands and kiss it.

"What is it, Stori?" he asks as if he's just as frightened as I am.

A train whistle from the station a mile away blares in the distance.

"I want to know the truth."

Father Ash's church is dim and empty. The stained glass windows are a patchwork of mauves and grey. Only candles light the way. We move through the solemn light down the west aisle toward the altar. "Your father came here long ago, Stori. My first day as pastor. He asked me to keep my eye on you. And to look out for strange people who might be looking for you."

"What strange people?"

"People who might do you harm. I told him he should let you know the truth about the Valley and about yourself. But he refused and he forbid me to tell you too. He was your father. There was nothing I could do."

Father Ash holds a large key ring and, as we approach a door near the Virgin Mary statue adorned with fresh roses and candles, he locates the proper key.

Through the door he leads me into his rectory. It's carpeted and, like the church, lit only by candles. "Don't you have electricity, Father?" I can't help but ask.

Father studies his key ring again. "One day I'll tell you about the candles," he murmurs. "For now, there's something more important."

As we pass through the living room and make our way to the end of a long hall he says, "But I told him, if you were to come to me and ask for the truth, I could not tell a lie to you."

At the end of the hallway is another door. Before he puts the key in I ask him, "Is that why my father always yelled at my mom when she wanted to come to church?"

"Probably."

"So what's this truth you want to tell me? That my father's been hiding?"

He slips the key inside the door and looks back to me. "It's not that simple. The truth I have to give to you… is more like… opening a door. Once I open that door, Stori, there will be several others you have to get through. And even then, it's up to you to come to the ultimate understanding."

"I don't understand already. I wish everyone would just speak in plain English around this place."

"Come with me. It's time."

He pushes the door and it opens onto a narrow stone staircase leading up. Candles sit in small shelves carved along the wall. The flames putter as we climb past them. Where is he taking me?

Father paces himself as if each step counts and I concentrate on keeping as close to him as possible.

"Have you ever heard of the Emerald Tablet, Stori?"

"No."

"It wasn't really a tablet. It was a book. The last it was seen was in the eighth century by a man named Baristos.

He found it in ancient Turkey in a vault under a statue. There was a corpse holding it. A corpse sitting in a golden throne."

At the top of the staircase we turn west to another ascending flight. As we climb the rough cut stone I feel my outer thigh muscles straining. (I better start taking stairs more often or I might find myself getting weak.)

"Who was the corpse?"

"No one knows. A king is what most assume."

"When was it written, Father?"

"Long before that king lived, or Balinas."

At the top of the landing he turns and waits for me. When I reach the landing too he puts a hand on my shoulder. "In ancient times, Stori, as ancient as the years of Moses, one of the greatest writers of all time lived. He was the mind who influenced Socrates, Plato, Aristotle…His works were the midwife to the birth of the Renaissance. All of his writings pertained to man's quest for perfect knowledge, also known as Final Sight. He himself had achieved it—all of life's mysteries were revealed to him. He knew the secrets to eternal youth, time travel, and visiting heaven while still on earth. He also wrote prophecies about the future and the coming end times. This man was named Hermes. Hermes Trismegistus."

The name sounds instantly like a scandal. "But that's not what the church teaches. You could get in trouble."

Father grins and grips my shoulder tighter. "I've

broken many rules I shouldn't have. But isn't that was living is for, Stori? Did not the greatest one of all show us that rules are meant to be broken?"

He picks up a candle from a shelf and hands it to me.

We move along another vestibule. At the far end is a stained glass window. When we reach it I see another door. It's arched wood and maybe ten feet tall and somehow frightens me.

"Is the book in there?" I ask him holding my breath.

"No. But the woman who knows about it is. The woman who remembers many of its verses. Who can tell you about a certain prophecy in it—concerning you." He reaches in his pocket and pulls out a single key. It's wooden, with three fat notches and a cut out triangle as the head. The triangle is big enough for me to put two fingers inside. He places it in my hand. "You will keep this from now on."

And with that said he turns on his heel and leaves me.

I stand there in his wake, listening to his retreating footsteps until I can't hear them anymore. I ponder all he just said. And then I face the dreaded door. I have the oddest feeling that once I slip the key inside, nothing will ever be the same again.

Am I ready?

I don't know.

Am I afraid?

Yes.

But still, I use the key and the door opens.

In a far corner, sitting on a footstool in front of a fire is a woman.

She has her back to me. Her hair is snow white and wooly as a lamb's. Her body is slight, like that of a child's, yet there's nothing childlike about her.

She's grand.

The blazing fire behind her, in what looks like an antique hearth, beats a blood-orange aura all around her. Her lamb's wool is illuminated with red. She looks like a vision, something too ethereal to be true.

I clear my throat to get her attention, hoping not to startle her. I wouldn't want to give her a heart attack or anything, seeing how old she is.

She doesn't move.

I rap lightly on the doorframe. "Hello," I call.

She turns and looks my way. The fire behind her has obscured most of her face. Then in all her glowing glory she asks me, "Stori? Is it you?"

How does she know? "Yes. My name is Stori."

Her hand flies to her mouth as if I amaze her. "I've been praying for days. My heart has been so burdened and all I could do is pray. That the right person would come. Some sign for what I must do."

"Is everything okay?" I ask her. "Do you need anything? From the store? Are you hungry?" It's not like me to get all caught up in the problems of a perfect stranger. I'm not acting like myself. I don't like it.

She stands and steps closer; she wears a cotton nightgown down to her ankles and the way it hangs about her gives her the appearance of a ghost. "Is it you?" she asks again. "The girl I named under the sycamore at first light?"

"Are you the Other Mother named Caroline?"

"Yes."

"You did name me. Stori. I'm Stori Putzarella."

"Yes. I have been waiting for you to come to me. At last you have."

"I hope I'm not bothering you—"

She puts a hand up to silence me, but I don't take offense. I shut up for her on cue. "I wanted to call for you. But I couldn't. These things can't be forced. You had to get here in your own time. Come closer, into the light." She's making little scoop motions with her hand.

I'm back to being nervous again. Actually, I'm scared. What a trip this is, that *I*, Stori Putzarella, fearless in the Valley, am afraid of an old woman locked in an attic.

"Come," she beckons.

For a split second I want to get right straight out of here. But I find that I can only obey her. So I take a few timid steps over the threshold.

"Closer," she says.

Wow. Look at this place. How cool is this? It's like a medieval attic or something. Towering columns lead into beautifully crafted archways. Stained glass windows feature lovely silhouettes.

And over in the farthest corner is a small kitchen table before a massive stone wall covered in shelving. Pots and pans and all kinds of containers clutter the shelves. I get the strongest desire to rush over there, put on her little coal burning stove and ask if I can make her dinner.

She allows me my time to marvel at her little habitat, not speaking a word.

"This place is cool," I say. "I never knew you were up here. I just thought it was a regular attic."

"Come to me, child," she says. "We can't waste any more time. I need to look into your eyes. I need to see who you are."

I obey. Now I'm up close and personal. She's so tiny but if she's old I can't see it. She doesn't look a day over sixty. Her olive skin shines and her eyes are violet with a piercing light deep inside them. A majestic beauty she is. Suddenly I'm no longer afraid but overcome by a desire to fall at her feet and cry. To tell her everything. Everything I have been holding inside. The things I only write in my diary, or tell Amanda. The things I'm afraid to tell my parents, for fear of breaking us, the Putzarellas. If it's even possible to break a thing that has already been shattered into dust.

Caroline's eyes dive into mine. She cranes her neck and concentrates. She goes on like this for a little while and

I stand still imagining she's working some kind of magic on me. But then all of a sudden she says, "I see." She says it just like a doctor does when he checks your tonsils and is about to tell you you need surgery.

"What? What is it?"

She shakes her head in disapproval. "Sadly, it is not what I hoped for. But I should have known. I should have known."

"What? Should have known what?"

"You have been hardened. The world has gotten to you, and it's gotten to you bad. You've got a bad case of fear. It's terminal."

"Fear? Terminal? What do you mean?"

"There are lots of ways to die, young Stori. Most people die before they ever find their graves. Oh, I have been so lonely. And the darkness is growing all around us. We are not safe anymore."

"Yes," I tell her. "That's actually what I'm here to talk to you about. You see, my father went missing and people are talking about Cosimo. If I don't find him soon this social worker might put me and Regi in a home. I have a friend at Pilgrim's Island and she told me some really horrible things."

Caroline's ears prick up. Something I've said has sparked her interest. "Tell me about the Island," she insists.

"Well, my friend said the mayor is going to make all the girls his wives. And she said the mistress in charge there…well…" I stop myself because I don't want the same catastrophe with Miss Van Patten to happen with Caroline. We've just met and I don't want to ruin it already. I'm sick of sounding crazy. I'm sick of the visions and the mania and the feeling like everything that I see or believe is not really there.

"Don't be afraid. It's not crazy." How does she know what I was thinking?

"She cut herself and didn't bleed. I know it sounds crazy but I can't stop thinking about these things, and wondering if there really are such evils in Redemption. And if my father disappeared, I need to know if the evil stuff had anything to do with it. It's hard to explain but the morning I woke up and read his letter I kind of felt like he was being forced to put those words down. But I get paranoid sometimes, you see, because of my illness. It makes me so suspicious of people and it makes it real hard for me to make friends. But still I believe something's up. So I came to Father Ash looking for the truth and he sent me to you."

I'm not even aware my head is hung until Caroline lifts my chin with her finger. "Why girl. You've been crying over the best parts of you."

Her touch is what I needed. Her voice, her words are a balm. Yet still I fight it. "Yeah right."

"Who told you aren't special?"

"Never mind that. I'm supposed to ask you about some book called the Emerald Tablet. Written by some guy named Hermes."

"Oh yes, the book," she says somewhat resentfully, like I just brought up an ex-boyfriend.

"Why are you sad about the book?"

"If I had seen something better in your eyes maybe I could start to feel happy again about the book. You see, I was called by an angel of the Lord to be a keeper of it's versus. I am called a Keeper. If I knew back then what it would mean for me, I would have never accepted. You're too young to hear about things like that, but all you need to know is I chose the Keeping over having a family."

"You mean you never had children?"

Now it's her turn to be ashamed. Her eyes drop to the floor. Something about this infuriates me. I want to find whoever told her she couldn't have a family and bash their face in. "So what," I challenge, no longer afraid to speak plainly. "Who gives a shit. Having a family isn't everything. And it makes people miserable. Most people I know who have children, it doesn't make them better. It only makes them worse. It makes them more selfish, more afraid." I think of my father, "More cruel."

Maybe this helped. For she picks her head up a little. I don't want to hear that she's hurting. Someone like her, all alone doesn't deserve it. But she says it anyway. "I am a broken hearted woman, Stori. I have never gotten over it. I always wanted a child."

"You have something better. You're a Keeper. Who else can say they have that!"

"Yes. I have Hermes' words passed down from my ancestors. But it is not a gift, as I thought it might be. For when the rest of the world is living in lies, what does knowing the truth give you? Burden. Burden is what it gives you. I know many things about this city. I know many things about what's going on. And I know the prophecy about what is to come. The knowledge has left me lonely and with no one to call my own. But I made the sacrifice, because I believed. I believed that one day my time would come. To help this city. To help the world."

"Can you tell me why you were waiting for me?" I ask, hoping to distract her from her pain, but also remembering what Father Ash told me about myself somehow being involved.

She goes to one of the stained glass windows and I sit at the kitchen table. At the base of the windows are two iron cranks. They squeak as she turns them. The panes open away from each other. Once open, I can see stars in a clear night sky and the edge of the billboard hanging over the expressway. "Hermes Trismegistus, the Thrice Great Prophet of ancient times, was the first living man to ever visit the Kingdom of Heaven and achieve perfect knowledge and prophecy. He lived at the same time as Moses, and he wrote many books. Within these books were the secrets of ancient history, wisdom, prophecy and true magic. All of the books are still out there, for they were forged by an alchemical process that rendered them indestructible, but where they are I know not. One in particular was called the Emerald Tablet."

"Yes. Father Ash told me. There's a prophecy in it. About our city."

"Would you like to hear it, Stori?"

"Yes."

She clears her throat and begins.

Oh, sweet and sullen Tat, my pupil who gazes at the stars. You have asked me a question I do not want to answer: Will Man return to Eden soon and be absolved? Sadly, I have glimpsed into time. Far far into the future and this is what I see: There will come a time, long from now, when all our studies and ruminations will be locked away from the world. Science will sadly be reduced to the mundane observation of matter. Men will hunch their backs over their studies of objects and have completely forgotten the mystical universe above. So they will lose their magic completely, their abilities to commune with the Divine. They will not mourn though, Tat, as I see you mourning now. For they will believe themselves Masters. Masters of the Universe they will claim as their title. And we cannot blame them, for they will, through science, achieve power over nature. Tat. Stand this very instant. Do not let fear overcome you. Our work will still be done.

Yes, nature will succumb to the Scientists. The Scientists will get so good at building towers and physical technology, that they will brush aside beauty, blot out nature, cover their eyes against the Heavens. They will actually believe they are in an age of enlightenment. In truth they will be in darkness. And where there is darkness, evil arises.

Yes. In a year called 2014, above a glittering city called Redemption a Giant Beauty will rise under the moon. She will be the newest object of the people's adoration. She will be the gateway. The gateway to the darkest times our earth will ever see. Men living in secret, very powerful and very sinister, will be in control of this city even before this Giant Beauty appears. These men will be part of a Night's Council. She will be their design. She will be a mechanism of suppression and a weapon against the people. They will hypnotize Redemption with her. 'Be like me,' that young woman will taunt. 'Be young, rich and shamelessly beautiful.' This is the only thing that will be valued in not only Redemption, but in the entire world.

And in that time of the Giant Beauty under the moon the Council is going to steal children from the streets, outlaw history books, hypnotize the citizens, and eventually rid that sleepy city of every kitchen table, because of all the things in the world the Night's Council will hate this the most. For the family, the family BEING TOGETHER, it will keep their powers at bay. Without their kitchen tables the last of the citizens will fall under the Giant Beauty's spell. Beset under her powerful trance, the Dark Council will be free to worship the Darkness in the open. All of the worst crimes throughout history will be repeated and this time there will be no one strong enough to stop them.

But fear not Tat. For our writings, although locked away, will still be remembered by some. And before the Night's Council will be able to take over they will be aware of this prophecy I now tell. So, beware, I say to you, whoever pure hearted that hears this now—for the Dark Ones have heard it too. They will know as you are about to know that the only way to end the Coming of the Night in the city of Redemption is to find the Crown of Final Sight. A most Holy and ancient crown forged before even I, the Thrice Great, was born. It is inlaid with the first stones of creation and it must go back to Babylon and return to the mighty summit—the Tower of Babel—and be placed upon the head of the One—the Great Ancient of Days, who will come down out of Heaven, and Heaven and Earth will become one.

I say to you now, a girl from the slums, a Daughter of Shinar, must find this crown. My only hope is that she finds it and when she does she will know which way to run.

If she does not, Tat, the Night's Council will find it. They will place it upon the head of a dead man and he will rule out in the open. The NEW LAWS will be enforced for good and the final age of darkness will descend. Like a moon being eclipsed permanently Man will not return to Eden. Man will know enslavement, suffering and famine, until the last day comes.

Caroline comes to the table and sits across from me. "You are the Daughter of Shinar."

"How do you know that?"

"The day I named you, I saw it Stori. Right in your swaddling clothes I saw the truth."

"Who told you this prophecy?" I demand. "Did you

make that up?"

"These are the words of the Thrice Great Prophet Trismegistus. The first man to step foot inside the Kingdom of Heaven while still on earth. His teachings and writings were so powerful, Stori, that many men and women died in the efforts to hide them."

"I'm so confused. Who is this Night's Council? Is that the mayor and the mistress? And the dead man, is that Cosimo?"

"You need not know yet about all their players. That will just set you to worry. All you need to know is there is a group of them who make the whole of the Night's Council."

"Well I'm not afraid of those assholes! I'll get the crown. Tell me where it is."

"I don't know. Only you can find it."

"Is there a treasure map somewhere?"

"No. It can only be found through the magic inside of you. But from what I have seen, Stori, your magic is all gone."

"Don't tell me that. My God! My father! All this talk about the city and the book and the crown and I almost forgot the most important person. What about my father?"

"I don't know. He could be involved. After all, he knew you were special. He must have witnessed your magic. He could have told someone. They could be using him to get to you. To draw you to them. But I don't know for sure. I only know the crown is the truest hope for all our safety."

"Maybe I can get my magic back. I have to."

"Oh, but it's been too long, Stori. Too long for all of us. The magic. The magic is nearly all gone."

Caroline slumps over the table like she's fainted. I'm by her side instantly, holding her upright. Her chest is heaving. She can barely get an arm up, "The bed," she croaks.

I scoop an arm under her knees and lift her to my middle. I carry her like a child to the bed and place her on it. I pull the covers down with some effort because she can't even move to help me get them out from under her. Then I cover her up. She's looking at me with those violet eyes, all weak and tired. "My powers, they are fading, Stori."

"I know we've only just met, but I'll take care of you, Miss Caroline. I'll take you home with me. My mother will make room."

"No. I must stay here."

"Please just tell me what I have to do."

She looks at me and the sadness is back. She reaches out and strokes the side of my face. "I do not know. You are too weak yourself and scared. I fear, just like Tat. You better go. It's getting late. Your mother will worry."

Priscilla Van Patten

Nate turns thirty-three tonight. His parents are taking us to dinner. This will be my first sit down occasion with them and I want to do everything right. But before I go home to prepare myself I just want to check in on Regina.

I find her sitting on her front stoop alone. "How is everything?" I ask, taking a seat next to her.

"I got kicked off the cheerleading team. Netty did too."

"Why? What happened?"

"It was Alexandria Madonna. She got mad because I made Netty dance."

"She can't do that!" I'm infuriated and I've surprised myself.

"Yes she can."

"I'm gonna fix this. You better believe it. That little brat doesn't get to rule the world."

"It's okay."

Regi is awfully calm for having been kicked off the team. I know I personally would have been crushed. "Why aren't you upset?" I ask. "It's unfair and something needs to be done about it, Regina."

She puts a hand on my knee and pats it. "Actually I don't want to be on the team anymore."

"You don't?" I hope she's not starting to withdraw.

"I was just doing it because everyone else was. But I never really wanted to. And I was eating all those mean words every day that Alexandria was saying."

"Regi. Words can't make you sick, sweetie."

"Yes they can. I know they can. I don't want to be around them anymore. And besides. The angels told me that I'm not going to be here much longer."

"What do you mean?"

"They told me my father's going to die and I won't be able to live with mommy and Stori anymore."

"Please, Regina. Don't say that."

A tear rolls down her cheek.

"I'm going to find your father, okay." The words fly out of my mouth unexpected. I think I might even mean them.

Nate's father chose a charming little farm to table restaurant for his birthday dinner. It's reeking of Old Money and Nate and his family fit right in. Here the people are too filthy rich to care: the men dress in casual jackets and loafers. The women are just as informal, but the pearl necklaces they wear are real and so are the semiprecious jewels glinting from their fingers. This is the difference between Old Money and New—New tries to augment and flash its wealth in public, Old wears it comfortably and without effort like a second skin.

Nate's little sisters are one year apart and in their first year at Washington U. They haven't really warmed up to me yet, despite my best efforts. I'm still trying to figure out if they like me but they've got that whole *Yeah, Whatever, I'm Young and Totally Not Interested in Anything That Doesn't Involve Me* attitude. I've noticed that about a lot of young people in Nate's world—I mean Nate's and *my* world. At first it unnerved me, this sort of stale disenchantment that permeates today's youth. It's like they're kind of zombies. They even talk like them, with that whole froggy sounding shit they make at the end of each sentence.

I find it kind of interesting that half the dinner conversation was allowed to belong to them. I know things weren't perfect in Erie, but at least my parents didn't let me think I owned the world by the time I was seventeen. I can't help but wonder what Mrs. Putzarella would do if she brought her daughters out to dinner and they monopolized the conversation for the whole main course. But then I remember her daughters, as faulted as they are, would never do that to their parents.

These girls, however, have unapologetically taken center stage, chatting over the trillion trips abroad they've had and how many times they've gotten so wasted that they couldn't remember what happened the next day. They laugh at things that aren't remotely funny and ignore the wait staff and complain about the food—which, for the record, is out-of-this-world delicious. And their mother and father are letting them do all this! Nate is no help either, laughing at their stupid jokes and calling them the Fabulous Duo. I can't imagine myself becoming their sister one day and having to listen to their shit every time this family goes out to dinner.

Wow. I better stop drinking. I think I just gave myself a dizzy spell. I blink and take a sip of ice water. We have just ordered our dessert and I ask for an apple turnover and an espresso—Oh, make it double please.

"This late in the evening?" Jerry muses. Jerry and Deb are here at dinner too. Nate said that, thanks to all his wining and dining, Jerry has softened up quite considerably and just might actually let Nate and his dad in on a piece of the casino—getting them one step closer to joining that secret club Nate keeps talking about.

"I'm a social worker," I explain. "Coffee is my friend."

"Oh. How charming," Jerry says. "I've always wanted to meet a real life social worker." The table laughs and Deb elbows her husband in mock punishment. "Don't be rude."

I'm too drunk to even notice if he's being rude. "Oh no, not at all," I say to no one in particular. "I get that a lot. But I really love what I do."

"So what kind of social worker are you, Priscilla?"

The girls are occupied with their phones right now. They're *Totally Over* being present at this dinner and have switched their attention to their virtual friends on facebook probably. So I guess it's okay to talk. "Family Intervention. Children mostly. I work for CPS."

"Rough stuff," Jerry says wisely. Out of everyone at this table I like Jerry the best. It seems like you could have a real conversation with him if you tried for one. I know Nate calls him *richer than God and the most pretentious person he ever met*, but I haven't seen any of those qualities thus far. I see something different. There's a sadness lurking just about his shoulders. Some regret he's carrying and it's weighing on him. It makes him real to me and I'm thankful for this regret. It's the buoy that has kept me afloat in this torrential sea of unfamiliarness.

"Rough indeed. I work in the Valley mostly. The people there are struggling."

"A philanthropist," Nate's father says indifferently. I can't tell what he means by it—if he's impressed or not. But in my present state, I don't really care.

"Well I think that's lovely," Jerry says. "Mayor Vaughn is all about improving the city. Have you heard of his new plans Priscilla?"

"No."

"He wants to start a second Renaissance. Right here in Redemption."

"A second Renaissance?"

"A new age of enlightenment."

"We already started," Nate adds confidently. "I mean, look at the progress that man has made in the past ten years. Information is at our fingertips now. Technology, industry, modernization. Thinking to the future and what we haven't discovered yet." Nate has been texting on his phone too, I have duly noted out of the corner of my eye. The other day I caught him deleting a text from Trish. I haven't said anything about it yet. But he's in for some hell.

"I'm not sure about the Renaissance," I say dryly to Nate, trying to mask my fermenting jealousy by keeping my eyes on Jerry. "But wasn't it about going back? Not forward. Looking inward, not outward? They weren't searching for modernization, they were searching for..." I'm not quite sure what they were searching for but I know it had to do with divinity. So I say it, "Divinity?"

Nate scoffs. "That was because of the pope. If Leonardo da Vinci lived in our time right now, he would be contributing to the efforts of modernization."

I wholeheartedly disagree so I say it. "I disagree. He

would probably live with the people in the Valley.

"The Valley? Are you for real?" Nate looks to Jerry for support but Jerry only blots his mouth with his napkin. "Jerry," Nate says, "You should hear the stories Pris comes home with. These people live like animals. People throwing their televisions out of their windows and talking about Cosimo the Corpse."

Jerry shoots upright like he's beset with a sudden back spasm.

"They should just fly a bomb over that place," Nate continues "and drop it right in the center."

"Nate darling," I respond stiffly. "I think we're both aware of what income inequality means in this country."

"Yeah, it means there's a ladder to climb and everyone's got a shot at it but 95 percent of us are too lazy to try."

"Nice rationalization," I fire back. "I bet that makes all the wealthy feel better at night, sleeping on top of their mountains of excess while people in Soda Can Alley are dying of starvation. The divide is here because of greed, not laziness. And by the way, I think it's more like 99."

The dessert comes, and everyone is thankful to have a distraction from the awkward moment I've created.

Nate takes this opportunity to grab my elbow and whisper in my ear. "What are you doing? You are embarrassing me."

I'm making him look bad and making myself look like

a fool. I'm in way over my head here. I burst out crying and say, "I'm sorry, Nate. I'm sorry."

Stori

As I make my trudge of defeat home from Father Ash's secret attic, I don't know who I am anymore. Put me in the cage with pure muscle and blood-thirsty rage and my heart won't skip a beat. But don't put me in front of a fragile woman with a bleeding heart. Don't strike me with the suffering of another when you know I have no way to defend myself from—from what, Stori?

I fight back tears. If I thought my heart was broken when I found out my father cheated or that Tony didn't love me, this is a thousand times worse. My city is being corrupted by this Godless Council and the girl to save the city is me—except I don't have the magic to do it.

To hell with this city then. To hell with the crown. I've got to find out where this Night's Council is and get my father back from them. They can have the crown for all I care. Redemption isn't my problem.

So why does my mind keep returning to the crown? Why am I no longer thinking about my father first? Why aren't I that girl who strode the Valley stone-faced with only him on her mind? I've got to refocus. This is about my father, not about my city. Not about that old woman. I'm not supposed to care, do you hear me! I'm not supposed to even care.

Approaching home, I'm passing a playground where a little girl is swinging on the swingset. She's singing that Sarah Barreilles song, the one about being brave and saying what you have to say. I shake my head and mumble, "Yeah fucking right."

There's a street sweeper on the curbside. He tips his fedora hat to me as I pass. "Nice night for a stroll. Weather's getting warmer."

I give him the dirtiest look possible. Then he pulls his collar up over his face and says, "Too hot, too hot."

I'm beyond agitated now. I think I might go down to the Cage and sign up for a fight. Or maybe I'll turn around and, just for fun, knock that street sweeper right on his ass. I've done stuff like that before when I was younger. Just to pass the time.

Him and that dumb hat and that dumb broom, sweeping…"

Hey! Wait a minute.

I stop dead in my tracks. The sweeper. There was something off about him. Wasn't he sweeping away from the gutters? Away?

He was fake sweeping, wasn't he.

Why would he be doing something like that?

I turn and make my way back to the playground.

Clinging to the shadows I creep closer and duck behind a bench near the swing set. The girl is still singing her song. "Say what you wanna say…"

The sweeper saunters over to the bench and sits. I crouch down as low as possible, without lying flat on my stomach.

"Gotta rest these weary bones," he complains to the girl.

The swing set is rusty so I know that she's slowing down.

"Oh. Don't stop singing on account of me," he tells her. "You got a voice of an angel you know."

She doesn't answer.

"You got a name?"

Nothing. The squeaky swing goes silent. I hear feet on gravel.

The sweeper mutters under his breath. "Too fast. Too hurried."

Then he stands and I see his face again. He's looking at her. "Now don't get all in a fuss on account of me. Go on now. Get home. But look here. I think you've dropped something."

The footsteps halt and change course. She's coming back in his direction.

He smiles.

That's when I see it. His skin goes grey and hair blooms over his cheeks and forehead. His eyes shrivel up to tiny black beads.

The girl shrieks.

I get on my feet and leap over the bench. "Away from her, you demon!"

He whips around in my direction. He hisses. "Get lost."

"No." I plant my feet and gather all my strength.

The girl is struggling in his arms and I lurch toward them but a searing pain rips through my entire body. I stagger back and the pain subsides.

He laughs up into the sky. "You burn me, I gut you. We are not made for each other."

Something about him, I can't get close.

I stagger back further, terrified of the pain. I watch him hoist her off the ground and toss her over his shoulder.

I can't let this happen. I'll die before I do. I will not watch a child be stolen by a monster.

And then I remember the girl in the lavender dress. "I call your name!" I holler. "I call to you! I call to you!"

She appears. Right where the monster snatched up the

child, in the same dress. She says, "Go on, look again."

I look at the monster. He's on the curbside, crouching low to pick up his broom. Tears stream down my face. And then it comes to me. "Samuel," I call. "Samuel, come back here."

He stops and turns. "Gloria?" he says.

My knowledge of him is infinite. "No. I am not your wife. But I know you. I know the memories they suck out of you with that strange drink. You had a wife and a son who loved you. They were your second chance in life. Because you didn't know what it was like to feel loved before you had them." The words are like a lasso that pull his hands away from the girl. She falls to the ground with a thud. She gets up and runs as fast as she can down the street. "What?" he asks.

I wipe the tears away. "One of the last times you saw them they were standing on your front porch waving to you as you came home. But not long after they were killed. And so was your heart."

His hands fall limp at his sides.

Panic stricken, his lips disappear from his face.

"But they are not gone and they have a message for you. Stop doing these bad things. Or you will never be able to see them again."

"You some kind of witch," he hisses. "Some kind of devil's spawn."

"Your wife and son want you to stop."

"You stay away from me. You stay away from me."
His Timberlands pound the cement and the night's
shadows swallow him whole. I notice something on the
ground where he was standing. I rush over to it and pick it
up.

It's a gat.

I stuff it into my coat and just hold it there. My hand is
shaking as I feel the hard, cold steel under my fingers. I've
never held a gun before and it's frightening.

Back at Father Ash's, he leads me up to the attic, this
time in silence. He doesn't need to let me in, for I have the
key.

Caroline sits up in bed when I call her name. "What is
it?"

"A street sweeper. He was trying to steal a girl. He was
a bad man. I think he was gonna kill her. He changed into a
bat."

She gasps and covers her mouth. Her eyes grow wide
with terror. "A Hound. Did he hurt you?"

"Just a little. When I got close to him it hurt me inside.
But that wasn't the worst thing. The worst thing is when he
looked at me. I went cold all over my body like I was
covered in ice. I can't remember being scared of someone,
ever. But then an angel came, and I felt this jolt. Like an
electric shock. And then somehow I knew him, like I know
my own sister. I told him everything I knew, and then I
wasn't scared anymore."

"Ahah!" Caroline shouts. "Let me ask you something. How did you feel when you were telling him all these things?"

"I felt sad to know his pain but also…boundless. Like I wasn't in my body. I was lighter than spider's silk. Yet I was stronger than a lion. And fiercer too. And I was abounding in mercy. I couldn't hate him anymore. I could only love him. To the point that I wanted to weep."

Caroline nods in confirmation. "There are two eyes from which to see in this life, the eyes in your head and the ones in your heart. You are a Brave, Stori and the magic in you is still alive."

"I'm not sure," I confess.

She scoots to the edge of the bed, and slides over the side. Her bare feet hardly make a sound as they hit the floor. "What have you relied on most of your life, Stori?"

I don't have to think about that one. I show her my fists.

She shakes her head, not even giving them a glance. "No. It's here, my girl." She points to my head. "And here." She points to my heart.

I shake my head right back at her. "No. You don't know me at all.

"Or is it that I do know you. Better than you know yourself."

I'm impressed by her briskness, as she hastens to the kitchen and takes something off one of the bottom shelves.

It's covered in a red satin cloth and she respectfully places it on the kitchen table and sits. I know to sit across from her, the covered thing in between us.

She lifts the red satin and I see a golden tabernacle, half the size of a mailbox. The doors are facing me, and I want nothing but to open them. But I restrain myself and wait for her cue.

"I am going to tell you one of the stories in The Emerald Tablet. Hermes' student, Asclepius, asked him how the art of writing began. Would you like to hear his answer to Asclepius, Stori?"

"Okay," I say as I fight the woozies. I haven't been this excited since the day I told Tony I loved him.

Caroline pauses, then begins:

And so, Asclepius, I have been made privilege to the stories of old. How I came to this story is for another time. But I will tell you briefly that I know it through one part dream, one part memory and one part vision. In a time before both of us were born there was a tower being built in ancient Babylon. The Tower of Babel.

I have heard of this tower, teacher.

It was a magnificent city, never a dull moment. But in the outskirts—in a mountainous place called the Caverns a tribe of people lived. One of the tribe was a young girl named Bilhah. She had the heart of an innocent and so she found favor with the Lord. He often visited with her.

One time when he came to visit he found her sitting despondent by a riverbank.

"What hurts you, child?" he asked.

"Oh Father. How much I love you. I have sung it at the top of mountains, I have danced it in the fields and before friends. I have sat over the fires of the tribe and told it in legend. Yet still I yearn."

"What is it that you yearn?"

"To carve it into the sacred caverns. The blessed wombs. To make it eternal. But I know not how to do this or what it would look like."

He beckoned her to rise and said, "Come. Follow me."

He led her to a cave and they stepped inside the blackness. "Although your flesh is temporary, child, there are eyes in you that are eternal. These eyes lead into caverns such as this, which enter into eternal worlds. Close your eyes. Do you feel it?"

"Yes. Yes, father. I feel it."

"I am going to show you your destined artwork. It is what you desire and I love you so, my child, that I will make this art form for you. Put your hand up to that rock, for this art is one that issues from the hand. Not that of painting but that of words."

"Words coming from my hand?"

"It is too dark, but if you asked for light you would see me smile."

"Father, how can words come from my hand?"

"Oh faithless child. You will write them."

"Write them? What does this mean, write?"

"You are about to learn my child."

"What should I do?"

"Pick up a stone at your feet and place it to the stone of the wall. Concentrate on that love you wish to express. With your eyes closed, become that love and let it move your hand."

And so the young girl gave herself to the abounding love she had in her heart and she began to move the rock upon the stone. The carving was effortless and the symbols appeared.

But when she opened her eyes she couldn't see them, for the darkness was too thick.

"I want to see it," she said.

And the Lord said, "And so you will have light."

A flame burst from the center of the room. A floating flame that came from no ember or spark. It floated in midair. It lit up the first written words of man so beautifully. The girl could not contain herself that she let out a gasp at what she just created.

"And so it will be," said the Lord. "That all true writing will be written not in logic but in spirit and emotion. And love. This is the truest form of writing. It can only be achieved by the abandonment of self, the closing of the earthly eyes and the opening of the eye eternal. You will connect to the divine this way. It is given to you for worship, testament, and prayer. And all endeavors involving the pursuit of knowledge that is just and true."

"I will honor this custom, father."

"See that broken dish in the corner?"

"Yes."

"Bring it here."

So she picked up the dish and brought it to him and he placed his hand into the flames. When he drew it back a single flame puckered from the tip of his pointy finger. He put the flame to the dish and there it stayed. Without a drop of wax, without a wick, the flame persisted.

"Bring the flame home. Keep it going. Make it eternal. Tell your mother if you have to."

"I will Father."

"From this fire you will be given sights, young girl. This is the first fire that illuminated the first writings. You will be blessed as they came from your hands. You may not understand the meaning of all that has just happened but you are but a spoke in a great wheel."

"What if the light goes out?"

"My beloved faithless. It will not. The fire I light is ever burning. Preserve the flame by preserving the ancient traditions. It will never go out if you remember your past. If you honor all the things that came before you."

Caroline taps the table and I return to myself. Is it possible this story is true? If it is I feel blessed to know it. For the first time in a very long time, I feel grateful.

"Is that flame inside there?" I ask her.

"Open it and see."

Oh little tabernacle, whose tiny door I see.
What can be in there?
What is waiting inside for me?
Is it another life, a better one than the one before?
Is it my father and my mother embracing as I walk inside
my kitchen door?

255

I only want a family. I only want to be.
The kind of person I was when I ran with the angels.
The better side of me.

I open the door and inside is a single flame in an indigo dish. It's the size of a finger. Inside the yellow white a deer is prancing. Then it disappears and a buffalo storms forward. Then children are running through a field of lilies.

"Is that the flame?" I whisper, frightened that my voice might extinguish it.

"Yes."

"Holy Father."

The dish is cracked on one side and as Caroline, who stands over me now, reaches in to bring the flame out I fear the dish will break. "Be careful," I whisper. "Please."

She places the tabernacle back on the shelf and leaves the flame in the center of the table. Then she comes back and sits down. "I have chosen my destiny, Stori. To be a Keeper of the flame. With this flame I can see many things. I might be able help you find your father, if you like."

"Yes. I would like that."

"Give me your hands."

We hold hands around the flame and I no longer see the changing shapes, but Caroline must see something, for she picks up her eyebrows as she stares and says, "He is chained up in a basement of some sort. Cosimo and the Night's Council are nearby and they are going to kill him."

"No!"

"Only your magic, Stori, can bring you to him. You must grow your magic. The more you grow it, the closer you will get to finding him."

"Show me how to grow it! I'll do anything."

Caroline thinks it over. "Come here once a day and help me around this place and when the time is right I'll show you how to grow your power."

"No. There's no time. Show me now and I'll come for the rest of my life. I promise."

"It's not like I know myself. We need to spend time so I can figure it out."

"I'll be here tomorrow. After breakfast."

Sleeping with the gat under my bed, I dream the most vivid dream.

I'm in a desert sandstorm at night and someone is leading me with the same dish and flame from the tabernacle. I marvel at how the whipping wind and sand do nothing to extinguish this magical feather. I lean my weight forward and shield my face with a scarf. A girl my age leads me. She keeps telling me that it is just ahead. The land of Shinar and the Tower of Babel. "Our people, the Braves, are there," she yells through the wind. "We live just outside the city in the caves up in the hills. My people are wise and humble. You will know them as soon as you see them. They will welcome you with gratitude and if there is an item they carry and you want it, they will give it to you, no questions asked."

"Even if they love it? Even if their father gave it to them?" I ask.

"Even if their father gave it to them," she answers.

We never reach the land of Shinar, though, because my dream gets interrupted by the terrifying face of my uncle. He's laughing and has me pinned to the ground with his knees straddled around me—the way I straddled Christina Dexter. He holds a gun to my temple. "You stupid Putzarella. You crazy, crazy girl!"

I'm grateful to awaken safe in my own bed, to a brand new day. I want to skip school and go straight to Caroline's, but there's one thing I must do. Ernestine needs to know what I've learned. She needs to know that I believe her story now and that I know a way to fight the evil things going on in Redemption. I will not only get my father back, I am going to save Ernestine from the mayor too. He's in that Night's Council for sure and I have to get her away from him!

I can't wait to tell her! I can't wait to look her in the face and say, "You don't have to be scared anymore. We are going to get through this. We have Caroline on our side and she's gonna teach me the magic to fight all this evil!"

But then I find Ernestine and it's not good. She's at the hooky spot, outside the building. That's where all the weed-heads and druggies hang out. It's kind of like the

Soda Can Alley of my high school.

Ernestine's plopped on a milk crate, leaning against the building with her eyes closed. "Ern," I say, standing over her. "Ern. Wake up."

She doesn't respond. So I kick her foot.

Still no response.

A girl in a skullie cap and a fake fur coat is smoking a joint and talking to some football players. "Yeah, man. That shit is wild. They're like not even gonna be growing our food from the soil anymore. It's gonna come right out of these test tubes and shit. Test tube veggies."

I crouch down next to my friend. "Ern. It's Stori. I have something really important to tell you. Ern?"

Finally she opens her eyes. Oh, no. My father doesn't even look that high when he drinks a bottle of gin. "I know you," she says all slurred. I wonder if she even recognizes me.

The girl behind me, smoking a blunt says, "She was like that when I got here. Poor thing."

"Thanks for the update." Dumb bitch. Nobody cares in this world. Nobody. "Ern. It's me, Stori. Your best friend. Listen. I spoke with Caroline, the prophetess. Remember her? She told me lots of things and I can't tell you everything now, but the main thing is that Cosimo is here in the city and he might have my father captive. And he's also got these people who work for him. Hounds. I'm pretty sure the mayor is one of them. But don't worry.

Because she told me about this crown, you see…"

"Uhhhhhhh," she moans like she's dying or something. Her eyes roll into the back of her head. "Get me a bucket," she croons. And then she leans forward and pukes all over my shoes.

I drop Ernestine off to the nurse's office and duck out of campus before security catches me. It takes me an hour to get home—I take two city buses back the Valley and I have to go home and change my shoes.

On my way out of the house I hear a voice calling, "Sullen."

It's Richie Ramera, the Valley pervert.

"I told you not to call me that."

He falls into step alongside me. "I want to show you something, Sullen."

"So do it."

He digs in his pocket for something and draws it out. It's one of the VIP casino chips.

"Where'd you get that?"

"My mom's cleaning company got contracted to the casino. And now she's banging the head of maintenance. Nice move, Ma."

What a creep. He even talks bad about his own mother.

"Nice, Richie. Real nice."

"Come on, lighten up," he laughs. "You only get one go-around on life."

"What does that have to do with disrespecting your mother?"

"I can get you in there. After hours."

"In where?"

"The casino?"

"Why would I want to go in there after hours?"

"Have you seen it? The VIP heaven lounge? It's a fucking palace. I'll take you. If you let me kiss you when we get there."

"In your dreams."

Some of his friends are approaching us from the other side of the street. One of them calls, "Yeeeo!"

"My main man!" Richie shouts and then skips off to his buddies.

I get to Caroline's a little late and she's already sitting on the front steps of the church. She stands as I approach, not bothering to say hello. She's ready for business. I'm glad because I am too. "Ready?" she says.

"Ready."

I'm not sure where she's taking me. "Where are we going?" I ask. "Are you taking me to Forest Boom?"

"No."

"But isn't that where the angels live?"

"Yes."

"So why aren't we going there?"

"Magic is in the most unexpected places, Stori. Learning it starts right at home."

"So you're taking me home?"

"Just come on."

I shrug and trail behind her as we make our way out of the piazza. We wind down onto the cobblestone avenue, right to my house, to Mama's Door.

Mama's Door is a restaurant run by the Pecorinos. They've been in business for over forty years and are known for their celebrated baked chicken and their hearts of charity.

I bet what I tell you next won't even surprise you. By now, you know the Valley pretty well. It's an unwritten rule at Mama's Door that the prices on the menu only apply if the diner has money to pay. It runs on an honor system and anyone who is found abusing the rule is talked about all over the Valley and blacklisted from every wedding, christening and annual feast.

In my lifetime I've never heard of anyone taking advantage. My mother always said that thieves attract thieves and an upright place like Mama's Door would never have to worry about getting robbed.

This is where Caroline has brought me. And I'm confused. "What are we doing here?" I ask her.

She looks at me and says. "We are going to help."

"Help?" I ask.

"Yes. Help."

"But I thought you said you were gonna teach me magic today."

"Yes. I did."

I've never been anyone's fool and, old lady or not, I'm not gonna let her get by on me either. "If you think this is some kind of joke…"

"It's not a joke. It's where you need to start. You're a real diamond in the rough if I ever saw one. There's a lot of basic stuff you need to address before we even begin."

This is never going to work, I think. But I don't have time to dwell on my despair for the head chef, Mama, appears and smothers Caroline in kisses and asks her how she's been all these years.

Then she throws her affections on me, calling me baby and telling me how beautiful I'm getting. She hugs and squeezes me and stares longingly into my eyes and leads me with an arm around my shoulder into the kitchen.

There I'm donned in a red apron, capped with a ghastly hair net and sent to the sink to scrub my hands.

The hustle and bustle of the kitchen is like a dance. I've never really been inside of a working culinary kitchen before and I have to say, I'm impressed. Everyone has a job to do and diligently working at their task. Their hands are chopping, pounding, tossing and sorting all kinds of meats, fruit and vegetables. A large stove is opened and the fire inside roars. Trays and dollies are sweeping by. People are walking backwards and sideways and all the while no one ever crashes into anything. I find it unbelievable. An orderly chaos; a battle and a peace offering at once.

I'm assigned the task of buttering biscuits. I have to work fast for the trays keep coming. There are dozens and dozens. Caroline is seasoning a stew and exchanging some important words with Mama. Mama nods her head intently. "That's great," I see her mouth. "That's just great." Then she looks at me and smiles.

I suddenly feel important. Like maybe they're talking about me. I've never been discussed where it didn't involve some kind of brawl or moment of unexpected mania and it's nice to think that for once people can see me in a different light.

Just when my hopes are up, though, Caroline hands me a basket of bread and says, "Table three. By the wall fountain." I know where she's talking about. It's in the bar area. I take the basket and push my way out of the swinging doors. As I approach table three I see a single man sitting. I take a closer look and realize it's no other than Sidewinder, the man who called my father retarded. I pivot and storm back into the kitchen.

"What is he doing here?"

Caroline looks at the basket in my hand. "He's down and out. He's hungry."

"He should starve. He called my father a name once."

Caroline doesn't flinch. "Nevertheless you are going to go over there and ask him if he wants a piece of bread."

"I hate him."

"Let it go, Stori."

"He hurt my father."

"You are bringing him the bread."

"No I'm not."

"Yes you are."

"No. I'm. Not." I shove the basket back at her.

She takes it but says, "Yes. You. Are." She might be a small woman but she's pretty stubborn. I snatch the basket from her and head back out to the dining room.

He takes a while to notice I'm there. His head is in his hands and he's staring into the tabletop. I can see and smell that he hasn't showered in days. He looks up at me finally and says, "Oh. I'm sorry. I didn't see you there." He looks at the basket like Regi does when she's really hungry and she's waiting for my mother or me to serve her.

Yes. It's him for sure. I'll never forget the curl of his lips as he sneered at my father's retreating back. My father, who couldn't get the words out to defend himself.

I don't give him any bread, but say. "You hurt my father one day. You called him a name. Just to be mean. He didn't do anything to you."

The man struggles a little to emerge from his shell of despondency. He's trying to place my face and then at last he does. His face opens with memory only to close again. "Are you here to hit me again?" he demands.

I don't know what is starting to happen to me. Why am I not knocking him on the ground? The old me would have rejoiced over this opportunity to get him back. To let him have a good piece of karma along with his slice of sesame. To let him know what it feels like to be kicked when you're down, just how my father felt.

But for all my might, I can't. I just can't get my hatred going for him.

What's more I feel bad for him. I realize that people like him, who hurt other people's feelings aren't doing it because they are evil. They're doing it because they're scared. Somewhere in life this guy wasn't loved enough. He wasn't told he could amount to something—something much better than a bully and now a poor and forgotten bum.

It's not my job to tell him, but it is my job to help. To feed him. So that when the day comes for him to choose hope he will have a little of it already from the olive leaf I am now offering. I feel embarrassed just doing it and pray to God no friends of mine are around to see my pathetic little tender moment.

He scowls as he takes my offer. He snatches the biggest piece he can find.

Back in the kitchen I'm pretty ticked off at Caroline. "Okay. So I didn't hit him. Is that lesson number one?"

She's pleased. "Stori. I can see your magic growing already. Maybe there is hope. Maybe there is hope indeed. There are two ways to hone your powers, Stori, and the choice lies within you."

"What are the ways?" I ask as the dancing around us

continues in all its chaotic perfection, as Mama's voice is shouting, "Get those greens blanched up pronto. I need them in five."

"The first way is simple. Just keep using them as they come. You will grow more powerful and at a very quick rate. You will be able to manipulate people and get your way wherever you go. But if you hone them this way the powers will eventually overtake you and lead you to commit yourself to darkness."

"What is the other way?"

"Through me. But it has its perils also. The more you grow as a Brave, the more Cosimo will be able to sense you. And he will send his Hounds out to kill you."

"So I have to choose."

"I cannot force you to make a choice either way. It has to come through you."

"If I choose the first way, will I find my father quicker?"

"You will find him, and it will be easier. But I can assure you it will not be a good thing."

"You mean for my soul, don't you."

"Yes. I do. And for the city."

"The other kind of power is much more difficult. It requires selflessness, Stori. Selflessness—the very thing that makes us truly wise and truly brave. A bravery and fearlessness to face many perils. But, oh, the riches that can be discovered. The great things that can be born from it."

I look back at the swinging doors. They never cease swinging as waitresses and busboys keep rushing in and out. I look at Caroline. "I want to learn it from you."

"Come, then. Follow me."

Bilhah

I come here at dusk to revisit myself. When the rest of my friends are swimming in the Tigris, I choose a separate path to the quiet lookout point and gather my thoughts unto myself. In the city out beyond, they have looking glasses called mirrors where women gaze for hours. They see their own reflections and become enchanted.

But I have a different looking glass from which to gaze, to behold the image of myself. And the girl who appears every time is not the girl I've glimpsed in the dark still waters or even from the corners of those finely polished mirrors. She is a blazing light with a heart that beats on the outside. She is the image of the Father himself. And she can fly. She has wings of the white dove.

What is the looking glass, you ask? It is everything. It is

the sky, it is the massive tower off in the distance, it is the rocks of the caves that hold my family here in the mountains, it is the little crawly things that live just under the rocks.

It is the sum total of all things. And when I am out here in the dusk and marveling at the beauty of each and every item that surrounds me, I can see the girl I really am. The true girl. The one who was born of the light.

You see, there is a universal truth that exists. A mass consciousness. All are aware of it, from the crawly thing, to the roaming beast, to the pondering man. All are under its influence, whether they know it or not. It is the singular motivation behind all actions, whether good or evil. It is the brightest light ever seen. A thousand leagues beyond the sun and moon. I can see it now, way out in the beyond. A blue so deep and lovely and it shines. It is called the Father Light.

Truth is singular. It does not exist outside of itself. It does not rest on anything, but the Great Mysterious, our Lord.

My mother tells me not to love the city of Babel. Not to love the tower and the people who live within its gates. She says they worship false gods there. They are governed by a man who calls himself King. They are devising evil ways and manifesting selfishness and vanity. And to admire such debauchery is to be just like them—to have fallen prey to their ways.

But when I am this girl of fire, who bears white wings of the dove, I love even the tower. I love even the waywards who worship the false gods. I love all things. All women. All men.

The Great Mysterious knows my love. For he comes to me at dusk sometimes, when I am wrapped up in the universal truth, the One Light, His Love.

"They have called for you again," He says, sitting in the place where the rock face juts out into the sky.

"My Glorious and Awesome," I say. "And I bow my head to the ground in honor of Him."

"Be at peace," He says. "Be at peace."

I know Him. I have always known Him. We did not have to greet one another in the usual custom at our first meeting. He appeared. I bowed my forehead before him. And at once we were friends. But more than friends, we were one. "I am You," I told him. "I am You and only wish to be You from here on until eternity."

He smiled and said, "My child. You are mine."

This is the way it is between the Great Mysterious and me. I may be shy with the rest of the world but I am as open as the sky when I am in His presence.

"Yes," I tell Him this evening. "They have called for me. I will go at sunrise into the city. My mother will make the provisions for my journey."

"Make sure you behold the lilies on your way down."

I don't know if the Great Mysterious has been down to see the tower. If He has, He has never mentioned it. When I am called by the wisemen, to come and perform the ancient dance, my mother is never pleased. "They drain her of her powers. They use it for their God."

"Nonsense," my father tells her. "They only wish to preserve and honor the ancient ways of our God. They use it for good. Bilhah, do you like to visit the Tower of Babel? Does it please you?"

"The city is full of fascinating people. And the wisemen have mapped out the stars that lead to the heavens. They are making a crown. They will place it upon our Great Mysterious, once the tower reaches into heaven. And have discovered many wonderful things. But my place is home. Nothing pleases me more than to be with my people." He smoothes my hair at the side of my head and says, "You are a good girl. Your father is pleased."

I am a worker of magic. I know the dance that holds off rainstorms. This comes in use for the residents of the city, for the bricks they bake in the ovens need time to dry. If they are not yet going to be dried and the wisemen read the stars to see that a storm is coming, they call for me. They have also called for me in recent days to dance as they draw their drafts of the crown. It has not yet been forged but they are still working on it."

I don't know why the Lord gave me such a gift as

dancing, for I don't like people looking at me. I was named Bilhah by an old prophet woman. *The girl will be painfully shy.*

Our people don't have to use the wisemen to know when it will rain. We have visions of storms before they happen. Even in our dreams. The animals tell us too. They know much about the land and without their guidance we would not be able to survive. The wisemen who work for the king call our way of living the Way of Faith. They place great value on it and always give me many blessings and send me home with gifts after I dance for them. I think that's kind of funny. That men with such knowledge, who can read the stars and draw out the mathematics to answer life's mysteries would be appreciative of someone like me. But Lazarus, the Mathematician, always tells me this: "The infinite knowledge is in all men. But it cannot be drawn out without the fearless love. *You* are the fearless love my child. You still possess the powers of those who commune with the earth. We have been kept here very busy in the city, working our calculations, ruminating in our minds. We write, we read, we ponder and discover. But the city walls we are building are a double edged sword. They protect us and build us a name, but they also dull our hearts and minds from the memory of being children! Dancing, playing children of the earth! For the greatest mysteries cannot be unraveled without the child's heart. Without the wonder and imagination and awe of the great wide world. You are a great spoke in the wheel of Babel, Bilhah. Your reverence and effortless unity with the cosmos have blown the very life into our studies. You are integral to the building of the tower and of the crown. We cannot do these things without you."

In the morning I will go. I will go to the Tower of Babel. But in the dying dusk I will watch the massive fires being lit. They can be seen from a great distance. They billow white smoke that is eaten up by the black sky.

Men are capable of such mighty things and it amazes me. I take it all in, I hold it in my heart. I become the girl the great Lord intended me to be. One of the universal truth. Of an everlasting all encompassing love.

Stori

So I've got these powers now, right? I mean, I don't really know how this Knowing works yet. I've only used it once. That monster was the scariest thing I've ever had to face, but I was able to stop him. Telepathy. It's fucking awesome. I've always been able to read people, a good judge of character, but when the magic takes over, it's beyond that.

Caroline's right. Knowledge is power. The more you know about someone the more you own them. I wish I knew everything about Tony. I wish I knew just what hurts him inside. Just what he likes. The kind of kisser that makes his knees buckle.

I'm almost tempted to go over to his place right now and see if I can use the magic on him. But the grand opening of Strive is tonight and getting down there to see the mayor is more important. Before I left Mama's Door Caroline told me I need to get to him somehow, read him the way I did the Sweeper. Caroline is deathly afraid of the mayor. I pray he knows where my dad is, and I get it out of him. If my powers don't work, I have my gat with me.

Forget Tony. I've got work to do.

The grand opening is advertised all over town. In every newspaper, in every storefront and, of course, the billboard hanging over our town. Even in the Valley people are talking about it. People want so badly to win a black chip. To get up to the Heaven Lounge and see what it's like to be catered to by robots.

It's also my birthday today. I've just turned seventeen. My mother is feeling better and has the house decorated with balloons and streamers. We're not really having a party because I told her I don't want one. But she promised tonight she's going to make me dinner and bake a cake. There's a present on the kitchen table and my mother even replaced the vase I shattered with a new one—and added even more pussy willow to it. The present is in a small box wrapped in pink wrapping paper. I haven't touched it yet.

"You can open it if you want Stori. You don't have to wait for cake."

"It's okay, Ma. I'll wait. What are you making?"

"Your favorite of course! Anchovies Pizza and Ice Box Cake!"

I'm happy she's feeling better. But I'm also scared she's just faking it. "You feeling better, now, Ma?"

She comes over to me and touches my head. The flour on her hand smells sweet. "I've still got you and Regina don't I?"

"Daddy too. He's coming home."

Just the mere mention of my dad makes her eyes water. She can't live without him. I know she can't.

"Don't cry. I'll get him back for you, Ma. I promise."

She turns away from me and retreats to the stove.

"Tonight is the grand opening. Of the casino."

"Are you going, honey?"

"Yeah. I'm bringing Regi with me. But we'll be back for pizza and cake."

"Of course you will." She says it like she doesn't expect us to come back at all. People leave and never return sometimes. She's already surrendered herself to that fact.

I make a pit stop at Mr. Delfi's butcher shop before Regi and I head out. Regi's hungry and I have to feed her before we go. I ask Mr. Delfi for a Cappy and Swiss on white to go. He obliges kindly, all the while whistling a happy tune. His son in law is nowhere in sight and I'm silently thankful for his absence.

Arty Arm is over by the storefront window, hunched over his newspaper, sipping from a tiny espresso mug. His cronies are with him, drinking out of their own mugs and chomping on Social Teas.

Since Mo isn't there I go over to his table and say, "Excuse me. Mr. Arty Carp."

I don't know if he's still mad about me interrupting his business with Mo and calling him a Faccie Due. "What is it kid?"

"I had a question to ask you. About, you know, that stuff you were talking about the other night. What you heard? The mayor and Cosimo and all that."

He raises an eyebrow.

"I was just wondering where you heard it from. That's all."

He closes the paper and points to the front page. "You see this?"

It's a picture of the casino and a headline reads: "Grand Opening of Strive and the Highly Anticipated Heaven Lounge Expected to Bring in Millions on Opening Night."

"The mayor will be there, you know."

"I know."

"He's going all over town yapping about how it's the first time in 300 years Redemption has jobs for every single resident of the city. He's gunning for governor, you know. A real opportunist this one is."

"What?" one of his cronies comments. "You ain't ever heard of a greedy politician?"

Arty sucks his teeth, folds the paper in its standard three folds and tucks it under his arm. He looks at me and says, "Do you know where he got most of the money for this outside of his investors? 1.5 billion in emergency reserve, plus he deferred 2 million. He's selling a fantasy of a newer, better city but in reality he's put us in major debt."

"But the stuff you heard?" I gently remind him.

He sucks his teeth. "Yeah. I stand by it. Even if it came from Soda Can."

"From Soda Can?"

"That's right. Soda Can. That's where I heard it. From one of the canners. Can't remember which one. Had my hands tied up at the moment. But I heard it none the less."

"You mean your *hand*," his friend corrects him and they all laugh.

The streets of downtown Redemption are thronged. Everyone has come for the grand opening of Strive. Dressed in suits and gowns, the children in their church clothes. It's almost 60 degrees out and what with the arctic freeze we had, it feels almost like summer. The air is buzzing with excitement. I shoulder my way through the crowd with Regi trailing behind me clutching my hand. As I draw near the front I have to push a few people but I don't mind. I want to get as close to him as I possibly can. And here he is. The mayor.

He's standing about fifteen steps above everyone, clapping shoulders and hamming it up with a few friends who look just as important as him. The lot of them don

279

brand new suits and phony smiles. Police guards have formed a barrier at the bottom of the stairs for their protection.

After a while someone hands him a microphone and he taps it. The pounding echoes through the crowd followed by the sound of him clearing his throat.

The crowd settles down.

"Hello," he says robustly into the din. His voice is larger than God's and the people quiet down even more to listen. "I can not tell you how ecstatic and appreciative I am that all of you fine citizens of Redemption have come out to honor the opening of Casino Strive."

The crowd erupts in cheers. Everyone is clapping proudly. Men send out sharp whistles with fingers in their mouths.

The mayor beams and whispers something to one of his friends.

"What a creep," I say out loud, since no one can hear me. "I know the real you."

If only he would just look at me. Just look my way and I'll trap you just the way I trapped that monster; I'll get the information I need and then send you running as far away from Redemption as you can.

"Thank you, thank you," he says and waits another half minute for the cheering to die down. "No really, thank you. There was tremendous red tape involved in getting this project implemented. And tremendous sacrifice on you citizens as you had to deal with the budget cuts and construction. But we knew, my advisors and I, that the opening of Strive was going to be a day to go down in the history books of Redemption. Not only have we created thousands of jobs, but we have erected this fine tower to make a statement. To anyone who is visiting Redemption. It says, we are not a city of the past, no, not anymore. We are a city of the future. Looking up and looking ahead. We are destined for great things because for great things we Strive!"

A pair of shiny scissors comes out and the red tape is cut. The cheering swells. The police have to hold some people back from bum rushing the stairs as Mayor Vaughn and his men disappear into the building.

Then finally the police step aside and all hell breaks loose. I have to pick Regi up in my arms and carry her all the way up the stairs, lest the frenzied crowd tramples her alive.

It's nothing less than a palace inside. Grander than anything I have ever seen. Regi is jumping up and down in excitement as I keep a tight grasp on her hand. God forbid if I lose her and one of those Hounds snatches her up. I'm scanning the room for the mayor but I don't see him.

But I am in just as much awe as Regi and can't help but pause to marvel over this place. Marble fountains, live palm trees swaying under a soft synthetic wind. Acrobats are suspended in the air twenty or so feet above our heads.

They're in diamond studded leotards and they glisten as they spin and swirl, climbing up and down their ropes.

Show girls line the largest fountain that shoots out fuscia water. They wear sequence underwear and peacock hats almost as tall as they are.

Golden dollies manned by bellhops are escorting some of the wealthier guests who brought luggage and intend to stay the night in the hotel. I recognize one of them as Priscilla Van Patten. She doesn't see me as she places a Loui Vuitton suitcase on a dolly. The man standing with her is tall and tan and handsome.

Regi has hooked up with some of her friends already. They're squealing and dragging her by her free arm away from me and pointing. "Hold on," I tell them. "Where you going?"

"Tigers!" her friend shouts. "Tigers are back there!"

"No!" I tell them. "Stay here. We have to do something first."

But they're already dragging her away and there's not a chance in hell I'm leaving my sister by herself in this madhouse.

I try to catch up to them, but they're faster for their small bodies are better for crouching under armpits and boring through narrow slits. I trail behind, following them through a maze of restaurants and clothing stores into another foyer. In the center is a glass case as big as a house. Inside are three orange tigers. Two adults and a baby.

They're pacing back and forth obviously agitated by the crowd.

People are snapping photos on their cell phones, some come right up to the glass and tap. Children are banging and shouting and the parents are letting them. I'm disgusted and want to scream out, *Stop it people. Stop it! You are scaring these tigers. These tigers are afraid!*

With the crescendo of pandemonium no one will hear me. I wish with all my might for the glass to break right open and the tigers to come out and maul these laughing baboons to death. I hope the powers I have will make it happen but they're no help.

Regina is pressed up against the glass with her friends. I haven't seen her this happy in a very long time and I can't help but feel good about it. I have to let her enjoy this moment. I come up behind her and pull her frazzled hair away from her face and lift it from her neck so she can get some fresh air. "Oh, Stori. Look! That tiger there is looking at you!" I take a quick look. I don't really want to, trying to contain my anger. And I know what Caroline said about being angry. I have to let it go. It's just so hard to. Especially when there are so many things in the world to be angry about. The Night's Council, evil mayors, this mass hysteria over a dumb casino and a room with robots somewhere in it. As I'm going down the list of why I don't think I'll ever be able to let go of my anger I spot something.

There on the floor, by a palm tree near the ceramic cave. I blink several times. I narrow my vision. I blink again.

It's still there. Hallucination or not. I can see it plain and clear. My mother's lemon cookie.

My father asked her to make a batch the night before he disappeared. He brought them to work with him, saying he had a friend that was just dying for one. Oh Shit! Soldier Sonny! What was it that he told me? I was only half listening. Oh yes! Cookies. He wanted to bring some cookies to one of the tigers! And there it is. My father must have gone in there like a dummy.

My God. Did the tigers eat him?

My heart pounds in my chest as I contemplate the worst. But the tiger is looking at me with such intensity that I have to look back. He's staring deep into my eyes with a look on his face like he's reading my thoughts. Yes. He is reading me, the way I read the monster the night I saved the little girl. I let him look and wait for what comes next. It's a grin and a shaking of his head. No. He's shaking his head no. My father's not dead. My father's still alive.

I have to get into that cage and find out what happened to my father. How will I do it? I need time. To figure it out.

We stay another hour. I let Regina venture back into the petting zoo and the kiddy casino where slot machines give out sugared candies. In the meantime I search all the rooms I'm allowed in, but the mayor is nowhere to be found. But then I think I spot him in a gaming room. It's adults only and I'm not allowed in there. He's by a slot machine with his hand on the shoulder of a young woman who's about to pull on the lever. They're both facing a photographer and smiling. I'm up on my tippy toes trying to figure out how to get in there. Then I see my uncle. He's next to the security guard. He nods to me. "Valley. Keep your eye on that one."

The guard looks me over, chewing on a wad of gum. He smacks his black baton in his palm and makes a lurching movement like he's after me. I jump back and lose myself in the crowd. I can't take the chance of getting caught with a gun. Okay. So it's not gonna happen tonight—getting to the mayor. Getting inside the tiger's cage. I have to go home, gather my thoughts, regroup.

On our way out I spot Miss Van Patten again. She looks stunning in a red dress that in my opinion shows not enough leg and too much cleavage. She's walking hand in hand with her boyfriend and as she passes I can't help but let my anger get the best of me. "Wannabe." I shoot it at her like a spitball and it hits her hard.

Her nostrils flare. But she refuses to look at me. She stares straight ahead and keeps on walking.

On our way out I grab a brochure. The hotel stays open all night, but the main casino, where the tigers are, shuts down from 4 to 11am. I've got to get back in here somehow afterhours. I have to get back to that tiger.

When we get home, Rose, the Other Mother, is making her way out of the house. "Is everything alright?" I ask her.

Rose clutches herself like she needs consoling. "Your sweet Mama is sleeping. Tell her everything you want to tell her girls. Tell her before you won't be able to."

Priscilla Van Patten

Our big weekend has finally arrived. It's the grand opening of Strive and Nate planned a night of gambling and mingling, followed by an overnight in a penthouse suite. I've been getting ready since this morning; you'd think it was my wedding day or something. But I want to look my absolute best.

My bags are packed. Nate is on the phone in the kitchen arranging for the concierge of our apartment building to fetch his car. I'm standing in front of a full-length mirror in the master bedroom. The dress I chose is sexy but sophisticated—a red midi with a plunging neckline and flowy satin sleeves. I try on a pair of black strappy stilettos. I swivel my hips to inspect all angles and come to the conclusion that I look great.

Now all I need are pearl earrings and an understated clutch. I rummage for my finishing touches and return to the mirror one last time. A deep breath. Nate is mine, I assure myself.

We had a fight again.

Not about what happened at his birthday dinner. I apologized profusely and Nate only took a night to forgive me. (He's very good that way.)

This time I'm mad at him, and I'm notorious for holding grudges.

You see, he had another late night with Jerry. Nate said it was strictly business and I was fine staying home. I've been highly emotional lately and I didn't want to run the risk of making a fool of myself again.

But turns out it wasn't strictly business; *she* was there. And he kept it from me. Who did I find out from? None other than the little cunt herself. I bumped into her at Bloomies in the women's shoe department. "Hey Pris."

"Oh. Hi Trish."

"Ferragamos?"

"Yeah. Not sure if they have my size."

"Too bad you didn't make it out last night."

"Last night?"

"The dinner at the yacht club."

"You were there?"

"Nate didn't tell you?" She was totally eating it up. "That big record producer's in town for the grand opening.

He met up with Nate and Jerry to talk business. But he also wanted to meet me. I might get a record deal!"

I tried to play it off. "Wow. Congrats. That's great, Trish. I'm sure you'll do well."

But I was fuming.

Does he even know how bad he made me look? Now she has the upper hand!

I just can't forgive him. Even as he comes up behind me and places his strong yet manicured hands on my shoulders, I act like he's not even there. But then he leans his weight into me and we lock eyes through the mirror. "Damn," he breathes. "You look beautiful. I wish we could just freeze this moment. Stay here like this all night."

He runs a finger down my satin sleeve.

"I'm really excited about tonight," I tell him despite myself.

He sweeps my hair over one shoulder. He plants a warm kiss on the arch of my neck. Shivers run down my spine.

"You're going to be even more excited," he tells me softly.

"Why is that?"

"I think you have something behind your ear. What could it be?"

He pulls it out, twirling it between his fingers.

I turn to face him. "What is it?"

He holds it up between us. A casino chip. "The black

chip," he says like it's a dirty little secret. "With this chip we have VIP access to the Heaven Lounge and will be one of its official members."

I gasp. "How did you get this?"

He tucks the chip into my dress over my heart. "Remember those powerful people I told you about? The ones running Redemption? I'm almost in with them, Pris. I'm almost in the club. Wait till you meet some of the members tonight. Record producers, politicians and Sheiks. I'm not just gonna show you the finer things in life, Priscilla. I'm gonna show you the finest."

He pulls me closer and kisses me softly.

I want to know the finest. I really really do.

Before we head out I open my jewelry box and slide my finger down the side. I pull out a small photograph. It was taken when Grace was four and I was nine. We're both in our underwear and each of us have on one roller skate. Grace and I used to share everything. I look at myself. Big smile. Sparkling eyes. Happy as ever in that dirty kitchen with that one skate and no clothes. "I'll never let you go," I whisper to the girl. And then I slip her and her sister under my dress, where the chip is hiding; now they are all over my heart.

Strive is quite possibly the most extravagant casino I've ever seen. The acrobats dangling in the air above our heads, the domed ceilings of fretted ivory, inlaid with what looks like real gemstones, the chandeliers bigger than baby grand pianos. The halls leading out in all different directions. Which path to take? There are so many options and all of them look just as enticing as the next. The main hall is so grand the shouts of the guests echo off the walls. "Holy crap!" I yell into Nate's ear. "This is amazing."

We check our bags at the hotel lobby just beyond the foyer. The attendant hands Nate and I our key cards with an ear-to-ear grin. "Enjoy your stay here at Strive."

Nate is happy to be free of the luggage. He tugs on his jacket and smiles up into the ceiling. "Oh yeah, baby. Tonight is going to be a good night." Then he takes me by the hand and leads me through the mayhem.

We travel through a maze of slot rooms, bars and gaming rooms. In the dead center of the casino we come upon a tiger's den encased in glass. There are three tigers inside. People are pressed up against the glass in wonder. Mostly everyone is taking pictures with their iPhones. We don't stay too long for Nate says something about pleasure for peasants but as we continue I spot a familiar face in the crowd. It's Stori. She's coming toward me, leading her little sister by the hand. As she passes I pretend I don't see her, but she knows better. "Wannabe." She says.

What a wretch. I'm done. I'm totally done sticking my neck out for her. I went way beyond the call of duty there, snooping around in those missing files and getting all caught up at Rita's bar. And for what? So this little girl can call me a wannabe? Can tell me I don't have any real friends? I know I promised Regina I would get their dad back, but I have to face facts and stop acting on emotion. The Putzarella case is DONE.

Stori's just jealous because I'm here with someone important. She's trying to make me feel bad because I got out and she didn't. Even though I'm trying to help her. Trying to make her see that living at home will only ruin any chances of getting a shot at the ladder like I did.

Somehow being mad at her makes it better between me and Nate. I'm back to teasing and pinching his ass as he leans over the railing of yet another massive fountain to throw a penny in. I point out handsome men in tuxedos and tell him "You would look a thousand times better in that." Nate preens under my affection. He always has. He's just a big baby, is all. He just needs a whole lot of love. And he wants that love from *me*, not *her*. So she can just get over it.

We visit a few more gaming rooms, and peruse the menus of some of the restaurants. We stop and take a few selfies in front of a lifesize statue of David. Then he offers to take me shopping but I tell him no. I'm too excited to see the rest of this palace to be bothered with mediocre handbags and costume jewelry. "Okay, then," he says. "Are you ready for VIP Heaven?"

"Come on. I was born for VIP Heaven."

He leads me to a set of elevators guarded by a

doorman. I'm almost convinced that he's strapped under his tuxedo, but there's no time to investigate for Nate flashes his black chip and says "Heaven."

The doorman presses a button and the elevator doors open. Nate squeezes my hand and we step inside. I can feel my heart beginning to race. I'm so nervous. I'm so excited. Does my dress look okay? Is my pressed powder still holding up fine?

In the VIP Heaven Lounge, located on the 111th floor of Strive Casino, bubbly cocktails swim above four hundred heads on trays held up by robots. Yes robots! It's the sickest shit I've ever seen.

They're so human-like it's hard to believe they're machines. One is coming right toward me and I almost scream. I clutch Nate in fear and he laughs and kisses my head. "Don't be scared silly."

The robot is so quick and effortless I'm sure she's going to knock me over. But then she stops right in front of me and says, "Excuse me my lady. Would you like anything to drink?" Her shoulder length hair swishes around her face as she adjusts her facial position.

I'm speechless.

"Olive Martini," Nate tells her like it's nothing.

"Coming right up," she answers, and retreats to the bar. The back of her head is an open gash revealing a complicated mess of wires, chips and metal.

Nate knows like every other person who walks by. I

know a majority of them too and I kiss hello and hand out hollow compliments as we navigate the crowd toward the VIP section. (Yes, there is a VIP in the VIP.)

Great. Nate's mom and dad are here and his two little sisters. Over by a roulette table. Deb and Jerry too. I was hoping none of them would be here. I haven't seen them since dinner the other night. Luckily everyone is caught up with Mayor Vaughn.

"Nate!" the mayor cries, like he hasn't seen him in fifty years. They give each other a strong embrace and the mayor puts a fond hand to Nate's cheek. "A good man. Just like your father."

The mayor and Nate's family are tight. Nate's dad is holding a fundraiser for Mayor Vaughn as he will be campaigning for Governor next year.

"Damon," Nate says. (They're on a first name basis). "This is my girlfriend Priscilla."

Damon's looking at me now, lit up with curiosity. He takes my hand in his and I make sure to give him a dainty little handshake—because that's what ladies do. "Priscilla. Nice to meet you, indeed." I'm a little surprised. He's not as good looking as his photographs. From my up close vantage I'd say he's average in the looks department. I search but find nothing remarkable or noteworthy in his features. He's a little bit of a slouch too, with an unathletic physique—weak shoulders and a thin neck.

But he's cool to me, if that makes any sense. He's got

an air of self-importance about him that sets him apart.

Never underestimate a man who thinks he owns the world.

He keeps shaking my hand and his eyes have unapologetically descended to my breasts. He leaves them there and his hand grips mine tighter. Then he does something I haven't experienced in years: he scratches the inside of my palm with his finger. *He wants to fuck me*, I silently muse. *The Mayor of Redemption wants me.*

It turns me on. His objectification of me. Even though it's demeaning, there's something wild and forbidden about the way he's hitting on me right in front of my boyfriend. Something taboo. I can only imagine what he's thinking.

I want to fuck him too. It's not right. It's cheating. Cheating on Nate. God, maybe I'm the one who's unfaithful. Maybe the cheater is *me*.

"You must be an actress," Damon says, finally letting go of my hand.

"Me? No. I'm a social worker."

"Ahh. Well please allow me say thank you for the service you provide to our fine city of Redemption."

I suddenly remember what Stori told me about him— not that I believed her. But I can't help but wonder if someone so prominent could be involved in something so sinister. I'm pretty good at reading people but he's so intimidating it's a little hard. "I'm often in the Valley," I tell him. "The last few months have been tough, with all the children who have gone missing."

"It's a shame, I know."

"Priscilla's an idealist. She think there's hope for the Valley," Nate says, "But I'm a realist. So can't you send a wrecking ball to that side of town? I mean really. There would be no crime at all if we just got rid of that place."

"I've tried to explain to Nate that the culture is complicated," I say. I hope someone changes the subject now. Why the hell did I even bring it up?

"Much agreed," Damon says to my relief. "Many of the habitants are third generation. They preserve some very old customs originated from the southern regions of Italy and many of those traditions are quite special and I do believe they should be preserved."

"That's wonderful. I'm sure they would love to know you feel that way." I wonder if he knows how many people in the Valley don't like him.

"But the poverty is a problem. Rest assured, I have plans. I plan on making affordable high rises. Get rid of the small houses and build up. Up into the very sky," he raises his champagne glass with triumph. "You see, the people there just need some help. They don't know any other way of living. They can keep their traditions and their pride, and they can modernize themselves as well. Best of both worlds. And now, seeing amazing people like you already in the trenches gives me great peace of mind. I do believe we are on the right track." He raises his champagne glass higher. "To Redemption."

We raise our glasses and cheer, "To Redemption."

Curtains open and a man in a polka dot suit and bowtie is standing behind a microphone in the center of a stage. "Good evening. Good evening. I'd like to first start off by saying welcome to Heaven. All of you must have been very good boys and girls to have ended up here."

The room eats it up. Hoots, hollers and cat whistles are the reply.

"My Name is Michael the Great and I will be your host for the night. Please make yourselves at home and get ready to enjoy a night of singing, dancing and maybe if you're lucky, a few magical surprises. I'd like to introduce you to our first act, a new group that has just been signed to Blues Nation Records. Forever Young."

Everyone rushes toward the stage to get closer. They cheer as a trio of young girls march onto the stage in flapper outfits, their hair in pin curls and ribbons. Fabulous. If I could transport myself back in time it would definitely be the 1920s. Everything about that era seems so glamorous and fun. The rebellious women, the lavish parties, the short sequence dresses. The men and women as rich and outrageous as Gatsby.

The robot girl offers me an electric cigarette. I take it between two fingers. This time I notice the weary in her face. How strange that a robot could look worn, like it's done a lot of living. Almost like it once was a real person. I place the cigarette between my lips, wink at Nate and inhale. A band takes their places behind the trio. Drums pound, saxophones wail.

The song is a big hit. Everyone is dancing, including the mayor and what looks like his wife. Nate is spinning me around, holding me tight. And then something wonderful happens. The roof above our heads slides back like a sunroof and the open sky is above us. White clouds sail in the deep grey black. Little stars are winking. A spray of lilac petals come showering down around us. They are scented with a fine fragrance. "Heaven!" I cry. "Heaven!"

Tell me this isn't destiny. That God's hands are not in this, working his wonders, making this happen for me. I went from cleaning my father's vomit out of a J.C. Penny rug every other Sunday night, to dancing amidst lilac petals with a beautiful man in a palace fit to please King Solomon himself. I have politicians kissing the back of my hand, and women casting curious glances in my direction. Who am I, they are asking. She must be someone important.

Don't tell me I need to come back to Erie and finish old business. I paid my dues and then some. I am worthy of this place. I am worthy of this man. I am worthy, Goddamnit. I am worthy.

We dance until our feet ache and retire to a booth in the corner of the room. A mustached man in grey Armani and a handsome Middle Eastern man take a moment from their commiserating to greet Nate.

"This is my girlfried, Priscilla," he tells them.

"Quite beautiful," says the Middle Eastern man.

The mustached one snaps his fingers and shouts. "Get this fine beauty a drink!"

Nate settles into the booth and leans in to impart a new secret. "The one in the grey is Chuck. He's a big-time record producer for Blues Nation. The other one's an oil tycoon. See. I told you." He pats my knee, but is preoccupied with his phone. He starts to look nervous. I notice Trish has arrived with her usual entourage. "What is she doing here?" I demand.

"She's getting a record deal soon with Chuck. I can't help it if she's a part of this scene."

"It just feels like everywhere we go, she's there."

Nate gets serious, which happens only on rare occasions. "Prissy. You've got to stop. With the jealousy. It's taking a toll on us. I don't know where it's coming from. Why you feel so insecure, but you need to deal with it."

"Well how would you feel if my X was at every event we went to and still all chummy chummy with me?"

"I'd be fine with it."

"Really?"

"Pris. Did it ever occur to you that Trish and I are friends? And because of you it's been really hard for us to keep that friendship going?"

Is he effing serious? Please don't tell me this is happening right now. That I'm the one getting blamed for another girl's intrusion. I want to scream at the top of my lungs. So I abruptly make my way out to the balcony so I can be alone.

I find an empty space. I lean my elbows over the balcony and look out to downtown Redemption. It's only fifty degrees tonight and with how cold it's been for the past month I don't even need a coat. Nate comes up beside me and says, "Come back inside. You're gonna catch a cold."

"I just want to be alone with you," I plead.

"We will. In just a few hours. I've planned something really nice. A dinner at Jon Pierre's. Have a little faith, girl."

"That will be nice. Just us." I'm still not looking at him.

He gets a text. He's nervous again. He pulls out a napkin from inside his jacket and wipes his forehead. He hands me his glass and says, "Enjoy yourself. Order another drink. I have to make a call. I shouldn't be long."

I look for Trish; she's sitting by Chuck, looking at her phone. She looks dead at me, and smiles.

I don't smile back.

"Redemption is quite lovely from way up here, is it not?"

I turn and find Jerry. "Oh. Hi, Jerry." I fake a smile.

He takes Nate's glass from me and puts it on a table. "Everything alright?"

"Yes. I just needed a little fresh air."

"You know I've been thinking a lot about what you said the other night at dinner."

"Oh. Yeah. That."

"You don't have to feel bad. You were just telling it. Like it is."

"I do that sometimes. It doesn't always work out for me."

"What? Saying how you really feel?"

"Yes. Saying how I really feel."

"If you ask me I think that's what's wrong with the world right now—people DON'T say how they really feel. And maybe because they don't even know HOW they feel." He takes a sip of wine, then right out of the blue, says, "I know a lot of important people in this city Priscilla."

"I know. Nate told me. He wants to be just like you."

He laughs darkly. "I bet he does. And I bet he will." Then he comes out of left field and says, "You're from the gutter aren't you?"

"I beg your pardon?"

"It's not an offense. I can tell by the way you were talking about the Valley that you understand the hard life."

"I don't talk about my past. This is the city of Future Forward remember?"

"Did you know I was saved last year, Priscilla?"

"Saved?"

"Yes. Saved."

"You mean by God?"

"Yes. In a church by myself. I was lost in a wave of sorrow and then suddenly I fell on my knees before the cross and opened my arms wide. I was saved."

"My mother was saved," I say from the pit of my stomach. "She said it made things easier and harder all at once."

He smiles somewhat pathetically. "It complicates things, that's for sure. Some things have to get left behind."

I'm not quite sure what being saved even means. "I guess."

"You know I have a big stake in this casino. I have friends in high places. People counting on me."

"I know. Nate told me."

He puts his head down between his shoulders and says, "God. But I…" He's struggling with something. Some unnamed desire that's pulling him in a direction where he doesn't really want to go. He thinks too much, I conclude. The way I do. So I tell him, "Don't think too much, Jerry. Just drink."

He picks his head up. "Maybe you were better off where you came from. Maybe this isn't the good life after all."

Just then I notice Trish reading another text. She

smirks, slips off her bar stool and trots in her slinky dress the same way Nate went, right out of Heaven.

I lose my sense of direction as I try to navigate through the swells, but finally I find my way to the hotel lobby and I get detailed directions on how to get to our room. Up on the 60th floor, I slink down the hallway, grateful for the thick rug eating up the sound of my heels. I find our room, 240 and carefully slip my card inside. I take a good minute with the door and I have to say I'd make a pretty good cat burglar.

Nate's somewhere inside the room. I can hear him murmuring through the walls. I press my back into the wall and slide my way as close to the bedroom without being seen. I take a quick peek into the room, finding it empty. *Where is he?*

His voice comes in clearer. "I just can't stop thinking about you," he says. "So it has to be real. This thing we have has to be the real thing."

MOTHERFUCKER. I move to the bathroom and am ready to burst through the double doors and kill them both with my bare hands. But there's a crack in the doors and I look through first. Nate's kneeling in front of a full-length mirror. He's holding a ring box. He stares pleadingly into his own eyes and says, "Will you marry me, Priscilla? Will you be my wife?"

I stifle a gasp, latching my lips shut with two fingers. I

back away from the door and make my way through the hall. Not as quiet as my entrance, my exit is rushed and clumsy. I let myself out and run like hell back to the elevators, terrified Nate will catch me.

Joe

Damn. Look at that ass.

Holy moly. I gotta stop for closer inspection. Oh yeah, shift your hips again. Just like that. Round, firm, cushiony. That's the kind of ass shouldn't be let out in public. Can make a decent man like me think of beastly things.

I'm an assman in case you haven't noticed and when I see one that good I don't let it slide.

I cut some douche bag off waiting in line for a drink. "Hey asshole," he says but I ignore him. Men nowadays are not nearly as tough as they used to be. Especially young ones like that. Besides, I'm on my fifth Heineken and already hit a fat line in the bathroom. The combination brings out my pushy side.

"Buy you a drink?"

"Already got one."

Wow, she's a dime. Got a face to match the rest. (The face will usually take a backseat to the body or vise versa, but not this time.) But she's upset by something and from what I can see she's alone.

Jackpot. A broad alone at a bar upset by some insensitive man, no doubt. I live for moments like this. Today is my lucky day.

"My name is Joe, and you have got to be the most beautiful woman I have ever laid eyes on. Just sayin,"

She's shaking her head like she feels sorry for me, but I can see she's holding back a smile. No matter what girls say about being respected, there's nothing more satisfying than to hear that a man thinks they're fine. Or even wants to fuck them. I've done that a few times. Driving past a girl walking in the street. Just rolled my window down and told her straight out what I had on my mind. Each and every time I saw her smile against her own will. They like it. It's the animal in them. The one they try to suppress.

This animal is a brown fox and I'm looking to spend a little QT with her, even outside of the bedroom. From those shoes and that dress I can tell she's moneyed up. And everyone knows moneyed up pussy takes a little more time. "You look kind of sad for a girl who's in heaven."

"I was thinking. I'm over it."

"What were you thinking about?"

"Just life stuff."

"Boyfriend."

"No."

She's lying. But I play along.

"Work."

"Yeah. Let's go with that." She shifts the focus back to me. "You're not too subtle about your game."

"I ain't one of these little boys you're used to dealing with. Baby. You haven't seen nothing yet."

"What?" Oh, yeah. She's enjoying the attention. I can tell, she's the kind of girl who needs alot of it. The prettier they are the more attention they need.

I decide to switch gears to keep her on her toes so I divert my interests elsewhere. "Ahh. Look at the mayor hamming it up over there. I bet you he's just loving this."

"I wonder if he knows how many people in Redemption actually hate him."

"He's a good guy. Did a lot for Redemption already. Why would you say that?"

"I work for CPS. People in the Valley have horrible things to say about him. You can only imagine."

She's been to the Valley. "Oh yeah? What do they say?"

"Uh uh. I can't tell."

"Come on, it can't be that bad."

"One girl, only sixteen years old, thinks he's planning on making all the orphan girls at Pilgrim's Island his wives."

Okay. Keep it cool Joey. Keep it cool. How the hell did she get that information? "Crazy," I comment blankly, taking a sip of beer. "Just out of curiosity, who told you that?"

"Can't say."

"Whoever it is they're probably on crack."

"Not, Stori. No. She's tough. But she doesn't do drugs…" She bites her lip, instantly regretful for her unprofessional slip, but she doesn't know it's enough to send me over the moon.

That little brat. How did she find out?

I want to rush out of here, put a bag over that little girl's head, drag her back to the dam where she should have drown the first time and drown her. But I can't let this one pass. "You from around here? Originally?"

"No."

"Let me guess. You came out here looking for a better life."

"Maybe."

"Did you find it?"

She ignores the question. She strokes her glass, letting her varnished fingertips get wet from the condensation.

"Trust me. You didn't find it. None of us have honey."

Then finally she looks at me. There it is. The sweet spot. The opening. Note to any men listening: they all want the same thing—a man to understand them and be a better version of their father. "Do you ever feel lonely?"

"Shit. Everyone does."

"No. Like not just when you're alone. But all the time. Like right now. Talking to me. With all these people around us. Are you lonely?"

"No."

"A deep down lonely. Like the people who are supposed to be with you are not and never will be. Because they're all dead or far away or somewhere long gone in the past before you were even born."

Nothing like existentialism to ruin my buzz.

"Like this life we live is not the good life? Because any one of these people couldn't look in my eyes and know my soul. Because that's what we were put on this earth for. To be with each other and love each other, and know each others souls." She turns to me and crinkles her face like she's gonna cry. "I want to belong to something. A tribe I spend every day with from the day I'm born till the day I die. Same people. Noone goes away. Noone ever changes. The tribe always stays the same."

"Some guy did you good, didn't he?"

"We were made for each other. That's why we're here."

"You wanna belong to someone?" I pull out my Park's Department card and slide it over the bar to her. "It was nice meeting you. When you get tired of playing with the preschoolers give me a call."

Stori

I never imagined my first kiss like this. 3 hours before sunrise in a casino parking lot, waiting in the dank cold with a gun tucked into my pants. Five cleaning service vans pull up to a receiving entrance. The crew quickly unloads their equipment and make their way inside.

Richie Ramera stands in their wake. He doesn't go in with the rest of them. Instead he turns and stalks through the half empty lot over to garbage bins where I wait. He steps into the thick shadows and says, "Hi Sullen."

I always knew it wouldn't be Tony but never thought it would be like this. With someone I don't even like.

All that practicing I did and for what?

I've never been a complainer, but this one just doesn't

seem fair.

I'm this close to bursting into tears when he gets up on me and puts his hands on my hips. What a failure I've become. He's gonna tell everybody. I'm never going to show my face in the street again.

I step back and his hands fall to his sides. "Let me see the keys first."

He pulls them out of his pocket. "Got them right here." He holds them up like bait, jingles them with a shit-eating grin.

I hope it makes him feel real good about himself, taking advantage the way he does. The old me would have never let this happen. She would have been clever and come up with a way to get inside without ruining her reputation. And she would have put Richie in his place to boot.

But I'm not the old me anymore. I'm somebody else— a girl I don't trust—and it frightens me.

I'm ashamed standing in front of him. I feel like nothing. Like I deserve nothing. I can't even be mad at him because now I'm convinced he's better than me. If he wants it, I should just give it to him.

He grabs me by the back of the head and smushes his face into mine. It's rough and all I can do is open my mouth and let his tongue in. It's hard. Not soft the way Seventeen magazine said it would be.

I don't feel anything as I let him go at it. Not fear. Not

desire. Not even regret.

He stops and pulls my coat open. "Let me feel you," he breathes. "Come on. Just a little."

"That wasn't part of the deal."

"It is now."

"I don't have time. But tomorrow."

"You promise?"

"I promise."

He grabs my head again and kisses me so hard our teeth scrape. "I'm gonna fuck you too. Okay?" He says it with hatred.

"Okay."

Finally he gives me the keys. Adjusting his crotch he backs out of the darkness. "Damn girl." Then he turns and skips out into the lit up parking lot. He sails all the way back to the receiving door.

I have what I need now. The keys feel heavy as I lift my arm, wiping my mouth with my coat sleeve.

I run to the van and open the back doors. I climb in and rummage through some items before I find a vest that bears the words Happy Time Cleaners. Richie promised he would leave an extra jacket for me. The keys are marked too: Receiving Entrance and Cage. The only two I need.

There's a man in the receiving office shouting on the phone. "I told you that shit was supposed to get here yesterday, not today. Do you know how many heads are gonna roll because of this?" I dart by him into a narrow hall that brings me up a staircase.

Voices meet me as I crack the door ajar; I pull it closed again and wait for them to pass. They're speaking Spanish. I muster up as much of my intermediate Spanish as possible to make out something about starting at the top first and finishing at the bottom. I count to three before I make my way out and follow a good distance behind them as they drag several vacuum cleaners and those rolling shelves that maids push around at hotels. I hide again as they wait for an elevator and then get on. The doors close. I listen for signs of anyone else, but there's only quiet.

Pots are banging in the far distance. It must be a kitchen somewhere. Finally I make for the foyer and just my luck, it's empty.

The tigers are there. They're sleeping. I go over to the glass and tap. They don't wake up. I see a mirrored door to the back; this is where the animal keepers must get inside. I go back into the hallway and see another door. It's locked.

I pull out the keys and locate the one tagged Cage. I slip it in and turn my wrist. The door opens.

I enter a musty room cluttered with boxes and tools. I see the door. It's glass from this side and the tigers are just beyond it. I use the key again. It works.

I don't know if I'm afraid stepping inside the tiger's den. I'm not sure how they will react when they see me. This could be the very end. *I will die for you father. I will stand and face the mauling. You will see then how much I love you.* My love for him pushes me forward. Whatever secret there is to be uncovered lies within this den.

I step inside and one tiger instantly senses my presence. Her head pops up, her ears stiffen. She rises, looks at me and roars.

I stand and watch her, expecting to be afraid, but instead overcome by remorse. "Oh baby. Who put you in here like this? Who took you away from them? That's what they're gonna do to all of us. Take us away from each other. Oh baby. Don't cry. I don't think I can stand it. Here." I go back to the door and open it. "Come with me. I'll get you out of here."

She looks at the cookie and then back at me. And then she roars again. The others have woken. The baby rises, yawns and stretches. She pads her way over to me and rubs her powerful flank against my leg. I almost fall over, and brace myself against her power. I look at her mother. "Why don't you come? I'm trying to help you. I'm supposed to be looking for my father. But instead I'm helping *you*."

The male is behind her, but he's not paying much attention. He's sniffing in a bucket for what I assume is water or food. Then he bends his head down and begins lapping up water from a bucket.

The mother is full of pride. I can see it in the way she strides over to a small cave and disappears inside. I know to follow her so I do.

Inside is a blanket of hay scattered across the floor and

in the far corner I see something glinting. I kneel and brush my hands over the hay and see a silver groove with a latch. There's a door here. It's wooden and hinged to the planks of the floor. I slide my finger under the latch and lift and the door comes up. What I find below the wood is a stone staircase leading down into pitch-blackness.

The mother stands at my side looking down into the darkness with me. "Thank you," I tell her. And I make my way down into the dungeon.

As the upper door closes on top of me, wood scraping against stone, I look up into the shrinking square of light. After it shuts I'm left in deafening darkness. I stand completely still. I'm not thinking anything. Just allowing myself to be. Then I reach out and feel for the wall. I lean as much of my weight into it as I can, and begin my descent, sliding myself down the stairway, using the tips of my toes as feelers before each step. After I get to the bottom I proceed slowly, still clinging to the wall.

Water drips from above. I can hear the little pats and every so often I take a shot right on the crown of my head. At first it startles me but then I get used to it. Somewhere far in the distance there's work being done. The sound of clanging against iron or steel. There's no telling what I might come upon and I have to fight the panic rising under my heart.

Then I see a flicker of light off to the side. I spy a

narrow passage and someone in it, moving away from me, holding a lantern. I gasp, despite myself and the figure halts. They turn and the lantern shows itself in fullness. I dart into the darkest corner I can find.

"Who is it there?" the figure calls in a loud whisper. "Show yourself to me."

The voice belongs to a boy. *Is that fear I hear in him?* I open my mouth to answer, only to clamp my mouth shut again. *Could a child be danger?* He seems to read my mind for he says, "If you are hiding because you're frightened, I won't hurt you."

I peek over the corner of the wall and see the lantern again. I'm not sure if he can see me for the darkness is deep. "We don't have much time," he insists. "We're alone now, but who knows how much longer."

I have no choice but to answer. "I came from upstairs. I'm looking for my father, Frank."

I can see his hand go up to his mouth. He looks behind him and then hurries to where I'm standing. I don't know if it's the light of the lantern that comforts me or the face of a nine year old boy with the prettiest black lashes I have ever seen and flushed cheeks in a round pale face.

"What is your name," he asks breathlessly.

"Stori. Putzarella. What's yours?"

"Ben. Ben Bak."

"You're from the Valley aren't you?"

"Yes. You are too."

"What are you doing down here, Ben?"

"These are Cosimo's quarters. He's building an underground palace with tunnels that will channel out as far as they can take him. I was kidnapped by one of his Hounds."

"My God, that's horrible."

"It's even worse for some of the others. I'm one of his chosen. I fetch him water and food when he and the Mistress dine. The others are in the prison hall. They only come out when he calls for them."

"I don't understand," I say.

"There's not enough time to explain it all," he says. "But this man, you speak of. I've seen him. His name is Frank. Cosimo has been keeping him prisoner."

"You have to show me! You have to show me where he is."

"Are you crazy?" he says. "You can be killed. Go back up." He points to the direction from where I came. "Go back up and..."

"No," I insist, trying to keep myself from yelling. "I will not leave without my father." I've come this far and even if I die at least I might get the chance to tell my father I love him. Maybe, I will even get to feel his touch one last time. Oh, to feel my father's touch upon my face. To have him hold me again. I would die a thousand deaths just to have that one more time.

Ben's not pleased. He shakes his head. "You won't get

to him. I promise."

"I won't leave until I see him." I have nothing to lose and everything to gain.

"Follow me then, and do everything I tell you."

He leads me through a maze of limestone walls. Rats scurry along the edges, ducking into shadows and burrowing into open crevices. We get to an arched door of dark wood and Ben pulls the handle to open it.

Inside is a decent sized room with a four post bed.

"Is this your room?" I ask.

"Yes. Like I told you. I'm one of the lucky ones. Here. Put this on. You can maybe pass as one of the other chosen ones. If you keep your head down and don't look anyone in the eye."

I get the feeling we're safe in here, so I take this opportunity to get a better look at Ben. He's barefoot and wears white linen pants and a matching shirt. And on his head is a crown of grapes and vines. His body is slight and his shoulder bones jut out under his shirt. But from the color in his face I can see he's well fed. At least for now.

I kick off my boots and socks, undress and quickly change into the linen. The pants are way too short for me, but the shirt fits fine. There's no place to hide the gun on me now, so I wrap it in my sweatshirt, making sure Ben doesn't see.

"Okay," he says. "Now follow me and if anyone speaks to you, only answer with Yes or No. Do you understand?"

"I understand."

He leads me out of the room and we descend deeper into the belly of this dungeon palace until we finally come upon a massive circular prison with small rooms blocked off by rows of bars. The prison spirals down deeper inside the earth. We're only at the top. Looking down, I gasp as I see prisoner after prisoner, all of them children!" They stare out of their cells with the saddest eyes I have ever seen. I almost want to break down and start weeping, but I know I can't.

"We will go further down," Ben tells me. "To Cosimo's quarters. He has his Great Room there. Where he brings the children for singing and dancing."

"His Great Room?"

"No time to explain."

"Who put you down here?" I ask.

"I told you. The Hounds. They work for Cosimo and the Mistress. Cosimo is further down, in the bottom."

"Why do they have you here?" I ask. I can only imagine Regina and I are next.

We go deeper into the dungeon, all the while the little eyes of children staring out at us from behind black bars. Under the prison is another maze of hallways and more lanterns are lit, resting in small alcoves the size of windows. I hear rats squeaking and scratching to get out of our way.

We finally come to a place that looks rather civilized in

comparison to the rest of this dungeon. It has marble floors and leather couches. And standing lamps give off fluorescent light.

I hear people coming, so I move to duck behind a stone pillar, but Ben grabs my arm. "They will have to see you," he says. "It's the only way."

We step closer and there are men and women; I recognize some of them from the casino. The mayor's friends who he was whispering with. I knew it!

They kiss Ben on the top of the head and ask him to fetch some water. "Right away," he replies.

Adrenaline pumps through my veins. I don't think about what I'll do if someone catches me. The streets of the Valley have taught me that it's better not plan out a fight before it happens. So I decide not to think too much.

Ben points to a door and says, "That's the kitchen. We have to get the water now. Follow me." We fill glass pitchers and he leads me out of the kitchen down yet another hall without any doors, save for one at the very end. Ben comes to the door and does some kind of secret knock—three taps follow by two, followed by three again. A woman answers. She's slutty, wobbling in stilettos pumps and as we follow her in I see the mayor's friends lounging on couches with even more slutty women draped over them.

The room is covered wall to wall in a red rug. Ben and I go to the dining room table; it's draped in red linen, lit with candelabras and covered with steaming hot food. We begin to pour the water and then retreat into the corner of the room. Dinner hasn't started yet, so I assume they're still waiting for someone.

There's a ball of glass in here too. It's about ten feet tall in the center of a marble floor. What is that thing?

Two soldier looking guys usher someone in. He shuffles his feet and they leave him by the ball.

Oh, Jesus! It's him. My father! He's bound by chains on his wrists and feet, wearing his work uniform.

Ben looks at me and squeezes my hand hard. He whispers. "Is that him?"

I look at Ben, my eyes brimming with tears. "Yes."

"Do *not* move. Do you hear me? Now is not the time."

The boy's words have an odd affect on me. I don't move. I only watch, miserably longing to run to him and embrace him. I want to break the shackles from his body, cover him in kisses. I want to pick him up and cradle him in my arms.

I wish with all my might for my gun. I would kill everyone in this room. I would kill these rotten bastards for doing this to my father.

But I know I have to wait. I have only known Ben for less than twenty minutes but I already trust his word completely. I know, somehow, that Ben is my father's only hope.

If I reveal myself it will only mean more trouble. A

man stands and walks over to my father and kneels down to inspect him. It's Mayor Vaughn. "How did he get down here," he demands.

Another person is in the room and their very movement puts the fear of God in me. A man sits in a throne. His skin is grey and his nose stands out on his sunken face like a protruding knob. Is he dead? No, he's breathing. His hands move a little. A woman sits next to him. She stands and comes closer to my father. She's cloaked in black. I can't see her face cause she's wearing a masquerade mask.

"What do you see, my Lady?" asks the mayor. "Is he corruptible?"

She points a long slender finger and extends it toward my father. I have to cover my mouth as tears stream in abandon down my face. Don't touch him. Please, Jesus, don't let her touch him.

"No. Not this one. He fights for the side that is good."

The finger swipes down the side of my father's cheek. It run down over his collar bone and move his unbuttoned shirt back to inspect his chest. What the woman sees is what I know is there already. A heart of thorns over my father's chest. It's not a tattoo. It's some kind of scar he never wants to talk about.

"We'll dispose of him then," the mayor asserts.

Over my dead body. They will have to kill me first. I brace myself for what's about to come. I look at Ben with utter defiance and wish I had kept my gun with me.

"Not yet," the masked woman says. "We can't. This one has something I need. Now leave me alone with him. All of you. And have Ben send for another child."

Hastening through the halls to get back to Ben's room, Ben cautiously explains a little more to me. "The man in the chair was Cosimo. He's undead. The children. In the cells. All of us. We are very important to him. His Mistress has us perform our gifts in front of him, whether it's song or dance or poetry. Sometimes artwork. He needs our gifts. We still shine, Stori. And our light. When we let it shine before him that glass ball lights up. It's like a drug to him. He's all darkness. But he wants to be light. Not to let it shine but to crush it deep inside him. To possess it only for himself. The rest of the world under darkness and he has the light only for himself. But the Mistress keeps complaining it can only buy him time without the Crown of Final Sight."

Back in Ben's quarters I let my knees crash to the cold stone floor and I weep. "Wake me, up, Ben. Wake me up from this nightmare."

Ben crouches low by my side and strokes my back as I weep. His touch is gentle and reminds me of my mother's and the way she strokes me when I'm sick. "Shh. You're giving up hope. You can't do that."

I look at him. "They're going to kill my father. I have

to go back in there and end it."

"Violence isn't the answer. I'll help you, Stori. I promise. Look at me." He moves in front of me and takes my face in his tiny little hands. He stares deep into my eyes and I see that a boy no more than nine is braver than I am at almost seventeen. That trust feeling comes over me again and I could shout out a Hallelujah in response to it. But Ben's words are more important. "I am a prisoner just like your father. My nights are dark as well as my days. I know the way out of here, but I won't take it. Because I have to help the others. I know if I go out, there's no coming back in."

"What about the police?" I ask.

"They can do nothing. This is way bigger than that. But now, there's hope."

"There is?"

"Yes. You!" he says smiling.

"Me?"

I begin sobbing again.

"Stop crying. You got down here for a reason. And now we've just learned you're a Brave! The same blood that runs through your father runs through you! You have to go back up and find out about the Crown."

"I know about that Crown. And so does this woman. A prophetess. She can help."

"Get to her. Tonight. Tell her all you have seen and heard here. I'll be waiting for you. Your coming here has made me stronger."

"But what if I can't find it?"

"No time for doubt, girl! Have faith. Have faith."

Looking at him I realize his strength for only a young boy. "Oh, Ben." I caress his face and fear all kinds of danger that might be ahead for him. I fear the cold dark nights he spends here sleeping in this unfamiliar bed. My heart breaks open in a way it has never broken before. To a perfect stranger I say, "I love you."

A tear slides down the side of his nose, "I love you too. See? Nothing bad can ever come out of love."

Frank

My name is Frances David Putzarella, born to Concettina
and Pasquale Putzarella on the fifth of March, 1966.

I didn't know I was a Brave until the age of seventeen.
My mother was a trash picker at the time. She had a hard
life and she was dying from cancer. But she was one of
those women who never complained.

One night when she was very ill, she woke me from
bed and told me to dress and put on a warm sweater. Once
outside, she led me up Windy Way into Forest Boom.

Carrying a satchel, she guided me to a small clearing
where a silver maple sat by a stream. Under the silver maple
is where she gave me the news: "There is a world beyond
this one son. I am going to it. Tomorrow I will be gone."

"Mama, no."

"You are not to fight it."

"I don't want you to go."

"You have Papa and Joseph."

"But I don't like Papa and Joseph. They don't love me."

"Nonsense. They love you. Sit down on that rock."

I hated having to obey.

"This world is dying, Frank. It is like me. Under a dreadful curse that can't be cured. The people in it are dying too. They are living but dying all at once, because they are sick with the curse, the curse of forgetfullness. Look at me. I am going to show you who I truly am. I should have showed you sooner. You are not to speak a word of what you see to anyone. Do you hear me?"

"Mama. You scare me. Let's go home."

She took out something from her satchel. It was a crown. A crown of indescribable beauty. Too regal for even a mighty and just king. The moment she brandished this marvelous thing, her whole being was lit up in blue light.

She held the crown to her heart and closed her eyes and tilted her anguish up to the green canopy. The moon shone in fullness above us. Fireflies winked in the shadows. Then a gust of air hit us and the maple thrashed its boughs and sent a shower of green over our heads. "The law from your mouth is more precious to me than thousands of pieces of silver and gold. They are more desirable than gold, even the finest of gold. They are sweeter than honey, even honey dripping from the comb."

Still bathed in blue, she held out the crown to me.

I fell to my knees.

"This was forged after the great flood, when the Tower of Babel was being built. Our tribe, the Braves, smuggled it out of the city when the Lord came down and dispersed the people, spreading them out over the earth. During that time, men still had divinity in them. They walked with lions and spoke to trees and knew many secrets of the universe. Keep it always with you, Frances. But never place it upon your head. Let noone know you have it. Hide it Frances. For you are of the ancient lineage of the Braves."

I reached up and took it from her, somehow knowing by taking the crown I was allowing her to die.

And then an angel appeared. He walked straight through her.

I whimpered like a wounded bird.

He touched me on the top of my head. "You are anointed, my son. Do not fear in this life. Do not fear."

The clangor of bells flooded my ears and they were heavenly. A thousand gongs. All the bells that have tolled through time and all the bells that will toll after I'm gone, were ringing at once inside of me.

I was still mourning but also filled with a bone crushing ecstasy.

The angel spoke to me. "Son. The final battle has

begun. We have arrived at the time when almost the whole world will fall under the spell of the Brotherhood and their Dark Council—Cosimo and his immortal witch. The people will become like zombies. They will forget who they truly came from and what they are capable of. But fear not. For you will raise a daughter. She will fight the evil ones. She will race them through time and take this crown back to Babel. She will fight to bring the crown back to its rightful owner, the Great Ancient of Days. If she can achieve the final coronation the Brotherhood, Cosimo, the witch and the Hounds will be no more. The people will awake from their slumber and usher in the new age. The new age of abundance and enlightenment. The Dawn of the Second Eden."

"Will she get there? Will she crown Him."

"Let the story tell itself. In time, all will be known."

Then a sword appeared. It lay diagonally across his chest, the point facing up. The sword was also consumed by the blue. "If you choose this sword, you will suffer in this life. The world will scorn you. Your good deeds will go unrewarded. But you will be my child, a Brave, living the life of truth. You will help the Crown back to Babylon."

I spoke without even thinking. "I want the truth. I want the truth and no other."

He lay the sword out for my taking. I took it in my free hand, the crown still in the other. I felt its power, its weight. Its heat from the light consumed the grip. And then there was no longer a weight. For the sword became my very hand, my very arm. It became all of me. I was not separate from it anymore. We were one. I and the sword. One.

The skin on my chest, just over my heart began to burn. I looked down and saw a hole in my sweater with singed edges.

My mother died at dusk.

I did not weep. For after I stopped the hands of her clock in her bedroom, I opened the windows and leaned out into the quivering dawn. A bird flitted down from a rooftop and perched upon our neighbor's fire escape. It had just returned from the south, and its song was robust and almost violent.

She paused in her song and looked at me and I looked at her. Our souls were speaking to one another. "Is it safe?" she asked me.

"I have it hidden."

"We watch your house, in the mornings. Our songs fight away the Brotherhood's Hounds. The light snatchers, the demons of the night."

"I fear the Brotherhood and their Hounds," I told her. "I fear the witch and Cosimo. I fear they will all get me, get the crown in the night."

"Sit with us in the mornings, listen to our songs, and they will protect you."

"I never knew you could speak."

"I am the keeper of you, my child. I am the messenger of the Ancient One. I am the keeper of paradise."

"Stay always with me."

"For as long as I can, I will stay."

I never knew the birds were protecting me. Their songs were not just pretty to the ear, but were keeping the darkness at bay.

I never looked at life the same way again, after the death of my mother and all that came with it. With the burn mark on my chest and the crown in my possession, I was a different man. I was a better one and a weaker one all at once. My life was not going to be easy, but it was going to be full and of great purpose. It was going to be the life of the Brave. A life of truth and courage and love. I was going to make a difference for my city and perhaps the world. I took great solace in that.

But the world is a very hard place for a Brave to live in.

If I had known what it meant to take the sword, I might not ever have. That angel never told me my family would suffer too. You see Braves can only live lives of truth and honor. They cannot lie and hurt and steal. Because I was actively living as a Brave I turned down a lucrative job collecting for the Tapparellis. I knew hurting people for money was wrong. I got laid off several times and Anna had to go back to work. And then Stori jumped off the dam. I lost my speech because of that. I lost my agility, my quickness. It hurt my pride. Cut me down. Made me feel less than a man.

It hurt worse when some people called me names in the street. They must have felt real tough knocking down a man already on his knees. I'm a big guy and I've never been afraid of a fight, but with the sword fighting wasn't possible. Until Sidewinder called me retarded. I hesitated. I wasn't sure what I should do. That's when Stori stepped up and knocked him over. When I saw the knife I thought she would retreat, but she didn't. When I looked at her bleeding face I saw myself and I got scared. She was showing signs early, talking about angels and the children who live in Forest Boom. I knew I had to get it out of her. The Brave. I didn't want her becoming one like me. Before something really bad happened. I couldn't take losing someone again—especially my eldest daughter. So I brought her down to the Cage and made her fight. She wasn't going to suffer the way I was suffering. She was going to beat it all down, all the cruelty, all the mayhem, all the noise.

I tossed the sword after that. I got rid of the crown. (Hid it in a place where noone would ever find it.) And just like that the Brave in me was gone. I became more of a sinner than ever. I drank, whored and lied to my family. I even justified my actions by telling myself I was at essence doing it all for them. Hardening my heart was keeping my family safe from harm. I really believed being bad would keep them secure somehow—cause it seemed only bad things happened to good people.

But I knew it was only a matter of time before my sins caught up to me. I just never knew my karma would come in the form of a tiger.

I didn't know feeding an innocent little cookie to a hungry tiger was going to end up like this. The tiger was telling me for weeks that it was hungry. So one day I just stopped and looked at it and asked, 'Well what is it your hungry for?"

"A lemon cookie," he said.

How could I walk away from such a request, knowing Anna baked the best lemon cookies in all of Redemption? So I snuck in here one evening when I was doing overtime. The tiger was grateful and he told me as a gift in return he would tell me a secret. "Children are going down there," he said.

"Where?" I asked.

"Down there."

That's when I found the door. I guess my curiosity got the best of me.

When I saw that spiraling prison leading into the abyss I cut right out of there and returned to the streets a madman. I found a cop parked by the movie theatre. "Officer. There's a prison under the casino. Please. Call it in right away! A prison! A secret prison!" It took me a while to get it all out, since I was speaking the words, not thinking them as I am doing now. So of course, the cop thought I was drunk. "Get the fuck out of here, you Valley trash. Get off the streets and go home!"

There was no one else I could think of besides my brother Joe. I know we hadn't spoken in so long, but he had friends in high places. People who might listen. And I told myself, *Joe knows goodness. No matter what he's become.*

I was wrong. He told me the same thing. I was crazy and to get out of his sight.

Oh, Anna. I have so much to tell you and I don't know where to start. The night I woke up to see Mo standing over our bed, I thought he was going to kill both of us. He shushed me. "Just you I want."

I went with him, because I feared he might hurt you and the girls and I knew deep in my heart this was part of the plan.

You see my work as a Brave might have taken a detour but it is not finished. I am here for a reason. I am here not by chance, but by design. I am part of a story being told. A prophecy is being fulfilled and I am a spoke in the wheel of that prophecy.

I am dangerous to them, as all who are Braves are dangerous to those who aren't. We threaten the very core of their pathetic being. We represent everything they are afraid of.

Once I was brought here by Mo, a woman named Smyrna made me write a letter saying goodbye to you. I started to put down all the love I had in my heart but they ripped it up and told me to start again. So I wrote the note, hoping Stori would get the meaning and get to the crown.

He's having another child sent down. From what I've learned he lives for the children. He can't get enough of the light they bring.

This time it's a girl. Maybe 10 or 11, I don't know. She's carried in by a Hound and set before the throne.

Smyrna looks at the girl. "What is your name?" she asks.

The girl just stands there.

"It's okay, my love. Are you scared of that creature sitting over there? Don't worry. He won't hurt you. He won't even touch you if that's what you think. You have my word."

The girl looks at the floor. "Adella."

"And what is your gift, Adella?" she asks.

"She's a dancer, your grace," the Hound offers.

Cosimo seems pleased. He leans back into his golden throne and waits as they bring the machine out. This is his drug. Not wine, not the lines of white dust the minxes snort from the coffee table. Just the machine.

It looks like a humongous Christmas globe, made of some kind of glass or maybe it's crystal. They roll it out carefully and pull off the heavy blanket that keeps it covered while it's not in use. Dust rises and settles.

Cosimo's breath is even. Nothing puts him more at

ease than knowing he will soon get the drug.

Smyrna moves to a stereo and presses a button. Music plays. Classical symphony stuff. It's pretty and Cosimo approves with a nod.

"Dance," she tells the girl. "Go ahead. The faster you start, the sooner I can take you back to your cell."

The girl is still looking at the floor. She's not sure what to do. I can tell. I try to get her to look at me, by staring intently. I have found that people can always sense when someone's eyes are boring into them.

It works. She glances up to see who it is. She looks down but then brings her eyes back to me again. She sees my chains. I nod to her, the way I would if she were one of my own girls.

She takes a deep breath, tilts her head to the side and then slides an arched foot forward, pointing her toe.

The dance is a little timid at first. But then the music takes over and she finally gets lost, as children often do when the music gets down to their soul. The crystal ball lights up. A soft glowing white at first. But as the dancing continues it grows stronger. There is a spinning blue planet in the center of the light.

Then the girl lets off her own illumination. It shoots straight from her chest, beaming right through the darkness and travels straight to the crystal. The crystal receives it and is now even more brilliant than it was before.

From the opposite side, the beam of the child's light

travels, piercing out, flowing directly into the chest of Cosimo.

Cosimo grips his throne, the ropes of blue veins standing up on his decrepit hands. He isn't breathing. But is braced by some kind of personal ecstasy.

Sick bastard. He's stealing the light from this poor child.

When the dance is done the music cuts off and the girl collapses. Smyrna snaps her fingers and an attendant comes and picks her up in both arms and hurriedly carries her out.

Stori, if I could just get back to you and Regi and Mommy. I'd make up for hurting you. I'd make up for everything I've ever done.

And I'd tell you this, Stori: I will hold this guilt with me when they finally take my life. Because I was wrong for trying to take the Brave out of you. I was wrong for keeping your destiny hidden from you. One day when you have kids you might understand. How scary it is to think they might come to harm. You will do anything in your power to keep them from it.

But looking at the faces of these captured children, seeing their fear and knowing you might be the one to save them, I can say wholeheartedly I was wrong. If only I knew it then. I would go back and change everything.

Stori, remember the man who threw the TV out the window. The man who loved you and believed in all your goodness. Not the man who blamed you, ignored you, made you feel alone. It was not your fault, Stori, what happened to me. Forgive me, Stori. Forgive me. The guilt is too hard to bear.

Smyrna moves in a all her cruel elegance to where I am shackled. "Are you surprised they haven't killed you yet?"

"I am."

"It's only because I wanted to speak to you. How did you get past the tigers?"

"They were sleeping," I lie.

But she's not a fool. "You lie. You spoke to them didn't you?"

"What if I did?"

"You are a Brave. The blood of Babylon runs through your veins."

"So it does."

"It is written that a Brave, a young girl from this city is the one to find the crown. Could it be one of your daughters?"

"You stay away from my daughters," I snarl. "My daughters know nothing of their lineage. I've made sure of that."

"From what I've heard you don't lie about this. The eldest one likes hurting people."

"I saw to that. And I'll see to the younger one when the time comes."

"Who are the others? Where is this girl they call the Daughter of Shinar?"

"Torture me if you want. I don't know. My guess is that she's dead. My guess is that I'm one of the last Braves living."

"Very well. You've chosen your fate then."

As she turns to walk away I tell her. "I am not afraid to die."

She looks back and says," Everyone is afraid to die, Frances. Don't fool yourself."

"You know not of the wonders my soul has looked upon. For I have chosen the path of light. I have glimpsed the great beyond in my dreams and it is magnificent. But you…you have chosen darkness and corruption. You, who have kept a corpse alive by sucking out the innocence of the young—you are going to a black abyss after this life. And you know it. You fear death more than anything you have ever feared in your life."

"I'll be back. I want to think long and hard on just how I'm going to kill you."

Oh, Stori. Whatever you do, you must not be careless with time. Make haste and get yourself to the crown. The crown will take you far from this time into another.

For this world, this cursed age of forgetfulness is not a safe one. It does not have the things you will need. But the past will provide it. The days long gone. And you can get to them. You can find them. And you will. You are not to hold your head held low anymore. Rise it up. Up up up, young lady. Search for the angels you once spoke to—the magic that is out there speaking to you. And you will complete this prophecy. And I promise you, when you come to the end of your journey, when the last breath of life falls over your lovely lips, I will be standing there. I will be standing there, my daughter, waiting for you. And then, I will set every wrong against you right. I will tell you what you have always longed to hear.

Sweeper

I think I'm dead. Why else would they have summoned me to their private chambers?

I go willingly. My wife and son are dead. I am not afraid to die anymore.

Two Black Boots lead me through the tunnels, west of Cosimo's quarters.

I can try to make a run for it. Through the months I've made several mental notes on avenues of escape. There's no surveillance in the undercity. I know it's hard to believe in this day and age; you would think the place would be swarming with techno-intelligence. (Seeing how they control all the corporations who produce that stuff.)

But they don't call themselves the masters of the universe for nothing. Surveillance is a double-edged sword and the greatest kept secrets are only kept that way by plain old fashion privacy. Cell phones, cameras, computers are not allowed past the checkpoints. Black Boots are the eyes and ears of this place.

The door is solid stone. The Black Boot hits a buzzer. A few moments pass and then we are ushered in by a slouching, malnourished man with a napkin draped over his shoulder.

This chamber is furnished with only the necessities. Table, chairs, a single door leading into what appears to be a bathroom, a buffet table featuring cold cured meats and an array of glistening fruit. And a crystal chandelier above our heads, in the abstract form of Jupiter.

There are five men at the round table.

Who are these men, you must be wondering. Dear companion, if you are going to come along on this ride with me, you're going to have to suspend disbelief—even if you tell yourself it's for the sake of entertainment. What I'm about to tell you is going to sound absurd—so just get ready.

These are the five men who control the world. They control *everything*. Banks, government, organized religion, education, agriculture, media, sports, Hollywood, hospitals, the fashion, entertainment and car industries, real estate and property management, travel, advertisement, literary publishing, pharmaceuticals, science, space travel, technology, energy, museums, archeology, the antiquity trade—everything.

How do they do it, you wonder?

Why through plain knowledge. All of the ancient texts that are missing from the Coptic canon they hold. Great words of wisdom and keys of truth that speak to the true destiny and power of man.

All forgotten and suppressed knowledge. Forbidden knowledge. The missing philosophies and ancient prophecy texts that are some of the most powerful literary weapons that exist in this known world.

Mystic truth hidden away in the darkness. The light of the world, kept buried under a bushel. Much that is good and pure they possess.

I'm one of the only Hounds who have taken an interest. I listen to the whispers, I gather my knowledge in pieces, and the more I spend in this undercity the more I realize that these men are evil. They seem to be human, but I wouldn't be surprised if they were dark angels working for Satan himself.

They are all white, varied in age, but none are younger than forty-five I would say. They speak English and I assume they are Americans, but one can't be certain.

When they see me they indicate a chair that is placed opposite a large man with a nose of steel. I call him Iron Nose and I try not to stare, for fear I might offend him. Is he deformed somehow? Or is it part of the mask he wears. Yes. They all wear masks so I cannot see their faces. And they are covered in robes of assorted colors.

Iron Nose speaks with a solid voice that booms. "As our guest you are welcome. Bow your head in prayer."

I bow my head and slit my eyes, keeping them open just enough to sneak furtive glances at them as they bow their heads and recite in unison, "Assassins of the truth seekers, killers of the people's joy, sons of the fathers and forefathers of the keepers of wisdom and divine knowledge. We pledge our honor to the brotherhood, the unbroken silence. Our temple is one created by our own hands, where the mysteries of the world are kept. Amen."

"Amen," I come in a few milliseconds behind them. The prayer was said hurriedly and I'm still processing the meaning, but impressively it's managed to frighten me.

Iron Nose speaks again. "It has come to our attention that you let a girl go recently."

"I did not let her go, my Lord."

"Don't call me that. Call me brother."

"Yes, brother. I did not let her go."

"Then what happened?"

"I was seen. By another girl. I could have taken her too. But she was hot with something. I couldn't get near her."

They exchange glances. "The Mistress Smyrna has requested a private council with you?"

"Oh?"

"You will be taken to Pilgrim's Island where she lives."

"Whatever you like me to do."

"It's not what I like you to do," he says sharply. "It's what she wants."

"Am I to go, your...brother?"

"Yes. But listen here. You aren't to tell her we called for you. But you are to do this. Report back everything she says."

"I'll do it."

"As you know you're in a precarious situation. We're aware you still remember."

"If I could only explain—"

"—Explain it to her. She has special sights and will be able to see if you're lying. She's magical, so beware. If she weren't magical we would have gotten rid of her already."

"I will explain it to her."

"She will report back to us, her findings. We will then decide if you live. But you will also be reporting back to us. Find out anything."

"Anything in particular?"

"That's not your concern. Just bring back everything she does and says. Got it?"

"Yes, brother."

"Now be gone."

East of Casino Strive is the sound that leads out to the Atlantic Ocean. But in a small inlet a quarter mile off shore lives an island maybe 100 square yards around. Upon this island is a stone mansion fit for a queen. And that is where I'm headed.

We go by rowboat, a Black Boot at the rickety helm.

At the pier we get out and cross over a drawbridge that leads us onto gravel and then dry land.

Servants swarm the foyer and down a marble staircase comes a woman both beautiful and ugly all at once.

Am I to bow?

I glance at the Black Boot who remains stone faced so I do the same.

"Good evening," she calls in a dark, sultry voice. "Samuel the Sweeper. So pleased to finally meet you."

Her eyes flash to the Black Boot. "Leave us."

He turns and goes and Mistress Smyrna leads me into a large study just off the foyer.

She takes a seat on a blush pink chaise and a bowl of fresh strawberries are placed beside her.

I take a seat on the couch across from her.

It seems like an eternity passes as she nibbles her red meat, all the while observing me intently. Finally she breaks the silence. "Do you know who I am, Samuel?"

"Mistress Smyrna."

"I am the woman who will judge if you are to live or die."

"I'm not afraid to die," I challenge, suddenly feeling brave. For some reason this woman makes me angry. What right does a woman have, to be in such power? I will not grovel before her the way I did with Iron Nose.

"You don't like a woman being in charge," she observes wryly.

"Women are made for other things."

"Like what? Making biscuits? Making babies?"

"Yes."

She throws her head back and laughter so ancient comes out of her mouth I almost shudder. "Babies I have made, but biscuits I'll leave to another."

"I know you're powerful."

"Oh? Who told you that?"

"No one. I can see it. You must be some kind of witch."

"Isn't that like every man to assume a woman who doesn't give a fuck and lives her life her own way is somehow possessed."

"So you don't have powers? Then maybe I'll just walk over to you now and snap your neck."

"No," she straightens. "I have powers. But I'm not a witch, so watch it." She can't help but hiss her warning and I recollect myself.

This woman chooses whether I live or die.

I bow my head in repentance. "It is only because I fear you're gonna kill me. Just tell me you won't and I'll be good."

"I'm sorry. I can't promise you."

"But why?"

"I've heard of your work in the Valley. And I must say I'm impressed."

"I aim to please."

"Let's cut to the chase. I know you're not loyal. It has proved evident by your reports. The potion only takes your memories away for a short while. You seem to be immune to the drug."

"What can I say?"

"As you know, that makes you a wild card. You could flip. Go back to the good side."

"I don't think you need to worry about that."

"And why is that?"

"Because I was there already. And I was helping. I was a psychoanalyst. After I met Gracie I went back and got my diploma. My job was helping people find their biggest and best truths. Their best selves. And do you know what I learned?"

"What is that?"

"They aren't capable."

If I'm not mistaken she almost looks disappointed, like I've confirmed a hidden fear. "Interesting."

"We're killing each other every day, the animals, the earth. What is there left for us to do to prove that we are all heathens?"

"Perhaps make amends. Return to justice."

"It will never happen."

"You hate everyone. Not just the poor and the weak,

because they remind you of yourself. But you hate the oppressors and the rich. You hate Cosimo. And the Brotherhood, and the people of this town. And even me."

"I am an equal opportunist when it comes to my hatred."

"Tell me why. And then I will decide if I can trust you."

"Okay. I'll tell you why. I often ponder how feared Christ was. What was he doing that made him such a threat that Pilate would go out of his way to see him killed? He wasn't claiming a crown, even though it was offered to him by the people. He wasn't asking for his face to be placed upon the emperor's coin. He was simply saving people's lives, healing people who were hurt and speaking about love. Why should any man have to die for that?"

"We know that kindness is always blotted out in the cruel world. The world we live in is not kind to kindness."

"Not just that, though Smyrna. It is deathly afraid of it. We weren't good enough to be saved. Not then, and definitely not now. When I look at the totality of humanity from beginning to present I see a world where all of the good things are crushed down and beaten. I see a vain and Godless world that doesn't deserve redemption, but deserves death. Once I really had a grip on just how far this world will go to blot out and ignore all the good things in it, a world that could rip a child out of it's mothers arms and…"

She must know about my boy. But witch or not, she realizes mentioning him will send me over the moon.

"...I decided to come and work for the dark side. I decided to work as fast as I can in making even more evil so to bring on the coming judgment that much sooner. Smyrna. I want to look at their stupid faces when it comes. I want to see them swallowed up by tsunamis, ripped to shreds by hurricane winds. And I'll be there laughing. And finally, before I'm swallowed up myself, I'll get to say to them, *See how stupid you were. You had the chance to do the right thing. Now you will pay. And everyone you love will pay. And I will watch you as you scream.*

"I hate this world, Smyrna, and everyone in it. That's why I steal their children. Not because I want to be rich and famous like the other Hounds. I could care less for any of that. I do it because they don't deserve anything as precious as a child. Nothing gives me more pleasure than to know I have taken away from them what was never rightfully theirs. And I am too fucking smart to forget. So don't ask me anymore why I still remember."

"They asked you to watch me, didn't they?"

She's as wise as I am; I don't have to answer the question. Wise people know how to speak without words. I walk over to her chaise and sit at the edge, reach over and pluck a strawberry from her plate. I place it between my teeth and smile.

She smiles back by a glint in her eye and by these two

insignificant gestures we have become friends. (Or at least interested in each other enough to see where our relationship might lead us.)

I already know her story from the gossiping minxes. From what I've gleaned, she's in love with the Corpse. Whispers tell me she was once his slave, but he fell in love with her and she bore him a child. His death was sudden, maybe he was killed—I'm not sure—and she was able to use some magical book to keep him alive. Some say the book is written in ancient tongue and since she is of a line of the sorcerers who had something to do with making the book indestructible, she has the powers to read the ancient language. I'm assuming the hidden knowledge that the brotherhood possesses is mostly in this book and because she is the only one who can read it, they have to keep her alive. She has been blessed with eternal youth—that part I haven't figured out yet—and she also has the power to keep Cosimo Medici alive. Apparently the Brotherhood wants him back, because he was the greatest ruler to ever live and they will use him when the time comes to take over the world. He will be what they call the Final Emperor and they will be his council. But apparently they need some kind of crown. I haven't mentioned it yet, because I don't think anyone is supposed to know. For now, I'll keep it a secret.

She puts the plate down and leans back on her chaise. The way she leans her head back makes her unbecoming but also stirs my loins. She blows through her mouth like a horse, her pursed lips purring. "I hate the fucking waiting game."

Soldier Sonny

One of the laughing girls tosses a magazine at me. Maxim. A girl is on the front and I hate it already. I throw it back at her. "I don't look at those things. I don't look at magazines anymore. Sometimes I like to go to the library downtown and sit where it's warm. I used to love reading the magazines, but I can't even look at them anymore. They're mean to everyone. To everyone who looks at them. The women pasted to the front, in their bras and underwear. It sickens me, what they do to women.

"That's not what a woman is. Someone just to make your thoughts go low. Down to the dungeon. She's not just something to take to bed, put nasty thoughts inside your head. She's someone to pull a chair out for and place a homemade meal in front of. A meal you cooked for her special.

"She's someone to put thoughts of children inside your head. Children reading books with flashlights under the covers and running into your room during a thunderstorm.

"A woman is supposed to make you have higher intentions. Want to be better. To love more, to cry more, to help more. That's what a woman is. That's her purpose on this earth. Looking upon the vision of a woman, it's a sacred thing. A thing from God. A thing to bring you to your knees and make you pray.

"I can't stand it, this mean sickness all around me. I don't like these men saying that horrible word, bitch."

"Wasn't your momma a bitch?" Mo says.

"I can't even go to the free movies at the library anymore. There's stuff in those movies you know. Like arsenic. If you swallow it it makes you sick. Bad images of people fucking without love. I don't want to fuck without love."

"I do," the girl says and they laugh.

"I just want to be a good person now. I had to walk away from a starving child in Iraq. I had to walk away from him."

The girl comes over and wants to sit on my lap. I don't let her.

"Come on," she says. "I can make it better."

"Let her sit down," Mo orders. He made me come

here to Rita's Tavern. He made me come. I used to come here with him and treat the girls bad. Before I went to Iraq. But I don't want to come with him anymore. He's mad at me. Mo don't like what I just said. But Mo doesn't understand that I can't help these things anymore. The truth things that just come out. I see the world now, for what it is. Before I was blind, but now I see, and what I see, it horrifies me.

"You should be a lady," I tell her.

"I am a lady. More than you'll ever know. Come on baby. Let me sit."

"Get away from me!" I yell and I push her away.

She falls to the floor and I know I wasn't supposed to do that. I start to cry. "I just wanna go home. I just wanna go home. I just wanna go home."

Mo gets up and walks toward me. I know what he's gonna do now. He's gonna hurt me real bad. He's gonna hurt me and make it end.

He rolls up his sleeves and lifts me off my chair. "You're a dumb motherfucker."

"I just wanna go home," I tell him.

"Crying like a little bitch."

"Take me home, Mo."

"Alright. I'll take you home."

Stori

I knew it. That night I had to tape my father up there next to Ben. I knew it without really knowing. He was not going to be coming back to us. He was never coming home.

Yet still, I put him up there. Even then it felt so much more than just a headstrong effort. It felt like a finalization. A submitting to God's plan. I was allowing my father to die. And accepting my new responsibility. To take up the quest, right where he left off. To find the dungeon, discover the pure evil that lives. To walk away from him, when I had a chance to kill his captors and set him free.

I couldn't kill, daddy. I'm sorry but I couldn't kill.

I sit here now at my kitchen table, unwrapping the gift my mother left for me. I open the box and pull it out—a golden locket in the shape of a house. Inside, all four of us

357

together.

Someone is yelling in the street below. It's the only sound, for the world still sleeps. "Soldier Sonny! Found him up in Soda Can! Head bashed in!"

Nothing comes as a surprise anymore.

But I long for revelation.

I need to know what to do next. For I know the truth and knowing truth requires action. Shouting it out in the street like that idiot won't get me anywhere. The voices of those deemed crazy are never heard.

I have to use my silence now to make the next move, so I simply bow my head and run my palms across the kitchen table.

I hear the voice of Caroline. "He will rid the world of every kitchen table."

The sun is rising. It's spilling over the windowsills, a bright glowing orange. How I would love to just sit here forever like this, in the silence of the sleeping Valley, with the ticking of the clock my only friend.

My bones are already weary and the journey has just begun. I reach out and place two fingers around a pussy willow bud. I rub it gently, thankful for its smooth velvet. "How pretty you are," I tell it. "How perfect and pretty."

I've memorized his letter by now. I read it back to myself in my mind.

Dear Family,

Goodbye. I am never coming back. Forget me and move on. I have a credit of $14.65 at the bakery. Oh, And you better bless the kitchen table when Easter comes.

Love,
Frank

    The kitchen table.

    The kitchen table.

    Yes! The kitchen table!

    I look down and see the edges of his scratches. I move the wrapping paper aside and no longer see the mess my mother cursed my father out for, but a sign. This is what it reads: *The Crown of Final Sight is with the one who holds the most Ginger Ales.*

    The kitchen chair clatters to the floor as I stand. In my room I stuff Amanda in my backpack and set off without saying goodbye to Regina or my mother.

In Soda Can Alley the Dobermans are loose, rummaging through litter by the trash cans. They spot me coming and brace, with tails darted like daggers. They snarl. They're headed my way but I'm headed somewhere else. I rush up on him. He turns around unexpecting, but he doesn't have time to take a swing. I am prostrate at his feet with my head bowed to the ground.

"Forgive me," I say in a language altogether new yet somehow a part of me.

"Huh? What you doing? You crazy or something? Get up off the ground girl."

"Forgive me. For my judgments. For my blindness. Oh keeper of the crown forgive your sister this day."

A gentle hand comes to my shoulder and Charley lifts me back to standing. "Shhhh! Speak English." Then he leads me to the garbage cans where the Dobermans are. He shooes them off with slaps and kicks and they trot away whimpering in dejection.

Behind the garbage bins we are out of sight. "Tell me, how did you know about the crown?"

"My father gave it to you, didn't he?"

"Did he tell you?"

"No. I had to figure it out myself."

He's displeased. "No one is supposed to know. Do you know what this could mean? If the wrong people found out?"

"I know what it means. I know Cosimo is looking for it. He has my father. Trapped under the city. He knows my father's a Brave. He's using children also, to grow his powers stronger. I don't think he can walk right now."

"My God. My God."

"It's true Charley."

"How did you know the ancient tongue?"

"The prophet Caroline up on the hill, she helped me.

She helped me learn about who I really am and the powers I have."

"Have you told anyone?"

"No."

"You musn't."

"I won't."

He looks about him once again and then quietly and carefully opens his many red cloaks.

And there it is. In all its glory.

My breath goes out of me. It is pure gold and inlaid with blue stones all around. The blue is a color I've never seen before.

As I look upon it I see four rivers flowing out of one, I see a man with a black beard dozing against the trunk of an oak. I see a garden. It is beautiful. I feel a breeze. A soft and loving breeze. I know forgiveness in this moment. "Thank you. I have never seen anything quite as beautiful. I don't know why, but this crown gives me great peace." I look at him. "What do we do now?"

"It must go back, to the Tower of Babel. You must find the portal. I will have it in the meantime. No one will ever look for it here. I have placed it only a few times upon my head, Stori, and believe me its powers are mighty. I saw everything. All of the mysteries of this world were revealed to me. I saw so much that I can't even remember anymore. I suppose I even saw you being here in this moment, because with the crown on my head, I was able to escape the confinement of time. I was able to see the past and the future as well. But as soon as I took it off, I lost most of it."

"Put it back on," I tell him. "You'll be able to see where the portal is."

"Never. It's too powerful. The evil in me feeds off of it. It's dangerous on the head of anyone but our Lord. Go. You must go. See the prophetess Caroline and have her help you find the portal."

"You will be okay?"

"Yes. Now hurry. I will be fine."

"Wait. One more thing." I pull Amanda out of my backpack. "Give her to that little girl who runs around here with her brother."

Charley takes Amanda and slides out from the shadows.

No sooner do I dart out of the bins than I see my uncle Joe running toward me with his arms flailing above his head. "No! Stori! No!" Suddenly Mo is standing in front of me. I hear a whooshing sound right next to my head, and then before I know it, lights out.

Priscilla Van Patten

I don't know where to go. Who can I turn to? Who can I tell? I can't call Grace 'cause I'll just hear how horrible I am for starting a new life and leaving my old one behind. I can't tell Trish or any of her friends 'cause they're like vultures swarming above my head, waiting for this relationship to drop dead so they can dive down for their long awaited feast.

Fuck it. I'll just get in my car and trust as I shift into drive the car will take me where I need to go.

It takes me to the Valley.

I lock up and walk a block and a half to Rita's Tavern. Rita is at the counter organizing little stacks of forks and knives over a linen napkin. I don't have time to make her like me. I just need to tell her what's on my heart. "Where is everybody?" I ask.

"Cleared out. You don't want to know." She looks like hell too. "What's wrong with you?" she asks. "It's four in the morning."

"Look," I tell her in terror holding out my ring.

She drops her fork and comes over to me. She lifts my fingers into the light and her mouth falls open. "Damn girl," she breathes. "Now that's what I call a rock."

"It's freaking huge."

She looks up and registers my distress. She frowns. "He's rich huh?" she asks.

I nod.

"And he's handsome I bet."

"He's gorgeous."

"And people like him and he's a lot of fun. And he's mysterious and keeps you on your toes and makes you crazy jealous."

"Yes! How did you know?"

"Honey. I been around the block more than once."

I like this lady. With a little styling advice and some microdermabrasion I bet you she would even pass for pretty.

She pours me a drink. "This one's on the house."

I down half of it in two big gulps.

She shakes her head and chuckles. "Chasing a stray bullet. Can't say I haven't done it myself."

"Did you ever catch him?"

"Few times."

"And?"

"My whole world came crashing right down. Thought I would go spinning out into the beyond and never come back. But I stayed strong and learned that chasing a man I don't love is just a way to chase the one I did. My father. I had to let go of him. You know. My father. Before I could start wanting to be with the right man. Well don't feel bad honey if you don't like him back."

"He doesn't just like me. He wants to marry me!"

"Oh honey." Then she does something unexpected. She comes around the bar and wraps her arms around me. She presses my head into her bosom. She is as soft as butter and I never want to leave her embrace.

"I miss my father," I tell her. "I want to go home."

She spends a little time just rocking me back and forth and says. "You got a broken heart girl. And some man out there has the kind of love to fix it."

Later in the day I stop at the da Vinci School of Arts for Children and ask to speak with Janice.

I'm brought into an empty studio where Janice is sorting through some CDs in the middle of the floor. She looks up and smiles, "Hello Miss Van Patten. Back again?"

"I just stopped by to see if there was anyone who could answer a few of my questions."

Janice looks alarmed. "Is everything okay. Are any of

my babies hurt?"

"No," I assure her. "I'm sort of here on unofficial business. It's not a specific case."

"The police were already here last year asking about the Baks. I told you that already."

"Yes. I know."

"I wish there were something we could do. To help them. But I guess it's true what they say. If you don't find a missing child within the first 45 minutes..." Her voice trails off and she picks up a CD and just holds it.

"I get sick just thinking about it."

"I do too."

I peek at the CD she's holding. Glière. "I work with children too," I remind her. "Although I don't get to ever dance with them."

"You're missing out," she tells me. "There's a light they give off. When they're dancing. It's a real live thing. And if you open yourself up to it, you can actually take some of it for yourself." She stands up and looks at me. "Do you really love them?" she asks.

"Love?"

"Yes. I love my children. Do you love yours?"

"I try not to. But it never seems to work, Janice."

She grabs me by the hand and says, "Come with me."

Down two halls we turn a corner to an alcove with a door in it. She brings me to the door and says, "I was sworn to secrecy. They came and told me I would lose my job, my apartment, everything."

"Who?"

"Never mind." She takes out a key from her back pocket and slips it in the door. She opens the door and stands back.

Inside are instruments. Some are sitting lifeless on the ground. But others—a harp, a clarinet, a cigar box guitar—are floating in the air, playing some kind of strange yet sweet symphony.

"I think I need to sit down," I tell her. "I don't feel so good."

"They want the children," she whispers. "They won't stop playing until they get them."

I get a text and somehow I know it's not going to be good. It's Bill. The text reads: *A Putzarella was just picked up for trespassing.*

Stori

I'm sitting in the passenger seat of Miss Van Patten's car with a duffle bag of clothes at my feet, watching downtown Redemption sail by. I just spent the night in a juvenile detention holding cell. My eye is bruised from Mo but thankfully the puffing went down and it didn't close. Priscilla is taking me to Pilgrim's Island and a police car tails closely behind.

"I wish you would talk to me about what happened at the casino."

I don't answer her, just stare out the window. Sonny's dead. My father and mother aren't too far behind.

She's leaned forward, with both hands tightly gripped to the steering wheel. "What could have possessed you to break in there like that? Don't you know the world is under surveillance? Are you that dumb? Were you trying to steal something? And where did you get that gun?"

She's talking to me kind of like how my mother does after I've gotten suspended from school for fighting, or when she finds out I've been at the Cage.

"What are you gonna do?" I ask her. "Ground me?" I don't have the energy anymore. I'm giving up.

"You seem awfully calm for someone who's going to an orphanage. Just talk to me, okay. Tell me why you snuck in there?"

I look at her and note she's been through some kind of duress herself. She's changed. Broken down and scattered. Like a falling house of cards, she's falling and going every which way. "What happened to you?" I ask more for spite than for curiosity. That's when I see the ring. I smirk and say, "Oh. Now I see. Congratulations."

"Listen, you. I don't have time for your wise ass remarks about my so called phony life."

"And I don't have time anymore to care. So don't worry. I've got more important things to do. Like go to this orphanage and die."

"Please. Tell me. Stori. Look at me. I'm the only one now, who can help you. Your little sister, I tried to get her in here with you, but they refused it. I managed to get her into the convent, but she's gonna go crazy without you and your mother. If there's something you're not telling me, like someone forced you to go in there against your will, you have to tell me now. You just have to trust me."

Maybe I should. Regi is all alone and still needs me. What if she's waiting for me at the meeting place? "You didn't believe me about the mayor. You won't believe me about anything else. That's for sure."

Even though her blouse is perfectly creased from shoulder to wrist and her black pencil skirt has not one fleck of lint clung to it, her face and what is behind it exposes a heaping pile of mess. For the first time, I get nervous she might be giving up on me. That's what I wanted though, all this time, isn't it?

Maybe she senses my anxiety for she says, "Listen. That's it. I can't do this anymore. I'm gonna walk away from you, Stori. You have no idea what I've put myself through ever since I took on your case. You have no idea how it's effected me, my relationships, everything. And for what? You tell me. What have I been losing sleep every night for? A girl that will never open up to me in a thousand light years?"

We pull into a gate by the sound. Priscilla shows a security guard her city badge and he buzzes us in. We stop at a dock where a guard is waiting. She throws the car in park and looks at me. "I'll be back tonight for the fundraiser, but after that I don't know how often I'll be able to see you. So if you're gonna talk, you better do it now."

Here goes nothing. "I broke in there because there's a

hidden prison under the casino. The mayor was there. And so was Cosimo the Corpse and this woman who might be his queen. They have my father prisoner. And all of the missing children from the city. They're looking for a crown and I know where it is and if they find it they're going to start a new world order and take over all of Redemption."

She's stunned, the way the girls get in the Cage when I knock their brains into their skulls. "Say something," I tell her.

The guard patiently laces his hands in front of him.

Priscilla rolls my window down. "Hi. We just need a few minutes please. Is that possible?"

He nods.

Priscilla puts a hand on my thigh. "Stori. I'm going to confess something to you too. I take medication, for a condition similar to yours. Well it's depression. I've learned to live with my illness. I've learned to medicate myself; I fight it. I should have told you this earlier, Stori, but I didn't. I see myself in you. The old me, the one that was scared and never thought she could amount to anything. But there's a life out there, sweetie. One of opportunity and success and happiness. You can become something. You can become, well, *me*."

It's funny. While she's sitting there feeling sorry for me, I'm now sitting here feeling sorry for her. Not only is she lost trying to be someone she's not, she's denying a part of herself that longs to be her old self again. The better self.

Maybe all this time it was *me* who was supposed to be helping her. Not the other way around. "It's not a hallucination," I say unwavering. "I got to know a lot of this stuff because I have powers. Give me your hands. I'll show you."

She hesitates but then finally gives me her hands.

I stare deep into her eyes and let the information come. "Your father used to sing a song to you to get you to go to sleep."

"What?"

"Your father, the one from Erie."

"Who told you I was from Erie?"

"I know things. I'm a Brave. I'll tell you about it later."

She snaps her hands out of mine, but it's too late. I've seen everything I need to see.

"Don't ever talk about my father again," she says crisply.

"He was sweet to you in the early years, but addiction got the best of him. A lot of it wasn't his fault. But you blame him."

"Where are you pulling this from?"

"Your boss, his name is Bill."

"He told you?"

"No. I'm talking about something else now. Your boss."

"What about him?"

"Have you been to the office?"

"No."

She's confused. "What about Bill?"

"Bill doesn't make much small talk. He's very serious about his job. He's kind of boring to be honest. But every once in a while he comes into your office to ask you about a case, or how things are going. Sometimes he tells you you're doing a great job." I pause to see if she's listening.

Stone quiet.

"You wait for those moments. Because when Bill gives you a compliment, you want to giggle." I stop again. Wait for a response.

Still silence.

"Your boyfriend, Nate—that's his name right?—does not ever praise you and when he does, it is for superficial things. And even if he did, he wouldn't make you wanna giggle the way Bill does. But Bill is much older than you. And you are so afraid of what people will think you will never let him see you smile when he tells you you're doing a good job."

"What are you? Some kind of mind reader?"

"No. I'm a number in your file cabinet. I'm about to be dropped inside of a drawer and closed forever."

"I've never looked at you like that."

"You haven't?"

"Tell me how you came up with those things. That, by the way, are completely untrue."

"Why Miss Van Patten. I'm surprised. All this time

you've been spending in Redemption. All the studies you've done. Did you not know that there are Braves here?"

She tucks a stray lock of hair behind her ear. "You're trying to avoid the subject. The subject of your hallucinations."

"No. I'm not. I'm not afraid anymore like you are. I'm not ashamed of me. The real me that I was born to be. I haven't stuffed her behind a locked door and threw away the key. And you are jealous of me because of that."

Priscilla turns the car off and gets out. "That's it. I'm done." She comes over to the passenger side and opens my door. "I warned you, you had one last chance. I knew you would just use it to take one last final dig at me. Get out."

I get out and she immediately goes back to the driver's side. She gets inside and starts to drive off, leaving me there all by myself. But then the car comes to an abrupt halt. She gets out again and marches back to me. "What is Bill thinking?"

"He's embarrassed and doesn't think he would ever have a shot with you."

"So he likes me?"

"He doesn't like you, dummy. He loves you. He won't ask you out though. You have to make the first move."

"Damn it." And she storms off again.

As she drives away, something unexpected happens. I am scared without her next to me. I don't want her to leave.

A row boat takes me over. Two men who look like marines effortlessly sail us to the looming stone mansion in the middle of the sound. I'm sure as soon as I step foot inside the colossal mansion, I'll be locked in a closet and starved, or waterboarded, or beaten with a stick. But it's to my surprise that Mistress Smyrna, the woman I saw in the dungeon with my father, greets me with a kiss on each cheek and has me personally escorted by one of her million attendants to the west wing where, behind frosted doors with little swirly designs on them, there's a full spa and beauty salon.

There, a swarm of women surround me and strip off all my clothes. I try to cover my private parts but they don't seem to notice my embarrassment or maybe they just don't care. They put me in a steaming hot shower, where I'm scrubbed and sponged until I begin to fear that if I keep getting scrubbed my skin will go raw.

Out of the shower I'm covered in a plush cotton robe secured tightly around my waist and am then escorted into a hair salon. There my hair is shampooed and conditioned before I'm placed before the stylist. She takes a good hour of drying, teasing, powdering, spraying and fastening to make my hair look like it was thrown in a messy ball at the top of my head.

But everyone seems to love it, telling me how I have the most adorable little heart shaped face and how delicate my neck is and how I should put my hair in an updo more often.

In the dressing room are racks of dresses of various styles, colors and sizes. I only try on one. A one shoulder plum prom dress with crystal embellishments and a slit up the front. I think it's a little too small and I complain that when I take a deep breath my ribs hurt. They laugh and say something about beauty being pain and then drag me into yet another room to have my makeup done. As I sit and look into the mirror, watching the cosmetologist who smells like tic-tacs paint my face from plain to pretty, I want to ask what I'm getting ready for.

I want to, but I don't. Because I'm scared of the answer.

The red dining room is as elegant as it is spotless. The knives and forks glint brilliantly under the crystal chandelier and the linen napkins are freshly starched. Tonight we feast on roasted duck and red beet salad. When the duck is served by one of the many maids who scamper back and forth around this mansion, I take note of its golden brown color. They obviously have a chef who knows what he's doing. I might as well enjoy a good meal before I make my next plan, I tell myself.

Ernestine sits by my side and she leans in and whispers. "Isn't the mistress beautiful?"

I've already decided that I'm going to kill her tonight; I

should have done it when I had the chance. But I can't let Ernestine know. "She is indeed. Ern. Are you okay? I haven't been able to talk to you since that last time when you were sick."

"I'm fine now," she says smiling. I can't tell if she's faking it or not. "Really. It's not that bad here. As long as you don't go snooping. Everyone is really, really nice."

The Mistress looks at me and smiles. "Well, Stori. I just wanted to tell you how happy we are to have you here."

"Thank you, Mistress," I reply politely.

She's pleased. Nothing about her looks like she's not really human.

"Girls," she says. "I have some very exciting news. AMC has contacted the mayor about doing a reality show here at the mansion. A few of the representatives will even be here tonight at the fundraiser. Please remember that you are to be on your very best behavior. Remember that our image is everything. And just think, we might be famous soon! They think it would be a great story. A family like us. Now what does everybody think?"

The table breaks out in excited chatter at the possibility of instant fame.

The mayor comes in and sits and seems to have eyes only for me. He's looking me up and down and I curse the very existence of this dress. I can feel his eyes all over me. It's like a slimy slug sliding up my arms, over my face and down my neck to my very visible cleavage. *Let me feel you,* I hear Richie say. I want to stand up and ask him "What the hell do you think you're looking at you perverted little creep!" I would, and with great satisfaction, but where would it lead me? Back to juvenile detention I'm sure. It seems that since I've started this journey Caroline has sent me on my strength and prowess, which have served me so well over the past few years, are of no use anymore. I have to find a new way to get over on people and this is not going to be easy.

Silence is the first thing I try. I sit there uncomfortably, nibbling on a piece of white meat, waiting for him to get distracted and look away. But he doesn't. He's obviously quite smitten.

"Stori Putzarella." He rolls the name around in his mouth like it's something on the menu. "It's your first night here, am I correct?"

"Yes, Mayor Vaughn."

He laughs weakly and says, "Don't be silly. Please call me Damon."

"Yes, Damon. It's my first night here."

"I understand your father went missing some weeks back. I'm very sorry to hear that." He lifts his wine glass and a girl in a white frilly apron steps forward and fills it from a crystal carafe.

"Yes."

"Any word on his whereabouts?" His voice has raised

a few octaves and his eyebrows are peaked with interest. I know he's fishing for something. He obviously knows I was arrested for being inside the casino after hours. Is it possible that he knows I found the hidden passage?"

"No," I tell him. "I'm afraid it doesn't look so good for my family."

"Well, I'm sorry to hear that. But you can be rest assured that we will be more of a family to you here than anywhere else they might have placed you. Mistress Smyrna is like a mother to these girls. And I have taken a very personal pride in this establishment. I have great hopes for everyone. And feel it's my duty to get to know each and every one of you personally."

I look to some of the other girls. They're all watching me with a look on their faces that says, "Oh shit. Is she in for a surprise."

Ernestine looks me straight in the face. I look back at her. We don't have to say anything, because we're family. I know what she's telling me. *Just remember the good days, Stori. Just leave your body and focus on that.* I don't want to imagine what it would feel like to have this creepy man's hands all over my body. And I can't see myself allowing him to touch me. I will break every finger he owns and tell him to like it. The fumes are rising again, and I have to remember if I blow my fuse I will also potentially blow my cover. I am the unassuming dumb girl who gets bullied into breaking into casinos at night to avoid getting beaten up.

Does he believe me? Has Priscilla Van Patten spoken to him and blown my cover? I won't know just yet. All I do know is that he is very interested in me.

I long for someone to pinch me and wake me from this nightmare.

The Butler appears and says, "Excuse me, Mistress Smyrna. There is a young man who came over by speed boat. He's at the door. And he refuses to go away."

"Who is it, Tyler?"

"He says his name is Tony Carp. And he's here to see Miss Putzarella."

The Mistress looks at the mayor.

The mayor puts his napkin to his mouth with both hands and blots his lips. He passes a glance in my direction and then smiles. "Well of course. We would expect this kind of thing on a first night. Please have him come in. We'll send Stori into the parlor to meet him."

Tony is sitting on the edge of a low back leather sofa. He looks up as I enter and stands. The parlor is grand but not grand enough for him. He looks ten feet tall in his black hoodie and his unlaced timberlands planted firmly on the rug. Just because I hate him, doesn't mean I can't marvel at his beauty.

As I get closer, I can see his eyes going over my dress. I can't help but wonder what he's thinking. Does he like what he sees? Does he even recognize me?

But what does it matter? He's nothing to me anymore.

Absolutely nothing. "Hi Tony."

He doesn't bother to say hi back. "Oh my God. What happened to your eye? Are you okay?" His face is all drawn and serious, like he's really worried about me.

It hurts just looking at him. Knowing I love him and he doesn't love me back. I tell myself I will not cry. I will not crumble into a slobbering mess. Is this what love is? A pain that almost feels like pleasure. A deep yearning unfulfilled. Do I only love him because I cannot have him?

"It's nothing."

"Who hit you?" His nostrils flare and his fists ball up like he's ready to fight. "Who the fuck hit you?"

"It's a long story, but it's over now."

He's at a loss for words. What can he say now? He turned his back on me and it's over. He shakes his head as if in denial and then says, "Where did you get this dress?"

"The Mistress gave it to me,"

"Why are you dressed like this?"

"They wanted to make me look nice, because of this fundraiser they're having in a few hours."

"I've never seen you with your hair up," he says. "And in a dress." Even though he's pissed off, his lips are fighting a smile. "You look really nice."

"Well thank you. That's very encouraging."

"Would you stop talking to me like that. Like we hardly know each other. It's me."

"Listen, I'm sorry I've been so rude to you lately. It

wasn't right of me."

"No. That's what you don't understand. It wasn't right of me. To hurt you."

I put a hand up to stop him. "I was just hurt, Tony, because I like you. Or I thought I did. And when you didn't like me back, I was too immature to deal with it." I want to cry again, because what I'm about to say is shameful. "Everybody calls me crazy in the Valley. I know they do."

"That's not true."

"You would not want to be the guy who's dating the crazy girl. And you shouldn't have to be. The hallucinations I get have been a curse my entire life. But I'm okay with them now. And some of them I don't even think are hallucinations anymore. Some of them are real. So yes, I am crazy, and I'm okay with that. But—"

"—Please, Stori. I'll do anything. Just tell me what I need to do."

As hurt as I am by him, and as much as I hate him, I want to bury myself inside his strong embrace. And I know he'll let me, despite his love for Desma.

But I don't. I have to be strong. I have to get through this on my own. "You're not responsible for me."

"But I am. I feel like a brother to you."

I do need him. I need him more than I have ever needed him in my life, but I also know I have to let him go so he can be with the one he loves. And I'm done with the guilt trips. I'm done with the anger. I don't want to make him feel bad anymore. It's just not in me. "I'll be fine here," I lie. "The Mistress Smyrna will take good care of me. And you have to focus on your career now, Tony. And Desma. And starting a new life. You deserve that. I know you do. Desma's a nice girl."

"Something's not right about this place. Why does the mayor only have girls here? And all of you teenagers? You don't know guys like I do, Stor. You don't know the things that they can be thinking. About innocent girls like you. I'll get you out. I won't let anything happen to you."

"Don't," I tell him. I walk over to the window facing the garden and look out into the frosty night. The sky is lit up with stars. I think about the Crown of Final Sight and my father locked away in a cold dungeon about to die. I think about Ben and his little sister. I think about Sonny. "Tony Carp. I never imagined my life would take a turn like this. I always believed somehow things would turn out different for me." I'm aware that everything spoken is probably being listened to. I turn to him and say, "You better go."

"But I..."

"It's okay," I tell him. "Go and live your life. Go Tony. Just go."

PriscillaVanPatten

I won't look at her. She's over there by the band, with some of the other girls. I really tried to help. But all she did was judge me. I'm done.

But look at her!

My God. She looks beautiful. Like a grown woman. Like a million bucks. That's what I was trying to tell her all this time. There's a girl under there, Stori. One who's classy, sophisticated, a girl who can put on a cocktail gown and command the attention of the entire room. Don't sell yourself short, girl. Don't think you have to pledge allegiance to the Valley for the rest of your life. Look what the Valley did to you. It left you to fend for yourself, to raise yourself because your parents were too broken to be there for you. If I did it, Stori, you can too. God. Get that awful look off your face! Like you don't want to be here. Like this is the end of your life or something. The mayor is not who you say he is. He's an upright man. He's making this city better. It's all that conspiracy talk that goes on in the Valley that's getting to you.

But how did she know all that stuff? My feelings for Bill. I haven't spoken a word to anyone and she knew details. I don't know. I don't have the answers anymore to anything. Maybe she had some weird psychic moment or maybe she just guessed. But what she said about the mayor and Cosimo and her father and the kids under the city is just too far out there for me.

I'm sick and tired of this job. I think I need a vacation. Matter of fact, I think I need to retire. Some of the older girls told me this would happen. "You'll get burnt out," they said. "It happens to every social worker. There comes a time when you feel so stretched thin that you can't even get out of bed in the morning." That's how I feel now. I'm stretched thin and I just want to give up.

Maybe on everything. I know I'm wearing his ring, and Nate is still the best thing that's ever happened to me. But who am I kidding? I can't keep up with him. All of his dinner parties and Wall Street pals, and Trish and her blood thirsty entourage swarming over our heads wherever we go—I'm starting to feel like I just can't do it anymore. Stori is right. I'm just a wannabe. I may look and act the part to critical acclaim, but deep down inside I'm still from the gutter. How does the saying go again?—you can take the child out of the jungle but you can't take the jungle out of the child. That's me.

I've decided on it. I'm a failure.

I even failed at being a social worker. I came into this thinking I was going to change so many lives and intervene on young children falling into the pit of hopelessness. I guess I was doing it to redeem my own past—take control of it, place it all into those neat orderly files. But my efforts were fruitless. Stori might have on that nice dress, but who am I kidding? She's never going to stop being the cold bully she is and never going to stop having those episodes of paranoia.

Life is so fucking unfair.

The fifteen year old girl, Destiny, wears lavender chiffon and Swarovski barrettes in her hair. She comes up the wide white marble staircase of the mansion's great room and faces the magician at the podium. The magician is hosting the fundraiser and has been doing mediocre magic tricks for the past hour. He looks down fondly at Destiny as she comes up the stairs. He hands her a microphone, "And here is Destiny. Destiny please tell us about what the Pilgrim's Island Girls Home means to you."

The spectators gaze on the girl, quietly taking sips from their champagne glasses.

"My name is Destiny Sperance," she says. She looks nervous and I'm waiting with baited breath for her to continue. It's torture watching someone have to speak in public, knowing how uncomfortable they are. Just when I think she might drop the microphone and run out of the room she goes on. "I used to live in the Hills. My father worked at the die factory by the sound. But when he got sick he couldn't work no more. My mother tried her best to provide, but she's disabled. We lost our house. We didn't have nowhere to go and I was scared…" Her voice trails off. She's thinking maybe, of what to say next. Or is it that there's something she wants to say but can't. She looks almost frightened. She glances to Mistress Smyrna who fires a venomous look at her. She swallows, clears her throat and continues. "But Mayor Vaughn came and visited me at the shelter. He promised my parents that he would give me a safe place to live. It was hard for them to let me go, but they knew I would have a better future if I lived here at the home. I never dreamed it would be this beautiful. Mayor Vaughn has saved my life."

The spectators give a collective and sustained Aww.

The magician puts his hand on the back of Destiny's head and says, "Well thank you, Destiny. Why don't we hear what Mayor Vaughn has to say about your experience?"

The room claps proudly.

Mayor Vaughn takes the microphone. I roll my eyes. Another speech? This guy loves hearing the sound of his own voice. "Thank you, thank you. It's been quite a busy week. As all of you know the grand opening of Strive was just two days ago…" He doesn't have to cue the audience for them to start cheering. "Thank you, thank you," he says basking under their adoration. "Please. I'm not done. Oh, you're too kind, but really…" They're still clapping and he takes a bow and they clap some more. Finally it quiets down enough for him to speak again. "Ahhh, my fine people of Redemption. It's been a crazy ride. It really has. Getting Strive erected was nothing less than a miracle for this town. But Redemption is a city of miracles I believe. Yes. Miracles. Here in Redemption the impossible becomes possible. The unattainable becomes attained. The too far out beyond our wildest dreams becomes reality. And do you know why?" He points into the crowd at someone. Everyone looks to see who it is. But then he points somewhere else. And then somewhere else. Then he runs his finger in zigzags all across the room. "It is because of you. Redemption's finest. Your sacrifices, your contributions, your willingness to commit yourself to service—those are the miracles. You see, all you have to do is believe. Believe. And dreams really do come true. But we cannot forget the least of us. For has is not been said that 'What you do to the least of them you do to me?'

"This home here is just as important to me as any of my other projects in Redemption. In fact, if you want in a little secret, it just might be the closest to my heart. You see, I was raised to never forget about the little people. I was taught by my mother, God rest her soul, that the little people have a place too here in Redemption. And as hard as we work to make this place a monument to go down in history, we cannot forget those who have fallen on hard times. Those like Destiny. Those like the other girls you have had the pleasure of meeting tonight. Let's give them something they have never had before. Our compassion, our generosity. Let's teach them good things. Let's lead them by the hand into the future and show them that they can take each and every step with honor and pride. This home is a place where these girls have access to all the things they never did in the Hills or the Valley. I believe many of these faces are going to be prominent ones in Redemption's future. You will see their faces again. And the next time you do, you will be able to say, 'I was a part of that story. I believed in her and took a chance. And look how she has not failed me.'"

The crowd gives a roaring applause. Some of them, putting their champagne glasses to the floor.

"So how about it?" the magician says. "How about we join in on Destiny's story and become a part of her success too? Now it's that time in our live auction where we will give all of you a chance to contribute. Now is the time for our first paddle call. I would like to see how many of you can contribute one hundred dollars." Please, raise your paddles high. I see one, two, three four, woahhhh! Too many to count. Yes! Yes! That's right. Please, sir, keep yours up. Please wait and someone will come over and take your information and most generous contribution. It is much appreciated folks."

I take a sip of my champagne and watch as Nate lifts his paddle high up into the air. Jerry does the same. An attendant comes to them with a pen and paper. The mayor is off in a corner with the Redemption Press.

I'm standing with a group of wives, including Deb and the mayor's wife. Mistress Smyrna strides over. She wears a long sequence gown that lets out a moderate but fascinating train at her heels. It drags on the floor behind her. "This is a wonderful event, is it not?" she comments coolly.

I only smile. I'm trying not to have a nervous breakdown and not do what I always do—let my emotions get the best of me and say things I know I'll regret later.

I nod over to Stori. "Stori looks lovely. She's mine," I tell her.

"Oh?"

"Yes. I worked her case for a while before she came here. She's quite special. I hope you'll take good care of her. You will won't you?"

"But of course."

"Don't put too much pressure on her at first. She doesn't like that."

"Of course, dear. Of course."

Mistress Smyrna turns her attention to Deb and the

mayor's wife. "My two beauties. Do tell me. When are we going to have another one of those delicious little girl retreats again?"

"Oh," Deb complains. "I am so in need of a vacation, you have no idea. Jerry and I just came back from the Dominican, and already I've been bugging him for a weekend at the Keys."

"You should do it," the mayor's wife says, "The Keys are my absolute favorite. My husband's too."

"You have impeccable taste. As does he. I do believe your husband is the best thing that ever happened to Redemption."

Oh shit. Here it comes. "Nobody even likes him," I say. "They're all just faking,"

They twist their heads and blink simultaneously.

"Excuse me?" Mistress Smyrna replies.

"I said everyone here is so fucking fake. They don't even like the mayor. We don't like each other either. We're just pretending. All of this, everything you see, the laughter, the smiles, the pretentious little appetizers. It's all pretending."

"And the money that's being raised," Mistress Smyrna asks. "Is the generosity pretending too? Are they giving only Monopoly Money?"

"They are giving. Yes. But they are giving so that they can be *seen* giving. They are giving to their own egos. Look at how everyone's eyes are on each other. But are any of them even looking at Destiny? Or Stori? Or any of these young girls?"

The skin around Mistress Smyrna's nose twitches and she lifts her chin a little. "Honey, I think you've had a little too much to drink." She reaches her hand up in the air and it seemed to rise almost to the very chandelier hanging above her head. She snaps her fingers and a pretty girl with mild acne appears. "Water," Smyrna says. "As quick as you can."

Water arrives on a serving tray in less than a minute. The waitress takes it off the tray herself, presents it to Mistress Smyrna as if it were a newborn child.

Mistress Smyrna looks down her nose at her and said, "It's not for me."

The girl just stands there with a look of confusion on her face. "Mam?"

Mistress Smyrna does not deign to answer.

Then the girl finally turns and looks at me. "So it's for you Mam?"

I don't answer either. I look at the girl, I look at Mistress Smyrna. Finally I look at the glass, take it from the tray and fling it's contents directly in Mistress Smyrna's face.

Those who are in the vicinity gasp. Women touch their beaded necklaces. Even Stori has her mouth hanging wide open. A man in spectacles with no rims or earpiece, with only the glass floating about his small nose asks, "Too hot in here is it?"

I finally looked at Nate. For once in his life he is speechless.

I want to say it out loud, but I can't. So I only say it in my heart. As I slip my Ferragamos from my aching feet and back out of the room slowly: I'm sorry, Nate. I'm so so so sorry.

Stori

I lie in the dark waiting, wearing the white sleeveless nightgown that was given me by the maid who turned down my bed. The steak knife from dinner is at my hip, secured by a double knot in my underwear. Right next to Father Ash's key. When he comes in here, and tries his little perverted plan with me, he's getting shanked. That's what I'm telling myself. That I CAN kill if I want to. I swear I'm capable of it. I'm not afraid.

Mistress Smyrna is dead too, wherever she's hiding, for that's my utmost intention.

At last, the doorknob turns and I brace myself, prepared to unleash hell.

But it's not him. It's a Black Boot. He puts his head inside and says, "Get up. The Mistress wants you."

I rise, throwing off my covers. "Let's go."

The halls of Mistress Smyrna's estate are cloaked in silence and darkness. I don't think I've taken a real breath until we arrive at her door. So I allow myself a split second deep inhale-exhale. This is the moment of truth.

Black Boot knocks and a female voice calls from within, "Enter."

We enter.

Oh my God! I've been in this place before! In my dream!

The four post bed, the French doors opening onto the balcony. I can't let her see that I know this place. Mistress Smyrna stands under a fur coat on the balcony with her back to me. "Give her something for the cold."

The Black Boot looks around and finds a satin shawl draped over a chaise. He puts it around my shoulders. Like that's gonna help.

Outside the moon is full and snow is falling. The city is lit up, but under fog. If I had been brought here under different circumstances, I would have called it beautiful.

I step onto the balcony and wait. This woman is no match for me, so I'm not even worried.

She turns to face me. "Hello Stori."

I can't bring myself to respond.

"You must be wondering why I summoned you in the middle of the night. Let me explain. I want the truth. Tell me, what happened that night at the casino."

"Nothing. It was a dare. My friend Richie dared me."

She shakes her head regretfully. "Why is it that I don't believe you?"

I better play stupid for a while, until my chance to strike. "That's all it was. I promise."

"The cameras show you going inside the tiger's den."

"I didn't go all the way in."

"You didn't?"

"Okay. I was looking for my dad. But I didn't find anything. I'm sorry. For trespassing. I know it was wrong."

"Let's cut to the chase. You know about the crown."

How does she know? "What crown?"

"Don't play stupid with me. Is that what you were looking for?"

I think of her leaning over my father and no longer can hide my hatred. "I don't have to answer any of your stupid questions."

"Oh, that's where you're wrong Stori. Have you ever heard of waterboarding?"

"I'm not an idiot."

"Patrick over here," she nods to the Black Boot, "Spent three years working in Guantanamo Bay. And he's just jonesing to remember what it's like."

Maybe now is the time. If I kill her first, I might have enough space and strength to take a good jab at Patrick, ward him off at least.

My mind is already playing out how I will cut her open

and leave her there to bleed, when something inside the room by her bed catches my eye. It's glowing. But not like one of the red candles dotted all about the room. This glow is different.

It's emerald green and it's pulsing. Almost like something is coming alive.

Is it a book?

Yes it's a book.

Could this be the one Father Ash and Caroline told me about? The one that mentions me in it? The one from Hermes?

I don't have the luxury for distractions and I know killing this evil witch is more important, so I dismiss it.

But the book doesn't dismiss me! It starts to move. It floats up off its easel and soars over to us.

The book stops in the center of the balcony, low to the ground.

I feel something I'm not sure I've ever felt before: Obedience. One that trumps anger, revenge, cunning.

I forget the knife, the plan, the hatred and step before the book and kneel.

Oh floating book
Oh book so holy
Oh book I've never known

How is it that I know you?
For I remember when I held you in my hands
Your pages ever turning
Tell me a story again
That one you told when I was in the Father's home
What father's home?
Oh yes!
I am the daughter
I am the kindred
Oh holy book leading me inward
Back to self
Back to memory
Lead me back to home

"No Patrick," I hear the Mistress say. "Let it go to her. I need to see."

The book opens and upon the page are strange symbols. They make no sense. But I *must* know what those words are saying. Something inside me would give my very life to know.

Intent on Knowing I stare and stare and stare, and I believe in a girl within me who is able to read those words. It takes some time, but in the stillness and steadiness of my own intention, I meditate even deeper and that's when the magic happens—the meaning appears.

And so I read:

I, Hermes, brought my curious pupil, Tat, to the pyramids. I pointed to their grandeur and I asked. "What made this temple, my son?"

"Ingenuity," Tat said. "Matched with Science."

"Ahah. But what is it that came before this ancient art of Science?"

He could not answer so I told him, "Art. Art came before Science."

He conceded to my truth and then I ventured further. "And do you know what came before Art?"

"What came before Art?"

"Wisdom."

"Yes, great master. You are true to say that Wisdom came before all the great feats of man."

"And do you know from which way does wisdom come?"

He could not fathom an answer. So I wasted no time in providing it for him. "Innocence. It is the most ancient power, and the foundation of all progress from man. The Crown that every Pharos, every king longs to get their hands on, was forged through the heart of an innocent."

"Where is it?" Tat asked.

"I cannot tell you because I do not know. But I can tell you where it will end up."

"Where?"

"At the dawn of a new age, the Sons of Darkness will have besieged a glittering city far from this place where our feet our planted. Within that glittering city will be a daughter of Shinar. She will have an unsmiling face, yet a heart that yearns. Just when the war between

the dark and light is near finished, when the dark has all but annihilated the light, the girl will come upon these words. Find the Crown, girl. The one forged at the Tower of Babel long ago. Find the Crown and bring it back. Bring it back through time, for time and space is only but a mirage, you see. Release yourself from body; become spirit girl. Once you take up this task a purple moon will rise and the darkness will tremble. Bring it back to the Tower that was created to restore man to divinity.

If you do not, the final age of darkness will descend. Like a moon being eclipsed permanently your people will know destruction, war and famine, until the final flood comes. And all will be washed away from the desolate land.

The book slams shut and falls to the floor.

Smyrna rushes over to it and picks it up, cradling it to her bosom.

My hand flashes to my hip. Is now the time to strike? Something stays my hand. A voice inside tells me no, so I wait.

Then I see the mayor. He slides off the four post bed and saunters over.

"Well. Isn't this quite the surprise," he muses as he saunters our way, adjusting his briefs as he takes a seat on a nearby chaise. "I was just dreaming of how I was going to deal with you. And had lots of delicious theories on just how I would get the truth out of you, but this is all the better. You've come to me."

"She's the one." Smyrna utters with venom. "She's the one in the prophecy. She knows where the crown is!"

"Settle down my turtle dove. Or you'll wake the whole mansion."

"Don't let her out of your sight," she snaps before she slips into the shadows, taking the book with her.

I've been waiting days for this—to finally get the chance to stand face to face with the mayor and confront him with what I know. Staring down badmen is what I do best, and when I do it I am fearless. Nothing has changed. "I know all about you," I tell him. "Your plans to enslave all these girls here, and I will never let that happen."

"And I know all about you. How you found the undercity. How you know too much for Valley slum. And now it appears you know about the crown. And that's not looking too good for you."

His eyes go to my bare places and he gives a look that makes my skin crawl.

"Come now, Stori, you don't have to be shy with me. I'm going to make you one of my glorious girls before I get the truth from you and then get rid of you." He gets up and instinctively I fly forward to attack, but a white light flashes and I'm hit with a searing pain that radiates my entire body.

I can hear the witch laughing. "Got her. She won't move."

I'm locked where I stand and suddenly freezing. I try

to move my arms. I try and try with all my might but I'm frozen. Paralyzed. I'm panting now. I can only think of my breath. I have to get a deep one and soon. He's walking over to me, grinning, taking pleasure in my struggle.

"Stay over there," I say.

He sucks his teeth. "Oh Stori. I've heard about your freakish strength and quite frankly it turned me on. But I can't have you putting up a fight on your first night here. I would then have to kill you sooner than I planned and we all know what kind of mess is involved in killing someone. First there's the blood of course, and then the mere weight of your body as I have to stuff you in my trunk. Then there's the smell if I have to leave you in there too long."

He sucks his teeth again. He's right up on me now.

I'm all adrenaline, yet it has nowhere to go. Luckily my breath has returned.

He's not touching me but my skin crawls. I shudder and try to pull my arms closer to my body, but I still have no strength.

"Then there's getting your dumb uncle to dispose of the body without letting one of his painted whores see. Your uncle is a little bit of a stray bullet with his addiction and that pesky guilt he carries around from giving away his own brother. I do feel sorry for him. But not enough to not kill him too, if he doesn't do every single thing I tell him." He grabs me by my shoulders with angry fingers.

"But anyways, nobody put a gun to his head, Stori,

when he came and told me about your father. Yes. Your
father found the undercity. And he told his brother Joe.
Bad move. Very bad move on your father's part. Sadly,
cash is king in this world, not family. Even in the Valley it
seems. But apparently there's not enough cash for *you*. Joe
Putz has a soft spot for you Stori. If he knew what you
were up to we didn't get the information from him." Mayor
Vaughn laughs.

"I don't care about my Uncle Joe," I say. "He's not
family to me."

"Yes. This is true. Now I am." He slides a finger down
the side of my cheek and brushes his thumb over my lips.
"Now I'm in charge here Stori. And I have to say. I like it. I
like it a lot."

"Start the torture," comes the witches voice from the
shadows.

"Go get the other girl!" he barks back.

It's not my time to die. I want to live. There has to be
a way to get out of this. Without my strength, I'm nothing.
I'm nothing. The only thing I can think of is to stall him
with questions. "What are you going to do with me?" I ask.

Mayor Vaughn must love the sound of his own voice
because he won't shut up. "Well I'm actually glad you asked
that question. You see with the other girls it didn't take
much to get them to surrender. Even your friend,
Ernestine. Oh yes, she cried the first few nights, but she
came around. Just like the rest of them."

I want to tell him that she never came around; she just escaped, let go of her mind to get through it. But now is not the time to be winning arguments. Now is the time to get out of these invisible chains.

He must sense my thoughts, for he stops and narrows his eyes a little. "I know what you're thinking. The loyal and honorable friend that you are. You want to break my face for doing such a thing to your bestie. But let's consider something, shall we. Have you ever asked yourself, if your true-blue would do the same were the shoe on the other foot?

"What are you talking about?"

"Well haven't you wondered who put us onto you?"

"The prophecy. It's in that book."

"But it doesn't say a name. So we couldn't be sure. Even though your father confessed to being a Brave you seemed to have taken a different path, so we had already dismissed you. But do you remember the night you went poking your nose in Soda Can Alley?"

"I went to go see my uncle."

"There was a girl with him."

I think back. Yes. There was a woman. One of the whores from the cathouse. Although I never really saw her, but who else would it be?

"Did you ever wonder who it was?"

"I'm not nosey like that."

"Well. You should have inquired. For the girl I sent

him that evening to appease his beastly pleasures was none other than Ernestine. It was her first night here. I broke her in."

Rage overtakes me. I'll claw his face before I bash it in. I wish again with all my might for release. I push and pull but still there is nothing. "You lie. You are a dirty filthy liar."

"Oh really?"

He goes to the door and opens it and Ernestine is standing there in tears.

"Come in my little birdie with all the information. Come in."

She's shoved forward by the Mistress. She stands there, crying hysterically, with her arms hanging by her sides.

"Ern," I tell her. "Don't worry. I don't believe him. I never would! You've got to wake up and fight. Right now. Wake up and fight. Don't let them take everything from you!"

"I'm sorry, Stori," she says. "I'm sorry. They made me do it. They made me go to your uncles and get stuff out of him. They thought because I was from the Valley that he would trust me. I didn't get much from him. But I had to do stuff with him. I had to…" she breaks down into sobs and crumbles to the floor. She weeps, and I wait, not knowing what to believe, while she gathers enough breath to speak again. She looks up at me and says, "I hated myself. Ever since Richie. I didn't want to live anymore. I tried to tell you in the bathroom. Because I knew they had their eye on you. I knew if you kept snooping around for your dad they would get you too. But you didn't listen!"

"You could have told me. Why didn't you tell me? I would have helped you."

"I was mad at you. For being free. For not being me. For being so strong all the time. So when you came and told me you were looking for the crown, I hid it for a while, but I finally told. Yesterday before you got here. I knew it would keep them from sending me to your uncle too. I had to tell them, Stori. I had to. I'm sorry."

"No, Ern. No. No. You didn't."

"I did. So now you know. I did."

Mayor Vaughn is happier than a pig in shit. He goes to the bureau where a carafe sits and a glass. He pours something yellow, like Mountain Dew, into the glass and he comes back to me. "This…," he says waving the glass in front of me. "…is a special cocktail made by Mistress Smyrna. You are going to drink it now."

"I will not."

He's mildly displeased. He makes little clucks of disapproval. Then he goes over to Ernestine and in a flash he's behind her with a knife to her throat. "This one is almost no use anymore. I was going to keep her, but I think I'll kill her instead."

"Don't," I tell him. I'm surprised at myself. I hate

Ernestine. Don't I? Don't I?

"You have two choices. You either drink the drink. Or Ernestine dies."

More time. I need more time. Stall him, Stori. Stall him. "I can't move. Let my arms go free."

"Oh, but I'll help you." He takes a break from terrorizing Ernestine and brings the glass back over to me. He lifts it to my nose and says, "Smell it. Go ahead. Smell."

I take a small whiff, trying to be as careful as I can. It's stronger than turpentine and I have to hold myself back from gagging. It smells like bile.

He laughs. "I felt the same way when I first took a whiff. But trust me, Stori. You will never taste anything more sweet than the Cocktail of Forgotten."

"What does it do?" I ask, trying to calm my stomach heaves, trying to muster my magic, so I can use it on him the way I did with the sweeper. But the magic isn't coming this time.

"It makes you die. The old you of course. But a new you will be born. A you like me. I luckily, never had the need for even a drop of the potion because I always knew the kind of man I wanted to be. But people like you, the *trouble rousers*, always need a little persuasion. Drink it. And you will no longer feel the need to go running around Redemption causing your little troubles. Because you will be on our side."

I look at the drink. Who knows what's really in here.

"Free her arms," he says into the blackness.

I reach for it and find that my arms are now free.

Mayor Vaughn is pleased. "Yes. Yes," he says. "Go ahead and drink it."

I hold it there. I look at Ernestine. "Ern," I say. "Even though you hurt me, I won't let him kill you. You're my friend. You're my family."

"Don't drink it," she pleads. "Just let him kill me. I just want to die."

I don't know why but I think of Cristina Dexter, the last girl I defeated in the cage. I realize what a monster I had been for wanted to hurt someone unprovoked. "I'm sorry, Cristina," I whimper.

I'm free to reach for the knife now. I can draw it out and dart it at him. I've practiced that before on targets like trees and stuff. I'm a pretty good shot. My hand falls nervously to my side, my fingers brushing against the hard place as they descend. But when I reach under my skirt and take it out I do something unexpected. I fling the knife out over the balcony. My only hope for survival eaten up by the blanket of a winter night.

"I don't want to hurt anymore," I say. "I'm done hurting. I'm done."

I never thought it would end this way. I always imagined the day I died I would go out fighting. I've always prided myself on my warrior spirit, but to die like this is strange. There is nothing left in me now but forgiveness.

"It's okay. I forgive you, Ern. I forgive you. Do you hear me? No matter what, I'll always be your friend."

I can see Cristina Dexter bloodied beneath me. "I'm sorry Cristina. I'm sorry. I was wrong to hurt you. I'm sorry!"

And then it appears.

A blue light; suspended above our heads like one of the chandeliers in the dining room. It is that stunning blue in the stones of the Crown. Round and perfect like the sun, it beats out its flawless color with a magnificence too great to behold. "Jesus!" I exclaim.

Mayor Vaughn staggers back and stutters. "What...what...what the hell is that?"

It spins. A great white wind swirls around it and the room is overtaken by a loud ringing, like the sound your ear makes when you get water in there. And alongside it is the woosh of gushing air. The chair to the Mistress' vanity topples over and a lamp crashes to the floor, shattering to pieces.

Mayor Vaughn covers his ears against the sound. His briefs are whipping about his thighs furiously. "Make it stop!" he hollers. "Make it stop!"

But I can't hear him all that well because my every sense is fixed on the blue up there. It is the one and only blue that born itself from the Father's hands. The blue of creation. The blue of His endless love. His pouring out of adoration. His weeping weeping joy that sang as He made this place we call earth. It crushes down upon me and the agony I feel is euphoric.

A great love which came at a great cost. A stretching of the arms open wide and a beating heart that bled for all to see.

My sights are also on the girl inside that spinning ball of blue sky. It is the girl who led me through the sandstorm in the desert. She is dancing. Yes dancing. A man in a turban watches her, wiping away tears.

Now I am dancing too because I have been made free by the sight of her glorious joy and innocence. I will go back to this girl, whoever she is. Wherever she lives, I need to find her. I swear I will not rest until I get to where she dances. Until her dancing and mine mingle into one.

Hands up, hips wild and free, my face turned up to the sky. I dance. And I sing as well. And not in the language I am used to speaking. It is in the ancient tongue.

Hands up. Heart ablaze. Ready to find you
Ready to fall at your feet, my Lord
Ready to be your child.
Hands up
Hands up
Hands up

Mayor Vaughn is in some kind of seizure state as I step right over him. Mistress Smyrna is cowering in the corner, hissing like a snake.

Even though she doesn't deserve it, I can't forget Ernestine.

I pick up her tear streaked face and I kiss her widow's peak. Then I leave her back to her sorrow, for something even stronger is calling me. Joy is calling me. And a voice. A voice. I can hear it. It is calling out to me. It is calling my name.

They watch me as I go. All of them. The girls peeking out of their rooms, pointing in alarm and confusion. The maids and the other servants. I am surrounded now in the blue light and nothing can stop me. Not Mistress Smyrna, not the mayor, not the Black Boots.

Not the butler, Tyler, who is no longer looking at the floor but staring at me in amazement.

He opens the door for me, still with the dishtowel draped over his arm and just like that I walk out of that place knowing I will never return.

Stepping down the gravel driveway I see a lantern in the distance.

My stride falls into a trot and then I begin to run. And when I make it to the end of the drawbridge I see a small speed boat. It belongs to Arty Arm.

Arty is holding up the lantern and by his side is Tony. "Get in."

Bilhah

The Mathematician wears his many cloaks and his tall
turban that looks like a golden beehive sitting on the top of
his head. His beard is white and full and his back is
perpetually hunched from all his poring over his studies.

My mother met him once, for she requested a short
meeting with the one who often summons me to Babel.
His back was the first thing she noticed about him. "For a
man who studies the stars he bears the mark of one who
does not look to the heavens enough. But he is a good
man. He studies for the justice and the betterment of man.
I only fear those who employ him. Their motives are not
yet known to us. And this crown they are forging—they

could have ulterior motives other than the coronation of the Father."

It is said that when the tower is finished and the portal to heaven is accessed, the crown will be placed on the great Ancient of Days. Once the great Father is crowned he will come down and walk with man again. The false idols will be cast aside and man will be atoned for the sins of Adam. It is said, once the crown is placed on the Father, heaven and earth will be as one and man will be immortal again.

My presence is announced and the Mathematician has me ushered in. He is happy to see me, as he always is. His wooden sandals make funny little clicks on the marble floor. He is always funny to me. The way his hair coils out unruly, even the hair of his beard. The way his eyes sparkle when he smiles. The way he speaks like a child. "My dear Bilhah. Our graceful dancer of the hills. Tell me how your journey was this day?"

"It was quite fine. I stopped and saw the lilies."

"Very well. Very well."

There are many windows and terraces in the mathematician's study. There is a bed for when he needs rest, a harp for music, and a table where his parchments are laid out. He is trying to solve many mysteries of the earth and heavens. He is trying to figure out how the capstone of the tower should be built and how the crown should be forged.

He leads me to the table and I look over his strange

drawings and calculations. The table is messy and cluttered and I tell him. "How do you work with such a mess?"

He laughs. "Ahh. If only you knew my madness. This is only but a hint of what goes on inside my head."

There is a parchment with a picture of the tower and notes are scribbled on all sides. I brush my hand over it. "I like to watch the tower at night when the fires are lit. It is quite beautiful from the Caverns."

"Is your mother well?" he asks me.

"She is."

"And your father?"

"He is."

"Good. Very good. That the heavens will protect them and keep you from knowing the loneliness of motherlessness, of fatherlessness, as I have known." He looks sad now. He misses his parents, I can tell. I hope to cheer him. "Maybe when the portal is reached, you will see them again."

He smiles. "Yes, maybe. Maybe."

The woman who plays the harp comes in and she sits at her stool and waits. The mathematician looks at me and says. "Today I will have you dance to the melody of the creation."

"I love that one," I say.

"I have been blocked," he tells me darkly. "My mind has been overworked and tired, maybe. But I have not worked in almost three days."

"Maybe you just needed a rest," I encourage him. "Don't be too hard on yourself."

"Yes. I forget sometimes. I forget sometimes to just be."

"My mother always tells me not to fight my lazy moments. She says when I am daydreaming I am letting the true light in."

"Your mother is wise. If she were not so opposed to the city I would have you all live here behind the golden gates."

"We have lived in the Caverns since before the flood," I tell him. "Our ways are sacred to us."

"Yes. Yes. I forget. I shouldn't forget. Your ways are powerful indeed. Your dancing, Bilhah. It is ethereal. It is the very light your mother speaks of. And it is a magnificent inspiration to me. I would call you my muse but you are much more than that. You are the messenger. The messenger of light. Your fearless dancing calls down the light. It opens my mind, sweet Bilhah. It calls forth imagination. For imagination is the only way to access the ancient sights. Not memory, not calculation, but unbridled dreaming. Laughter and dance of the soul." He cues the woman at the stool with a gracious nod of the head and the music starts to play. He shuffles back on his funny shoes and seats himself upon a chair.

I feel a little nervous at first. I always do when I know he's watching me. But then the music starts to take over and my feet betray my inhibitions. The sway of my heart becomes my very body. It floats me up and down, and sends my fingers out in waves. The music is life now. And I am intent on living.

The music is inside of me, outside of me. To the right, to the left, above, below and always always in the center.

When the song is done I am refreshed and tingling like I've just emerged from the cool waters of the river under a blazing midday sun. I'm tired. But not the kind of tired from not feeling well. It is the kind of tired that makes me feel like I can run right out onto the terrace, swoop my arms out and up and take off right into the sky.

The Mathematician is up on his feet, clapping. He is beaming with happiness. With pride. He is looking up into the corners of the room like he has just spotted something. "Yes! Yes!" he cries. "I have got it! I have got it! The crown must be inlaid with the stones of lapis lazuli. The gold must come from Havilah! These items were created in ecstasy. These items will open the portal of ecstasy that leads to the gates of heaven. I must be alone now, to work on the plans. I have so much running around inside my head. Guards. Take her down to the city gates. Let no one in after she's gone."

The guards are not quick enough for me, though, for I dart out of their sights as soon as the Mathematician's doors close behind us. I know he would be displeased if he found out I left the city unattended, but I just have to get down there in all that bustle, all that brilliant color. I don't want the guards telling me I cannot stop to listen to the women and their gossip at the water well or watch the fires burning in the furnaces where the bricks for the tower are made.

Today I stop at the jewelers. Inside the men are at their tables, working diligently. They are tapping, sanding and polishing all kinds of magnificent gems. The Mathematician says that the men who carry the stones for the tower all wear necklaces of crystal—it augments their power and makes them stronger than the average man.

I just think the stones are pretty and some of them are hanging in the windows for the women to see. There are classes in the city of Babel. Not every woman is as wealthy as the next. The ones who have the money are able to stop inside the shop and commission the jewelers to make them ornaments for their bodies. My mother tells me these women are vipers and their desire to adorn themselves in lavish things is a great sin. My mother says the city dividing the people according to wealth is the greatest iniquity of all. My people—the Braves of the Caverns—do not believe in possessions. All things inside our dwellings—our clothing, our animals—are not considered belongings. We share all things in the Caverns.

But oh how some of the gems sparkle. How I do secretly wish to have a green ruby sitting above my breasts.

"Do you like it?" someone asks me.

A boy is standing beside me. He is taller than me but looks younger. He is studying my face and I find this quite unsettling. Why is he looking at me like that? He does not even know me. I'm insulted and turn and walk away from him at once.

But he follows me.

I quicken my steps, but he is still there. Now he is right beside me. "You are not from the city. I can see."

"The Caverns," I tell him quickly. Maybe he will find this offensive in some way, as others here in the city have when I told them where I live.

"Oh. The Caverns. So you are a girl of earth and clay."

"I am."

"Don't tell your mother you were dreaming of necklaces. She might bash your head in with a stone."

I am frightened. The words themselves are like stones and I can feel my insides drawing tight. I am not a fighter. I have never used my hands to harm another living thing. Why would a stranger say such a thing to me? That my mother would want to kill me? What kind of thoughts live here in the city? Spoken out loud without a care for who around will hear?"

"I beg you. Please let me be." I quicken my steps and it seems he has stopped walking. Good. Get away from me, you evil boy with the evil words living upon your tongue. Get away.

Then I feel something bite me in the back of my head.

I look down and see a stone behind me. I reach to the hurting place and feel that it is wet there. The boy is trying to stone me. I want to call for help, but I can't. The fear has stifled my very speech. People are rushing in every direction around me. Women with baskets atop their heads. Men with leashed dogs and nets of fish. All of them are swarming and creating so much noise that the "help" that finally escapes from my trembling throat is eaten up, swallowed whole.

He runs after me now. I run, as fast as I can. I run from the boy. Another rock is hurled my way. It misses me by an inch. Then another comes flying and it gets me in the back of my heel.

Up ahead I see one of the guards. He stands close to the gates of the city. He spots me and puts his hands on his hips. I must get to him. I must get to him. I must. And then I hear a voice fall down from the very sky and it says. "Fear not. For there is another who is coming. A girl who will knock the stone thrower to his feet. A girl with fire upon her head and a heart that trembles."

Tony Carp

Me and Richie Ramera was talking about how we like them one night. Sharing a bone on the curbside, watching a few of them go by.

"Crazy," Richie said. "They let you put it anywhere."

"I like the soft ones," I said. "Soft ones are nice."

"You know what I ain't had yet? Gotta get a piece."

"Lemme guess."

"Sullen."

"Sullen's hard. Complicated. I don't do sullen."

"But I bet it would taste sweet. All that sadness. Yeah. I'd give her something to be sullen about."

It was all good until the night you came into the Cage and fought Christina Dexter. Richie was there and he was tanked. The second he saw you he said, "There it is, bro.

Sullen. Gotta get me a taste."

I pushed him off his seat and one of his boys took out a gat.

But Richie only laughed. "I thought you said you don't like it."

"Don't matter. That one's mine."

I'm looking at you now and I'm still wondering what those words mean. She's mine.

We stand in the middle of Windy Way. You still look so pretty and over your gown you're draped in my goose down coat.

"I never meant to hurt you Stori. I never meant to treat you like a possession. It's just that I wanted to protect you from guys like Richie. I know you've got a mind of your own and you know how to use it. I know your tough."

But as I look at her I also know she's not tough. She's just what Richie said she is. Sullen. And sullen girls are the softest of the soft. That's why I told her she's better than this. Better than the animals in the Cage. Better than me. You see I'm just like Richie and the rest of them. And I prefer it like that. I don't want to feel. I don't want to care. I'm an orphan. And orphans know better than anyone else, that people leave and never come back. And the worst thing you can do is care.

I would only hurt her. Maybe in another world we could be together. But not this one.

I take my necklace off. "I want you to have this." It's a

silver chain and a charm—two boxing gloves. My father gave it to me the day before he and my mother died.

"I can't," you tell me. "I can't take that from you."

"You have to. It'll keep you safe. Be your good luck charm. It has always been for me."

You look at me and there's no more of that anger in you anymore. The sullenness, yes. But the anger is gone.

"I'm sorry about all your losses, Tony. I know it hurts. And I'm so sorry about what I said—"

"—Shhh." In the Valley, friends don't have to explain.

We embrace. As friends. I know it's all we can ever be.

No. I never felt that way about you, Stori. As much as I wish I did. Because we could be perfect for each other. Maybe it's the destruction in it. You know. The lust part. Wanting to possess someone. I think that desire makes us animal. Maybe you're too good for the animal in me. Oh, Stori. If you only knew about the animal in me.

But know this. A friend in me you do have. And when the time comes I'm getting you out of this mess. But for now I'll go back to Nardo's and feed the beast.

I don't want to let go, but Caroline is waiting for you just beyond Windy Way and she told us we have to make good time. "I'll check on your fam," I tell her. "Anything they need."

"Thank you, Tony. Thank you."

Stori

Forest Boom is blanketed in brand new snow. Icicles twinkle like ornaments on the weighted down tree limbs. It's so quiet I can hear a single pinecone thump to the earth's floor.

"It sure is dark in there," I tell Caroline as we stand there together waiting.

"It is," she says with a frown. I'm not the only one who's nervous. "But you've got my warm boots and your lantern. And your matches and your sleeping bag here." She hefts my backpack a little.

My heart aches for Amanda. I still can't believe I gave her away.

I have one more thing I must do before I set off on my journey. "Caroline. I told Regina to meet me at the dam if she needs me for anything."

"I will watch her in the flame. Your sister will be fine."

"Do you promise?"

"I promise."

We turn to face the forest now, standing side by side. "I always thought I could protect her, and my family by being tough. But I've learned that I was wrong. All that did was make me small, weaker. I want to change. I want to be a better person, Caroline. I don't want to be small anymore."

"Just keep your heart open," she tells me. "No matter how tempted you are to close it. I wish I could go with you, to help you. But this journey can only be traveled alone."

"What do I look for?" I ask, peering into the unknown darkness, unsure of what lies beyond the dense grove of pines.

"I don't know. But the forest is still rich with many powerful things. If the answer to finding the portal is anywhere, it's in there. When you find it, I'll have the crown sent to you."

"Then I have to go," I say, hoping that speaking the truth will help in accepting it.

"Yes. You have to."

I take a step forward so that I'm standing separate from her. A wind picks up from the north and the branches of the trees go wild. Snow-dust scatters. Just when I think that I'll be too scared to do it, I see something appear beyond the first row of pines.

It's the boy.

The Native American looking boy I saw delivering firewood in the Valley that day. He moves from behind a black trunk and faces me. Draped in white fur to his ankles, he starts nodding his head like he knows my whole story and then he turns and retreats deeper into the forest. Then a girl appears. The one who appeared the night I was putting up my dad's signs. She's got the same dress on and her hair and face are shining. I move closer to see her better.

She is beautiful. And she is smiling. She is smiling at me. She lifts a sword in front of her and it bursts into flames.

I don't bother to say a final goodbye to Caroline because the place that I am going to is not a destination. It is a feeling. An experience. A place of wonder hidden deep inside the soul.

Oh you that have stayed this far to listen to my story, I wonder if you are curious too about the worlds beyond this one we have always called home. Will you follow me?

I take up my path and don't bother to wonder where it will lead me.

The angel is pleased. She turns and begins to lead me in, her flaming sword parting the darkness. Her steps are light and dainty. Her dress billows out behind her in the wind.

This is the beginning of my journey. It starts at the end. In what this life has taught me so far, I have found that most journeys begin this way. When all is said and done, when the sweet things have been crushed down, run away and vanished, there is nothing left to do but let go of who you think you are and surrender yourself to the light.

Note to Reader*: Thank you for reading the first installment in a series called **The Emerald Tablet. If you enjoyed the first book, make sure to look out for book two, **Ghost Dance Returns**. Coming Soon!

Here is an excerpt from **Ghost Dance Returns!**

Lone

The girl has been sleeping for days and does not wake. I keep her aloft, in the tree house, wrapped in many quilts. She is safe from snakes here and from the pranks of the Boom Babies down below. But her nightmares I cannot protect her from. She cries in the middle of the night. "No. Don't take them from me," she begs. "No. Don't take them." Her hands clutch the sack she brought with her from the Valley, fingers crushing pillowed cotton, making little dents. She is haunted by something. Some kind of loss tearing at her soul.

I have not been interested in someone in quite a long time. But the girl and her haunted dreams makes me wonder.

I want to rouse her from sleep and ask her how she

found this place. It is protected by the Great Mysterious and no one in history has ever been able to find us. I have been here since the year 1890, the year my grandfather Sitting Bull was killed. I am the last of his line and the world knows me not. I was named Lone Bull, a name whispered to my grandfather by a buffalo bull years before I was ever born. For short the Boom Babies call me Lone.

I carry the ancient gifts passed down by my mystic fathers. As my father, and his father before him, was able to speak to animals, so am I. It is not easy being the last of my family here, being without them. It has been over a hundred years, yet still I miss them with all of my heart.

The Boom Babies are my brothers and sisters now, and they are good people to live with. But still I am unsatisfied. I am a severed limb from a tree. Fallen away from the trunk and roots, I rot here alone. It is hard to keep the memories alive. The stories passed down to me from my father, from my tribe. The stories I myself have to tell.

I have killed men in battle and have shown them mercy in battle too. I have proven myself a great warrior amongst my people, touching the enemy with the coup stick without ever drawing blood. Only a few have been able to accomplish this, my father being one of them.

I hardly speak the stories to anyone. For they are too precious for others to hear. I only keep them in my heart and pray that I will always remember.

Sometimes I think I'm starting to forget. Who I am. Where I came from. The family I once had. It's like a bad dream. And I must wake.

I have to fight it. I have to fight for the memory.

The Boom Babies know that I must free myself into the forest when this happens. I must return to the Mother Speaker, I must unleash myself and run wild like the wolves.

I am running now; the girl is still aloft in the treehouse sleeping.

I leave her for the moment and start a good trot out of the Canopy. I pick up speed, a small hill trailing down toward the stream offers momentum. The path along the stream is roped with roots and I know each and every one like the purple ropes under the skin of my hands. I know the heart beat too. The heart beat of the land I am pounding my bare feet upon. The snow has finally melted and the first of spring is coming. The heart is open and calling out for its child. I am that child and I lift my face to the clear blue sky and shout my first cry—the cry of a ghost dance apostle, fearless in the art of warrior love. A hawk cries, joy is rising, it is rising from the earth. It is coming right up from the soil, up my legs and into my heart. I am strong and fast, like a fox. I am swift and deadly like the night. I am Lone Bull, the son of Sitting Bull, the big medicine man.

I am rising now, taking great leaps as I make my way

up the butte of the rising mountain. I am almost there. I am almost there. The last great leap and I have made it.

Panting heavily, I stand over Forest Boom in the secret place where my prayers are taken up to the Great Mysterious.

I raise my arms wide over my head and tell him. "Father! I am here!"

My call echoes, it booms off the rockface below, ricocheting from one side to another. It is as if my message has a life of its own. I wait for the silence. It comes in a great rush all around me.

The clouds above are puffy and white. The air holds the sweet promise of spring. I stand there with my arms out and offer my being to the Great Mysterious.

And then an eagle soars down from brilliant white, the sun is behind it and it blinds me. Its swoops down low right over me; its wings are as big as me when they are open. But as it perches in the narrow crags just above my reach the wings disappear. He nestles into the rock and blinks. He likes his little spot just fine.

There is no trick to communicating with animals. There is no practice, no method, no theory. There is only an opening of the spirit. My spirit has opened wide.

And then he speaks.

"Lone Bull. The waiting is done. In the treehouse she sleeps. It is time to awaken her. It is time to tell your story."

What a trembling is stirred within me when I hear the

message of the eagle.

It calls to memory words of my father before he died. I have never spoken of my father to anyone. To anyone. I will tell it to you, but you must swear secrecy. What I give you is more precious than gold.

Before my grandfather died he told me this: *The time is coming, Lone Bull. It is upon us. When the buffalo will return. The people will awake in the night to the pounding of their hooves. To the earth shaking. The ornaments they have collected for themselves will come crashing down to the floors and shatter. The windowpanes will break.*

The dead will rise that day. I will rise son. When the buffalo come, do not hide under your bed. Do not run to the oaks, to the bushes. Tear your garments from your body and run to them, naked as the day you were born. Run to them. And do not fear. For in their midst you will see me, your father who loves, you. Out of the very earth, you will see me rise.

At the death of dusk she finally stirs. She rolls on her side and moans, then her eyes open. She blinks. Then she blinks again. I don't move so as not to startle her. She needs to find me on her own.

She picks herself up on one elbow and looks down to her sack. "Ma," she croaks and places the satchel to her middle, under the covers. Then she turns her head and our eyes meet. If she is scared she does not show it. "What happened to me?"

"You were running from wolves. You fell down a cliff. You have been sleeping ever since."

She looks up to the window and sees the deep green boughs shadowing the coming of night. "Where am I?" she asks.

"You are in the Canopy. Welcome to your new home."

Jennifer Cipri would love to hear from you!
jenniferevecipri@gmail.com

Made in the USA
Charleston, SC
12 October 2014